Lady Munevver

The Opium Merchant's Daughter

D1712337

Eris Field Perese

Copyright

Dedication

The discipline of nursing is based on the work of a courageous woman, Florence Nightingale, who, during the Crimean War, struggled to save wounded Englishmen in Scutari Hospital, an old army barracks lying across the Bosphorus from Constantinople. Lady Munivver: The Opium Merchant's Daughter is dedicated to nurses all over the world who follow her teachings, and to the memory of a very special nurse, my mother, Emily.

Acknowledgments

I wish to acknowledge my gratitude to my copy editor and proofreader, Joyce Mochrie, for her review of this manuscript.

And thanks also for the never flagging support of the fabulous five—my children.

Chapter 1

September 1852: Surrey, England

The plush oriental rug silenced the sound of Munevver's uneven steps as she hurried down the hall toward the back stairs that would take her to the breakfast room. This early in the morning, there was no need to try to conceal her limp, and the day would go better if she were settled in her customary place before Lord George, the man she refused to call father, took his place at the head of the table.

After estimating the length of time it would take for him to come down the elaborately carved south staircase, Munevver asked Foster, who was checking the breakfast platters on the sideboard, to bring her a cup of hot chocolate and then fill a plate for her. Once his back was turned, she glanced at the stack of letters precisely arranged to the left of Lord George's place. Quinn, the butler who had been there for at least forty years, had fanned the letters slightly to reveal the return addresses, trusting Munevver to push them into a discrete arrangement before her father entered the breakfast room.

Scanning the envelopes with a speed honed by two years of practice, she paused as she recognized two from the Ottoman Empire. The one from Bursa was not unexpected, she decided, as she recognized Lord Sandison's angular handwriting. Lord Sandison, with his knowledge of the customs of the Ottomans and his fluency in languages, had been appointed consul to Bursa, where he was expected to further English commerce in the Ottoman Empire and, more specifically, to influence Ottoman policy to favor England over Russia in any trade dispute.

Lord Sandison and her father had been two of the original members of the Levant Company, founded in 1581 after trade between England and the Ottoman Empire—trade that was controlled and protected by the Venetians and the Italians—had been decimated by pirates. Merchants in England, now dependent on their own ships to bring in highly prized goods from the East, such as wine, spices, raisins, currants, carpets, silks, fine soaps, and drugs, had formed trading centers. These protected enclaves, *Factories*, included not only the trading areas and warehouses but also housing for the merchants and their families. The *Factories* were divided into several divisions: Turkish, Levantine, Venetian Littoral, Alexandria, Smyrna, and the most important of all, the magnificent trading center of Aleppo located between the Mediterranean Ocean and the Euphrates River.

When the Levant Company's charter was not renewed in 1825, Lord George and his father, Lord Clarence, were faced with the need to change, but they had disagreed on a course of action. After many recriminating discussions, Lord George had joined the rapidly expanding East India Company, and Lord Clarence had moved to Yorkshire, where he purchased a vast, secluded estate. Taking advantage of the estate's holdings—the Hull and Grimsly docks on the Humber River that could accommodate the largest cargo ships and had access to the North Sea—he established a new trading company.

After a quick glance to assure herself that Foster was busy selecting the items that he knew she would like, Munevver touched the letter from Aleppo, the oldest city in the world. Over eight thousand years old, with a history that could be traced back to the Stone Age, it contained ancient treasures: the Great Mosque, the Citadel of Aleppo, magnificent palaces, famous hammams, and enticing souks with their exquisite rugs, tapestries, and silks—the finest in the world.

Aleppo was the city Munevver had always dreamed of visiting. Someday she would go. It was all there waiting for her, but it would be up to her to make it happen. Lord George would never agree. He had insisted she leave her grandfather's home, where she had lived since she was a toddler, and "do her duty by contributing to the welfare of the family." With her knowledge of languages, international marketing, and accounting, which she had learned from her grandfather, she was free labor for her father's business. He would never agree to her leaving, but somehow, someway, she would escape from the prison of her father's home. She would make her way to Aleppo.

Munevver eyed the envelope. It was thicker than

normal. Her uncle must have sent more invoices with his customary detailed information about the seller, the quality of the goods, and the price. An uneasy thought made her frown as she considered its weight. It was possible that there were difficulties beyond the usual ones. Throughout the history of the Levant Company, Aleppo had served as the headquarters for the entire Middle East trade, and now it was still the center for all English trading.

She slid the envelope under the others as she thought of the story that she had heard so many times as a child. When he was only twenty-four years old and working for the Levant Company, one of her relatives, Anthony Jenkinson, had traveled as far as the city of Aleppo— the western end of the Silk Road—and had described the amazing quality of the silk that poured into Aleppo. Her lips tightened in self-disgust. *Twenty-four years old! Just six years older than I am now. He had seen the world, and I know just two places: my grandfather's home in Yorkshire and my father's in Surrey.*

The Levant Company's trade with the East had flourished, and although King Richard I, who followed Queen Elizabeth I to the throne, had engaged in a verbal anti-Ottoman crusade and had neglected to maintain relations with the Ottomans, he had regularly renewed the Levant Company's charter since the largest portion of his revenue was based on the taxes levied on its profitable trade. The English merchants exported rum and spices, cloth—cotton, woolens, and kersey—tin, pewter, and silver and brought back raw silk for Spitalfields' silk mills, cotton, velvet, the soft leather called maroquin, currants, raisins, nutmeg, pepper, and indigo. Soon they were bringing back luxury items that the upper class demanded: magnificent carpets, silks, porcelains, and wall hangings. They also brought back medicines and drugs—opium to be made into the laudanum that the English people demanded. Not only did the king not interfere with trade with the Ottoman Empire, but England's diplomatic policies were strongly influenced by this trade.

Munevver suppressed a sigh. The Levant Company had existed in less turbulent times. Yes, there had been competition from other countries, but English warships had ruled the oceans and her frigates had cleared out any challengers. The English ships were known as the *wooden walls* of England. Times had changed, and Lord George had resisted the need to adapt. *Will he start off this morning with his usual tirade about the widely forecast death of the Ottoman Empire, or will he go immediately to the more pressing problem—the steady decline in trade?* Either way, Munevver would be busy all morning determining what the latest problems in Aleppo were and what Lord Sandison wanted Lord George to do about them. She could only hope there was no further reference to his son, Douglas, as a possible candidate as a husband for her.

She could not help the bitter grimace that replaced her usual composed expression. Munevver forced herself to relax. She didn't have to worry about the outcome of that. No matter how attractive a bargain her father offered, Douglas would not accept her. She carried too great a liability. Besides, Lord Sandison did not seem to know her father's intention: a titled husband, a duke, or at least a future duke. He was determined to arrange a marriage for her that would benefit her brothers and her sister and, most of all, the family's social standing. He wanted a title in the family that would remove the stigma of his being a merchant. It affected everyone in the family. Munevver slid the envelope back in place. His dream was impossible! What titled family would accept a crippled bride, even one with a very generous dowry?

Holding her breath, Munevver nudged the heavy, cream-colored envelope of the next letter with the tip of her finger. It was from Constantinople—the enchantingly mysterious city that had played a vital part in history and continued to influence every country in Europe and beyond. How she would love to see the treasures of Constantinople! She gritted her teeth in a most unladylike manner. Grand Tours were for sons like her older brother, Ryker. Sons could travel, but young ladies were schooled at home by governesses.

Ryker would be returning soon from his two-year tour of France, Italy, and Venice and the additional excursions to Egypt, Greece, and the Ottoman Empire that he had managed to inveigle from his father. He would have seen Constantinople! He would have stood in the hallowed Sancta Sophia, at one time the most beautiful Christian church in the world.

Constructed over a period of five years, from AD 532 to AD 537, at the direction of Byzantine Emperor, Justinian I, it had been the most magnificent cathedral in the world and had served as a Byzantine Cathedral for over nine hundred years. Then, in 1453, when the Muslim Ottomans defeated the Greek Orthodox Byzantines and captured Constantinople, it had become a Muslim Mosque—the Aya Sophia.

Munevver struggled to hold back tears. Ryker would have been able to put his hand in the opening in the Wishing Column. He would have felt the moisture there that was believed to have the power to cure any affliction. Ryker did not have any problem! He did not need a cure. She shuddered at the memory of the day when Aunt Frederica, her father's younger sister, had told her of her grandmother's deformity—the family curse of clubfoot that had been passed on only to Munevver.

"Christianna, my dear, I want to see your progress on the tray cover you're embroidering for the Home for Distressed Governesses." Aunt Frederica looked up from her breakfast to greet her youngest niece, who was slipping silently into a chair near the end of the breakfast table. "I hope you haven't forgotten. The committee responsible for finding and furnishing a home for distressed governesses and seamstresses will be meeting here tomorrow afternoon. They will want to see everyone's progress." She studied the crumbled piece of linen with the few irregular stitches in green outlining the edge that Christianna pulled from the workbag on her wrist. "You don't seem to have made much progress." She frowned at her niece. "I can't even tell what design you've planned."

Munevver hurried to her younger sister's defense. "Christianna was telling me yesterday about her plans. She is going to add a cluster of fuchsias in the right-hand, lower corner."

"Fuchsias? What is she thinking of? The color would be too bright for a tray cloth for retired governesses."

"Perhaps not when you consider the whole effect." Munevver attempted to divert her aunt before her father lashed out, telling them to cease their prattling. She continued in a soothing monotone. "The corolla would be a bright pink. Worked in satin stitch, of course. The tepal right above the corolla would be a halo of very light pink. The stamens below would be a medium pink with touches of gold, and the stigma would be just a swollen bulb of warmest pink." Munevver paused at the thought of the stamen loaded with pollen-carrying sperms and of the stigma, ready, sticky, loaded with eggs, waiting to receive the pollen. She swallowed hard as an unfamiliar feeling curled through her lower abdomen and then added quickly, "Of course, there would be cool-green vines and leaves."

Christianna hissed at Munevver as her aunt motioned to Foster to fill a plate for her. "Why did you have to say that? You know I can barely do the outline stitch."

"Leave it in my room. I'll take care of it for you." She winced as she thought of the time it would take and then stiffened as she heard the snap of the newspaper her father was reading. "Is the news bad?" Munevver asked on cue as she hurried to finish her poached eggs. Once he challenged her to state her knowledge of the situation, there would be no more breakfast.

"Bad?" he snarled. "When is news about the Ottoman Empire ever good?"

When no one responded, Munevver asked cautiously, "What has happened now?" No matter what the news, Lord George would expect her to be able to discuss the historical background, the interests of the major European nations, any threat to English trade, and the potential for him to profit from the situation. As she waited for him to begin, she watched the endless glide of raindrops—cold, October raindrops as big as snowflakes, sliding down the windows of the breakfast room.

"Remember the Russo–Turkish War of 1828–1829?" Lord George marked a section of the paper for her to read later.

"Yes," Munevver answered dutifully. "It was set off by the Greek War of Independence, as I recall."

"The Greek Uprising," he replied, correcting her brusquely. "More specifically, by the Ottoman's closing the Dardanelles to Russian ships in retaliation for Russian support of the Greeks at the Battle of Navarino."

Munevver considered the chances of escaping from the breakfast room before her father began on the October 20, 1827 Battle of Navarino. Realizing it was already too late, she settled back in her chair, unable to stop shivering at the thought of the frigid, October naval battle that had been so disastrous for the Ottomans.

"The Battle of Navarino," Lord Arundal began, studying his daughter's face but, as usual, to his annoyance, could not detect her thoughts, "was the first of Greece's nationalistic uprisings." He sighed. "I was thirty-eight years old at the time and held the belief of most English scholars—that Greece still represented noble, ancient Hellenic values." He shook his head and added dryly, "It's been a long time since the modern-day Greeks represented Hellenic values, if they ever did."

Lord George flexed his hands in an effort to disperse the energy he felt rising in him. "To support the Greeks, Britain, France, and Russia sent squadrons to the Bay of Navarino. Just think of it! They sent their ships into the Eastern Mediterranean, into Ottoman waters. Their plan was to use a show of force to stop the conflict. When the Ottomans saw the combined fleet approaching, they agreed to cease fighting as long as the Greeks did the same. However, the Greek armies, commanded by English officers, continued to advance and the truce broke down. The Egyptians, part of the Ottoman Empire's force, and the Ottomans opened fire on the fleets."

"What did England, France, and Russia expect?" Munevver risked asking. "They sailed into a harbor that was Ottoman territory."

"The English Admiral, Sir Edward Codrington, had no choice. He had to lead the European counterattack." He refolded the paper precisely and laid it beside his plate before saying dispassionately, "The entire Turkish fleet was destroyed."

There was a moment of silence before Munevver trusted herself enough to speak. "The Ottoman ships were at anchor." She paused to take a breath. "The English fired on Ottoman ships at anchor in an Ottoman harbor! Seventy-eight Ottoman ships were destroyed and three thousand men killed." She measured his expression carefully. His reprisals could be brutal. "I remember you saying it was against accepted maritime rules to fire on ships at anchor."

Lord George shook his head. "A regrettable event! An English admiral, the Most Honorable Edward Codrington, gave the order to fire on ships at anchor. Unthinkable!" He rubbed his hand over his eyes. "I hope such an atrocity never happens again." After a moment, he continued. "At the time, the English thought they were helping the gallant Greeks gain their freedom from an oppressive Ottoman Empire, but in reality . . ." He stared at Munevver for a moment without seeming to see her. How could he explain how the English leaders had let their memories of the grace and beauty of ancient Greece—the Greece they had studied at Eton and Harrow—distort the reality of the Greek minority in the Ottoman Empire that had fought for more than ten years for independence, an independence that they were ill-prepared to defend?

He cleared his throat. "That was in the past. Now we have other problems. The Ottomans have not been able to rebuild their navy since that loss. They are without a strong navy, and Russia, ever greedy for warm-water ports on the Black Sea, is growing bolder every year. It is a very dangerous combination." Lord George glared at her. "Don't waste time this morning with household nonsense." He glanced dismissively at Aunt Frederica, who had sat silently throughout the exchange. "She can take care of whatever needs attention." He gathered up the papers and letters. "Come along! There's correspondence that requires immediate attention."

Munevver met the frantic gaze of her younger brother, Alexander, as he beckoned her from behind his father's chair and then slipped away. It must be something dire for him to have braved coming to the breakfast room when his father was there. What could have terrorized a seven-year-old? She tipped her cup of chocolate and watched the stain spread over her favorite morning dress. "Oh, dear. How clumsy of me. I must change." She managed to sound both flustered and sorrowful. "I'll be along directly," she called over her shoulder as she headed for the back stairway where she knew her brother would be hiding. "Tell me," Munevver said as soon as she reached him. "You know I'll help you if I can."

"It's multiplication." His voice wobbled. "Mr. Andrews said I have to know the sevens by this afternoon. All of them." He began to shake. "He said he has arranged for me to show Father what I've learned after tea."

Unable to resist the trembling little boy, Munevver put her arm around his shoulders and pulled him to her side. "Don't worry about it anymore. I'll join you for lunch in the nursery and we will master the sevens then." She hugged him tightly. "I know a magic way." She would have to find time to retrieve the box of Yorkshire buttons from the bottom of her trunk that had accompanied her from Yorkshire to London two long years ago. Grandfather had used the handcrafted, wooden-and-bone buttons to teach her the multiplication tables, and she would use them now to help Alexander.

Chapter 2

October 1852: Ryker Returns

"Ryker will be home soon," Munevver muttered to herself as she hurried down the long hallway, lined with portraits of famous horses her father had bred, to the dark-walnut paneled study that was her father's office. "It's time he took over some of the work."

As always, she could not help feeling envious whenever she thought of Ryker's Grand Tour. She let her mind wander. First France. He would have crossed from Dover to Calais and then by carriage to Paris. She smiled as she thought of the beauties of Paris that she had read about. Paris! Her godmother, Lady Sophiana, had asked Munevver to visit her at her villa in the South of France, but when Munevver had told Aunt Frederica about the invitation, she'd advised against mentioning it to Lord George, who had just received a request from Ryker to extend his time abroad.

She frowned, remembering her father's rage when he received the letter from Ryker saying he wished to extend his travels to the Ottoman Empire and the

Black Sea area. Although he had finally agreed to Ryker's request, he had made it clear that when Ryker returned, he'd be expected to take an active role in the family shipping business, participate in running the country estate, and manage the new program to train horses for the military. Lord George had been specific: Ryker would be responsible for learning Louis Nolan's method of training horses in less than two years and for implementing it.

For a moment, Munevver's spirits lifted. Ryker would be home and would take over as his father's assistant, but would she be able to go home? Could she really go home? Back to Yorksire, to her grandfather's estate where she had lived most of her life, where she was loved and accepted. She refused to let her mind wander to the extensive estate adjoining her grandfather's more modest property where William, the second son of Lord Richard Del Feld, lived and served as steward of the estate.

William. Tall, lean William with his crisp, auburn hair and hazel eyes. William, her childhood hero. It had been William who had taught her, along with his sister, Caroline, to ride, to shoot, and to play croquette. For a moment, she let herself relive the country dance her grandfather had arranged for her in honor of her seventeenth birthday. She had only danced once, but that dance with William had been as perfect as she had ever dreamed.

For a moment, she let the memory of that moment surface—the memory that she usually did everything to prevent. She could almost hear him vowing that he would call on her father the morning after her eighteenth birthday and ask for permission to court her. She swallowed hard to quell the rising nausea evoked by the thought of that painful year of waiting, hoping William would come and take her away, back to Yorkshire.

Finally, the day arrived, and the day after her eighteenth birthday, she could barely conceal her excitement. But there was no one she dared share it with. Not even her beloved Fayne, who had looked after her throughout her entire childhood and had returned with her to her father's home. She relived that dreadful, endless day of waiting for her father to call her to his study to tell her the wonderful news. The pain had become less sharp during the empty days, weeks, and months that followed but had never completely disappeared.

Another thought made her stomach churn anew. Ryker's passion was the cavalry, not shipping or training horses. Although there were moments when he treated her with consideration, underneath, he had his father's ruthlessness when it came to getting what he wanted. If he left to join a military unit, her father would never let her go back to Yorkshire.

The next morning, a disgruntled-appearing Ryker was already at the breakfast table with a cup of black coffee in his hand when Munevver hurried through the door. *Good. Lord George has not come down yet. I have just a few minutes to alert Ryker to his father's expectations.* She placed a slice of hot, buttered toast on a plate and quickly added scrambled eggs and a tiny amount of kippers. Lord George believed everyone should eat kippers to start the day off properly. The scent of kippers might appease him for a few moments. She slid into the chair opposite Ryker and took a bracing swallow of the hot chocolate Foster had placed by her plate.

"Father left a message," Ryker grumbled sullenly, not bothering to greet his sister. "He wants to talk to me in his study directly after breakfast." He shot her a wary glance. "I don't suppose you know what it's about?"

What does he think it is about? He has been granted more than two years of carefree travel to learn about the world, and now Father will expect him to settle down, to take an interest in the business, and to apply what he has learned to increase profits. "I imagine he wants to talk with you about your future."

"My future?" He snorted. "I've talked with him about it, but he refuses to buy me a commission in the cavalry. That's the future I want."

"Ryker! Be sensible! You're his heir! He has always planned for you to join him in the business. Now, you have acquired knowledge about other countries that can be used to expand his trade." Bracing for his explosion, Munevver used the time to eat her eggs. It would probably be the only peaceful part of a very long day.

"I am not cut out to be a bloody, penny-counting merchant!" Ryker snarled. "I have always wanted to be in the cavalry. He knows that."

Hearing heavy footsteps approaching, Munevver did not respond.

Striding into the room, Lord George motioned for the footman to fill a plate from the sideboard for him. He ignored Munevver's good morning. "So, what did you learn from your years abroad?" Lord George asked Ryker.

With an innocent expression of mild interest, Ryker picked the one topic sure to irritate his father. "Everywhere I went in France and Germany, the talk was about expanding the railways. They seem convinced it will be trains, not ships, carrying all commerce in the future."

"Humph! You are too young to remember the wild enthusiasm for railways in 1837. People rushed to invest but then the bubble popped." He rubbed his hands together as a sly expression crossed his face. "Fortunately, I was one of the few who refused to invest in them." He looked at his son sternly. "Even greater interest in railways surged in 1844. People—small landowners, merchants, and even household servants—rushed to invest. They borrowed money to invest in the land where they expected the railroads to be built. They took a chance on iron, coal, and even the labor needed to build the railways." He grimaced. "Of course, they had to cut back on other things, like repairs to their estates, number of servants, imported wines, and other goods. Then, in 1846, the price of railway shares dropped, and many lost all they had invested." He paused to study his son carefully. *Has he matured during his travels abroad? How far can I trust him with information about the business? Is he ready to settle down and take his rightful place as a partner?*

Lord George began cautiously. "We seem to be approaching a period of stability. The crops have been abundant. The banks are stable, and even the railways are making a profit at last."

"Not to mention that gold has been flowing into England's banks after it was discovered in California and Australia," Ryker added.

Lord George looked at his son with new respect. "It brings with it the challenge of wise investing."

"Yes," Ryker answered slowly. "It wasn't just railways arousing interest in Europe. In France, Germany, and Russia, there was a lot of talk about a new type of French weapon for naval battle—the Paixhans gun."

"There are always new guns," Lord George scoffed. "What are the supposed advantages of this one?"

"The guns are designed to fire explosive shells, not just inert cannonballs as they were in the past." Suddenly, Ryker seemed different, older. "The Paixhans guns fire shells that can travel much farther, tear into a ship, and set wooden ships ablaze on contact."

Lord George looked uneasily at his son. "Who else besides the French are using them?"

"I've heard the Russians are equipping all their naval vessels with them." Ryker paused and then continued slowly, "It is not only a matter of more deadly guns. I heard talk about Russia building larger steamships with ironclad sides that will make them invincible in battle." He hesitated and then decided not to repeat the gossip he had heard about the Russians planting round, metal devices in the Northern Azov Sea, which was connected to the Black Sea by a narrow strait. Those floating objects were said to have the capacity to cause an explosion if they came in contact with a ship. He needed more information about these strange devices before he exposed himself to his father's almost certain ridicule.

"The Russians are preparing for another war?" Lord George could not suppress a shudder as he thought of the cold steppes of Russia and the winters that had become colder each year since 1836 when England had snow fifteen feet deep and drifts of fifty feet. Last year, the winter of 1851, had been marked by the coldest temperatures and heaviest snows that had ever been known in England. He could not shake his worries about the coming year. "What else was being discussed in the coffee houses?"

Ryker seemed to consider the question carefully before responding. "There is talk of the possibility of revolutions—a desire for change in Germany, Denmark, France, and Poland."

Lord George was silent for a moment. "Any unrest in Europe will threaten English shipping, a loss of revenue we can't afford."

"Change is not limited to Europe. There was word

that a United States' clipper ship, the *Witch of the Waves*, had arrived in the East India docks."

Munevver stared at Ryker. "Why would an American ship be in the East India docks?"

"To pick up opium."

Chapter 3

Opium and the East India Company

"I can't stay! I've got to get away from here!" Ryker stormed into Munevver's sanctuary, a secluded room above the massive staircase with a recessed window that provided a clear view of the long approach to the manor. It had been Ryker's retreat as a little boy whenever he'd been reprimanded by his father. When Munevver had arrived from Yorkshire, there was something about her silent misery that had made him show her his hideaway and inform her that, since he was leaving, it was now her special place. Ever since that day, it had been Munevver's safe haven.

Ryker studied her carefully. He couldn't quite identify what had changed during the two years he had been away, but she seemed different, even more withdrawn, and yet, at the same time, more guarded. *How strange.* He was her older brother, but he had never known her, not until she arrived shortly before he left on the Grand Tour. He had not even known she existed. His father had offered no explanation. She had traveled from their grandfather's estate in Yorkshire accompanied only by her maid, Fayne. Ryker frowned. A grandfather he had never met, and a sister he did not know existed. It had been his aunt Frederica who had introduced her. His father had said only that she would be working with him.

Ryker felt an unaccustomed feeling of self-loathing. How selfish he had been. She had appeared sad and withdrawn, and he had done nothing to get to know her, to help her, before he left. Well, he had left her his bolt-hole. Now, she seemed closed over, sealed off in a world of her own. He should try to help her. What a ridiculous idea. He couldn't do anything to help himself. How could he help her? Lord George held the ultimate power over all of them and he hated him for it, for how impotent it made him feel.

"What's happened?" Munevver studied her brother. He had been moody since his return from the continent. "What's changed?" she asked more softly.

"Nothing has changed. Well, perhaps I've changed." He prowled around the small room, stopping in front of the corner bookcase. For a moment, the sight of his books soothed him. She had made the room her own, but she hadn't thrown away his things.

"Let me fix you a glass of Grandfather's *Lion's Milk*, and then you can tell me what's troubling you." Munevver pulled a gleaming, crystal glass and a bottle of raki from the depths of the pleated pouch of her walnut sewing table. She knew it was a hopeless dream that her grandfather would visit her, but she kept the raki ready just in case. Now, she poured out a generous two fingers and handed it to Ryker. "Sorry, I don't have any water."

He gave her a wicked grin. "I've learned, during my travels, to drink it straight."

"Grandfather would be proud of you," she quipped and then became serious. "Tell me what's wrong?" Munevver folded her hands in her lap and waited. Ryker had been home for a month, and she had noticed an increasing restlessness in him.

"The East India Company," he finally spat out. "Father seems to be blind to what they are doing."

"He's been a partner in the East India Company a long time, more than twenty-five years." She tried to read her brother and failed. "As far as I can see, the company is prospering. Each year's income is higher than the last."

"Prospering! It controls half of the world's trade! It's England's main source of income." A cold anger radiated from him. "Do you know how they manage to achieve those magnificent profits?"

"Of course I know. I spend hours every day with the accounts. The East India Company carries wool, cotton, silk, iron, and other goods from England and sells them in other European countries, in the Ottoman Empire, and in India." Munevver paused and then added slowly, "For some reason, they are selling more saltpeter recently—a lot more."

"Saltpeter? Potassium nitrate? They call it the mother of gunpowder." Ryker laughed at her shocked expression. "Even with increased sales of saltpeter, English goods account for only a small part of their profits. Their most lucrative product is the opium they pick up in India. More specifically, in Bengal." He scowled at his glass. "The esteemed East India Company controls the entire poppy production of India! Poppies are grown for just one purpose—they produce opium!" Ryker drained his glass. "Those wonderful profits come from the sale of opium!" He shook his head. "In 1836, the East India Company's opium trade was bringing in a profit of seven million dollars. The biggest share of that profit was from the sale of opium to China." He held out his empty glass. "Who knows how much it is bringing in now."

"But the East India Company doesn't sell opium to China." Munevver shook her head. "I remember Lord George telling me about the agreement with China. The English could buy Chinese tea, spices, silk, and porcelains at the Port of Canton, only the Port of Canton. They could unload their goods there, but they were not allowed to sell opium in China. Selling opium in China is punishable by death."

"How do you think the East India Company pays for the tea, spices, silks, porcelains, and oriental rugs that the English people demand?" Ryker asked.

"With the products we sell them: cotton, wool, coal, iron, and other goods."

"Their silk and cotton are much finer than anything we produce. No. The only thing they would accept in payment for their goods was silver, and England could not afford to keep depleting her silver supply."

"The East India Company would have lost their license

to trade if their ships carried opium to Chinese ports." Munevver frowned. "I remember Lord George was very firm about that point."

"The East India Company ships do not carry opium to Chinese ports. They use other ships—*country ships*. There are about six men with very fast clipper ships that pick up the opium from India where the East India Company controls the production. In exchange for smuggling opium into several ports along the coast of China—the Portuguese-controlled Macao, Larks Bay, and the island of Lintin—they demand 10 to 20 percent of the amount the East India Company receives." His laughter was tinged with cynicism. "It's rumored that a few of the *country ships* are so corrupt, they siphon off some of the East India Company's opium and smuggle it into smaller ports along the Northern Coast of China," Ryker explained.

"I can't believe an English company is involved in selling opium to the Chinese. I've read about the devastating effects of opium on users. You know my friend Louisa. She's living with her brother Edmund, who's the vicar in the village. I know that Louisa's father, who is Grandfather's vicar in Yorkshire, was against opium. In fact, she told me that religious leaders—Quakers, Congregationalists, Wesleyans, and Baptists—had all approached him, asking that he do everything he could to stop the opium trade." Munevver paused. "Louisa said that officials in the Chinese government had made several attempts to rid the country of opium. They claimed it was having a destructive effect on the people of China—the military, government workers, merchants, farmers, teachers, and even schoolchildren."

"England not involved in opium trade!" Ryker jeered. "In 1833, after the English Government ended the East India Company's monopoly on trade with China, our foreign minister, Lord Palmerston, knowing full well that England made money from the tax on opium flowing into England, as well as through its sale of opium to China, chose to ignore the opium problem. The English people were demanding opium in the form of laudanum for their use to treat everything from depression, women's problems, and as a sleeping aide for young children and even babies. Lord Palmerston sent out a new superintendent, Lord Napier, with instructions to establish trade through the Southern Port of Canton and also to find a way to extend trade to other parts of China."

"He didn't specify opium?" Munevver inquired.

"No, but other than saltpeter, which is used to make gunpowder, there was nothing that China wanted in trade for the tea and luxury goods the English were demanding." Ryker shrugged. "Lord Napier knew what was meant by extending trade to other parts of China, and he targeted the northern coastline for expansion of trade in opium."

Munevver frowned, lost in thought. "There was a threat of war as I remember."

"It was China that raised the stakes," Ryker said. "You have to admire them for doing it against such odds. Fourteen years ago, in January of 1838, Envoy Lin put a ban on the import of opium to China. His goal was to prevent the use of opium by the Chinese people and to rehabilitate them. A year later, on February 26, 1839, there was an uprising, resulting in destruction of the English merchants' *Factories*—the warehouses and living quarters of the English merchants. Of course, the merchants were furious at the destruction of their property and for endangering their families. They appealed to the English Government for military aid."

Ryker moved restlessly in the small chair by the window. The retreat of his childhood had shrunk. "Envoy Lin told England to give up the opium trade and to rely on legal trade. In response to his demand, English warships were sent to defend the *Factories*—to protect English lives, property, and what they saw as their right to conduct business."

Munevver motioned for him to continue.

"As you might expect, Envoy Lin imposed a blockage of the *Factories*. English Foreign Secretary Lord Palmerston was told that the English must give up all their opium to secure the safety of the foreign community— the merchants, their families, their workers, and their products. When news reached England of the Chinese blockage of the English merchants' trading centers and the threats to their families, Lord Palmerston declared that China had engaged in an act of unprovoked aggression against English life, liberty, and property."

Munevver moved restlessly. "You said that the new superintendent was charged with finding more markets. They would have had to be north of Canton." She paused and then cautiously resumed speaking. "The northern provinces speak a different dialect. It would have been difficult to do business with them."

"Oh, Lord Napier found a way. He convinced Protestant missionaries to translate for him in return for his support of their missions. He had the missionaries translating information about opium all along the northern coastline." Ryker shook his head. "England's sale of opium in China soared, but the situation in China was drastic. The economy, military services, government services, and the health of the people all declined. The Daoguang Emperor issued an edict banning both the importation and the use of opium throughout China. Too late. By then, there were approximately twelve million Chinese opium addicts. The emperor charged Viceroy Lin Zexu with the task of stopping the flow of opium into China. Viceroy Lin Zexu wrote a letter to Queen Victoria, appealing to her moral responsibility in stopping the opium trade that was destroying the people of China."

"How did she respond?" Munevver studied her brother.

"As far as I know, there was no response." Ryker paused. "Lin confiscated 20, 283 chests of opium. Dumped them into the sea." His voice was grim. "You could say that the incident precipitated the Opium War of 1843." He slumped against the back of his chair. "I was sixteen. I asked Father what it was about, and he said it was a matter of a dispute with some pirates but that the English Navy had settled the problem." Ryker gave a halfhearted laugh as he got to his feet. "I suppose his praise of the navy's success aroused my interest in a military career."

"Was that what your argument with him was about? You mentioned your desire to join the cavalry—again?"

"Munevver, you know how I feel! I am not cut out to be a merchant. You know every detail of the business. You can estimate the profit of any cargo, the best ships to use, the length of time to deliver the merchandise, the likelihood of weather disasters, and the effect of political disturbances." Ryker shrugged and continued with an element of defeat in his voice. "You even speak five languages! I can barely make myself understood in French. You may not believe me, Evie, but I've tried. Since I returned, I've tried, but I can't stand hours shut up in the office with Father. I'll never be the merchant he wants me to be. War is coming and I want to be part of it!"

"Oh, Ryker! You are his oldest son, his heir. He would not want to risk losing you by letting you join the cavalry. Of course he wants you with him in the business."

Ryker's voice was harsh. "I don't want to be involved in shipping opium to China."

"Surely Lord George is not involved in that." She could not force herself to use the word father, and even as she spoke, she remembered her grandfather's sharp criticism of England's involvement in the opium trade.

"You know the business. He claims that commerce is down. What do you think has accounted for his increase in revenue each year?"

She paused as she realized that Ryker was right.

Revenue had increased each year. Ryker's probing questions made her uneasy. Each day, Lord George sorted out a certain part of the business papers that he said he would take care of. Surely, he would not deal in something that injured people.

Ryker tried to soften his reply. "You know he only thinks in terms of making a profit. He would tell you that selling opium to China is not new." Trying to diminish her distress, Ryker began in a more neutral tone. "It is said that the Arabs were the first to introduce opium to China. Why by 1659, the Dutch were trading opium for Chinese silk, tea, and spices. Then there were the Portuguese, the Spanish, and the French. The latest are the Americans. They pick up opium in Smyrna, Turkey, then they offload it to other ships and sell it in China." He gave her a rueful grin. "For a long time, Turkish opium was not considered to be as good as Indian opium, but over time, as the traders adulterated the Indian opium with leaves and other material, more of the Chinese buyers preferred the unadulterated Turkish opium."

Ryker groaned. "Evie, to be entirely honest, it's not just the opium. I'm not cut out to be a merchant. I have always dreamed of a career in the military. I've asked Father again and again to buy a commission for me in the cavalry, but he refuses to even talk about it." A truculent expression made him appear little more than a boy. "Besides, I am not his only son."

"Alexander?" Munevver gasped. "He's only six years old, well, almost seven years old." She looked at her brother in disbelief. "He dreams of becoming a doctor." She tried to keep her voice steady. "You know he rescues every wounded bird and animal he comes across."

"He won't be seven forever." He grinned for the first time. "I suspect he would be a more worthy heir than I ever would." Suddenly turning serious, Ryker studied her closely and then said, with lethal softness, "You can't even bring yourself to call him Father."

"It is not because of his business dealings," she responded slowly. "He has never been my father. The only father I knew as I was growing up was my grandfather. He cared for me and taught me everything I know. He never regarded me as a cripple, something shameful to be hidden away."

Ryker patted her shoulder clumsily. "We did not know each other as children, but I am your older brother. I should have protected you through the years and I did nothing." He groaned. "I should protect you now, but I can't even help myself."

"Don't worry. I'm safe as long as my presence helps his business." Munevver tried to reassure her brother.

"Or until he finds a way to use you for a greater benefit," Ryker added cryptically.

"How could that be?" Munevver dropped down to the chair she had just vacated.

"An arranged marriage," Ryker mumbled, wishing that he had never overheard the servants' gossip.

Chapter 4

November 1852: Unrest in the East

"Exactly how many guests will be descending upon us?" Lord George inquired, addressing a piercing look of displeasure toward Aunt Frederica.

"There is so much fervor about attending the Duke of Wellington's funeral." She paused, hoping the gambit she had offered would curb his irritation at the thought of guests disturbing his preferred solitude. "You know how it is. Everyone wants to come to London to honor him."

"Humph! He died two months ago. Haven't they had enough time to express their sorrow?"

"Yes, but they want to be part of the queen's honoring of him. They want to be in London on November 18th. They are asking if they can stay a few days in order to be close to the ceremony at St. Paul's Cathedral."

"Close to the cathedral!" he thundered. "We're miles from there. How will we ever transport so many guests?"

"Well, perhaps some will decide to forgo the crush in

London," Frederica added in a soothing voice.

At her aunt's pleading look, Munevver began in a neutral voice, "There has been a letter from Lady Florence Nightingale. She'll be joining us."

"Yes, yes," Lord George interrupted. "Good family." He glanced at Lady Frederica. "I remember her mother was your close friend. Lady Florence is always welcome," he said more enthusiastically. "She's invariably up to date on what's going on."

"My goddaughter, Georgette, will be visiting for a few weeks," Aunt Frederica murmured.

"Again?" Lord George scowled. "I thought she just had a season?"

"Yes, but when her uncle went north for the shooting, he took her with him. She says she is lonely."

"Am I correct in assuming she didn't take during her season?"

Aunt Frederica ignored his question. "Her uncle's lands are so isolated." She looked pleadingly at her brother. "I couldn't refuse her request." At his reluctant nod of acceptance, she turned to Munevver and waited for her to continue.

"Uncle Charles will be here, according to his last letter."

Lord George nodded impatiently. "Yes, I am expecting

him. Go on." He frowned as he remembered his brother telling him in confidence that he was being sent to the Crimea in December to evaluate the availability of medical care. "He didn't say his son or daughter would be accompanying him, but plan accordingly."

"Ryker has invited Rauf, his classmate from Eaton, to come for a few weeks, and he will be here then."

"Is that all?" he ground out impatiently.

Aunt Frederica spoke more confidently now. "I understand our sister, Lady Patience, is planning to visit her godson, Edmund." When Lord George did not indicate that he had heard her, she said, "Even if she is staying at the vicarage with him, she will expect that both of them, and his sister, Louisa, will be invited to join us here for dinner."

"No doubt," he growled as he considered the list of guests who were of little interest to him.

Munevver hesitated. "I believe you mentioned this morning that Ari Hakuz, the Ottoman envoy, has accepted your invitation to visit." When her father nodded briskly, she added, "As I was preparing a response for you, I noticed he had referred to your meeting last year at the Great Exhibition of the Works of Industry of All Nations." For a moment, she allowed herself to re-experience the hurt she had felt when she had not been included in the family's visit to the Great Exhibition. Now, she let herself visualize the displays, the competitions, the lectures, and the dazzling ceremonies she had read about but had not been able to experience. "It seems that he is seeking information about schooling for his young cousin, Davud."

"Yes, yes, I remember. He wrote that he had recently been appointed minister of finance in the Ottoman Empire's Tercüme Odasi—the Translation Bureau."

Munevver dropped her eyes. She did not find it necessary to mention that, according to her grandfather, the Translation Bureau's real mission was to prepare well-educated, young men from distinguished Ottoman families to be statesmen for the Ottoman Empire. Grandfather had added that they were experts at gathering information.

Lord George sat, lost in thought. He was sure Ari Bey's real purpose in England was to secure help in rebuilding the Ottoman Navy for a future face-off with Russia, which everyone feared. He would find time to talk with the young man away from the inquisitive ears of London. He gathered up the papers beside his plate. "You can spend one hour helping your aunt plan the accommodations and activities for the guests." In a put-upon manner, he added, "We will have to resume our work an hour later than usual."

Munevver hesitated. She hadn't told him that her friend Louisa had come from Yorkshire to live with her brother, the vicar. She would need to be invited, too. Munevver shrugged. It was unlikely her father would object to one more. At least she could depend on Louisa to help with the other guests. As the daughter of a vicar and sister of another, she was skilled in managing visitors of all ages and temperaments.

Munevver exchanged a speaking glance with her aunt. One hour? It would take days to make arrangements for so many guests. Rooms would have to be aired and made ready. Each fireplace cleaned. Menus planned. Provisions ordered. Wines selected for each course of every meal. And, most troublesome of all, entertainment for a houseful of visitors in November would have to be arranged. It might be gorgeous weather with crisp, sunny days that fostered riding, walks, visits to neighboring estates, croquet, and even picnics. Or it could be day after day of grey skies and drizzling rain. She would have to make contingency plans for several days of indoor activities for their guests. Reluctant to worry her aunt even further, Munevver hesitated before saying what had to be said. "Knowing the family, we had better be prepared for at least one or two unexpected relatives to descend upon us as well."

Friday evening, Munevver was to remember her words as Quinn announced the unexpected arrival of Lord Cardigan, a cousin of Munevver's mother. Quickly, Munevver ran through the number of people who must be seated correctly at dinner according to their title or degree of importance. Lord George would escort Florence Nightingale, of course. Lord Cardigan would escort Aunt Frederica. Uncle Charles would be a safe partner for the unpredictable Christianna. She bit her lip. It would have to be Ryker's friend, Rauf, who would take in Georgette. She would probably be dressed outrageously and would flirt with every man there, but Rauf was surprisingly experienced for his age. Ryker would be relieved to have the gentle Louisa on his arm, and Aunt Patience would be escorted by her godson, Edmund, the vicar.

Yes, that would do it. She would have to explain to Ari Bey that he would be expected to offer his arm to her and see that she was seated on her father's left side. For a moment, she felt uneasy. She knew it would not be considered proper for an Ottoman gentleman to touch a woman not of his family, but he had been in London for more than a year, overseeing the Ottoman Bazaar in the Great Exhibition. Surely, he must have become aware of English customs to some extent. Besides, if her memory was right, Ari Hakuz was a Circassian name, not a Turkish one. The Circassian language, customs, and religious practices were different from those of the Ottomans. She suppressed a smile that accompanied a pleasant thought. *At least tonight, I will have an interesting dinner partner. While Lord George insists that I be seated near him as the correct placement for the eldest daughter of the family, he usually ignores me for the entire dinner.*

* * *

With a sense of relief, Munevver watched Aunt Frederica catch Lady Florence's eye so that they could rise from the table together and lead the ladies to the drawing room. The other ladies rose in silence and followed Aunt Frederica and Lady Florence from the dining room. The only sound was the whisper of the ladies' wide, crinoline-supported skirts as they glided toward the drawing room. They would wait until they were in the privacy of the drawing room before they shared the delicious bits of gossip they had heard during dinner. The men would remain for their after-dinner port and a chance to discuss what they considered to be the important matters of the day.

While Georgette drifted to the pianoforte, and Aunt Frederica and Aunt Patience settled into their favorite chairs by the fireplace, Munevver, Louisa, and Christianna clustered around Lady Florence. They knew from previous visits that she would provide the most interesting conversation of the evening.

For Munevver, Lady Florence was a revered model of the woman she would like to be. Although Florence came from a wealthy, aristocratic family with expectations that she would marry well, she had refused all offers of marriage that her father had conveyed to her. She insisted that she had received a calling from God, telling her she was destined to carry out some special work.

From her twenties on, Florence had taken an interest in how the sick people in the villages around her home in Hampshire were cared for, and she became convinced that God wanted her to become a nurse. Her parents, shocked and angry when she told them she wanted to learn more about nursing, had reminded her that nurses were often uneducated women from poor families, or they were drunkards or even prostitutes.

Florence had persisted in what she believed was her mission in life. It was her friend Elizabeth, the wife of Lord Sidney Herbert, the secretary of war, who had used her position on the board of a small hospital to gain permission for Florence to study with the other nurses.

Later, Florence had visited the hospital at Kaiserwerth in Germany to learn about their program for preparing nurses, and in 1851, against her parents' wishes, she received three months of training in Germany. Munevver could barely conceal her eagerness to learn what Lady Nightingale was planning to do.

"Please tell us what you are involved with now," Munevver asked as soon as they were all seated.

"Well, as you know, I've spent the last few years nursing my father, my mother, and then my sister." She lifted her hands and let them fall into her lap. "Hampshire seems to have more illnesses than other counties, especially those that affect children. There was a dreadful Scarlet Fever epidemic that caused twenty thousand deaths. The deaths were horrible, but there were also the side effects of the illness—ear infections, kidney disease, rheumatic fever, and endocarditis. So many children were left handicapped for life, and their parents had little means to care for them." She sighed. "I did what I could to help, but it was not enough." She brightened. "There is good news! A wonderful opportunity has opened up for me. I have been asked to take over the running of a small private hospital in London."

"That's wonderful news!" Munevver reached over and grasped Lady Nightingale's hands. "What about your parents?"

"My father finally realized I was serious about my commitment to nursing, and he offered to support me financially."

Florence had her dream and her father supported her. How many times had Munevver tried to tell her father of her dream of going to Aleppo to work at the headspring of their trading business with her uncle? She had tried so hard to make him understand that she wanted to see the world as Ryker had. She had reminded him that she knew their business thoroughly and was fluent in the languages of the people they traded with: French, Italian, Turkish, Persian, Arabic, and even some German. But all her father had done was hand her another report to read, summarize for him, and file. He had no interest in her dreams.

When the gentlemen joined them in the drawing room, Lady Florence opened the discussion by asking Ryker for his observations of the situation in Europe.

"As I told my father, there seemed to be a great uneasiness everywhere I went. Russia has been speaking more openly about the Ottoman Empire as the "Sick Man of Europe." He shrugged. "It is rumored that Tsar Nicholas has plans to partition off the Ottoman Empire before it reaches the anticipated demise on its own."

Lord George moved uneasily. Only a few people knew that the tsar had visited England for several weeks in the spring of 1844, seeking cooperation in dealing with the collapse of the Ottoman Empire that the tsar believed was imminent. He also wanted a commitment from England that she would take action if the Ottoman Empire was attacked by another power. The tsar's plan had not been rejected, but no action had been taken. "Although there are differences of opinion, I believe the majority hold the view that it is important to help the Ottomans maintain their empire."

Ari Bey waited for a pause in the conversation. "The Ottoman Empire has been weakened by several events—

external but also internal." Lord Charles nodded in support of Ari's comment but said nothing. Ari continued. "Yes, there have been almost constant wars with Russia over her attempts to seize territory in the Crimea that would give her warm-water ports on the Black Sea, but there have also been internal problems in the empire. The revolts in Serbia, Greece, and Egypt required military interventions that drained our resources." He took a deep breath. "On the other hand, the Ottoman Empire has made serious attempts at reorganizing—changes they hope will stabilize the minorities within the empire."

"Yes," Uncle Charles said quietly. "As I remember, the latest was the Reform Degree. It was truly an astonishing undertaking." Realizing that he had captured their interest, he continued. "In the summer of 1839, the sultan and high-ranking officials drafted the Tanzimat Degree, also known as the Reform Degree. It was an amazing plan, and even the Ottoman elite, the ruling class, supported it. They wanted to ensure the integrity of the empire, and they were willing to use all of the empire's resources— political, military, fiscal, and ideological resources—to achieve their goal." He hesitated and then added, "They saw reform as the best chance for the empire's survival."

"The changes were drastic and far-reaching." Ari's enthusiasm for the topic Uncle Charles had introduced was evident by the flush covering his cheeks. "They created a disciplined army, limited the power of provincial rulers to reduce corruption, standardized government practices, and used their newly created European Embassies to achieve a more equitable trade balance. It was a very ambitious plan. It was also a costly undertaking and the people suffered. They faced heavier taxes, inflation, and loss of their sons and husbands as thousands were pressed into military service. Several sultans had supported similar reforms, but none more strongly than the current sultan, Sultan Abdulmejid." Ari studied the faces of the men grouped around Lord George. "There are always factions that are opposed to change, and certainly, the Ottoman Empire has many of them. There are the usual religious and ethnic enemies, but there are others: rural versus cosmopolitan, educated versus traditionalists, and wealthy versus the poor."

It was Lord George who broke the silence that followed Ari's comments. "Yes, there were many problems, but there were also some advances. In 1838, there was the Anglo-Ottoman Commercial Treaty that increased trade between England and the Ottoman Empire. The Ottoman Empire was sending us more raw silk, wool, wheat, raisins, and currants, and we were exporting more cotton cloth, refined sugar, iron, steel, hardware, and cutlery." He raised his head proudly. "England's exports to Constantinople tripled between 1840 and 1851."

"Yes, trade was flourishing, but the Ottoman Empire was vulnerable," Ari said. "The military was weak and the navy outdated and in poor shape." He decided to forgo saying that the Ottoman Navy had not recovered from the terrible 1827 Battle of Navarino when the English Navy, eager to assist the Greeks in their fight for independence, had destroyed most of the Ottoman Navy—destroyed them while they lay at anchor, moored in the Ottoman harbor of Navarino. Although he was not certain they were following what he was saying, Ari Bey resumed. "Now we find ourselves threatened by a Russia that has the largest land army in Europe. Yes, their weaponry is out of date and their men poorly prepared, but they have a limitless supply of manpower that they can mobilize."

"Their navy is smaller than the Ottoman Navy," Lord George said firmly.

"Perhaps, but the Russian Navy has steam-powered, ironclad ships and cannons that can deliver explosive missiles," Ryker interjected grimly. "They do not have to depend on the uncertainty of the wind to navigate and the dead weight of short-range cannonballs to inflict damage." Barely able to contain his impatience, Ryker glared at the men surrounding his father. "Everyone knows there is going to be war. The question is, when will it start?"

"A young man's question," Uncle Charles offered dryly. "Older men ask what will be the cost?"

Chapter 5

November 1852: Teaching Horses to Swim

"We've been most fortunate to have the warmth of summer linger into these late days of fall," Aunt Frederica offered in an attempt to engage the guests gathered at the breakfast table as Lord George ignored them while he directed his attention to the newspaper folded by his left arm.

When no one responded, Christianna, glowing with pleasure at being allowed to join the adults, beamed at her aunt. "Yes! The days have been warm, and Nolan says that if it stays warm a little longer, he'll be able to teach the horses he's been training to swim." When no one broke the silence that followed this news, she decided to offer further information. "Of course, some of the horses know how to swim instinctively, but not all know how." She looked around at the startled breakfasters. "It's important they be able to swim if the water level is high when they disembark."

Assuming the silence that followed was an indication of interest in the topic, Christianna continued with enthusiasm. "Horses have been transported by sailing ships for a very long time, but there has always been the problem of getting them off the ships when they reach their destination." Well pleased that she had been able to remember some history, her father's favorite subject, she directed her words toward the head of the table. "The ancient Greek, Herodotus, described horses being brought to Greece on sailing ships by the invading Persian Army in 1500 BC."

She bubbled on. "If you look at the Bayeux Tapestry very closely, you can see horses disembarking from the Norman ships of James the Conqueror." Suddenly aware of her father's grim expression, she remembered that the Bayeux Tapestry depicted not just horses disembarking, but also the act that all Englishmen found deplorable— the Norman conquest of England in 1066. She rushed to finish. "During a sea voyage, horses are usually suspended in slings on deck or tethered tightly and boxed into compartments in the hold. It's very stressful for the horses." She glanced around the table at the fascinated guests. "As you can imagine, getting them off the ship can be perilous, especially for those that cannot swim."

Without looking at her father, Munevver knew he was bristling with rage. She turned toward him now in an attempt to deflect his wrath from her sister. "How very interesting, as I believe you said that Nolan had already achieved a remarkable feat in training your horses for the military in two months instead of the usual two years." She raised an eyebrow at Ryker for help, but it was Ari Bey who came to her aid.

"My lord, you have accomplished a truly amazing

feat." Ari had early on recognized that Lord George was one of those men who would want all the credit for an achievement and would never acknowledge that it had been accomplished by someone in his employment. "I had heard that the Austrians have a system that uses a shorter time period, but nothing like you have taught your man to do."

"Nolan says that horses are best taught not by harshness but by gentleness," Christianna offered in a low voice.

Ari directed his request to Lord George. "I would very much like to meet this man Nolan before I go back."

"His name is Louis Edward Nolan." Christianna, suddenly aware of her father's mounting anger, risked adding, "He's with the 15th Hussars."

"You have a man who can train horses in two months?" Ari shook his head. "I would have believed it to be impossible. I have always heard it takes at least two years."

Lord George responded to the not-so-subtle flattery. "No. Monsieur Baucher of France wrote a book about his methods of training—*Methods of Equitation*. He emphasized the use of a two-month training period." He paused, lost in thought. "He was an interesting man. He believed very strongly in the power of a cavalry attack. He insisted that the cavalry attack should be used in conjunction with sustained artillery firing and against a *routed* enemy." He looked around the room at the fascinated listeners. "Monsieur Baucher could bring his horses to do in two months what years of training using old-school methods could not accomplish." His voice lost its tone of approval. "This man, Nolan, adapted Baucher's approach to training horses for the cavalry."

"Nolan? Who is he? What's his background?" Rauf asked Ryker in a low voice. They had been schoolmates at Eaton and, as a frequent visitor at Lord George's home, he sensed that Lord George did not approve of Nolan.

"I don't really know," Ryker murmured. "I've been away for two years, and I don't believe he was here before I left."

It was Lord George who supplied the information as he addressed the table in general. "The man's a Scot. His father was an educated man who moved around a lot. It's said he spoke Italian, German, and French. Nolan probably learned those languages from him." He shook his head disparagingly. "He's a clever chap. He picked up the language wherever they lived—Hungary, Poland, and Russia." Lord George shrugged his shoulders dismissively. "I hired him because he had trained with the Austrian Imperial Army for a time." He frowned. "That's all I know about him."

Christianna unwisely added to her father's description. "Nolan's father knew Lord Raglan, and he helped Nolan apply to the Army Riding School at Maidstone," Christianna beamed proudly. When there was no response, she added helpfully, "It's near Kent, near the coast." Slightly subdued by the continued silence, she added in a low voice, "He was appointed riding master of his regiment."

"I wonder what method he uses to train horses in such a short time," Ari Bey murmured. The thought of the Ottoman Cavalry being able to train horses in two months was intriguing. He had to learn more about Nolan before he returned to Constantinople.

"He has just finished writing about his method." Christianna paused. "Did you know the earliest manual on horse training was written in 360 BC?" She nodded vigorously, hoping this bit of historical information would placate her father. "Nolan's book is titled, *The Training of Cavalry Remount Horses: A New System*. He says the trainer should never punish young horses, should never shout or hit them." She continued as though reciting from the book. "Cavalry horses must be versatile. They must be trained for reconnaissance, raiding, communication, supply, and, of course, for cavalry charges." She paused. "Nolan says they have to be taught to swim, too."

"Taught to swim? Don't all horses know how to swim?" Ryker asked.

"No. Most do but some panic." Christianna studied Ari before continuing. "Nolan says we will most likely have to transport the horses by sailing ships, but when it comes time to get them off the ships, there may be no ramps. They will have to swim to the beach."

"Did Mr. Nolan say where they would be swimming?" Ryker could not resist teasing his younger sister.

"No." She glared at him. "Where else but the Black Sea?" She turned her back on him. "Even I know there will be war there any day now."

Intercepting her father's thunderous glare in Christianna's direction, Munevver turned to Georgette and spoke quickly before her sister could continue on what appeared to be her favorite subject. "Has your mother completed her plans for her gardens?" When she did not reply immediately, Munevver turned to Ari. "Georgette's mother has the most beautiful gardens in all of England, and each year she designs them to feature different flowers."

"I believe she has finalized her plans." Georgette smiled at Ari. "Perhaps you would like to view the gardens in the summer?"

"That sounds delightful, but unfortunately, I am not certain that I will be here then."

Chapter 6

November 1852: Threat of War

The hours working with Lord George had seemed endless to Munevver. He had ordered trays for lunch, but there had been no other interruption. *There is one good thing to look forward to*, Munevver thought as she stretched her aching back. *Today is Aunt Frederica's at-home day, and she expects me to be at her side, ready to receive the ladies who will come to call.*

Munevver hurried to scrub the ink stains from her hands and change from the black skirt and grey blouse she wore while working with Lord George into the only afternoon dress she had—a worn, mauve silk that she had worn in Yorkshire during the second year of mourning for her grandmother. Now, as she hurried to join the others in the drawing room, she let the gentle elegance of Aunt Frederica's voice calm her.

"Traveling and learning foreign languages have long been traditions in our family." Lady Frederica settled back into her chair before taking a sip of her tea. "My cousin, Lady Montague, married Edward Montague. He was fluent in French, of course." She looked around the circle of listeners, most of whom had heard the story many times. "In 1716, when he was appointed ambassador to the Sublime Porte, Lady Mary traveled with him to Constantinople. They were only there one year, but she made many visits to the Royal Harem at Topkapi Palace and learned to speak Turkish."

"Indeed," Ari Bey murmured as he balanced his teacup and saucer on his knee with newly acquired expertise.

"Lord Montague was supposed to bring about peace between the Ottoman Empire and Austria." Lady Frederica took another sip. "Unfortunately, the Ottomans did not agree to the English proposed terms, and Lord Montague was forced to return to England the following year."

Munevver smiled fondly at her aunt. "I remember you telling us that after they returned, Lady Montague worked tirelessly to encourage people to be vaccinated against smallpox. Her brother had died from smallpox, and although she survived the disease, she had been left with scars. When she learned that Turkish women followed the custom of Circassian mothers— vaccinating their daughters in order to safeguard their beauty—she was determined to bring the practice of vaccination back to England. She did not want other girls to suffer the disfiguring effects of smallpox as she had. She described how the Turkish women would gather for tea, and an old woman would come to the harem and inoculate all of them." She paused, and then when she had their full attention said, "Just imagine! Lady Mary Montague managed to bring some of the vaccine back to England in a walnut shell."

"They say there is hope that by next year, smallpox vaccination will be required for all the children in England." After their murmurs had subsided, Aunt Frederica added, with a twinkle in her eye, "She also brought back Balm of Mecca. She said it was the finest face cream she had ever seen." She rubbed her hands together and then added crisply, "To give credit where it's due, it was her son, Edward, who taught my grandfather Turkish, Arabic, and Persian."

"I know most English gentlemen learn Latin and French and some Greek, but it is most unusual for one to study Arabic and Persian. I wonder what drove him to do that?" Ari Bey inquired, managing to keep his voice carefully neutral.

"Oh, Edward loved to travel." Aunt Frederica paused and then added delicately, "He lived in many places, but he always returned to England." She frowned at her cup as she tried to recall something. "Yes, I remember now. He lived for some time in Smyrna where he studied Turkish, and then he lived in Leiden in Holland for a few years. Leiden has a very old and highly esteemed university. He studied languages there. But as I said, he would always return to England, and it was during those times that he taught my grandfather Arabic and Persian."

"Ah, the young Edward Montague!" Lord Charles said caustically as he and Lord George joined the ladies in the drawing room. "Famous for his facility in foreign languages, and infamous for his tendency to marry a succession of women without obtaining a divorce between marriages." Lord Charles's voice was sedate, but his eyes sparkled with mischief.

"As I've heard, the family considered him to be officially insane." Lord George sought to conclude the discussion about one of the black sheep of the family.

Chapter 7

November 1852: Golden Cages

The following evening, Munevver relaxed slightly as she surveyed the dinner table during a brief lull in the conversation. Everything seemed to be proceeding as her father would wish, and then she heard Christianna break the silence as she directed a question to Ari Bey. "Is it true the sultan's brothers are imprisoned in golden cages?"

"Ah, I think you are asking about the Kafes, the princes' apartments," Ari Bey responded smoothly. "In the third courtyard of the harem, in the innermost part of the sultan's household complex, there are pavilions with beautiful apartments. Each apartment is decorated with the most exquisite blue, green, and aquamarine ceramic tiles, Iznik tiles. There are white, marble fountains and large, brass fireplaces. The apartments are furnished with magnificent oriental rugs, velvet divans covered with bolsters, and huge, brass mangals in the center of the room to provide heat."

"Yes, but do they have to spend their entire lives in the

cages?" Christianna persisted despite a hissed warning from Aunt Frederica.

"Not their entire lives. Until the age of twelve, they live with their mothers in the harem, the women's section of the palace." He hesitated. "If a boy's mother dies and no one is willing to adopt him, he may be placed in the Kafes at a younger age."

"How young?" Christianna probed.

"I believe there was one instance of a three-year-old prince." He straightened his shoulders and continued. "The princes are educated in history, philosophy, and languages—French, Turkish, Persian, and sometimes Italian—and they also have lessons in music, art, and leather or woodworking, if they wish." He paused, surveying the ring of silent listeners. *How can I explain an expedient Ottoman custom to a roomful of English gentry who have never ventured from the island of England?*

Ari decided to use a gentle lecturing approach. "The custom of secluding the sultan's brothers began about two hundred fifty years ago. In 1603, to be exact. Before then, in order to prevent revolutions whenever a new sultan succeeded one who had died, the new sultan would have all of his brothers put to death. Since it is against the Muslim religion for one Muslim to spill another Muslim's blood, princes and brothers were usually strangled with a bow string." He looked at Munevver for guidance, and at her slight nod continued as though recounting a well-known period of history.

"It may seem violent to you, but in 1402, after Sultan Bayezid's death, there was a ten-year war between his successor, Mehmed I, and his three brothers. During those ten years of fighting, many civilians and soldiers lost their lives and the empire lost territory. For a sultan to lose Ottoman land was considered to be an unforgiveable failure." No one spoke, so Ari proceeded in full lecture mode.

"On October 6, 1553, Sultan Suleyman the Magnificent left Constantinople with the army for his third campaign in the East against the Safavids—the main opponents to the Ottomans in that area. He asked his son, Mustafa, to join him. Later, the sultan accused his son of conspiring against him and had him strangled. This was the beginning of the tradition of Ottoman sultans committing filicide, killing their sons, or fratricide, killing their brothers, by strangulation with a bow string or by poisoning. Fratricide had been officially endorsed earlier by Sultan Mehmed II, who conquered Constantinople in 1453 as a way to maintain public order, prevent succession wars, and ensure the safety of Ottoman territory.

"The policy remained in place for nearly one hundred fifty years. Then, in 1595, Sultan Mehmed III killed nineteen brothers and half brothers. Seeing nineteen coffins, some very small, carried through the streets of Constantinople was too much for the public and they protested. The next sultan, Ahmed I, did not strangle his brothers. If they were under twelve years old, they continued to live in the harem with their mothers and were educated there. As soon as they reached puberty, they were placed in the Kafes, the pavilions within the most secluded court of the harem, and their education in government and world affairs ceased." *How can I tell a roomful of prim English ladies that the princes are well supplied with wine and beautiful but barren women?*

"Although the princes were not allowed to learn administration or to have political, military, or economic experiences, they did learn a craft. Some made beautiful jewelry. Some became experts in cabinetmaking. Some were very skilled in calligraphy or poetry." Ari felt compelled to end on a more optimistic note. "Sometimes, despite his lack of education, knowledge of the world, or experience in governing, one of the princes would be taken from the Kafes to serve as sultan."

"They were imprisoned for life?" Christianna gasped.

"Yes, unless they were needed to replace a sultan who died or was killed." Ari hesitated. "When Sultan Abdülhamid I died of a stroke on April 7, 1789, Selim III became sultan. He had lived in the Kafes most of his life, but he was well educated. In fact, he brought about many changes. He created a more just tax system, modernized the military and the navy, and opened Ottoman embassies in the major European capitals. Sometimes he went too far. When he accepted help from England and France in training a new branch of the military, the Janissaries, the elite military division of the Ottoman Army, and the religious leaders did not approve, and Sultan Selim III was returned to the Kafes in 1807, where he was strangled on orders from his successor, Sultan Mustafa IV."

"He had eighteen years of freedom," Munevver said softly. "Did any of his reforms last?"

"Yes, some did, and the idea of reform was not lost."

"The Kafes," Christianna shuddered. "I can't think of anything more horrible!"

For a moment, Ari thought of the special method of death reserved for sultans—twisting or compressing their testicles until they died from shock—but he decided against sharing that information and instead introduced European customs. "During the same period of time, France was well known for using *La Guillotine*, beheading." He paused, lost in thought. "England used beheading into the 1700s. Norway, Sweden, Denmark, and Germany used it longer."

Munevver responded in a soft voice. "I believe the Tower of London has served a similar purpose as the Kafes—seclusion. There were some Frenchmen held there in the 1100s, and the Earl of Kent, a Welch Prince, in the 1200s." She paused. "As I recall, there was also a Scot, David II of Scotland. Then, of course, there were the two young princes, twelve-year-old Edward and his brother, ten-year-old Richard. They were incarcerated there in 1470 by order of their uncle. It's said they died there."

As she watched Christianna fidget, Aunt Frederica tried to stave off whatever she was so eager to ask. "As I recall, Ann Boleyn was imprisoned there in 1533, but I don't remember for how long."

Christianna could not let the topic go. "The cages are not still in use, are they?"

Ari raised an eyebrow in Munevver's direction. What was he supposed to do? "As I said, the Kafes are a very beautiful part of the harem section of the Seraglio. Some princes live there and some live in remote palaces, far from Constantinople." He felt himself relax as Munevver nodded in approval of his response.

"What is this recent nonsense I'm hearing about the French demanding a key to one of the church doors in the Holy Land?" Lord Charles, who seldom raised his voice, spoke loudly enough to divert Lord George, who was scowling at Christianna.

Lord George rose to his brother's challenge. "You know how that upstart Napoleon is trying to gain the support of the French. He's using an old issue. The Orthodox Russian Church has the key to the main door of the Church of the Nativity, but the French do not. They have a key to the side door."

"What does it matter?" Ryker asked.

"It matters because the Russians can enter the church first," Lord George stated flatly.

"Would they go to war over a key?" Ryker asked.

"Nations have gone to war over less," Uncle Charles answered.

Chapter 8

November 1852: Medical Readiness for War?

The next day, after dinner and after the ladies had retired to the drawing room, Lady Florence Nightingale began the conversation with a topic that was uppermost on her mind. "I'm sure the men are discussing the likelihood of war." She straightened her shoulders and looked around the silent room. "If there is war in the East—and it looks very likely there will be—it is almost inevitable that we will be drawn into it. All wars have been associated with death of the nation's young men, but there is also the extremely high toll of wounded and ill soldiers. What I am trying to say is that there will be many English soldiers who will need medical care." She ignored the shocked murmurs around her. "There will also be many who require care after surgery on the battlefield, and there will be even more who become ill with cholera, dysentery, typhoid, malaria, and other infections. Who will care for them?

"I don't know the state of military medical care, but I've seen what passes for nursing in London. It is a disgrace! The hospitals are filthy, and the so-called nurses are drunkards, thieves, or worse." Her voice dropped. "It's true. They use foul language, extort money from the patients, and steal from everyone. They know nothing about caring for the sick or wounded." Florence looked at the elegantly dressed women in Frederica's drawing room, drinking expensive tea from China.

"When war breaks out in the East, it will be our husbands, brothers, and sons who will be called to fight." She spoke in a strong, clear voice. "Many will be wounded or maimed. The army surgeons will do the amputations where they fall, but who will care for them?" The room was silent now, the women staring at her in shock. "You have heard me talk about what I feel is my calling, to serve the Lord by nursing those who need it." She looked at the group defiantly. "I know it is not considered respectable for gentlewomen to do such work, but I believe that it is my destiny." She straightened her back.

"Last year, I went to Kaiserswerth in Germany to observe the hospitals and nurses." She quivered with excitement. "It was amazing. The hospitals were spotless. Each patient had clean linen and was cared for by skilled nurses—women who had been trained to tend to the ill and wounded." She nodded vigorously. "I've heard it is the same in Paris. Yet, here in England, we have not improved the care of those who can't afford to be looked after at home or in doctors' homes. When war comes, it will be our loved ones who suffer from lack of care." She looked at the women surrounding her. "They will be thousands of miles away, in a foreign land, and in desperate need of attention. Who will tend to your wounded husbands, brothers, and sons?"

In an attempt to diminish the shock that followed Lady Florence's words, Aunt Frederica began a rambling description of how the ladies' sewing circle was now focusing on meeting the needs of distressed governesses and seamstresses and how they were trying to find a suitable home for them. She concluded by saying that they spent one afternoon a week embroidering tray cloths for the home they were planning to furnish once they had located a suitable one.

Munevver addressed her words directly to Lady Florence. "It is not just a need for trained caregivers on the battlefield or in field hospitals that war brings. There is an unfortunate residue of every war—the huge number of returning injured and disabled soldiers who need care. The fortunate ones may find a retirement home like the Royal Hospital Chelsea or the Royal Hospital Kilmainham in Dublin. They will have a six-foot by five-foot room, food, and clothing. They are the lucky ones, but it is the streets of every city in England and Ireland that are the homes for the less fortunate, and those streets can be very cold in the winter." She reached for her bag that was always nearby. "If I could, I would join Florence in learning to be a nurse, qualified to provide care for our soldiers, but I can't. Instead, I spend the spare moments of my days knitting socks and mufflers for the soldiers of the streets."

The silence that followed her words was broken by the men entering the drawing room.

"Lady Florence has been telling us about her experiences this year when she went to Paris to train with the French Sisters of Charity at the Maison de la

Providence." Lady Frederica's voice was steady, although the slight color in her cheeks betrayed her worry about what Lord George's response would be. She continued. "She has been alerting us to the need for nursing care for our men if there is war."

"Well, Foreign Secretary Lord Palmerston considers Lord Stratford de Redcliffe, our ambassador to Constantinople, to be the highest authority on the Eastern Question." Lord George rambled on, trying to avoid the subject of war. He paused and then added, "Lord Stratford de Redcliffe is not speaking about an imminent threat of war."

"He has spent many years in the Ottoman Empire, as I recall," Uncle Charles murmured. "He was sent there for the first time in 1808. Then in 1814–1818, he served as an envoy to Switzerland, and in 1820–1824 as envoy extraordinaire to the United States. After that, he was dispatched to Constantinople to serve as our ambassador to the Ottoman Empire. Five times he has served as ambassador to the Ottoman Empire. It would appear that there is no one better qualified to know the thinking of the Sublime Porte. In fact, the Ottomans call him The Great Elchi, The Great Ambassador."

"You didn't mention that he was appointed ambassador to Russia in 1832, but the tsar refused to accept his appointment." Ryker supplied this bit of information with a mischievous glance at his father. "The tsar called him a *persona non grata*. I remember Palmerston saying it was an outrageous act. Not surprisingly, relations between de Redcliffe and Russia have been strained ever since."

Uncle Charles studied his nephew. "Yes, those hard feelings have not changed, but the world has been changing. Not too long ago, the Ottoman Empire reached from the Crimea in Asia, to Austria in Europe, and to Algiers in North Africa. Then several provinces rebelled—the Serbs in 1804 and the Egyptians in 1805. That was the beginning of the decline of the Ottoman Empire, but the Greeks really lit the fire of independence. They fought over ten years, from 1821 to 1833, to establish independence, an independence they are in danger of losing."

"Yes." Lord George nodded slowly. "There has been an uprising for independence in several provinces, but it is Russia that is the biggest threat to the continued existence of the Ottoman Empire. Russia has fought the Ottoman Empire again and again in desperate attempts to acquire warm-water ports like Odessa on the Black Sea. Now, Russia wants what they consider to be rightfully theirs— the Byzantine city of Constantinople. Lord de Redcliffe is determined to prevent Russia from seizing it."

"Stratford de Redcliffe is a very clever man," Lord Charles offered cautiously. "Not of the ton, of course. There was that unfortunate marriage of his father." Lord Charles frowned and then refocused. "He is astute, devious, and dangerous. He has maneuvered the young Sultan Abdulmejid into the position we're all in now— the brink of war!"

"Well, it might be more accurate to say that Russia orchestrated the situation," Ryker risked adding to the discussion. "She has been urging the Danubian provinces to seek their freedom from the Ottoman Empire for years."

"It didn't take much urging," Lord George snapped. "Years of heavy taxes and forced conscription of their youth into the Sultan's Army, in combination with oppressive local governments, were powerful incentives. Ever since Greece won her independence in 1833, Russia has been quietly supporting the Balkan provinces in their desire for independence."

"Yes, and now Albania, Serbia, Wallachia, and Moldavia are almost independent," Lord Charles offered in a neutral voice. "They are all ripe for Russian acquisition. In truth, since 1830, the Ottoman Empire has had only nominal control over them." He gave a hopeless shrug. "Nevertheless, they are Ottoman provinces, and the Ottoman Government will have to protect them if it comes to that."

"You say Russia is supporting them in their desire for independence!" Ryker scoffed. "Russia didn't support independence when Hungary tried to break away. In fact, when Hungary was defeated and Kossuth, Bem, and other leaders of the Hungarian uprising fled to the Ottoman Empire seeking sanctuary, the tsar demanded that the sultan return them to Russia. When the sultan refused, the tsar was furious."

"As I recall, he cited the 1774 Treaty of Küçük Kaynarca." Lord Charles spoke before Lord George could challenge his son. "According to the treaty, the Ottomans were not to give refuge to rebels and evildoers."

The vicar, who had been following the interchanges

intently, spoke up for the first time. "There was an exception. Refugees who escaped to the Ottoman Empire and converted to Islam could not be returned to Russia."

"Did the provision specify how long they had to remain Muslims?" Lord Charles needled the vicar gently.

Ryker came to the defense of Edmund. "The sultan said he would rather give up his throne than endanger the lives of those who had fled to him seeking protection." He glanced at Ari, who had been silent. "England and other European countries supported the sultan."

"I'm sure Lord de Redcliffe had some role in the sultan's decision." Lord George smiled cynically. "I've heard that the tsar found the European nations' praise for the young sultan's gallant stand to be especially galling."

"The Russian tsar should find the possibility of both England and France supporting the sultan terrifying," Lord Charles added. "France and England seldom agree on anything."

Ryker joined the conversation of the older men more confidently. "The sultan is facing threats on two fronts. The Russian desire for warm-water ports is not new. Russia and the Ottomans have fought over that issue many times." He exchanged a look with Ari and, at his barely perceptible nod, continued. "The greater threat to the Ottoman Empire comes from within—the emergence of an educated elite—young men who do not agree with the current Ottoman administration. They are demanding social, political, and economic reforms."

Turning suddenly to Ari, who had remained silent during the heated exchange, Lord George asked, "How do you view the situation?"

With only the barest pause, Ari replied, "The Russian threat is of great concern. As you are well aware, the Ottoman Empire's Navy is obsolete. It was never rebuilt after its destruction at the Battle of Navarino. The army— ill fed and unpaid—has scattered across the plains of Anadolu and the treasury is empty." He sighed as he surveyed the group of wealthy, aristocratic Englishmen standing in the comfort of an elegant English manor house. "History tells us that Russia is likely to begin hostilities in late fall or early winter." He shrugged. "Traditionally, sultans led their troops into battle after the spring planting was completed and hoped to return for the harvest. It is the Russians who consider winter to be their ally."

* * *

As soon as the gentlemen drifted into the drawing room to join the ladies, Georgette settled herself on the settee beside Munevver. "What a delightful opportunity to learn what my dearest friend has been doing since I was last here." She spoke in a voice trained from childhood to be charming as her eyes evaluated each of the men entering the drawing room. Before Munevver could reply, Georgette whispered, "I didn't meet the man wearing the red fez before dinner. Who is he?"

"That would be Ari Bey, Ari Hakuz." Munevver did not offer any more information until Georgette hissed, "He's very attractive! Who is he?"

"He's an envoy of the Sublime Porte."

Georgette managed to smile sweetly as she jabbed Munevver with her elbow. "And what, pray tell, is the Sublime Porte?"

"It is the term often used when referring to the government and officials of the Ottoman Empire."

"Oh my! He is important as well as handsome. What is he doing here?"

"I think it is safe to say that he is in London on business related to the Ottoman Empire."

Georgette's eyes flashed with anger but she spoke softly. "What is he doing here in your father's drawing room?"

"He and Lord George became acquainted last year when he came to supervise the Ottoman Hall in the Crystal Palace." When Georgette made no response, she added, "The Great Exhibit."

"Yes, yes, of course. I want to meet him." Georgette covered her demand with a demure smile. "Let's take a turn around the room and find your brother. We'll ask Ryker if he and the handsome Ari would like to join us in a game of bridge."

"Ryker hates bridge."

"It doesn't matter. He will have to introduce Ari to me." She gave a slight shrug designed to call attention to the ivory smoothness of her shoulders and the shadowy hint of cleavage enhanced by the crimson satin of her dress. "After that, I'll manage well enough."

As Munevver had predicted, Ryker politely declined the invitation to make up a table for bridge, but he was forced to introduce Ari Bey to Georgette, adding that she was Aunt Frederica's goddaughter. Lord George overheard the conversation and, aware of Ari's uneasiness, invited him to play chess.

Munevver hurried over to sit beside Aunt Frederica. She intended to tell her she would like to retire early, but before she could speak, Lord George called her to take his place at the chess table. "There's a messenger waiting for me in my study." He motioned to the chess table. "I've started with the English opening. You can't go wrong if you follow that."

Ari Bey stood courteously as Munevver approached the chess table. When she was settled, he politely asked if she would prefer to start over. With a quick nod, her fingers began to fly over the board. Ari settled back in his chair and asked the question that had been constantly in his thoughts. "How does it happen that an English lady knows languages, history, and international business?" Ari studied her opening as he awaited her reply. "And chess?"

"My grandfather taught me what he thought was important for an educated person to know." She paused, not certain how much to tell him, and then added cautiously, "Not everyone shares my grandfather's views. Most members of society believe education for females has just one purpose—to prepare a young woman to be a desirable candidate for marriage. The greater the wealth, the higher the rank, or the more ambitious the family, the more preparation is required of the young woman.

"When I came to live at my father's home, Aunt Frederica informed me it was expected that an advantageous marriage would be arranged for me and that I must be prepared for such an eventuality. She told me that it was my duty to be prepared to attract the notice of the eligible men I would be introduced to. While my knowledge of languages was admirable, she said I needed accomplishments that could be displayed. I must learn to play the piano and to sing. I would also have dancing lessons and lessons in painting, water colors only, of course. She expected me to improve my skills in fine embroidery. I had to memorize the peerage of England, read classical history, and learn the geography that was pertinent to the English Empire." At the incredulous expression on Ari's usually inscrutable face, Munevver added quickly, "I failed miserably." An awkward silence followed this statement, and she hastened to rectify the situation. "I suppose it's the same in your country?"

"Marriages are arranged." He spoke slowly with his eyes on the chess board. "But it is the man's mother who does the selection." At her questioning look, he continued. "Daughters are educated at home—languages, music, embroidery, and managing a home." He hesitated and then proceeded with his eyes lowered. "Mothers have the opportunity to meet the daughters of other women during their afternoon visits, at celebrations, and, of course, at the hammam."

"Hammam? The bath?"

"Yes. Some homes have their own hammams, but most women prefer to go to the larger hammams with their relatives and friends. They reserve rooms and spend the whole day relaxing, feasting, and sharing the news. The women with sons are accorded deference by the mothers of daughters as they try to present their daughters to their best advantage. The mothers make notes of potential brides for their sons." He shrugged. "It is the mother who decides who the bride will be."

At his first mention of the hammams, Munevver had felt a blush creeping over her. Unmarried ladies did not discuss such things with men. "I see," she mumbled.

"In our society, it makes sense. A young man and his bride usually live with his family, often in a section of his father's house, and so it is his mother who has the most contact with his wife."

"Doesn't that ever cause problems?"

"Perhaps, but girls learn this system from a very early age. They know that someday they will be in a similar position."

Realizing she had participated in a conversation that should never have taken place, Munevver hastened to move a chess piece as she saw her father returning.

He glowered at the board. "You started over." His voice became colder as he surveyed the bold flank opening she had chosen. "You used the Hungarian opening? I told you to stick to the English opening. I knew it was all you could handle." He slid into the chair she had vacated and began to rearrange the pieces.

Chapter 9

Christianna: Banished to Yorkshire

"Dinner last evening was a disaster!" Lord George shouted over his shoulder at Munevver as she followed him into the study. "First horses and then cages! Your sister is not to join us for any meals when we have guests until she learns how to act like a proper young lady." He shook with anger. "It's your job to teach her how to behave. It's simple! Three things: She must be an obedient daughter, a charming wife, and a devoted mother. That's all that's required of her." He misinterpreted the stricken expression on Munevver's face when she heard him declare the expectations he had for her little sister. He added gruffly, "Don't worry. You'll be a wife and mother. You'll be a duchess. I'll make you a duchess somehow, and then you can help launch your sister. For now, manage the situation."

He settled at his desk and glanced at the headlines of the newspaper. "It looks like the Russians have activated their Southern Army. They are moving their fleet into the Black Sea." He frowned at the paper and then said, in a more urgent tone, "They are fortifying Sevastopol!"

He stared at her. "I think it is best if your marriage is arranged as soon as possible."

Arranged as soon as possible? Munevver tried to suppress a shudder. She did not want to marry—ever—and she definitely did not want a marriage arranged for her by a man who had never had any thought for what she might want in life, only for how she could benefit him and the family.

"Yes. If there's war, and it looks as though there very well may be, there would be no sense in wasting money for a season for you and Christianna. Most of the eligible men would be away serving in the army or navy." He appeared to look older as he passed his hand over his face. "A war could last two years . . . or more. Many young men will be killed." He straightened in his chair as though he had reached a difficult business decision. Motioning for Munevver to take her usual place at the small table near his, he handed her a bundle of mail. "Start with these. We have a lot of work to do today."

Even now, when her fate hung in the balance, she could not bring herself to address him as father. "I would really prefer not to marry." She glanced down at the clumsy boot partially hidden by her skirt. "I am not what young men dream of when they consider a bride."

"Nonsense. I'm an earl. It may not be a grand title, but at least it's a title accepted by the ton. You have a respected, old family name and an excellent dowry, an outstanding dowry." He paused. "I'll take care of the details."

"You have been very thoughtful in providing such a generous dowry, but it cannot change the fact that I am a cripple—a woman who can't dance, can't even walk into dinner gracefully." She lifted her head and forced herself to continue. "Even worse, I am considered to have tainted blood. Any family would worry that a child I give birth to might have the same affliction."

Lord George studied his shoes. How could he tell her that he felt driven to make up for her clubfoot? His mother had also had a clubfoot, and he remembered how people treated her, his beautiful, gentle mother who led the life of a recluse, ignored by his father and her social contacts limited to the family. "Think carefully. If you do not marry, you will be a burden to your brothers and sister. Do you want to live as a dependent in Ryker's home when he marries? Would you want every aspect of your life arranged by his wife? Do you want Christianna's husband to be responsible for your care?" He frowned at her. "Or will it be Alexander's fate to have to provide for his unmarried older sister?"

"Please, Father," she said desperately, not realizing that she had called him father for the first time in her life. "Let me have the dowager house. It's small and secluded. It could be a home for me and Fayne. Please!"

"No. You are being selfish. Think of the help you could give your brothers and your sister if you marry the son of a duke." He smiled at her gasp. "Yes, that's my plan. You will marry the son of a duke. People will be well aware that someday you will be a duchess, and they will treat you and your family accordingly. You will be in the enviable position of being able to help your sister make a good marriage, and your brothers, too." He settled himself and spread out the mail. "Enough talk. We have a great deal of work to do today." He paused and then stated flatly, "I am relying on you to deal with Christianna. There must be no more disgraceful episodes." His expression was icy. "It's time she visited her grandfather."

As soon as she could, Munevver escaped to her special province within the household—the still room. She would deal with Christianna later, but now she could work here and no one would disturb her. No one would see how her father's words had devastated her. In the back of her mind, a vague plan was forming. Ever since her father had brought her here, she had known she must find a way to leave, but now her father's words about arranging a marriage for her made her realize that time was running out. She didn't know when or how, but she knew she must leave or she would be trapped in a horrible situation for the rest of her life. She had to find a way to free herself.

Somehow, the thought of actually escaping calmed her, and slowly, she began to fill a tin box with herbs she had been taught to use by her grandmother: white willow to reduce fever and pain, lemon balm for discomfort and to promote sleep, comfrey to heal bones and wounds, lavender to calm, agrimory to reduce inflammation, feverfew for headaches and fever, and rosemary for depression and arthritis. She touched the round, brown, papery globe at the end of the branch of rosemary—seeds. Nature had so carefully protected the potential for new life. She added several branches to the box. Suddenly, she remembered an herb essential for cold climates—horehound. Horehound tea was known to eliminate congestion of the respiratory passages and to soothe coughing. As she surveyed the neatly arranged tin of herbs, she felt her spirits lift. It was hers. No one knew about it. She had taken a small step toward her freedom, but first she must help Christianna.

Chapter 10

Sacrificing One's Happiness
to Save Another

"Perhaps I can be of some assistance?" Quinn paused in the doorway of Lord George's library, watching Lady Munevver lift one bottle after another from the liquor cart, study it carefully, and then put it back.

"I'm looking for raki. Grandfather always had some, but I can't seem to find any."

"Ah, yes." Quinn opened a small closet door that blended into the oak paneling of the library wall and pulled out an unopened bottle of the clear liqueur. "I always keep it ready for when your grandfather comes to visit."

Comes to visit? Grandfather and Father have not been on speaking terms for as long as I can remember. She reached for the bottle and added it to the basket on her arm.

Without speaking, Quinn handed her two small,

crystal glasses. After a moment, he murmured, "Might I suggest some cheese and crackers?" When she hesitated, he added, "I would recommend a Cheshire cheese . . . or perhaps a Wensleydale cheese would be a better option?"

For a moment, Munevver could almost taste the crumbly, slightly sweet, Wensleydale cheese that was a specialty of the northern part of Yorkshire. *Cheese and crackers will require a trip to the kitchens. I trust Quinn, but I dare not risk alerting anyone to what I plan to do.* "The Wensleydale cheese would do very nicely." She paused, hoping he would offer to procure it.

"Shall I also add a bottle of spring water?" He motioned toward her basket and she handed it to him. "Where would you like me to carry the refreshments?"

"To my retreat, and would you please ask Lady Christianna to join me there?"

She could hear Christianna stomping along the hallway. Of course, she would be furious at being summoned by her older sister, but better to talk with her in the privacy of her refuge than risk someone overhearing them in the morning room.

"What did I do now?" Christianna, still wearing her riding outfit after her usual morning ride, flounced into the room.

Munevver motioned to the two chairs in the window alcove with a low, round, brass table in front of them holding the bottle of raki, a small jug of cold water, and a plate of pale, slightly crumbled cheese and crackers. She poured two fingers of raki into each glass and paused. "It is colorless now, but when I add water, it will turn white." She didn't add that it was a very old liqueur used for centuries to heal the heart and comfort the mind. "It's called *Lion's Milk*, and it's consumed to give courage."

"Why should I need courage?" Christianna inquired, glaring at her sister.

"I'm the one who needs courage." As Munevver raised her glass to her lips, she breathed in the familiar scent of anise and remembered the first time her grandfather had let her have a tiny sip of Lion's Milk. One of the older girls on the estate had made fun of Munevver's limping gait. Munevver had run away and hid in her room. She remembered his words: "No one can belittle you unless you let them."

"Your father is annoyed that you are concentrating so much on horses and not on what he considers the proper pursuits of young ladies."

"My father!" Christianna snarled. "He's your father, too."

Munevver lifted her glass and motioned for Christianna to join her. Christianna gasped as the heat of the anise-flavored liqueur spread through her. "Horses?" she said in a strangled whisper. "You've ordered me here to talk about horses?"

"Not just about horses." Munevver regarded her sister in a new light. Nearly seventeen, she had lost her childlike trust but had not yet gained the confidence of a young woman. Her father treated her with condescension. Aunt Frederica hovered over her but could not seem to connect with her, and Ryker ignored her. She was adrift in the household, and if allowed to continue, she would be severely hurt. "Fortunately, your father thinks the problem is horses, but you and I both know it's not." She sat down in one of the chairs and motioned Christianna to the other. "I invited you to join me to talk about Captain Nolan. If your behavior continues, and your admiration for Nolan comes to Father's attention—and it will—Nolan's reputation will be ruined. Father will dismiss him without a reference, and no one else will hire him."

"You are hateful! You don't know what it is to love!" Christianna finished the rest of her drink in a gulp that made her gasp for air.

Munevver hesitated. How much dare she share with an angry, vengeful Christianna? "You're wrong. I know what it is to love, to have loved."

Christianna seemed to deflate as she regarded her sister with new eyes. "You lost your love?"

"I am not sure I ever had it, but I know what love feels like." She passed the plate of cheese and crackers to Christianna and then poured them each another finger of raki. As she added water, slowly watching it turn milky, she prayed that the right words would come to her. "Our father is not a kind man. He's not a just man, and he definitely is not a forgiving man. Not only will he dismiss Nolan, he will destroy him. He will spread word that the book he has put so much effort into writing is worthless. It will never be accepted."

"What can I do?" Christianna whispered. "I love him so much."

"When you love, you want what is best for the loved one." Munevver paused, waiting for Christianna to speak. After a moment of silence, Munevver continued. "I know you do not want to harm him, but it will be difficult if you stay here, seeing him every day." After a moment, she took Christianna's hand in hers. "I think you should go to Grandfather's. Go to Yorkshire."

Munevver choked as the memory of the countryside covered in heather, the rolling, green dales dotted with grazing sheep, and the drives lined with massive elm and sycamore trees filled her with longing. For a moment, she was back in her grandfather's magnificent, old manor house, listening for the sound of the Humber River as it raced toward the North Sea. She remembered her first smell of the ships arriving with their cargoes of fish when her grandfather had allowed her to accompany him to Grimsby Dock, and she could almost hear the rumble of the trains carrying coal to the docks where his ships waited. Her grandfather had loved the bustling docks and the sight of his ships full of coal, iron, lumber, and wool. All good, clean, English products he often said. There would be no opium on his ships!

Gripping her glass, Munevver let her thoughts wander for a moment. Her grandfather and father had both been members of the Levant Company until its charter was not renewed in 1825. Her grandfather, wishing to return to his native Yorkshire, had established his shipping company on the Humber River so that he could live full time on his estate in East Riding. Her father, accustomed to the bustle of the Levant Company's docks in London, Southampton, and Bristol, had joined the rapidly expanding East India Company with its busy dockyards in London along the Thames.

"I couldn't leave here!" Christianna sobbed. "I've lived here all my life. Grandfather's whole world revolves around coal, sheep, and . . . fish!" She glared at Munevver. "I'd die of loneliness if I were to go there."

"You've never seen Grandfather's home. It is an elegant home in the most beautiful setting. His land stretches from the North Sea westward to the Yorkshire Dales, where he raises horses."

"Huge, plodding, farm horses, no doubt." Christianna crossed her arms over her chest defiantly.

"Grandfather has always raised and trained horses for the cavalry." Munevver studied her sister. How alone she must have been growing up. Ryker was much older and Alexander was just a baby. "Didn't your father ever tell you what his father did?"

"He doesn't talk to me about anything. He just freezes me with a disapproving look, and then Aunt Frederica tells me what I did wrong."

"I think you will like it at Grandfather's. His land seems to go on forever, and there are marvelous riding trails."

"When would I go?" Suddenly, she froze. "Will you go with me?"

"I am hoping to accompany you," Munevver answered cautiously. "I've already written to Grandfather, telling him you would be leaving tomorrow."

"Tomorrow?" Christianna gave a panicky look in the direction of the stables.

"Yes, early in the morning." She linked her arm with Christianna's. "I mentioned to Grandfather that you would be able to introduce some of the latest methods for training horses in a short time." She smiled for the first time. "Grandfather may be old, but he is still a fierce competitor in business affairs. And if he can train horses in less time for the army, he will see it as a victory over his competitors."

"What about Nolan?" Christianna could not meet Munevver's eyes.

"He will have the chance to enjoy the benefits of his years of hard labor. He will be recognized for his expertise." Her voice softened. "It is very important to a man to be recognized as outstanding among men." For a moment she faltered. *What is important to a woman? To be loved? To be cherished?* "If it is meant to be, it will occur in time, but if you try to force his commitment to you now, you will destroy the man you love and he will resent you for it every day of his life."

Christianna bowed her head. "I'll go to Grandfather's. I couldn't bear to stay here, near him, yet forced to ignore him. It is better that I go away . . . for a while."

Munevver held out her arms to her sister, and the fiercely independent Christianna rushed to her for comfort. "I hope I'll be able to travel with you, but if not, I'm sure Aunt Frederica will." Munevver stroked Christianna's hair as though she were still a child. Her voice trembled as she said, "It's been a long time since I saw Grandfather." Munevver held back the angry tears that threatened to escape. Her father had always refused her whenever she suggested visiting her grandfather. He had said there was too much work for her to leave for a social visit. She wiped angry tears from her eyes. *Father has used me to solve a problem that threatens his way of life, but this is the last time I will do his dirty work! Somehow, someday, I will find a way to sever his control.*

Chapter 11

Yorkshire

"Be sure to pack your favorite riding outfits," Munevver said over her shoulder as she hurried from the room.

"Does Grandfather really have decent riding horses?" Christianna asked in a sullen voice. "Why would he maintain a stable in such a desolate part of England?"

Pausing in the doorway, Munevver turned and regarded her younger sister. *She's going through a very difficult time. She is being forced to give up her first love, or her dream of a first love.* "I rode every day when I lived with Grandfather," Munevver replied briefly. Then she relented, "He has magnificent horses and he trains them himself."

"I didn't know you rode." Christianna stared at her sister in disbelief.

"Riding in the park is not my idea of riding," Munevver snapped. "Now, riding over the dales covered with pink heather that stretches to the horizon . . . that is a different matter." *Oh, the scent of a field of heather—the dry, slightly mossy and woody smell. Will I really get to see it all again?* She stiffened as she remembered her father's expression when she said she would accompany Christianna. It was the coldly calculating look she had learned accompanied a harsh decision. *Surely life cannot be that unkind. He won't forbid me to go back, just this once, to see my childhood home again.*

"We are nearly the same size." Christianna ran an appraising glance over her sister. "I'll pack all of my riding outfits and we can share."

Munevver linked her arm with her sister's. "That is very kind of you. I know it seems as though you are going to a strange country, but I think you will love it." *How can I make Christianna see the beauty of Yorkshire as I see it?* As you may remember, Yorkshire was captured by the Normans when they invaded England in 1066. They fought all the way from the channel to the north of Yorkshire. Many of the leaders were given vast estates by the king. You will see magnificent, old homes, and in the greenest pastures precisely demarcated by ancient, dry, stone walls, you'll see masses of white sheep. If you're lucky, you'll be able to spot red grouse, golden eagles, and even Eurasian nuthatches. You may even catch sight of short-eared owls on the moors."

When Christianna did not reply, Munevver hurried on. "Grandfather has superb streams stocked with salmon and trout. And of course, there are excellent walking trails that will take you to beautiful waterfalls. Oh, there is so much to see and do!" *The image of Woodware, the small shop that offers exquisite, handmade, wooden toys and figures comes to mind. Grandfather seems to have an endless supply of tiny, wooden horses, sheep, dogs, and kittens in his pockets and knows just when one will lift my spirits. No, I will not tell Christianna about Woodware. It will remain my secret delight, as it has through my childhood, the tiny figures a source of comfort and courage. Even now, I always carry one or two in my pocket.*

A whimsical thought made her smile. She carried the wooden figures in her left skirt pocket, and the old, Muslim, amber prayer beads with their thirty-three beads in the right pocket. Grandfather had given her the prayer beads one day as he was describing the different religions of the world. He had told her that Allah had one hundred names and believers would finger a bead as they recited the names in their prayers. "I'm sure you will like the local cheeses. They have the most delectable flavors."

"What about people?" Christianna's voice was flat. "Who are our neighbors? Who will visit us?" She turned to Munevver. "Tell me about the household. I have to know what to expect . . . and what is expected of me."

"Grandfather's home is Barton Hall, a magnificent, old manor house in a beautiful park-like setting far from any village. It's seven hundred years old." At Christianna's irritated sigh, Munevver hurried on. "It's a pink brick country home with two large end wings that have crenulated towers." She smiled at the sulky Christianna. "When I was very young, I thought it was a castle."

At Christianna's defiant stare, she continued her description, trying to make Christianna see it as it existed in her mind. "The middle section is slightly recessed and has nine windows across it." She whispered, "It is so beautiful." She allowed herself a moment to feel its calming presence again and then continued more briskly. "Each of the three levels has nine windows across the front, although the top ones are much smaller. There's a Great Hall and a Long Gallery that are used for exercise when the weather is unsuitable for outdoor activities." She wiped sudden tears from her eyes as she remembered racing down the Great Hall with Louisa and Caroline while William stood guard to warn them of approaching maids.

"There is a long, straight drive lined with trees—elm, ash, sycamore, and evergreens. As you approach, you will see the house becoming larger and larger until it seems to loom against the sky. As I said, it is three stories high in the middle with a West Wing for family and guests and an East Wing for less important guests and for some of the servants—the lady's maids and valets. The third story has the nursery and quarters for the rest of the help."

"The stables?"

"There is a brick stable block with gleaming, black, double doors at the back of the mansion, near the West Wing." She was relieved to see Christianna's increased interest in what she was saying. "The stables are kept in pristine condition." She fought against a hot wave of envy. "I think you will find them to be everything you could ever hope for."

"Who is in charge of the stables?"

"Grandfather has several men who work directly under his command. Many are returned soldiers who were wounded. They are Yorkshire men who fought in the war in India."

"You said that Grandfather trained horses for the cavalry. Who supervises that training?"

"Grandfather does. He has been doing it for years." She met Christianna's challenging gaze firmly. "He is very well regarded by the military."

Christianna moved restlessly. "Who else lives there?"

"There are many household servants and a steward. Most have been there for years."

"No other family members?"

"No. As you know, Grandmother died two years ago. Grandfather has five living children: our father, Uncle Charles, Aunt Patience, and Aunt Frederica. I've never met his youngest son, Uncle Harris. He lives in Aleppo and manages the business from that end."

"You mentioned two friends—Louisa and Caroline. I am assuming Louisa is the Louisa who lives here now with her brother, the vicar? Tell me about your friend, Caroline Del Feld.

Does she live near Grandfather's?" Christianna tried to appear nonchalant, but Munevver recognized the fear of possible rejection.

"Well, nearby is relative." Munevver managed to keep her voice steady. "She lives at Sledmere House in East Riding." She paused as memories swept over her. "It is the most enchanting estate I have ever seen. There is a large deer park, and, of course, there are sheep, goats, horses, and dogs. Lots of dogs. You approach Sledmere House by way of a curving drive that reveals different glimpses of the house and gardens. Then, at last, you finally see a three-level, light-grey, stone building with recessed windows across the front." Munevver sighed. "Her father's estate is about six miles from Grandfather's. She used to drive a pony cart to come to visit me. Every one of Caroline's visits was a delightful treat." She put an arm around Christianna's shoulders. "I'm sure you will become great friends."

"Does she have sisters?"

"No sisters, but she has two older brothers."

"Oh. Much older, I suppose?"

"Somewhat." Munevver put an abrupt end to the questioning. She could not bear to think of William, the younger of the two brothers. She had adored him from the time she was three and had just been found by her grandfather. William had been the center of her world from the first moment he had entered her grandfather's office and had knelt in front of the special chair she occupied beside her grandfather's desk. He had placed an orange-striped kitten in her arms, a beautiful, soft kitten that had curled up and purred as though she belonged there.

Two brothers. So different. Richard was Lord Del Feld's firstborn son, his heir, the golden boy who could do no wrong. William was Lord Del Feld's second son, the son who worked with the steward to manage the huge estate while Richard spent his time in London with his friends.

No matter how carefully the land was managed, there always seemed to be a list of things that needed William's attention. Yet, he found time to repair Caroline's pony cart and watch over them when they insisted on wading in the cool streams that crisscrossed his father's land. It had been William who had taught Caroline and her archery, croquette, and how to ride. So many happy memories.

And then there had been the day when her grandfather told her that her father was demanding that she be sent to him. She was to return to Surrey and work with him. The days after she returned to Lord George's house had passed in a grey blur for Munevver. She was no longer treated as the beloved daughter of the house. Her father insisted that she spend her days working with him in his study. Day after day, she toiled without any word of thanks or commendation. The only bright light in her life was William's promise that he would call on her father the day after her eighteenth birthday and ask for her hand in marriage. But there had been no mention of William's call. Not the day after her birthday, not ever. She had finally convinced herself that he had not come, that he would never come.

* * *

It was at the end of their workday when Lord George placed both hands on his desk and, without looking at Munevver, said, "I've made the arrangements. Christianna will leave tomorrow morning while the weather holds. Your aunt Patience will accompany her." At her involuntary gasp, he added, "It would not have made sense for you to be gone so long. The work would have been hopelessly delayed." He frowned and then added as an afterthought, "It wouldn't have been appropriate, either. Two young women traveling alone. No, it's better that she be accompanied by someone older, by her aunt."

For the first time since she had been brought back to work for her father, Munevver swept out of the room without waiting for his usual, brusque nod of dismissal. She hated him! Anger so fierce, so burning that she could hardly breathe swept over her. Somehow, she had to get away from him. He had discarded her at birth and had only reclaimed her because of her ability to assist him. He had never been a father to her, and now he had denied her the thing she wanted more than anything—to go home, to see her grandfather again.

She owed him nothing! She pressed her hands against the faded, blue serge of her morning gown. Two years ago, when the dressmaker in Yorkshire had made it for her, it had been the deep, clear blue of the violets that hid under the hedges around her grandfather's garden. She had loved the color, but now it was more grey than blue. She had been here two years working for her father, and he had not offered her a single new gown. The tiny amount of pocket money Aunt Frederica gave her each month would never cover the cost of a new dress. A surge of rage swept over her, leaving her shaking. She had to leave. She could not stay here, letting him humiliate her. She would go so far away that he could never reach her, to the end of the world, if possible.

* * *

At the sound of a soft knock on her door, Munevver slid the small pile of coins under her skirt before saying, "Come in." Surprised to see Aunt Frederica instead of the maid, Munevver motioned her to the chair by the bed where she was sitting. *What could have prompted Aunt Frederica to come?*

Without speaking, Aunt Frederica picked up the petticoat that lay on the bed and examined the side seams that Munevver had opened. "What size coins are you planning to hide?"

"Are you going to tell him?" Munevver's voice shook with pain.

"No," Aunt Frederica said calmly and then repeated, "what size coins are you going to use?"

Munevver slowly drew out the pitifully small pile of coins she had been able to save from her pin money.

"I'd suggest starting with half sovereigns." Aunt Frederica enlarged the slit in the seam with her finger. "They are used more widely and will cause less attention."

"Half sovereigns!" Munevver gasped. "Where would I get them? It's taken me months to save these."

"I have a hoard of them," Aunt Frederica stated softly as she sat down on the bed beside Munevver. "You are welcome to them."

"You were going to use them?" Munevver asked in disbelief. "To leave? To slip away?"

"I waited too long, and then it was no longer possible." She patted Munevver's shoulder. "The coins are there for you if you choose to use them."

For a long moment, there was silence, and then Munevver put her arms around her aunt's shoulders. "I remember now! Grandfather told me. When my mother died, you came to take care of Ryker, Christianna, and Alexander!" A stricken expression accompanied the words that burst out. "Alexander was just a baby. You must have been so young!"

"Enough talk," Aunt Frederica said firmly. "I'll just take these petticoats to my room. Tomorrow, bring me your cloak, traveling outfit, and bonnet." She turned at the door. "Sew the smaller coins into the lining of your knitting bag. They'll be easier to reach quickly."

Chapter 12

January 1853: Prelude to War

The first days of the new year seemed endless to Munevver as she spent more and more hours shut up in Lord George's gloomy study. Prices were rising steadily, and there appeared to be a greater urgency to the correspondence that arrived daily. Lunch on trays was standard practice now, and most days, it was impossible to get away to join Aunt Frederica for tea.

The unwritten message pulsing behind each communication from the East was fear of war. If there were a war, what would it mean to Lord George's shipping? What would it mean to the markets? Ryker chaffed at his father's brusque commands, but Munevver just worked on, one letter after another. They both knew that if war broke out, prices would explode, but neither dared to question how Lord George would meet the contracts he continued to make.

By late January of 1853, there were rumors in England that Napoleon III, Emperor of France, was about to seize the Channel Islands—Jersey, Guernsey, Alderney, and

Sark. The archipelago of islands, just eighty miles from the southern coast of England, had been dependencies of the English Crown since the Norman Conquest of England in 1066. By February, Lord Palmerston, believing the danger of a French invasion was real, said that the best way to defend England from the French would be to fortify the islands. Others believed a strong defense against a French attack could be achieved by adding to the existing number of Martello towers, the massive, round, stone towers that had been built by Henry VIII to protect the southern coast of England against an attack by France. Seventy-four of the indestructible towers, thirty feet tall and fifty feet in diameter at the base, with guns mounted on top, still safeguarded the coast of England closest to France.

In addition to the fear of a French invasion, there were rumors that Russia was gathering troops on the borders of Ottoman principalities in support of the tsar's outrageous demands: one, recognition of his right to be the custodian of the holy places, and two, acceptance of his role as the protector of all Orthodox Christians in the Ottoman Empire.

As the new year began, England was politically split. The Conservative Party, staunchly supported by Lord George, wanted to keep the Ottoman Empire alive and strong—a protective fence along England's routes of communication and trade with other European countries and with the East, with India, and China. They believed that with Lord Stratford de Redcliffe at the Sublime Porte in Constantinople, the Ottoman Empire would become more tolerant and conditions would improve for the minorities within the empire. The Liberal Party was adamantly opposed to this view. They wanted England to agree with Russia's desire: to liquidate the Ottoman Empire and divide the spoils. To placate the people, Secretary of War Sidney Herbert proposed two actions— establish a military training camp at Cobham in Surrey and hold a huge naval review, one that he believed would dispel the public's fear of imminent war.

"The situation is becoming more difficult and we have to plan accordingly." Lord George straightened the edges of the letters that had arrived that morning. Although Munevver was his only companion in the study, he lowered his voice before saying, "The country is split. Lord Palmerston has a strong belief in the regeneration of the Ottoman Empire and absolutely no faith in Russia. The Conservative Party wants to keep the Ottoman Empire alive and strong." He paused. "Well, at least alive. They don't seem to realize that the Ottoman Empire has shrunk considerably since it was defeated at the Second Siege of Vienna." He shifted uneasily in his chair. "Also, there is such turmoil in its provinces. As soon as Greece became free, Macedonia started clamoring for autonomy, and now it is raging for independence." He groaned softly. "The Macedonians don't have the slightest understanding of what it would take to achieve independence and hold it."

Lord George rubbed a hand over his eyes as he mentally ranked the challenges facing England. "The problem of Macedonia belongs to the future. We face more urgent ones right now. The Liberal Party wants England to agree with the Russians that the best approach is for the major European powers to come to an agreement on how to liquidate the Ottoman Empire instead of letting it dissolve from internal strife. They say it has existed for over four hundred years, and now it's time for a change." He wiped his forehead with a square of white cotton and then shoved it back into his pocket.

Munevver's thoughts drifted as she watched him put the handkerchief back in his pocket. There had been a single line of plain machine stitching around the edges of the cotton square. In contrast, the snowy-white handkerchiefs that Ari Bey used were made of fine linen and had a double band of handcrafted hemstitching around the edges, giving the handkerchief an elegant appearance. For a moment, it puzzled her. Such attention to detail for so unimportant an item. And then she realized that it was the perfect example of the differences between the ancient complexity of the Ottoman culture and the movement toward efficiency and utilitarianism of English society. Certainly, Lord George represented the new thinking—minimum expenditure of labor and time to produce maximum output. Ari Bey, on the other hand, represented the wisdom of the ages by appreciating the beauty of an object created by talented individuals.

"The tsar has made it known that he wants England to join Russia in dividing up the Ottoman Empire before it collapses." Lord George snorted. "Their family relationships may be distant, but the tsar believes he can influence the queen. According to his plan, Russia would take the Black Sea, the straits, and Constantinople. England would have Egypt so that she could maintain her trade routes to the East." He paused and then continued in a softer voice, "There are many in England who do not accept the imminent demise of the Ottoman Empire. They believe it is in the best interest of England to maintain the Ottoman Empire . . . at least for the immediate future."

"And the others?" Munevver could not stop herself from asking.

"Prime Minister Lord Aberdeen and his friends believe in the good faith of Russia. They think war can be prevented by meeting some of Russia's demands." Lord George's voice revealed his cynicism. "On the other hand, Lord Palmerston of the Foreign Office has no faith in Russia. He believes peace can be achieved only by convincing Russia that, if war breaks out, she would face more than just the Ottoman Empire." Lord George seemed to shrink in his chair. "It may already be too late. Russia practically owns the Black Sea, but they are determined to have the straits! They've always wanted the straits! If they gain control of the waterways—the Bosphorus and the Dardanelles—they would control Constantinople, all commerce within the Ottoman Empire, and access to India and the East." His voice dropped to a whisper. "Russian control of the straits would be ruinous for us."

"It appears that a decision will have to be made soon," Munevver offered tentatively.

"Or we wait too long and the decision is made for us by either the Russians or the Ottomans."

"What about the Ottoman's reorganization, the Tanzimat?" Munevver suggested cautiously. "Modernization was supposed to strengthen the Ottoman Empire and put an end to the interference of foreign powers like Russia, France, and"—she risked a quick glance at her father—"England."

"Ah, yes. The Ottoman intellectuals thought that if they integrated the non-Turkish Ottoman subjects— Bulgarians, Armenians, Greeks, Jews, Albanians, and Kurds—enhanced their civil liberties, and granted them equality throughout the Ottoman Empire, they could reduce their accelerating demand for nationalism. It didn't work. In fact, the cry for nationalism in the Ottoman Empire is louder than ever and spreading. At first, it was expanding westward to the Serbs, Romanians, and Bulgarians, but now it is emerging in the East among the Armenians, Albanians, Arabs, and even the Kurds."

Lord George paused for a moment and then said, "There is another internal threat that may be more immediately dangerous: a fledgling, secret society in Constantinople. They call themselves *The Young Ottomans*. They believe the Tanzimat reforms did not go far enough. They want a constitutional government. They even believe they can bring about reconciliation between the West and the East." He gave a cynical laugh. "Some, the more outspoken, have become active in Ankara. Only the young, pampered Ottoman aristocracy would believe they have the ability to determine the fate of the Ottoman Empire."

"To be fair," Munevver said softly not to anger her father, "the Tanzimat did bring about some reforms that benefited the people. It abolished the ancient devshirme system of conscription. The military can no longer seize eight-year-old boys from the non-Muslim population, force them to convert to Islam, and then serve in the Sultan's Army. They created a more just system, a universally conscripted army."

"Yes, and they replaced religious law with secular law. Their most ambitious move was Ottomanism. They attempted the impossible . . . to unite the population of the Ottoman Empire: Turks, Greeks, Armenians, Jews, Kurds, and Arabs." Lord George scowled. "It is said that the Ottomanism movement is backed by certain young men—members of the translation office and the embassy secretariats—who believe they can change the world."

After a moment, Lord George shrugged. "The changes were almost certainly doomed to fail, but out of failure, some modernization was accomplished. The Ottoman Empire gained an excellent telegraph system that facilitates communication, and their railroads will be reorganized and running efficiently soon." He nodded. "Those changes are good for business, but the minorities are still a problem, restless and dangerous. They watched the ten-year-long Greek Revolution eventually end in a free Greece, and they've been inspired by the recent revolutionary uprisings sweeping over Germany, Denmark, France, and Poland." He allowed himself to slump in his chair. "Even closer, they can see the Bulgarians, the Serbs, and the Macedonians crying for freedom." He shook his head in discouragement. "The lives of the subjects in the Ottoman Empire have improved. They have more freedom than ever. Even the tax collection process is more just after they abolished the ancient tax-farming system, the iltizam."

Munevver nodded. "The old practice of giving the right to collect taxes to powerful, local men in exchange for a lump sum paid to the Ottoman Treasury was always rife with corruption."

"True, but that had been the method of tax collection for centuries. Now there are official salaried tax collectors. The people no longer have to fear for their lives if they don't pay the taxes demanded by powerful families or that their sons will be seized and forced into the army. Yes, the Tanzimat reforms benefited the population, but many are intoxicated by the thought of being free, independent nations." Lord George straightened in his chair and began to arrange the papers on his desk. "Independent nations for how long without strong armies to guarantee that independence?"

"You've used the Silk Road that winds through different provinces of the Ottoman Empire all these years." Munevver thought of the camel caravans bringing the treasures of the East—magnificent silks, rugs, fine wool, delicate porcelains, teas, spices, gold, jade, perfumes, tobacco, and coffee—from China to Aleppo, across the Anatolian Plain to Scutari, and then from Scutari by ships to England. "Won't it be endangered if there is war?"

"Transportation of goods is always a concern, but it is not what worries me the most." He paused and then added, by way of explanation, "It's always been a matter of bartering. It can be fixed." Lord George hesitated and then the words burst out. "It's this asinine dispute between France and Russia over the right to protect the holy places in the Ottoman Empire, especially the right to protect the Church of the Nativity. Just think of the absurdity, arguing about who has the right to maintain a church built over the stable where Jesus was born." He groaned. "Even worse, there is the dispute over the matter of a key. At first, it seemed like such a small thing—France's demand for a key to the main door—but it could plunge us into war."

"War over the right to protect the holy places?" Munevver could not keep the disbelief from her voice. This did not seem like her father's usual astute understanding of the world he commanded.

"Yes, the holy places in Jerusalem," he answered impatiently. "There have always been disputes between the Latin Catholic Christians and the Greek Orthodox Christians in one part of the Ottoman Empire—Palestine. Now, the French Catholic monks want to expose a silver star in the Church of the Nativity in Bethlehem and have a key to the main door of the church. At the present time, the Orthodox Christians—Greeks and Russians— hold the only key to the main door of the Church of the Nativity. The Latin Catholic Christians have a key to the side door but not to the main door. Of course, the Russians supported the Orthodox Christians and are opposed to the French monks having a key."

"Could a disagreement over a key precipitate war?" Munevver's voice was incredulous.

"Yes," he snapped, and then, seemingly pleased to find an area in which his knowledge of European history exceeded hers, continued in a pedantic manner. "It's not a simple matter. Since 1740, France has had a treaty with the Ottoman Empire giving France the right to custody of the holy places in and near Bethlehem and Jerusalem and control of the pilgrimages of the Catholics and Orthodox Greeks."

"And the revenue generated by the pilgrimages?" Munevver did not expect a reply.

"The French had neglected the upkeep of the holy places, and the Russian government asked the Sublime Porte for permission to clean and repair the holy places that were falling into decay. The sultan granted their request and they repaired the shrines.

"Then, in 1850, Napoleon Bonaparte's nephew, Louis Napoleon III, soon to crown himself Emperor Napoleon III, found himself in desperate need of public support. He wanted the backing of the Roman Catholics in France, so he asked the sultan to renew France's claim as protector of the holy places."

"That would have put the sultan in a difficult position," Munevver murmured.

"Yes. The sultan tried to please both. He granted the right of protector to both of them, but recently, in 1852, Napoleon III demanded that the Sublime Porte recognize France as the sole protector of Christian monks and pilgrims in the holy places. To strengthen his demand, Napoleon III sent a warship up the Dardanelles to the Marmara Sea. The Sublime Porte had a key made to the main door of the church and gave it to the French Catholic Christians."

"I don't suppose that settled the matter." Munevver glanced out the window. The warmer spring days had prodded the lilacs to bloom earlier than usual. For a moment, she let herself visualize the gently rolling fields of her grandfather's Yorkshire estate—fields covered with celandine and anemones and, tucked under hedges, there would be violets with their fleetingly sweet scent.

Lord George rubbed his hand across his face. "The tsar of Russia was furious and demanded that the Sublime Porte confirm Russia as the protector of the holy places, and then he added another request."

"What else did he ask for?" Munevver was startled. She had read about the argument over the key to the main door but had not heard of any additional Russian demands.

"On May 3rd, Tsar Nicholas sent Prince Menshikov to Constantinople to ask that all Greek Orthodox churches be placed under Russian protection as had been granted eighty years earlier."

"That was not a new claim." Munevver frowned, unable to understand why he was making such a point of it.

"Menshikov also claimed that Russia was the protector of Orthodox Christians in the Ottoman Empire from oppression—all Orthodox Christians."

"All Orthodox Christians?" Munevver choked on the words. "Orthodox Christians in the Ottoman Empire would include those in Egypt, Palestine, North Africa,

Bulgaria, Macedonia, and Syria. That would be millions of Ottoman citizens!"

"About fourteen million Ottoman citizens." Lord George spread his hands out on his desk in disbelief as he forced himself to state the unthinkable. "The tsar wanted the sultan to agree that the tsar had control over half of the population in the Ottoman Empire."

"The sultan could never agree to that." Munevver shook her head in disbelief. "The tsar must know the sultan would never agree to that!" She stared at Lord George. "That leaves his other demand—the right to protect the holy places. Would the tsar really go to war over the question of protection of some holy places?" She paused and then said slowly, "It appears that the tsar is looking for a reason to attack the Ottoman Empire again."

"It's not about protecting holy places," Lord George snapped. "It's an old feud. Russia is huge—and landlocked. She wants year-round access to shipping lanes. Russia has ports on the northern shore of the Black Sea, but to get to the Mediterranean Sea and the major shipping lanes, she needs to be able to send her ships through the Bosphorus, now controlled by the Ottomans, across the Marmara Sea, through the Dardanelles to the Aegean Sea, and then to the Mediterranean." He looked at her and said simply, "If Russia were to gain control of the straits, it would threaten our shipping. It would imperil our trade with India and the East."

India and the East. Those two areas constituted the majority of their trade. "We'd be ruined." The words slipped out before Munevver could stop them.

She was stunned when Lord George nodded in agreement and then said softly, "It looks ominous." He stared at the floor before continuing. "Prime Minister Lord Aberdeen, and his friends, continue to believe in the good faith of Russia and have little confidence in the Ottoman Empire. They think peace can be achieved by placating the tsar by meeting some of the Russian demands." He shrugged. "On the opposite side, Lord Palmerston in the Foreign Office has no faith in Russia and a strong belief in the Ottoman Empire. He says maintaining peace depends on convincing Russia that, if war breaks out, Russia would face more than the Ottomans."

"They would face the English?" Munevver asked softly and then added, "and likely the French."

"While they bicker, Lord Stratford de Redcliffe, our ambassador to Constantinople, is doing everything to convince the Ottomans not to agree to Russia's demands. He fears it would give Russia the right to interfere in every Ottoman province where there is an Orthodox Church." Lord George pulled himself to his feet and, for the first time that Munevver could remember, seemed ready to leave his study early. "I've always believed that de Redcliffe has more power than most realize. I'm counting on him. They say the sultan listens to him."

Chapter 13

March 1853: Russia Issues Ultimatum to Ottoman Empire

The gloomy days of February seemed endless to Munevver as she spent hour after hour in the study with her father and the sullen Ryker. It was a relief when the first day of March finally arrived. Ryker found the time his father expected him to spend working in the office unbearable, and now that the weather had improved, he took every opportunity to travel to London, supposedly on business. But today, as he entered the breakfast room with a spring in his step, Lord George had handed him a thick folder and said that the work was to be completed by the end of the day.

Sensing that Ryker was about to refuse, Munevver rushed to divert her father's attention. Pointing at the paper beside her father's plate, she asked, "Is there any news of the East today?"

"The tsar appointed Prince Menshikov to the embassy in Constantinople a few weeks ago." Lord

George, having addressed his reply to Ryker not Munevver, now waited to pounce on Ryker's ignorance of the delicacy of the situation.

"Prince Alexander Menshikov?" A startled expression crossed Ryker's usually inscrutable face. "Wasn't he the Russian admiral in the war against the Ottomans in 1828–1829?" Ryker stopped suddenly as he remembered the gossip. *Supposedly, while Menshikov was distinguishing himself at the Siege of Varna, a Turkish cannon shell had exploded, castrating him instantly. Dear God! The Russians had sent the man the Ottomans had made a eunuch to the Sublime Porte with an ultimatum that could strip the sultan of his empire.* "Obviously, an unfortunate choice," Ryker responded in a bland voice, unwilling to accept the bait his father had cast out.

"Yes," Lord George continued. "He has already presented Russia's grievances over the rights of Greek and Latin Christians in the Holy Land." He glanced up from the paper with a wary expression. "Our foreign secretary, Lord John Russell, had been assured by the Russian ambassador that it is Prince Menshikov's intention to demand recognition of Russia's rights over the holy places. Nothing more."

The last words, "nothing more," made Munevver stiffen. Her grandfather would have commented on them, questioned them, and turned them inside out, but her father had not. Munevver's apprehension increased as she watched Lord George's expression change as he continued to read the article. "It says Menshikov has been sent to demand that the sultan grant Russia the right to represent all Orthodox citizens in the Ottoman Empire." Lord George closed the paper, folding it precisely. "This is terrible. It's an insult of the greatest magnitude." He pushed himself away from the table. "The Sublime Porte, acting on Lord Stratford de Redcliffe's advice, has already issued a refusal to agree to such a Russian protectorate."

"Dear God!" Munevver felt the blood leave her face. "What will happen next?" It was one thing to talk about war in the abstract, but now it was filling every corner of the study. "The Ottoman Empire will have to go to war to defend her sovereignty," she whispered. *How long will it be before England is compelled to join her?*

Lord George began to speak with cold decisiveness as he paced the library. "War would be disastrous. It would upset the balance of power among the European nations. There would be long-term, detrimental effects on trade." He stopped suddenly. "The Europeans must make an attempt to prevent war."

Within days of the news, England and France had joined Prussia and Austria in sending representatives to Vienna to try to find a compromise that would enable the Ottoman Empire to avoid war. The four powers developed the Vienna Agreement, which guaranteed Russia's rights at the Sublime Porte while, at the same time, ensuring the sultan's rule. However, when the sultan was asked to sign the agreement, he refused unless certain modifications were made.

The sultan insisted that Prince Menshikov's demand

for protector status of the Greek Orthodox Church, clergymen, and all Greek subjects in the Ottoman Empire was not acceptable. England pressured its ambassador, Lord Stratford de Redcliffe, to convince the sultan to sign the Vienna Agreement. Ambassador de Redcliffe, who had spent years in Constantinople, actually supported the sultan's refusal. Outraged at him for taking that position, England was about to recall him when a private dispatch of a Russian, Count Nesselrode, was printed in a Berlin newspaper. The dispatch indicated that Russia interpreted the Vienna Agreement as giving Russia the right to intervene to protect the Greek Orthodox Christians in the Ottoman Empire. The Vienna Agreement was not accepted by the sultan.

The days slid by, and Munevver was almost lulled into believing that the threat of war had passed. Then, the headlines of the newspapers screamed the news. On May 21, 1853, Russia had given the Ottoman Empire an ultimatum: Agree to Russia's right to protect all Greek Orthodox Christians in the Ottoman Empire, or Russia would send troops to invade Ottoman territories. The Ottomans refused, and on July 2, 1853, Russia sent troops to the Ottoman provinces of Moldavia and Wallachia on the Danube River.

Munevver hesitated and then decided to risk it. "Some of the newspapers are calling for England to continue to offer protection for the weakened Ottoman Empire. They say Constantinople will be in danger if Russia reaches the Bosphorus."

Lord George glanced at Munevver with respect.

"England has already acted on that fear. On May 26th, an English fleet"—he paused and added grudgingly—"and a French fleet arrived at Beşik Bay, the entrance of the Dardanelles. They are poised there, ready to sail up the Dardanelles, cross the Marmara Sea, and force their way through the Bosphorus to the Black Sea the minute war breaks out."

"Is there nothing else England can do?" Munevver's mind was racing. "Must we just wait to see what Russia does?"

"Or what the Ottomans do," Lord George responded without looking at her.

Chapter 14

March 1853: A Marital Bargain

While the suites of Aunt Frederica, Christianna, and Ryker were located in the luxuriously appointed West Wing, which also contained the master suite occupied by Lord George, Munevver, when she had been brought from Yorkshire on Lord George's orders, had been placed in the East Wing, which had guest suites and smaller rooms for unimportant guests. Since no one appeared to take any interest in the spartan state of her rooms, Munevver had explored the vast attics to remedy the situation.

The sheen of the pearwood furniture she had found lent an air of serenity that was counterbalanced by the exuberant colors—uncountable shades of reds and blues, lightened by thin waves of ivory—of the room-size, Lavar oriental rug she had found rolled up in the attic. Aunt Patience, her father's older sister, had been horrified when she saw the rug, denouncing the colors as too vibrant and the design as too erotic, but Munevver had insisted on keeping it. At some time, someone in the family had appreciated the forceful beauty of one of the finest of Kerman rugs. Now she paced the room, following the pattern of golden scrolls. There had been something different about her father's demeanor today. He was even more guarded than normal, and he had checked the clock frequently before he finally dismissed her nearly an hour earlier than usual.

Pausing in front of the window overlooking the courtyard, Munevver spotted a sturdy, black Brougham making its way up the long, tree-lined approach. It was too far away for her to recognize the crest on the side. A carriage of that size suggested that the journey had been long. She shivered as she felt an unaccustomed sense of danger. Who would be coming to see her father so late in the day? Obviously, neither her father's solicitor nor his estate agent. She would have known if her father was expecting them. He would have instructed her to prepare the documents he wanted to discuss with them ahead of time. No, this carriage belonged to a man of distinction—or at least of power.

As the carriage drew closer, she could see that it was no longer new and there were signs of neglect. She straightened her shoulders. There was no reason to assume that the visit involved her, and there was nothing she could do about it if it did. If her father summoned her, her mauve morning dress was spotless, although many launderings had dulled the original, vibrant color she had loved to a greyish lavender. Fayne had made sure that the lace-trimmed collar and cuffs were starched to perfection. That morning, Fayne, after brushing Munevver's hair until it gleamed, had arranged it in an ebony coronet. As the day wore on, tiny curls had escaped, but there was nothing she could do about that now. Perhaps her father would not need her. With luck, she would not have to limp into her father's study in front of his caller. She concealed herself behind the curtains of the window overlooking the drive and waited to learn the identity of the occupant of the carriage.

As the coachman opened the door and the thin, bent form of the Duke of Leinster stepped out, Munevver gasped. The duke and her father knew each other, but they did not move in the same social circles. Why would the duke be calling on her father at his home? Her father had been elevated to the position of earl upon his older brother's death, but he was still a merchant, and dukes did not socialize with merchants. In fact, she recalled Fayne telling her about the time the duke had not acknowledged Lord George in public. Her father had been furious. *What is the duke doing here?*

She remembered her grandfather telling her that her father's land in Ireland—land he had inherited from his mother—adjoined the duke's estate at a certain point, but her father's holdings were extremely modest in comparison to the duke's. A question about land? Unlikely. The duke was known to have huge estates in Ireland. It was equally well known that the potato famine had left the estates in desperate straits. He had been forced to sell what he could, but most of his holdings were entailed. They could not be sold but would pass to his heir, his oldest son, James. Her stomach churned as she considered possible reasons for his visit. It was rumored that he had mortgaged the land repeatedly. She could think of only one reason for him to be calling on

Lord George—the duke needed money urgently.

Motioning for Fayne to accompany her, Munevver sped down the back stairs and entered the small estate office adjacent to her father's study. It had been designed for the master of the house to use when he needed to meet with his steward or men of the estate who wished to bring problems to his attention. Now it was hers. She had appropriated it for her own use.

The pain of the day that prompted her to take that action was still sharp. She had been at her small desk in a corner of her father's study, working on correspondence as usual. Munevver remembered every detail. Ryker had been standing at Lord George's side when a businessman had been shown in by Foster. Lord George had introduced Ryker as his son, and he had waved a hand in her direction and said, "My clerk." She had never forgiven him for the slight.

Munevver moved quickly to the wall of bookcases separating the room from Lord George's study. She removed a heavy volume and motioned for Fayne to put her ear close to a crack in the paneling. Then she took her usual place at her desk and began to read the correspondence Foster had left on her desk. Later, Fayne would be able to tell her what had transpired between the two men, but for now, all she could do was wait and work.

Just before going to join her aunt Frederica for tea, Munevver took the last of the correspondence to her father's study. Lord George addressed her without raising his eyes from the papers he was studying. "I've arranged a marriage for you. In time, you will be a duchess, able to provide the help you owe your family."

If she could get to her room without falling apart, Fayne would tell her what she needed to know, what had actually been arranged. Now, two thoughts throbbed through her: Her father had sold her for a title, and why would a titled family accept a crippled bride who carried tainted blood? *Please God, let Fayne know what was arranged!*

Fayne was pale as she helped Munevver change. It was Aunt Frederica's at-home day, and she would expect Munevver to be there by her side, dressed appropriately and appearing pleased to greet their callers. Munevver clenched her teeth as she thought of the next two hours. On Aunt Frederica's at-home days, there were always the same older ladies who called and always the same questions. *When will she be having her season? Has any particular young man caught her eye?* She could not wait any longer. She met Fayne's eyes in the mirror. "Tell me."

"Lord Leinster's two sons are insisting that their father buy them commissions in the cavalry. They want to join the cavalry now—the Light Brigade, no less. There is a rumor that they will be shipping out soon, and they are worried about missing out on the coming war."

"Two sons?" Munevver whispered. "Cavalry commissions are very costly."

"He was insistent. He had to raise enough money to buy two commissions." Fayne let her hands rest on

Munevver's shoulders for a moment. "Lord George and Lord Leinster finally reached an agreement. You are to be engaged to Lord Leinster's oldest son, James, with the marital date to be decided by Lord George. Although the marriage will not take place immediately, the funds to purchase the commissions were made available by Lord George today."

"Is that all?" Munevver forced her voice to be noncommittal as she tried to hide the anguish that was twisting through her.

Fayne hesitated, thinking of the rumors she had heard from the footman, and then said, "It was all I could hear."

Munevver hurried toward the stairs. Aunt Frederica was depending on her. She straightened her shoulders. The pain was so acute that it hurt to breathe, but no one would ever know how devastated she felt. Lord George had destroyed the nebulous dreams she secretly cherished of finding love and happiness with William. Her father had arranged a marriage from which he would profit and her brothers and sister would benefit. She stood erect. *Someday I will find a way to hurt him as he has hurt me.*

Chapter 15

June 1853: Cobham Training Camp

Munevver was surprised to see Ryker entering the breakfast room so early. He was dressed for riding and seemed to radiate energy. She could only hope he wasn't going to try to talk to his father while he was reading the newspapers. If he did, he would be unsuccessful, and she would pay the price for the rest of the day.

"Father, is there any news of the military camp they are constructing at Cobham?" Ryker could hardly contain his enthusiasm. "In Surrey Heath? I've heard they are going ahead with the plans to create a battlefield with redoubts and ravines. They want to be able to carry out full- scale maneuvers." He shook his head. "It's hard to believe, but now our men train in small units scattered across the country." He could not keep the disgust from his voice. "Many are even bivouacked among the population." He brightened. "Just think! Ten thousand men will be there at the camp to learn new ways of fighting!" He could not suppress his eagerness. "They say the construction is going well. Despite all the problems, there is going to be an opening!"

"Nonsense!" Lord George thundered from the head of the table. "It's all nonsense. The Duke of Wellington has said that there is no need to change our training methods. My father fought with the duke at the Battle of Mysore in 1799 and at the Battle of Waterloo in 1815. The duke was never defeated by Napoleon! If there is war, the Iron Duke will guide us well."

"Yes, Father, but the Duke of Wellington is in his eighties now." Ryker hesitated, knowing that his father would reject anything he had to offer, but then felt compelled to say, "During my travels through Europe, I saw how other countries—the Germans, the Austrians, and the Russians—were changing their training methods and updating their weaponry."

"The Iron Duke has never failed us. I see no reason to change." He picked up his newspaper again, indicating that the subject was closed, and then lowered the paper. "Cobham? It's heathland. You can't build anything there. There are swamps, bogs, and quicksand when you try to dig."

"Prince Albert has approved the plans and work is already underway." Ryker reached for the pitcher of cool, fresh water that Lord George insisted must always be on the table at every meal. "There appears to be an extraordinary concern about water. They are damming up streams and locating natural springs. Where there is no water, they are digging wells for the soldiers and creating ponds for the horses. People have been traveling to Cobham just to see the construction." Ryker ignored Munevver's kick under the table. "They say there will be four regiments of the cavalry training there." He appeared alive with anticipation as he added, "The infantry and the guards will be training there, too."

"Enough!" Lord George glared at Ryker as he prepared to launch into his usual, blistering response to Ryker's interest in the military. "I provided you with tutors to learn languages, mathematics, and history. I sent you on the Grand Tour to learn about other countries and how to expand our trade with them—a tour that I might remind you was extended at your request and my expense. Nearly three years! I did not spend all that money to prepare you for the military!"

Lord George rose from his chair and, with his hands clenched behind him, began to pace. "Military glory! It's a myth. Men who should know better think battles are won by valor. Actually, battles are determined not so much by one side winning as by the other side losing, and the losing side is usually the one with the most filth, disease, and incompetent leaders." He jerked his head erect and glared at his son. "I expect you to join me in the library in ten minutes. You will start contributing to the company today."

"Oh, Munevver," Ryker grumbled after his father had left. "What am I going to do? You have such an aptitude for business, but I am hopeless with languages and have no interest in trade."

"I don't think I have a special aptitude. Grandfather drilled it into me from the moment he found me and now"—she struggled to keep her voice neutral—"I help your father with his work." She would never give the power to anyone, not even Ryker, of knowing how much she hated Lord George, the man who had fathered her, discarded her, and then reclaimed her when he learned she had been taught business skills he could use.

"I want to be in the cavalry." Ryker sounded like a petulant schoolboy. "It's all I've ever wanted."

"He'll never buy you a commission in the cavalry." She struggled to hide her irritation. Ryker was the eldest son, heir to his father's title, and yet his father treated him much the same as he treated her—a pawn to be used. Her voice softened slightly. "You've always known he had plans for you to join him in the business."

"You don't have to buy a commission in the navy," Ryker replied without meeting her eyes.

"No, you have to train and work your way up." No point in reminding him that most seamen started at the age of fourteen. "I've heard that it's a very tough training . . . and a dangerous life." She thought of the wounded seamen she had known on her grandfather's estate, handicapped seamen who had found their way to her grandfather's estate knowing he would offer them work and a place to live. She turned at the door and regarded her brother with pity. Everything he had ever wanted had come to him so easily. "Ryker, you are the heir of an earl. Sons of the nobility, even minor nobility, do not join the navy."

"Not true. There have been some who have served in the navy."

"Yes, perhaps the son of a marquess and sometimes

second sons." Munevver's expression softened. "You're a firstborn son, Father's heir." She shook her head. "You've always known he planned for you to join him in the business."

"He thinks he is still part of the Levant Company— the Levant Company that was dissolved in 1825; the great Levant Company that bought half of all the opium produced in one part of the Ottoman Empire, Smyrna, and then sold it directly to the English people and to the Americans. What they did not sell to them, they offloaded to other merchants for sale in China." He shook his head. "More than twenty-five years have passed, and he still thinks he is carrying out the traditions of the Levant Company."

"Well, it was a very important trading company in its time. The English people developed a taste for beautiful fabrics to make exquisite dresses, for oriental carpets to be used in their homes, and always more tea and currants. In exchange for these luxurious goods, the Levant Company traded English products—cloth, tin, lead, and furs." She scowled at her brother. "It didn't just sell opium."

"But its most profitable commodity was opium," Ryker stated flatly.

"The Levant Company wasn't the only trading company dealing in opium." Munevver struggled to defend the glorious old company that her grandfather had loved. "It's well known that the East India Trading Company grew opium in India and hired smugglers to take it into China."

Ryker grunted. "It's true that England wasn't the only country trading in opium. France and Spain were involved, and early on, an American from Boston bought opium from England and sold it to China. He didn't do very well, but a few years later, another American purchased ten tons of Turkish opium and, using his fur company's clipper ships, transported it to Canton, China. He even sold Turkish opium to England!"

Suddenly aware of his sister's shocked expression, Ryker softened his approach. "Yes, there were others, but the East India Company's opium trade was much larger than any other company. They bought opium in Bengal and Bihar, India and sold it to China in exchange for tea and other luxuries. In fact, they had a monopoly on the opium trade through their control of all the poppy growers in India. They controlled the source of all of India's opium. The growers were forbidden to sell the opium obtained from their poppies to other trading companies."

Ryker laughed cynically. "You could say their very successful opium trade was due to the English people's love of fine tea. China was the only producer of tea at that time, and the English people's demand for tea was ever increasing. China would only accept silver in exchange for its tea. In fact, Queen Victoria awarded the East India Company a monopoly on the opium trade." His voice was tinged with a bitter cynicism that Munevver had not heard before. *Is it possible that underneath Ryker's callous manner he really cares about others?*

"China knew that the use of opium was spreading and that opium addiction was interfering with her merchants, workers, army, and even the running of the country. It was destroying their agrarian foundation as a way of life. Crime and civil disorder were increasing. Taxes were rising and there was increased unemployment. Chinese officials tried again and again to prevent opium from being sold in China. It's hard to believe but, in 1839, England went to war with China to maintain England's opium trading market. That war lasted three years!" He scoffed in disgust. "We knew what opium addiction could do to a nation, but we went to war to make sure we could continue to sell opium to China!" Ryker shook his head. "By 1840, England was becoming wealthy from the sale of opium."

Munevver looked at Ryker with new respect. She had suspected that he was better informed than he let his father know, but she had not known that he had a real concern for the welfare of others—people in the world he did not know. For a moment, she thought of Louisa and her father, the vicar, who were outspoken about their opposition to England's trade in opium.

"As I said, you don't have to buy a commission in the navy," Ryker said over his shoulder as he hurried toward the door.

She stopped at the door and regarded her brother with a sense of pity. Everything he had ever wanted had always come to him.

"Please don't do anything in haste."

"I've invited Ari Bey to join us to visit the Cobham Camp in July," he said as he paused in the doorway.

"Perhaps he will have news of the East that will change Father's mind."

Munevver limped down the hallway toward the study. Lord Arundal would be fuming. Maybe she could distract him by asking what news there had been in the morning paper. At the sight of Mrs. Coates bringing fresh rolls to the breakfast buffet, Munevver remembered she would have to find time to talk with her. Earlier that morning, Mrs. Coates had stopped Munevver to tell her that she was worried about her fourteen-year-old son, Gordy. Large for his age and with a caustic wit, Gordy had worked for the last two years as a stable boy. Recently, he had started hanging out with the men at the inn, and now he was talking about joining the navy. Munevver shuddered. *Just seven years older than Alexander. How can he possibly survive in the navy?*

* * *

"It's too late." Mrs. Coates sobbed. "Gordy is bragging that he took the queen's shilling! He's just a boy!" Fear roughened her usually placid voice.

"How old is he?" Munevver asked. Gordy had been here when her father had brought her back from her grandfather's, and the young boy had been eager to tell her about his adventures. He could shimmy up the tallest trees. He could walk across the highest beams in the barn. He was fearless and endlessly cheerful. She would miss him.

"He turned fourteen last month."

"Was it impressment?"

"No. He said some men at the inn offered him a shilling, and he took it."

"He has twenty-four hours to change his mind." Munevver's mind was whirling. Gordy was Mrs. Coates's whole world. Her husband had been the game warden on one of Lord George's country estates, but he had been killed in a shooting accident, and Gordy was the only family she had.

"He has already left." She wiped her eyes with her apron. "He said he has always wanted to be in the navy." She slid into a chair. "He listens to all the stories the men tell. He is certain that he can be a "Top Man.""

"Top Man?" Munevver suppressed a shudder. The most respected man in a ship's crew. It was the Top Man who was the best at climbing to the top of the mast and managing the canvases. "He's big for his age, but he is still only fourteen." She tried to remember what she had heard about life in the navy. "It is hard work, constant work." She thought of Gordy and the other stable boys swimming in the pond when their day's work was done. Gordy, who loved his mother's cooking and could identify every aroma coming from the kitchen. In the navy, it would be hard biscuits, salt pork, and watered-down grog. "Did you speak to Lord George about it?" *Does my father even know that Mrs. Coates has a son and that the boy worked in his stables?*

"I am going to speak to him this afternoon." Mrs. Coates straightened her cap. "I will ask him if he can do anything to get Gordy back for me."

"Let's talk with my uncle Charles." Munevver put her arm around Mrs. Coates's shoulders. "He's been in the navy all his life."

"How long ago?" Lord Charles knew from the expression on Mrs. Coates's face that the twenty-four-hour grace period when a man could withdraw his acceptance was over. It was likely that even the more lenient ninety-six-hour limit had also expired. He felt a great weariness as memories of harsh treatment, deprivation, and loneliness came rushing back. *A boy. Her only son. What can I do to help?* "I will make sure that he is placed with a fair master."

"A kind master! He's so young, and he's never been away from me. Please put him with a kind master." She sobbed.

"A kind master?" Lord Charles stared at the floor. "A kind master often endangers his men, his ship, and his mission. No. A fair master is a seaman's best chance of survival."

Chapter 16

July 1853: Russia Invades the Ottoman Empire

Quinn had made the unusual move of laying the newspaper open by Lord George's place so that Munevver could read all of the headlines. On July 2nd, Russia had crossed the Danube River, the boundary between Russia and the Ottoman Empire, and on July 3rd, she had invaded the Ottoman provinces of Moldavia and Wallachia. Munevver struggled with a sense of outrage. Russia, after proclaiming such interest in protecting the holy places and all Orthodox Christians, had chosen Sunday as the day to attack the Ottoman Empire.

She forced herself to scan the paper as quickly as possible. According to the article, Russia claimed that under a treaty between Russia and the Ottoman Empire, Russia had some rights and interests in Moldavia and Wallachia. However, the Sublime Porte had not accepted Russia's claim and had declared the Ottoman Empire to be at war with Russia. With its declaration of a state of war with Russia, the Ottoman Empire was no longer bound by the treaty with Russia that prevented foreign warships from traveling through the Dardanelles.

With a sense of dread, Munevver heard her father's footsteps on the stairs. She hurried to read as much as she could. Allied ships had passed through the Dardanelles and were in the Sea of Marmara, prepared to come to the assistance of the Ottoman Empire. Russian ships were in the Black Sea. As she arranged the paper in its customary folded position, she visualized the situation. To the north, Russian ships in the Black Sea, and to the south, Allied ships in the Marmara Sea with only the fragile, nineteen-mile-long Bosphorus Strait, two miles wide at some points, but only half a mile wide at the narrowest point where two great Ottoman fortresses— the Rumelihisan and the Anadoluhisan—faced each other.

By July 9th, the English newspapers were sounding the alarm, declaring that Russia wanted to gain control of the failing Ottoman Empire. The papers warned that a Russian conquest of the Ottoman Empire would threaten England's Eastern Empire. The newspapers raised the fear that, if Russia were to seize Constantinople, English trade routes, naval supremacy, and national honor would be destroyed. Prime Minister Lord Palmerston went so far as to state his fear explicitly: Russian expansion into the Ottoman Empire would threaten England's trade routes to India and the East. The public responded by insisting that action be taken to prevent this from happening. The more outspoken journalists demanded Russia's immediate evacuation of her forces from the Ottoman provinces of Wallachia and Moldavia.

Chapter 17

Summer 1853: England Fears War

After the ladies had withdrawn from the dinner table and Foster had placed glasses and decanters of port, brandy, and cognac on the table, Lord George settled into his chair with a sense of relief. He no longer felt the need to act as though everything was under control. He glanced around the table, estimating each man's understanding of what war would mean.

His brother, Charles, as a military doctor, knew more about the nation's readiness for war than he had shared. Vicar Edmund Ashley, his longtime friend's second son, would have heard rumors in the village of the need for defense and the mothers' fears of their sons' recruitment. He studied Ryker uneasily. He had gained a wider understanding of the nations he had visited than Lord George had anticipated, but he did not display the bone-deep, all-encompassing commitment to the family business that Lord George expected of his oldest son.

It was with a sense of reprieve that he turned to Ari Bey. He was an outsider. He would not be as influenced by the public's rabid demand for a war to uphold England's honor. It was more likely that he would consider the situation within a different perspective—what it would mean for the Ottoman Empire. "There was a time when the English Empire stretched around the world." Lord George hesitated before continuing. What he was about to say could not be unsaid. "It has always been held that, if any country threatened English communication, travel, or commerce throughout the Middle East, that country must be stopped."

Ari sensed the tenseness in the room and tried to dilute it by introducing a more benign approach to the subject. "At the same time that England was expanding her vast empire, the Muslim countries were expanding internally, developing their knowledge of mathematics, medicine, sciences, geography, astronomy, and philosophy."

"The English Empire is far-reaching, but Russia also has a vast empire," Ryker offered in a neutral voice, "and she has long wanted to extend her . . . influence."

"Extend her influence?" Ari's voice was carefully devoid of criticism. "I think it's more a matter of her constant efforts to gain warm-water seaports. With her only ports ice-locked during the winter months, she is desperate to gain ports in the Crimea."

"She has Vladivostok," Lord Charles murmured.

"Vladivostok is enclosed by the Sea of Japan," Ari continued, as though delivering a lecture. "The Japanese control access, and in the winter, Vladivostok requires icebreakers to keep it open. Without warm-water ports,

Russia is landlocked for half of the year."

"I have no sympathy for Russia," Lord George said in a firm voice as he reached for the bottle of cognac with its amber glow promising the smoothest of drinks. He studied the bottle in his hand and suddenly realized that his favorite cognac came from the southwestern part of France. *War could disrupt all trade.* He made a mental note to tell Quinn to order more French cognac.

"It is more than warm-water ports. The tsar has long wanted to see the Ottoman Empire ground into the dust and Constantinople a Russian city. He dreams of making Constantinople a Byzantine city again—a Russian Byzantine city." Lord George's voice escalated, filling the room. "We have Russia to thank for the precarious position we are now in. Russia is determined to divide up the Ottoman Empire!" He shook his head in frustration. "The threat of war is real, and our Parliament is divided on the issue. The Conservatives want to keep the Ottoman Empire alive and strong—a protection for our trade routes."

"And the Liberal Party?" Ryker asked dryly.

"The Liberals!" Lord George snarled. "Aberdeen agrees with Russia that the Ottoman Empire should be liquidated." He lifted his glass of cognac and looked around the table, challenging each man to disagree. When no one spoke, he added, "I think it's safe to say that England is not ready to see the Ottoman Empire divided up as Tsar Nicholas wishes." With a glance, he took the measure of each man. "England, France, Austria, and Prussia do not want any change in the current balance of power." He added softly, "It would not be in anyone's best interests."

"The Duke of Wellington is still commander-in-chief of the English Army, I believe." Ari broke the silence that followed Lord George's words.

"Yes, but he is over eighty now." Lord George poured himself more cognac and slid the bottle down the table. "It's generally accepted that Lord Raglan will succeed Wellington. Even though Raglan lost an arm at Waterloo and is in his seventies, he will be in command." Seeming to relax slightly, he added, "Young men praise the Duke of Wellington while secretly hoping to achieve a similar status."

"I think every country has its ambitious young officers," Ari offered diplomatically.

"Yes, young officers who dream of attaining military glory in battle." Lord Charles sighed. "They don't know the truth. Even great armies have been defeated by disease, deprivation, and lack of medical care."

"The unheralded challenges of war that every army has faced," Ari said as he thought back to the two failed Ottoman campaigns to capture Vienna. "One must also include the distance the army must travel, overstretched supply lines, hostile native populations, shortages of water, lack of provisions for the horses, and freezing climates."

"Yes, and yet young men are convinced they will achieve honor and acclaim." Lord George shook his head. "Two such dreamers are family relatives. There's Lord Lucan, who visualizes himself as commanding the cavalry. He was the eldest son, and when his father died, he inherited his father's Irish estates. He exploited the people to pay for his luxurious style of living in England and to purchase advancements—very rapid advancements—in the army." He paused, lost in thought.

Lord Charles continued the tale. "His parents have divorced, you know. Terrible scandal for the family."

Ignoring his brother's attempt to lighten the mood, Lord George took control of the conversation again. "It took Lord Lucan two years, but by the time he was twenty-six, he was a lieutenant colonel in command of the famous 17th Lancers." He reached for the port, then shifted to the bottle of brandy and half-filled a new glass. "He's a miserable bastard, constantly worrying about his estates in Ireland but only to the extent that they bring him revenue.

"Ireland is a wild, beautiful land, but much of it is a land of bogs, rocks, and mud huts. To make matters worse, it has been plagued by failure of its main crop, the potato, for several years. Potatoes are the primary source of income that the peasants need to pay rent to greedy landlords, and potatoes are the only food available for the people. There were more than four years of failed potato crops, and during the worst of the potato famine, Lucan evicted over two thousand of his tenants—tenants who had worked the land for his father and grandfather. Each family had lived on one acre of land and worked it to produce potatoes for them to eat to survive and to sell to pay the rent, but when the potato crops started to fail in the 1840s, the tenants could not pay their rents. Lord Lucan evicted them, even though they had no place to go and were starving. He was known as the "Exterminator."

"What did he hope to accomplish by evicting them?" Vicar Ashley asked.

"He wanted to sell the land so that he would not have to pay taxes on it." Lord George scowled at the glass in his hand. "Mark my words. He will find a way to be in command of the cavalry."

"Has he had any experience in war?" Ari asked quietly. He had heard stories about young men of the aristocracy with absolutely no military training or experience who bought positions of command.

"Yes," Lord George answered grudgingly. "He fought against the Russians in 1828 in the Balkans." He raised the brandy to his lips and savored it before continuing. "He is a combative, irritable man. He even hates the swans the queen protects. He complains that there are seventy swans on his land and they foul his fields." He slumped against the back of his chair.

"Now, my other cousin, James Brudenell, Lord Cardigan, dreams of nothing but the glory of being a military hero, another Wellington. He is a vain, reckless, irresponsible man." Lord George stared at the glass in his hand. "The best that can be said of him is that he's an excellent horseman, outstanding in a foxhunt. He has bought his way up to lieutenant colonel of the 15th Hussars. The word is that it cost his father more than forty thousand pounds. I'm sure that it was far more." He sniffed disdainfully. "It appears as though he is always involved with some other man's wife, which leads to a duel or a divorce proceeding for *criminal conversations.*

"The Brudenell family has always been close to the king, accepted in the innermost circles of the court." Lord George's voice held a seldom heard note of admiration. "Like most powerful families, they married their children into other first families." He seemed lost in thought. "They live at Deene Park, an old country manor with a magnificent library. It has the original manuscript of Chaucer's *Canterbury Tales.*" He shifted restlessly in his chair.

"But I was talking about the family's young dreamers. James was born in 1799. He had one older sister and six younger sisters. Harriet, his older sister, protected him from his father and the younger ones idolized him. He was a headstrong young man who crashed through life disregarding society's rules." Lord George hesitated, seeming uncertain whether to continue and then pressed on.

"He met and fell in love with Elizabeth Johnstone. She had married Captain Johnstone against her family's wishes, but after they married, she could not stand being poor. She asked her father to arrange a separation, but before he could act, she discovered she was pregnant. After she gave birth to a daughter, she ran away to her grandmother in Paris and married James Brudenell. Captain Johnstone started divorce proceedings. He brought an action for damages against Lord Brudenell." At the puzzled look on the faces around the table, he hurried to explain. "It's the first step in the long process of divorce that involves a special act of Parliament. It was the only way a marriage could be dissolved. Two years later, after the divorce was obtained, they were married, but from the beginning, their marriage was a disaster."

"Criminal conversations? I am not familiar with that term." Ari felt compelled to break the deadly silence that followed his host's long monologue, but he was unsure what an acceptable inquiry was into family affairs by an outsider.

"Adultery. That's what it means." Lord George stared at his empty glass. "According to the eighteenth-century BC Code of Hammurabi, adultery should be punished by drowning. Young men are sometimes so blinded by lust that they are willing to risk death in a duel for a few moments of pleasure. What fools! Why, after they were married, they fought all the time." He shook his head. "It is well known that Brudenell had several mistresses and had fathered numerous illegitimate children in the villages of Northhamptonshire."

Uneasy with this turn of the conversation, Ari repeated the question he had asked earlier. "Has he had any military experience?"

"None. He believes the only skill he needs is to be the best rider in a hunt. James is an arrogant, haughty, vain man. He's driven by his ambition and nothing else matters." He shuddered. "He took over the 15th Hussars by displacing an experienced and well-liked commander, Colonel Thackwell." Lord George groaned.

"There you have it. Two men in our family, dreaming

of gaining military glory. They are very similar, but George, although three years younger than James, has achieved more in the military and outranks him." He paused, staring at his empty hands. "Even worse, they are brothers-in-law. In 1829, Lucan married Cardigan's youngest sister, Anne. Lucan and Cardigan have detested each other ever since. They hate each other more than they will ever hate the Russians."

Ari hesitated to comment. In Ottoman society, the male head of a household would never criticize family members in front of strangers. He considered his options. He could wait in respectful silence or he could leave the room, but he definitely could not comment on what Lord George had just disclosed.

"Then there is another problem," Lord George muttered. "That damn exhibit! Prince Albert had planned it to showcase England's advancements in science and modernization of industry, but instead, it has been interrupted by others—Austria and Russia—as England's universal interest in peace."

"If peace was the intent of the exhibit, there seemed to have been a great deal of interest in advancements in weaponry," Ari offered cautiously, relieved to be on safer ground.

* * *

After they had joined the ladies in the drawing room, Lord George abruptly resumed the subject that had upset him earlier. "That damn exhibit! Because it was described as a peace incentive, the tsar is convinced

England has such a strong desire for peace that she will not go to war. To make matters worse, he knows very well that England has allowed the army to decline and the navy to be neglected. The deplorable state of our army and navy emboldened him to send Prince Menshikov to Constantinople, demanding that the sultan grant Russia protectorate over all Orthodox Christians in the Ottoman Empire. What audacity!" He sprang up and began to pace. "Of course, we had to respond, but in a way that would not precipitate war. In the end, we did the minimum. We sent ships from Malta to the Dardanelles. They are there now, ready to assist the sultan, if necessary."

Lord George paused and then spoke in a more placating manner. "England has always understood the danger Russia poses. For Russia to be a world power, she needs access to the Black Sea and the Dardanelles in order to enter the Mediterranean. As early as 1699, Russia began its push to the Black Sea." He looked around the room. "There have been three Russian–Ottoman wars since then. In each war, Russia had the same goal—to gain control of the Black Sea and the straits, and after that, the conquest of Constantinople. Eighty years ago, when Russia pushed to gain control of the Black Sea in the Russo–Turkish war of 1768–1774, she had a strong ally, Austria." He paused, frowning. "At that time, only France came to the aid of the Ottoman Empire against the combined forces of Russia and Austria."

Vicar Ashley entered the conversation for the first time. "In fact, in 1774, the Russians were at the gates of Constantinople and, although Russia did not capture Constantinople, under the terms of the 1774 treaty—

the Treaty of Küçük Kaynarca—Russia gained official status as protector of Orthodox Christians living in the Ottoman Empire."

After a moment, he continued. "A few years later, in the 1787–1792 Russo–Turkish War, the Ottoman Empire tried to get her land back. This time, both England and France supported the Ottoman Empire, but the Russians fought fiercely. In fact, when they captured Ottoman cities near the Dnieper River, they killed all the civilians. In the end, the Ottomans failed in their attempt to regain their lost land and had to accept the peace terms of the Treaty of Jassy that recognized Russia's annexation of Crimean territory." His voice became a rasp. "It set the stage for more Russian aggression . . . and for where we are now."

"I remember that Lord Stratford de Redcliffe was sent to Constantinople with Robert Adair in 1808 to restore peace between Russia and the Ottoman Empire," Lord Charles mused. "It took four years, but de Redcliffe brought about the Treaty of Bucharest between the Ottomans and the Russians."

"Well, de Redcliffe was in a strong bargaining position." Lord George nodded at his brother. "The Sublime Porte did not want to be involved in a war between France and Russia, and the Russians wanted to clear up problems with the Ottomans in case there was war with France. De Redcliffe got the Ottomans out of a war they could not win with only a few concessions."

"His efforts served him well," Lord George added cynically. "In 1825, he returned to Constantinople as ambassador."

"Well, Viscount Stratford de Redcliffe's good fortune did not follow him. When he was appointed ambassador to Russia in 1832, Tsar Nicholas refused to receive him." Ryker chuckled. "He got his revenge. Later, when de Redcliffe was ambassador to Constantinople, he persuaded the Sublime Porte to reject the compromise agreement Russia proposed—putting Greek-controlled churches under Russian protection."

"He's a man who holds a grudge," Lord George said with admiration in his voice. "Definitely not a man to cross."

"Nor a man to be indebted to," Lord Charles murmured.

* * *

After dinner, as they waited for the gentlemen to join them, Munevver retrieved her workbag from its hiding place behind the floor-length drapes pulled over the windows to shut out the grey shadows of evening. Settling into a chair in the corner, she began to knit the wool socks she made each year for the soldiers of the streets—the soldiers who, unable to find a place to live, huddled in doorways during England's cold, wet winter months. Louisa moved a light chair nearer to Munevver and reached into the bag to find the wool she knew would be there, waiting to be wound into a ball.

It was Georgette who broke the silence. "Munevver! You are such a paragon of virtue!" Her voice was melodic, but her words did not disguise her animosity. "My dear godmother," she said, smiling sweetly at Lady Frederica, "is constantly reminding me of all you accomplish." When there was no response, she continued. "She says that every day, you manage Lord George's correspondence, help Alexander with his lessons, and supervise the still room." She laughed prettily. "Oh, yes, I almost forgot." She dipped her head to the side so that the golden ringlets slid forward. "Most marvelous of all, you are fluent in foreign languages." As she noticed the gentlemen entering the room, she spread her carefully tended hands out to show them to their best advantage. "I try so hard, but I am simply useless with languages. I always have to ask a gentleman to translate French for me."

To relieve the awkward silence that followed Georgette's comments, Aunt Frederica began a rambling and often-repeated description of her grandmother's friend, Lady Mary Montague, and how she had set the custom for the family to learn languages. She had just begun to recount Lady Mary's experiences in Constantinople when Lord George took over the conversation.

"Our connection to the East goes farther back than that." Lord George raised his voice slightly so that he would have the attention of everyone in the room. "In 1553, a distant relative, Anthony Jenkinson, traveled to Aleppo, a magnificent city on the Silk Road that crossed Asia Minor. He was there in November of 1553 to watch Sultan Suleyman I enter Aleppo at the head of a huge army." He looked around the room proudly. "By December of that year, Jenkinson had asked the sultan for permission to trade everywhere in the Ottoman Empire, and amazingly, he was granted it." His gaze was cold as it landed on Ryker. "That was an amazing feat for a twenty-four-year-old to accomplish. It laid the foundation for our family's business connections with the Middle East and Asia."

"Yes," Ari Bey spoke slowly. "Sultan Suleyman I captured Aleppo, a city that has been in existence since the stone age." He looked across the room to meet Munevver's gaze. "After he seized the city, he restored the Aleppo Citadel, which dates back to the third millennium BC." Sensing that Lord George was not interested in the history of the city, he changed the thread of the conversation. "Are the trading connections with Aleppo still in place?"

"Oh, yes." Lord George beamed at Ari. "My youngest brother, Harris, has lived in Aleppo for years. His son, Rupert, took over when his father became ill, and now it is Rupert who manages the shipping of goods from Aleppo." He looked at Ryker again. "In time, Ryker will manage things from this end."

"Ah, a widely accepted arrangement," Ari murmured as he watched Ryker stiffen and Munevver cringe.

Chapter 18

August 1853: News from the East

The newspapers in early August were full of Queen Victoria's reassurances that England and France were united in their efforts to avoid war with Russia. However, there were reports of other troublesome issues. In Europe, there had long been an accepted brotherhood of sovereigns—Russian, Austrian, Prussian, and English—all related in some way. When the tsar of Russia refused to call Louis Napoleon, who had been declared Emperor of France in November of 1852, mon frère, my brother, and instead insisted on calling him mon ami, my friend, Louis Napoleon was outraged and never forgave him for the insult.

However, gossip about this slight was soon replaced by more pressing issues. It was being reported, in colorful prose, that the real cause of the hostility between France and Russia was based on old issues related to the holy places—the Church of the Nativity in Bethlehem and the Church of the Holy Sepulchre in Jerusalem. There were also dramatic reports that the hostility between Russia and the Ottoman Empire had been aggravated by

Russia's demand for the right to protect the Orthodox Christian population in the Ottoman Empire.

The newspapers declared it an unbelievable demand: Russia wanted protectorate of all Orthodox Christians in the Ottoman Empire, fourteen million people, nearly half of the population. England and France were acutely aware that Empress Catherina of Russia had claimed a similar protectorate of Poland in 1772, and soon after, Russia had dominated Poland. By September 1853, the public learned that the Vienna Agreement, designed to lessen tension between Russia and the Ottoman Empire, had been abandoned, and on October 9, 1853, they learned that the Sublime Porte had notified the tsar that unless Russia removed her troops from Wallachia and Moldavia, a state of war would exist.

It had been a long, hot day of work in Lord George's study, and now, after dinner, while waiting for the others to gather in the drawing room, Munevver glanced at her reflection in the mirror over the hall console. The violet, silk twill of her new dress, an early birthday gift from Aunt Frederica, complemented her eyes. She examined the neckline critically. It was Aunt Frederica who had ordered the dress for Munevver and had approved the lower neckline.

Despite Aunt Frederica's reassurances, the modest décolletage had made Munevver uneasy. Using the lace-making skills her grandmother had taught her, she had created an insert of Honiton lace to fill the top of the bodice. The delicate star stitch, Antwerp diamond stitch, and Flemish stitch that she had used to form a pattern of scrolls, flowers, and ferns brought a look that she thought was demure but actually emphasized her fragile beauty. She smiled at her reflection. Her dress might not be as fashionable as Georgette's, but at least it was more elegant than the dinner dresses she had brought with her from Yorkshire two years ago, she reassured herself as she slipped into the drawing room and made her way to the circle of people gathering around Florence Nightingale.

Lady Florence addressed herself to Lord George as soon as he entered the drawing room. "Although there is much talk about the probability of war, it appears that the military has not considered the crucial subject of providing medical care for the wounded." She lifted her chin defiantly. "The French, on the other hand, learned valuable lessons from the Peninsular Campaign. They know the importance of organizing medical care—evacuation, triage, and surgical care—and they have accepted the concept that medical care must be provided promptly, close to the front line." She smiled for the first time. "One of the French doctors designed a *Flying Ambulance* to take the wounded from the battlefield to the field hospital."

"I've heard stories about them," Ryker said quickly. "It's an enclosed, wooden cabinet mounted on a two-wheel frame and drawn by two donkeys. They can transport the wounded with amazing speed."

"It's not just the French who have been making preparations," Lady Florence added swiftly. "The Russians started to build military field hospitals in 1830 and now have over fifty." She met Ari Bey's gaze in a silent challenge. "I know little about Ottoman medicine and even less about their preparations for caring for their wounded."

"Ottoman medicine?" Ari hesitated. He had no desire to talk about the nearly non-existent military care of the wounded. He decided that it would be safer to use an academic approach in responding to Lady Florence. "Ottoman medicine has been influenced by the different cultures within the Ottoman Empire—Byzantines, Anatolians, Arabs, and Asians. It's based on a rather unique belief that it is everyone's duty to conscientiously promote their own health." He frowned, not knowing how much detail she wished to know. "There's a great emphasis on cleanliness. Muslims wash their hands, face, and feet before each of the five daily prayers. They make frequent visits to the hammams, and they always take off their shoes when they enter their homes to keep the filth from the streets and the marketplace from their home and family."

"You mentioned the influence of the Byzantines. As I remember, they believed in humoralism—the body's four humors—blood, phlegm, black bile, and yellow bile. Is it still followed?" Florence prodded.

"Yes. There are still those, a small number, who believe in the four humors and the importance of keeping them in balance." He continued slowly. "However, what may be less well known is the Ottoman belief, an almost universal belief, that six elements—light and air, food and drink, work and rest, sleep and wake, excretions and secretions, and disposition—are the foundation of health. Ottomans accept the need to follow a way of life that keeps these six elements balanced in order to avoid illnesses."

"How interesting!" Lady Florence beamed at him. "That's a very broad prophylactic approach to health." Her questioning became more intense. "What about hospitals? In 1851, I spent three months training as a nurse at the Institution of Protestant Deaconesses at Kaiserswerth, Germany. I spent time in their hospital and orphanages. Since then, I have been particularly interested in the hospitals of different countries. I've heard that Italy has excellent hospitals. They are clean and the patients are well cared for . . . and well fed."

"We have hospitals in five of our largest cities. One of the oldest is in Aleppo."

"Aleppo?" Munevver, who had been following their exchange closely, murmured.

"One of the hospitals in Aleppo, the Nuri Hospital, dates back to 1154." At Munevver's slight nod, Ari Bey continued. "Hospitals were built around a large, enclosed courtyard that had a pool and a fountain. Paved areas around the pool had lattices to provide shade for the patients."

"Were they just for wealthy patients?" Lady Florence's words had a cynical tinge.

"The hospitals were ordered to be constructed by sultans, their mothers, or influential families as acts of piety. They had areas for the wealthy and also for the poor. They even built special sections for the insane, and of course, there were separate hospitals that served to isolate lepers from other patients," Ari explained.

"Amazing! Is it the Ottoman Government that funds the building of hospitals now?"

"No. Hospitals are still built as a charitable offering by a sultan or by the mother of a sultan to be available for all. They are based on the theory of integralistic medicine—promoting physical health, mental health, and quality of life. Promoting the health of these three areas of one's life is believed to prevent illnesses. Cleanliness, peace of mind, and good nutrition are paramount features of treatment."

Ari grew less cautious as he became aware of the depth of their interest. "We believe that water is powerful in healing, and most hospitals are built with warm baths—hammams—for the patients' use. It is accepted that frequent treatment in the hammams will restore the balance of patients' humors, and thus, their physical and mental health. Our hospitals also include gardens with sweet-smelling flowers and aromatic herbs. They often have fountains that produce a melodious sound that soothes the mentally ill. We believe that sound is energy."

He smiled at the skeptical looks on his listeners' faces. "The drumbeat of the Mehterhane-i-hagani band, the Imperial Military Band, provides the energy that arouses the troops' fighting spirit as they go into battle. It is believed that the energy of music helps in promoting health." Ari shrugged. "Like most hospitals, our hospitals employ physicians, but there are also attendants to wash the patients, their clothing, and their bedding as well as cooks, musicians, and gardeners."

Ari stopped for a moment, uncertain whether to make an important point. "The Ottomans are practical people. They know that two things are crucial for hospitals: clean water and an efficient sewer system. To gain these and to save costs, they tend to build hospitals as part of a larger complex, such as a mosque, school, or marketplace where the engineers have already arranged for these two essentials."

Georgette felt she had been ignored long enough. "Tell me, Ari Bey, of all the beautiful things you have seen in London, don't you agree that the Elgin Marbles are the most exquisite?"

Munevver froze at Georgette's question and then forced herself to respond when Ari remained silent. "During the time my grandfather spent in the Ottoman Empire as a young man, he collected detailed drawings of the Greek treasures, including the marvelous statues and the friezes of the Parthenon." Munevver glanced around the circle for support and, when none was forthcoming, pressed on. "For centuries, those priceless pieces of art were not ravaged. They passed the years in Athens' sunny, hot, dry summer days and the cloudy, cold, windy days of winter. They existed as they had been carved in all their magnificent glory during the Byzantium Empire and continued to be revered when Athens was conquered by Ottoman Sultan Mehmed II in 1458." She took a deep breathe. "They did not need to be stripped away to 'preserve' them!"

Ari's voice was uncharacteristically crisp. "In fact,

as the conquering sultan rode into Athens, he was so impressed by the beauty of its ancient monuments that he issued a *firman*, an official edict, forbidding their looting or destruction on pain of death."

"Yes, but Lord Elgin dedicated his life to saving them," Georgette insisted. "He brought them here to England to preserve them and so we could all enjoy seeing them." When no one responded, she tossed her head and continued petulantly, "I think it would be a wonderful idea if we all went to the English Museum tomorrow to view them." She glanced at Munevver. "Perhaps the trip would be too troublesome for you, but I'm sure others would enjoy visiting the Elgin Marbles."

"Save them?" Ryker broke the silence that followed her statement. "Lord Elgin chiseled the most beautiful friezes ever created from the Parthenon. He ripped statues from their pedestals. He plundered the metope panels of the Parthenon, the Temple of Athena, built in the 5th century BC. It is said that he removed about one-half of the remaining sculptures of the Parthenon and transported them to England." Ryker's face was grim. "He had been a trusted English ambassador to Constantinople, and he ravaged her treasures under the guise of a firman, a permit. That firman allowed him to copy the works, to make models of them, and to excavate where necessary to discover inscriptions that may have been hidden in the ruins."

Ryker covered his face with his hands for a moment. "Under Lord Elgin's orders, priceless artwork was crated and transported from the Ottoman Empire to England, where it sat for years in dark sheds on the estate of Lord

Elgin's mother until the English Museum finally bought the collection from him in 1816. I, for one, do not wish to visit the product of Elgin's looting of the Parthenon."

Munevver read Aunt Frederica's raised eyebrow correctly and took a deep breath. Her plans would seem insipid in comparison to the attraction of Georgette's proposed day in London. "It appears we are to have rain for most of tomorrow, so I thought that it would be a good time for a scavenger hunt." Glancing at Alexander and Davud, huddled in the window seat, she added quickly, "As I recall, there are two velocipedes in the carriage house that could be put in shape for riding along the drive. If you start early in the morning, you will have them ready by the time the rain stops."

"Oh, splendid, Verie." Alexander beamed at her. "We can start working on them right now."

Uncle Charles, standing quietly on the edge of the circle, met Munevver's pleading glance. He had raised two children and knew well the perils of a rainy day and unoccupied boys. "I will be glad to go with you boys to check them out in the morning." He looked at their disappointed faces. "It is too dark to do much work today, but I promise to go with you as soon as we have finished breakfast, and I will be happy to offer any assistance you might require." He was rewarded with their quick grins.

"Have you created a new scavenger hunt?" Ryker asked. Before she could answer, he had turned to Louisa. "You remember the last one? We were a team. It was devilishly challenging, but we won."

"It's a new one and requires teams of two people. Ladies who wish to participate will write their names on slips of paper, twist them closed, and put them in the jar on the mantel." She gestured toward the fireplace. "In the morning, each gentleman wishing to join in the activity will select a twist of paper and will discover who his partner is to be." When no one broke the silence, she said, "The search is difficult. It covers the entire manor house. The contestants must find the article, sketch it, and describe where they found it."

"It sounds delightful, my dear," Aunt Frederica said with a relieved sigh.

"For those who prefer a less vigorous challenge, there will be new Parisian jigsaw puzzles set up in the Long Hall. The two partners who complete a puzzle first win."

From the gleam in Aunt Frederica's eyes, Munevver knew it had been worth all the effort she had made to get the latest puzzles from France. She suppressed a smile as she visualized the Grand Exhibit's

Crystal Palace puzzle. It would be very challenging, but Aunt Patience would love it. "The chess table and card tables will be set up in the Long Hall for those who prefer those activities." She glanced around the room. How could she compete with Georgette's proposal?

"Will there be prizes for every activity?" Ryker asked.

"Of course." Munevver felt relief sweep over her. "Prizes will be awarded at tea time."

Chapter 19

August 1853: An Itinerary Shared

With the scent of coffee reassuring her that the day had begun as her father demanded, Munevver hurried down the narrow back stairs and slipped into the breakfast room. A swift glance revealed that Quinn had placed the freshly ironed *Morning Post* and *The Times* on the table to the left of Lord George's place setting, as usual, but he had left them open instead of folded.

Munevver filled her cup with hot chocolate and slid into her regular place. She could read the headlines without moving the papers, but she would have to wait until Lord George left to go to the city to fully satisfy her curiosity. She murmured a quiet good morning in the general direction of Lord George as he strode into the room, followed by Ari Bey in his customary, black frock coat and scarlet fez with its black tassel dancing a greeting to her.

Hearing her father's coffee cup hit the saucer with unusual force, Munevver strained to hear what he was saying to Ari. "Leaving?"

"Yes, evidently my work here is finished." Ari spoke in his usual, measured tone, but there was a slight flush across his cheek bones and he raised a crisp, white handkerchief to cover one of his frequent bouts of coughing. "I've been requested to return to Constantinople."

"What will you do? What will be your assignment? Not Macedonia, I hope!"

Munevver's mind worked rapidly. Macedonia, lying north of the Aegean Sea, included some of the most rebellious Ottoman provinces—Salonika, Monastir, and Kosovo. Among these mutinous provinces, it was Salonika that was generally accepted as being the birthplace of the revolutionary movement, The Young Ottomans' dream of democratization. It was also the site of Bulgarian terrorists' activities as the Bulgarians attempted to undermine Ottoman rule in Macedonia.

Lord George rubbed his left eye, which was twitching again. "The entire province of Macedonia is a cauldron of Albanians, Greeks, Bulgarians, Serbs, and Rumanians infected with the Greek fever for independence." He shuddered as he remembered what he had read about rumored uprisings and Russian unrest. After a moment of consideration, he nodded at the younger man. "You could stay here and work with my company."

"Thank you. I am most honored by your offer, but my duty is to the sultan," Ari Bey replied. "I will serve wherever he sends me."

Quinn leaned over Lord George's chair and murmured something.

"Excuse me. It seems my steward has an urgent problem." He bowed to Ari. "After you finish your breakfast, I hope you will join me in my study. I have some new papers from Constantinople that I would like to discuss with you." Lord George glanced at Munevver, who was sitting quietly with her eyes on her plate. "Leave the household matters to your aunt this morning," he said with thinly disguised irritation. "There is correspondence that requires your attention as soon as possible."

With a glance at the footman, who was replenishing the covered dishes on the sideboard in anticipation of the boys coming down to breakfast, Munevver ventured to ask Ari Bey for the information she needed if she was going to carry out the escape plan forming in her mind. "How will you return?"

"How will I return?" Her question startled him. *Why would she want to know how I intend to travel? What does it mean?*

"Yes." Munevver asked hurriedly with her eyes fixed on the piece of toast she was crumbling. "How will you return to Constantinople and . . . if you wanted to go to Aleppo, how would you go?"

"Aleppo?" Ari's head shot up in surprise, and then he regained his customary composure. "Aleppo's a long way from Constantinople."

"Well, tell me how you will go to Constantinople." She fought the urge to tell him to hurry, to give her the information she needed so badly as fast as he could. Every time her father had stared at her without speaking, she was terrified he was going to announce that he had arranged the date for her to be married. Her escape plan was taking better shape in her mind, but she needed time—and information. She knew that Uncle Harris was unwell. Surely, he would welcome her help. She had to know how to get to Aleppo.

"I will take a ship from London to Marseilles. Once in France, I'll travel overland by train and carriage to Vienna. In Vienna, I must find a steamship that will be traveling down the Danube River to the Black Sea. I hope to find one that goes as far as the Port of Varna." He smiled slightly. "It's the closest port to Constantinople." He resumed his description of his itinerary. "Then I will take a ship across the Black Sea and down that beautiful, narrow, treacherous strait, the Bosphorus." Ari's voice became husky. "Suddenly, I'll see the minarets of Constantinople and I'll be home."

"You've been away a long time." Munevver kept her eyes on the napkin she was folding and refolding. "You must be very eager to be home again, to be back with your family."

"There is only my mother, but yes, I will be very happy to see her again." He spoke without meeting her eyes. "You asked about Aleppo. To get to Aleppo would be a very difficult journey." Ari paused for a moment. "It must be over 1194 kilometers, 742 miles, from Constantinople to Aleppo." He met her eyes and smiled. "If I were ever desperate enough to make that journey, from my home in Constantinople, which is located on the European side of the Ottoman Empire, I would take a brief ferry ride across the Bosphorus to Scutari, and when I got off the ferry, I would be in Asia—the first step toward Aleppo."

"Scutari?" The tension that had been making it hard for her to speak lessened. "Scutari is the terminus of the caravan routes that bring treasures from Asia Minor to Constantinople. I know the markets of Scutari."

"From Scutari, I would have to travel southeast across the vast, primitive Anatolian land that we call Anadolu." Ari shook his head. "It would be a long, hard trip with very poor accommodations or none at all."

"Yet, pilgrims travel that route when they go to Mecca," Munevver stated quietly.

"They go in organized caravans with protection." Ari gave her a warning look. "It is not a journey to be taken without protection." He changed the subject as Alexander and Davud hurried into the room, making straight for the buffet of hot dishes. "My mother asked me to express her appreciation for all you have done for Davud. He's her brother's son, but she has cared for him since he was a child. He is very precious to her." At her questioning look, he continued. "His father was killed fighting the Russians, and his mother died of consumption when he was three."

Ari moved uneasily in his chair. "My mother also asked me to extend an invitation to you to visit her if you are ever in Constantinople." He handed her a small, white envelope. "I have written down the directions to her home."

"Thank you." This act of kindness brought tears to her

eyes, and she had to clear her throat before continuing. "Please convey my warmest greetings to your mother."

Hesitantly, Ari pulled a slim book from his inner pocket. "I think you might enjoy this book." He extended the book to her. "It contains some information about traveling in the East."

As she accepted the book, the sound of Aunt Frederica's footsteps approaching made her slip it into her bag of knitting. *I'll have to wait until I'm alone in my room to discover what it is that he has risked giving me.*

* * *

The leather cover was as fine as the chamois covering of her nail buffer. The pages were tipped in gold, and the endpapers were a scroll-patterned gold and crimson. She lifted it to her face and captured the orange scent of bergamot and the smoky, medicinal aroma of Oud—the fragrance associated with men from the Middle East. Her grandfather's library had always held that scent.

Munevver glanced at her bedroom door. *Shall I lock it to prevent anyone from entering while I scan the pages? What will I say if Christianna or Aunt Frederica try the door and find it locked?* She shuddered. *What if Georgette decides to drop in for one of her 'special times' together?*

Georgette. On the outside, she was flawless—a slender but curved form, hair the color of April sunshine, and light-blue eyes that could look so innocent. When they were with others, Georgette pampered Munevver in ways that drew attention to her limp, but when she was alone with her, she was malicious, mocking Munevver's interest in trade and making pointed remarks about her unwed state. *A house this big and not one place of privacy for me!*

Memories of her grandfather's home brought tears to her eyes. She had been cherished in her grandfather's home, and after her twelfth birthday, her grandfather had arranged for her to have her own sitting room. Now in her father's home, even though she was the oldest daughter, she had no sitting room of her own, no library, and not even a small writing room. Well, she did have the tiny retreat bequeathed to her by Ryker, but someone was likely to see her on her way there.

Munevver glanced at the window seat with its thick draperies and piles of cushions. If she heard anyone enter, she could slip the book under a cushion. She wanted privacy so that she could savor every bit of information she hoped the book contained. She stood uncertainly in the middle of the room. *It was wrong of me to have accepted a gift from a man, but it is just a book. A book is not a personal item. Still, I should have shown it to Aunt Frederica.*

She removed the folded paper and smoothed it out carefully. Yes, it was Ari's precise handwriting. She had read his communications to her father often enough to recognize it at first glance. At the top of the page was written *Vienna to Constantinople on the Austrian steamship, Galatea.* Below that, Ari had described the trip minutely.

Vienna to Pest. Approximately twenty-four hours, depending on weather.

Pest to Drekova. Two to four days. Beds are benches that slide out from under divans. No mattresses, blankets, or pillows are provided. Problem with fleas and mosquitoes.

Drekova to Skeia Cladova. A short distance of fifty miles, but this part of the Danube has rapids and stony reefs with only eighteen inches of water over them. Could take two days.

Skeia Cladova to Galatz. Three to four days.

Galatz to Constantinople on steamship Ferdinando Primo. About two and a half days.

Conditions: Crowded, malodorous, and noisy with the incessant sound of paddlewheels. Men spend their time playing cards or gambling. Women sit together and knit with four double-pointed, lethal-looking steel needles. Food is indifferent. Water is scarce. The biggest problem is the swarms of malaria-carrying mosquitoes that invade every space in the evening. Wise travelers bring insect repellant nettings for cover.

Chapter 20

September 1853: Constantinople

The magnificent length of the old, wooden yali stretching along the waterfront gleamed like silver in the late afternoon sun as Ari stepped from the caïque that had brought him the last lap of the journey from Constantinople to his mother's home on the Bosphorus. He paused on the steps at the top of the embankment to admire the open balconies and loggias with their ornately sculptured roofs placed strategically along the front of the yali so that there was maximum opportunity to watch traffic making its way down the treacherous strait that linked landlocked nations around the Black Sea to the Marmara Sea, and then through the Dardanelles into the Mediterranean Sea and the rest of the world. He never tired of the view, and now he had the oddest desire to share it with Munevver.

Ari cast one last look at the prow-shaped middle part of the yali jutting out over the water. His mother would be waiting for him. He hurried up the last steps and into the main hall that traversed straight as an arrow from the waterfront to the outside door leading to the gardens that his mother adored. He entered the vast hall with its many doors opening off it. As a nod to European influence, formal chairs and tables were set precisely along the length. Ignoring the labyrinth of halls and rooms that enabled men on their way to the men's section of the house, the selamlik, to avoid the haremlik, the private section of the house allocated to the women, Ari hurried to the marble staircase at the end of the hall. It would take him directly to his mother's rooms.

He tapped lightly on the door before entering the dimly lit salon with its wall of windows overlooking the Bosphorus. Low, broad divans covered in crimson-and-gold brocade encircled the room, meeting to create welcoming corners under the windows that bowed out over the waterfront. Plump, silk-covered cushions in bright colors and decorated with intricate embroidery were piled in the corners and along the broad expanse of the divans.

Ari stepped inside and bowed to his mother, who was sitting in her favorite corner where she could see the traffic on the Bosphorus going down the strait with its treacherous currents toward Constantinople. He smiled grimly at the old saying: "He who controls the straits, controls the world." It had been true for four hundred years for the Ottomans, and it would continue to be true as long as they held the two straits, the Dardanelles and the Bosphorus, that connected three seas—the Black Sea, the Marmara Sea, and the Mediterranean Sea—and two continents, Europe and Asia. The Bosphorus linked the Black Sea to the Sea of Marmara, and the Dardanelles linked the Marmara Sea with the Aegean Sea and the

Mediterranean Sea. The Ottomans had been challenged again and again by landlocked Russia for possession of the straits, but they had always managed to hold on to their most prized possession—the straits.

Ari felt a chill creep over him. The empire was heavily in debt. The army was in tatters, and the navy had not been rebuilt since its destruction at Navarino on that terrible day, October 20, 1827, when the Allied Forces of England, France, and Russia had come to the aid of Greece in its fight for independence. They had entered the Ottoman-held Bay of Navarino and opened fire on Ottoman ships at anchor—seventy-eight ships destroyed, and three thousand men of the Ottoman Navy killed.

He had to conquer the despair he felt before he talked with his mother. It was pointless to frighten her. She knew the threat of war as well as he. Russia's desire for control of the straits was stronger than ever, and the Ottoman Empire was in a desperate state. But if war came, they would fight to defend their homeland. There would be none of the fanatic excitement over the glory of war that was stirring the people in England and France, and none of the religious fervor of the Russians. The Ottomans would call up the sturdy, uneducated farmers and shepherds from Anadolu, and those men would answer the call to fight to protect their country.

In the last one hundred years, the Turkish peasants had left their lands many times to fight against the Russian enemy when it had attacked their country. Each time, ill-equipped, seldom paid, and poorly fed Ottoman soldiers had gone forth to defend the Caliph against the infidel. Only this time, Ari reflected, it was likely that the

Ottoman Muslim soldiers would be fighting beside the Giaours, the non-believers, the English, and the French.

"Mother," Ari said softly as he hurried to her side, his eyes registering the lovely picture she made in her dark-blue tunic over a creamy, silk blouse with lace trimming at the neckline and at her wrists. As usual, she had donned the traditional, blue-silk, loose trousers that were gathered and tied at her ankles, and a plum-colored, velvet entari or dress embroidered with silver thread that reached to the floor. It had a low neckline and was open from the waist down to allow for ease of movement. Around her waist was a four-finger-wide, silver, mesh belt embellished with sapphires and diamonds. She wore the standard golden silk, backless slippers and a small, black, velvet hat perched on one side of her head. Her needlework was resting on a low table decorated with mother-of-pearl in front of her.

"I trust your health is well?" Ari said as he knelt to kiss each of her hands and raise them to his forehead.

She murmured, "By the goodness of Allah, I am very well." As she cupped his face with her smooth hands, he inhaled the familiar, clean scent of Limon Kolonyasi and knew he was home.

"Come. Sit beside me and tell me all your news." She raised a beautifully shaped eyebrow in the direction of one of the women at the end of the room, who slipped soundlessly from the room. "We'll have coffee in a moment, but for now, it is enough to know you are home and safe."

He began in the traditional way by asking about her health and the health of her household. It was not until the maid had returned with tiny cups of coffee and a plate of baklava that he began on the topic he knew she was eager to hear about.

"My efforts in London did not yield the results that were hoped for," he began in Turkish, and then, at his mother's glance at the maid, changed to Persian, which they often used to discuss family matters. Not just hoped for. He had been instructed to convince the English to extend more credit to the Sublime Porte so that the Ottoman Navy could be strengthened. Everyone in Constantinople knew that it was only a matter of time before the great polar bear that was Russia would make another push to gain the waterways to the Mediterranean Ocean. Everyone also knew that the Ottoman fleet was old and in need of repairs. It had never recovered from the disastrous Battle of Navarino twenty-five years earlier.

"I am sorry, my son. I am sure that it was not due to your lack of persistence."

A sigh of frustration escaped his control. "I was more than persistent. I trampled on the rules of diplomacy. We must have credit so that we can restore the navy well enough to handle the next Russian onslaught. They are already spreading word that they are deeply concerned about the plight of the Christian subjects in the Ottoman Empire."

"Christians and others—Armenians, Jews, Circassians, and Arabs—have lived together in the Ottoman Empire for centuries. The Greeks, too, until they insisted on independence." Janan Hanim sniffed delicately, remembering the Greeks' long rebellion against the Ottoman Government. The Greek War of Independence had begun one year before she was born, in 1822, and had lasted until 1833. Her father had considered it to be an act of treachery, and she had watched it claim his life and the lives of many Ottoman soldiers.

"The Greeks were well supported in their fight for independence by the blindly idealistic English and French." Ari frowned. "Even the Russians helped them." He straightened his shoulders. "We didn't have any support then, and we don't have any now. Yes, the English and the French want us to believe they are our friends—friends who arrogantly dispense suggestions, plans, and arrangements that benefit them, not us."

"They will support us if the Russians attack again, won't they?"

"They will act to safeguard their very profitable trade with India and the East, and that means preventing the Russians from gaining access to the waterways. You know well that it has been a Russian dream for centuries—capture the Ottoman ports on the Black Sea, seize the Bosphorus, command the Sea of Marmara, and control the Dardanelles entrance to the Mediterranean Sea. If they achieve that, English shipping will be in peril." He shook his head. "The only reason England and France will support us would be to preserve their shipping lines." He stood up and offered her his hand. "Let's go out on the balcony. The walls have ears in Constantinople."

She whispered, "You saw Davud?"

"Yes, I saw him twice." He smiled at her gently as he noticed the quiver of apprehension that she was not able to suppress. "I will tell you everything you want to know in a moment, but first I must advise you on what must be done."

"The bitter before the sweet?" she murmured, moving closer to the edge of the balcony as her eyes followed a huge cargo ship going down the Bosphorus headed toward Constantinople.

"Mother, listen carefully." Ari moved so that his mouth was close to her ear. "We will be at war soon." He felt her tremble. "This is what you must do, but you must do it without anyone realizing what you are doing. Store enough food—rice, beans, lentils, olives, dried fish, figs, raisins, olive oil, and so on—to last two years, if possible. Store water, too." He wiped his forehead with his handkerchief. "This is most important. You must hoard all the gold you can. If we survive the war, our situation will be desperate. Ottoman money will be worthless. You will need gold." How could he tell her that, if war came, it was unlikely that he would be able to help her. "Your survival depends on it."

"It's come?" Janan Hanim shuddered. The menace of war with Russia was always in the air, but now it was on her balcony.

"Russia has given the sultan an ultimatum."

"What is it this time?"

"The Tsar wants to have the power of protectorate over all the Greek and Russian Orthodox Christians in the Ottoman Empire."

"He wants the empire!"

"He doesn't care about the empire, but he does want the straits and Constantinople. He wants to make it a Byzantium city again." Ari's shoulders slumped. "It was five hundred years ago, but he is convinced that the marriage of Byzantine Princess Sophia to Russian Grand Prince Ivan III makes it imperative that he free Constantinople from the infidels. He sees it as his duty to make Constantinople a Byzantine city again."

"Princess Sophia? Wasn't she the grandmother of Ivan the Terrible, the first tsar of Russia?" Janan Hanim asked with a mischievous smile and then added urgently, "Surely the sultan will refuse?"

"English Ambassador Stratford de Redcliffe believes it is best for the Ottoman Empire to survive a little longer. I think he has convinced the sultan that England and France will back him against the tsar."

A shrewd expression reflecting years of experience made her seem older. "Tell me, my son. Do you believe they will send their young men to die in a foreign land just to help us defend our sovereignty?"

"Yes, but not because of their desire to support us. They want to keep their trading routes open. They want the straits and the Mediterranean Sea to be open for their commerce, not under Russian control."

"When will it begin?" Janan whispered. "How much time do I have?"

"I'm not sure, but as you know, Russia has a history of using the power of winter to her advantage."

"Yes, and winter came early last year. I don't have much time." She stood, lost in thought. "The storerooms are supplied, as always, but not for a two-year period, and there is the matter of accumulating more gold without attracting attention." She pulled herself erect. "For this evening, we will forget the approaching war, and you will tell me all about England and the lovely family that has offered a home to my Davud."

Janan Hanim noticed that, despite his efforts to draw a broad picture of Lord George's home and family, her tall, handsome son returned again and again to Lady Munevver. "Munevver is a distinguished, old Ottoman name," she said hesitantly. "It means enlightened or intelligent. How does it happen that an English lady has such a beautiful Ottoman name?"

"The family has very old ties to the Ottoman Empire through trade and through its connection with Lady Mary Montague, who lived in Constantinople for a time when her husband was ambassador." Ari frowned, puzzled by a sudden remembrance. "I believe she said that it was her grandfather who named her, not her parents."

"Tell me more about this English Munevver?" Janan Hanim hid her smile. It had been several years since Ari's wife had died, and he had refused all of her attempts to convince him to even consider marrying again.

"She is taller than most women." He held his hand under his chin. At his mother's exasperated sigh, he started again. "She is the oldest daughter."

"Still unmarried?" Janan Hanim's brief inquiry carried many sub-questions. Why had her family not arranged a marriage for her? Were the negative factors due to the girl or to the family? What possible connection could there be between the young lady and her beloved son? She knew that social customs were different, but surely, he could not have spent time alone with a young lady, an attractive, unmarried young lady?

"Yes." He found himself struggling to provide the information his mother was seeking but not asking. "She has a clubfoot."

"It wasn't corrected when she was an infant?" She thought back to the infant with a clubfoot whom she had seen. Loving women in the family had taken turns gently manipulating the infant's distorted foot to a more normal position, and then splints covered in soft cotton that had been soaked in beaten egg white mixed with alum would be applied. They knew that, although the bones and joints were malleable enough to bring about change until the child was ten years old, it was crucial to start in infancy to minimize the deformity.

"It wasn't spoken of by anyone in the family." He found it hard to relate the story he had been told by his valet. "I know it's hard to believe, but Hasan said that the servants told him Munevver had been cast off by her parents when they learned she had been born with a clubfoot."

Janan Hanim nodded. Valets knew everything that was going on in the family. How could a family reject a child? It was unthinkable. Families accepted whatever challenges life presented. After all, it was the will of Allah.

Ari continued. "She had been sent away to the country and lived there for the early years of her life until her grandfather, her father's father, found her and raised her."

"Who could discard a baby? A clubfoot is not the child's fault. It is the will of Allah." She nodded briskly. "Tell me more about this English lady."

"She is well educated. In fact, she speaks five languages."

"Is Turkish one of them?" Janan Hanim asked with a twinkle in her eye.

"Yes, and Persian, too." His voice softened. "Her French is impeccable."

"You said she is the oldest daughter and not yet married." Janan Hanim paused as she pondered what could have prevented the proper marriage of a family's oldest daughter. It was a difficult question, but she had to ask it. "How old is she?"

Ari struggled to suppress a smile at her question. In his mother's world, marriage would surely have been arranged for a daughter by the time she was eighteen. "She was eighteen when I met her."

Ari could almost see the questions rippling through his mother's logical mind as she continued her questioning. "What does she do? Does she manage her father's household?"

"Her aunt Frederica, her father's younger sister, manages the household. Evidently, she took over after Munevver's mother died." He hesitated. It was unusual in England for a woman to engage in business and, in the Ottoman Empire, even rarer. But there had been Valide Sultans who had managed vast businesses . . . even empires. "During the day, she works with her father, Lord George, on matters related to the family business."

"I'm sure you told me there was an older brother. Wouldn't he be the one to work by the side of his father?"

"Ryker is the oldest, the firstborn son." Ari sighed. "He's the heir and has just returned from the Grand Tour." He hesitated. "He doesn't appear to have settled down yet."

"Humph!" Janan Hanim scowled. "So, this intelligent, young lady works for her father?"

"Yes, and she assists her aunt Frederica in caring for the children in the household." He added clumsily, "She spends time with her younger sister, Christianna, and helps her younger brother, Alexander, with his lessons." Ari quickly added, "Of course, she also helps Davud with his lessons."

Janan Hanim looked around her richly decorated salon. Her lute awaited her in the corner. The low tables, intricately inlaid with mother-of-pearl, held small boxes of the honey lokum she loved. Light from the windows overlooking the Bosphorus slid across the many pillows on the divans that she had spent hours embroidering, making them sparkle. After considering her world as it might be seen through the eyes of an outsider, she asked hesitantly, "What else does she do?"

"She knits scarfs and socks for the soldiers wounded in the Peninsular War who have no families . . . no homes." He waited, not knowing how his very conservative mother would accept the information that a young lady would knit items of clothing for men not of her family.

"It is taught that we should help one another," Janan Hanim said softly. "Now, my son, you have told me what she does but not what she is like. Tell me more about this lovely, young woman."

"How did you know she was lovely?" Ari could not help exclaiming. When his mother just smiled, he began. "She is slender with black hair, very fair skin, and she has the most beautiful violet eyes. She rarely smiles, but when she does, it makes the day better."

"She is beautiful, educated, and devoted to her family, but yet, she is not married?" Janan Hanim summarized gently but persistently. In her view, a judiciously arranged marriage of a daughter was the most important responsibility a family faced.

Ari turned away from his mother to hide his discomfort. "I've heard that her father intends to arrange an advantageous marriage for her."

"Her father? Her father would arrange her marriage?" She raised her eyebrows in disbelief. "What do men know of such things? It is the women of the family who must consider every aspect in arranging a marriage. It is they who gather the necessary information about the young woman and her family to determine whether a merge of the two families would be right. The hammam is always buzzing with news, and of course, the mothers are able to meet many lovely, young ladies there."

"In England, it is the male head of the family—father, husband, brother, even an uncle— who controls all of the assets of the family and makes all of the decisions, including the marriage of daughters and sons." He paused. "It is the custom in England for the male head of the family to arrange marriages that will benefit the whole family. Because Lord George has wealth from his trading company but only a very minor title, it is believed he will try to arrange a marriage that will bring him prestige among the aristocracy." He paused, and then said more crudely than he had intended, "He'll try for the highest title he can buy, a future duke if he can find one."

"Marriage is more than increasing status or wealth. It is a question of selecting a partner who will be the best fit for the young lady and her family. Every mother knows that!"

"According to the servants' gossip, Lord George will arrange a marriage for Munevver that will not only enhance the family's social standing, but will also increase her sister's and her brothers' chances of making more splendid marriages."

"What about Munevver? What does she want?"

Ari allowed himself a brief smile. "Lady Munevver wants to escape to Aleppo."

"Aleppo? It's the end of the world!"

"It is the wellspring of their family's trading business. She has an uncle there whom she thinks will welcome her."

"No one will welcome a daughter fleeing from her father." Janan Hanim's sharp comment made Ari squirm as he considered if he should share the gossip about Lord George's likely choice, the duke's son. His voice was low as he divulged the rumor that the man Lord George was considering preferred young boys.

"A pederast! That should not be!" Her emphatic words were accompanied by a firm stamp of her foot. "A daughter is a family's greatest treasure, and her happiness is to be assured in arranging a marriage. No family should subject a daughter to such a humiliating situation."

"Well," Ari mumbled sheepishly, "when she asked how one would travel to Aleppo, I gave her directions to you."

Janan Hanim studied her son. While he hadn't indicated a preference for this girl, he had always refused to even listen to her describe the many lovely, young women she knew. "What is she really like?"

Ari studied his determined mother. "She uses the Hungarian opening when she plays chess."

"Hmm." Janan Hanim lowered her eyes to hide her excitement as she began to plan the arrangement of a home on the Bosphorus for the young couple.

Chapter 21

October 1853: Ottoman Empire Declares War on Russia

The broad windows of the breakfast room that usually provided a view of blooms or at least succulent greens now framed a dismal display of rain-flattened shrubbery. Munevver paused on her way to the sideboard. It was almost time to start planning the year-end festivities, and she could not even bear to think of them. Christianna was still in Yorkshire, and Ryker was more morose as each day passed.

As Munevver scanned the headlines, she gasped, unable to believe the news. She quickly opened the newspaper folded beside her father's place setting. There it was! On October 4, 1853, the Ottoman Empire had declared war on Russia and had sent troops north to the Crimea to drive the Russians out of the Ottoman provinces they had occupied. The Turkish declaration of war had appeared in the official newspaper, *Takvim-i Vekayi*, on the fourth of October. However, it was quickly followed by a 'Manifesto of the Sublime Porte,' stating that the government had been forced to declare war because of Russia's refusal to evacuate the principalities. Additionally, as a sign of its peaceful intentions, the commander of the Rumelian Army, Omer Pasha, would give the Russian forces an extra fifteen days to carry out the evacuation before the commencement of hostilities.

What will it mean for England? What will it mean for my family? She stared at the paper. Russia had fifteen days to leave the Ottoman provinces. If she did not, the Ottomans would be at war with Russia. *How long will it be before England is at war? Ryker? What will he do? Uncle Charles? Will he have to go with the army? Young Gordy is somewhere with the navy. And what of Ari Bey? Had he been able to get to Constantinople before war was declared?* Munevver had lost all desire for breakfast, and now she huddled in her chair, sipping her hot chocolate while she waited for her father to take his place.

There was a long moment of silence while Lord George read the paper, and then, with a snap, he folded it and put it beside his plate. "It has come at last. The Sublime Porte has declared war on Russia." He looked around the room. "Everything we know is going to change, and it is too late to do anything. The Bursa has already taken the events into consideration. Our markets in Aleppo have been making adjustments for this eventuality for months." His hand trembled as he tried to smooth the newspaper. "There's no question but that we will be drawn into this war. It is just a matter of time."

"Is there more news?" Munevver could not resist asking.

"Not in the paper." Lord George turned to Munevver. Although he never acknowledged it, he recognized that her understanding of affairs in the Ottoman Empire was greater than his. He continued grudgingly, "I've heard the Ottomans have risked sending ships to Sinope, one of their ports. It's on the northernmost edge of Ottoman land on the Black Sea. They sent ships carrying supplies for their troops stationed there and for the new troops they sent there to help push the Russians back. It was crucial that they send supplies to them before winter set in." When she nodded, he added, "Lord Stratford de Redcliffe advised the Ottomans not to send their large ships—the line-of-battle ships. He thought that the larger ships would be more likely to infuriate the Russians and to instigate a Russian attack. The Ottomans sent smaller ships, frigates, with supplies for the Ottoman troops." He sighed in frustration. "What they sent is not enough to support the troops for the winter. They will have to send another convoy."

"It will be even more dangerous now that they have declared war," Munevver said softly.

"Yes, but for the soldiers, winter in the Crimea without supplies would be a death sentence." Her father could not meet her eyes.

It was on the 5th day of December that Munevver remembered her father's grim words. The papers carried the headlines—Massacre at Sinope. On November 30, 1853, the Russians had launched an attack on the Turkish fleet anchored in the Ottoman harbor of Sinope. The Ottomans had sent a second fleet of small ships with supplies for their troops to their lightly defended harbor at Sinope. Because it was so late in the season and the weather had deteriorated suddenly, they anchored there for the winter.

Russia sent line-of-battle ships into the Ottoman harbor. The Russian ships were armed with the newly developed Paixhan guns, which fired explosive shells. The much larger Russian ships attacked the smaller Ottoman ships while they were at anchor. After all the Ottoman ships, except one, had been destroyed or rendered useless, the Russians turned their attention to the Ottoman shore defenses and destroyed them as well. The Ottomans fought valiantly but were defeated. Their entire fleet, with the exception of one small steamer, was destroyed. Only four hundred Ottoman seamen out of four thousand survived.

The one Ottoman ship, the twelve-gun steamer, Taif, that managed to escape the battle reached Constantinople with the news of the Russian attack within four days of the disaster. The news aroused panic in Constantinople as the people learned that Russia now controlled the Black Sea!

The English press called it the *Massacre of Sinope.* They declared that *war crimes* had been committed by Russia! They insisted that the attack on ships at anchor and ships of lower class was a war crime. Public opinion urged England to declare war on Russia. The English newspapers were adamant. It was impossible for England to accept the situation without betraying the Ottoman Empire. They demanded that England act quickly to help the Ottomans clear Russian troops out of Ottoman provinces.

"What were the losses?" Munevver whispered as she lowered the newspaper.

"The Ottomans or the Russians?"

"It's the Ottomans who are our Allies." Munevver leveled a look at her father. "What were their losses?"

"According to one newspaper, there were 2,960 Ottomans killed and one hundred fifty taken prisoner. Many are missing. Omer Pasha was one of those taken prisoner. The Russians destroyed two of the Ottoman shore batteries and sank a frigate and a steamer."

"The newspapers are calling it, *The Massacre of Sinope*. How could so many have been killed?" Munevver asked.

"Sultan Abdulmejid knew he had to send more supplies to his army in the Caucasus before snowfall. As you know, earlier in the fall, he had sent troops to the Caucasus with orders to push the Russians back. Once there, they would have to survive the merciless winter months.

He had to establish a supply line to get them what they needed. The first convoy he sent got through. The Russian fleet that was stationed at Sevastopol could not intercept them. The sultan risked sending a second convoy in late November under the command of Omer Pasha. He really had no choice. If his troops were to survive until spring, he had to get supplies to them before winter set in. The weather worsened, and the fleet was forced to seek shelter, to anchor in Sinope Harbor, an Ottoman harbor, where it was destroyed."

"Weren't the Ottomans prepared to defend themselves?" Munevver inquired.

"Actually, the Ottoman Empire was already in desperate shape when the Russians seized the Ottoman provinces of Walachia and Moldavia." Lord George paused. "But when Russia attacked Ottoman territories, the Ottomans had no choice but to defend them." He passed a hand over his eyes. "The Ottomans had twenty-five thousand men in the infantry and cavalry. Twenty-five thousand men to deal with internal uprisings and to defend the vast empire from outside attacks. They also had a corps of four thousand irregular cavalry. They even used the Bashibazouks, unruly bands of cavalry fighters." He shrugged. "It wasn't just a shortage of men and equipment. The Ottoman Government has been heavily in debt to the English and the French for a long time. Because of that debt, the Sublime Porte had to agree to reductions in the Ottoman Army and Navy that the English dictated. So, no, they were not prepared for war, but when the Russians seized Ottoman property, the sultan had no choice but to defend Ottoman territory."

Chapter 22

December 1853: Massacre of Sinope

"It's hard to even think of the approaching holidays," Aunt Frederica said as she settled into her favorite chair by the fireplace and motioned for Aunt Patience to join her. "The news is so dreadful! The Russians destroyed the entire Ottoman Naval Fleet, a fleet that was anchored in an Ottoman harbor for the winter." Aunt Frederica's voice was calm, but her eyes sparkled with anger. "They caused the death of three thousand men! The papers say the Russians even fired on the men in the icy-cold water, trying to swim to shore. Just think! Men swimming for their lives in late November! The Ottomans were not attacking the Russians. They were just trying to bring supplies for their soldiers, provisions that they would need to survive the winter."

Aunt Patience glanced around the drawing room with the beautifully dressed women waiting for the gentlemen to join them and then spoke softly to her younger sister, "The question is whether our world, the civilized world, will ignore such an atrocity!"

"It is unfortunate that the Russians destroyed the Ottoman fleet, but I don't understand why people are saying we should rush to help the Ottoman Empire. This talk about sending our soldiers and sailors to defend them is so upsetting," Georgette said, lifting her chin defiantly as Aunt Frederica raised an eyebrow in silent reproach of her goddaughter. "It's so far away," Georgette wailed, and then continued petulantly, "it's inconsiderate! The season begins in just a short time! How can we prepare for it if we don't know if we will be at war? It takes time to find a suitable house to rent in Mayfair or Belgravia."

She looked around the circle of women who had remained silent. "We have to plan for so many activities. My cousins have been telling me about the invitations for balls, parties, dinners, and even breakfasts that they expect to receive. And then, of course, there are the rides in the park, the exhibitions we must visit, and the afternoon calls." She glanced at Aunt Frederica. "How long can we wait before we commission our wardrobes?"

Georgette frowned. She had not yet asked her father for a new wardrobe. Surely, he would realize she could not wear the same dresses that she had worn last year. She would need to order for the activities of the new season—walking dresses, riding outfits, dinner gowns, and several ensembles for the balls. What if she ordered them and there was no season, or if there was a season and all the eligible, young men were in the military? If the country was at war, she might not be successful in finding a husband. Her wardrobe would be outdated and could not be worn the next year. The next year? Panic flooded her, making her turn pale. What if the war lasted more than one season?

At nineteen, Georgette was already older than most of the young girls who would be having their first season. She did not understand why she had not been taken during her first season—not a single proposal. She was fluent in French and Italian. Her singing was not remarkable, but she played the piano proficiently. Her portfolio of watercolors was better than most, and thanks to her father's endless drilling, she could discuss both classical and modern history.

It would be tragic if the next season was unsuccessful. She would be seen as desperate, approaching the age of being considered 'on the shelf.' A horrible thought made her feel faint. It was unlikely that her father would expend the funds for a third season. He would simply negotiate a marriage for her. She struggled to put the grim thoughts away and smiled prettily. "My father says we are already carrying the Ottoman Empire financially and have been for years." She tossed her head with a practiced skill that made the silky, golden ringlets dance across her shoulders. "What has the Ottoman Empire ever done for us?"

"An interesting question." Aunt Frederica answered slowly, "Although most of the ladies have heard how the Ottoman Empire helped England, perhaps you have not had that opportunity." She directed her words to Georgette. "If you go back to the early years of Queen Elizabeth, you will find that an Ottoman sultan helped her survive when she was very young and in a precarious position. She was facing Catholic opposition to her rule.

"As you may remember, her father, King Henry VIII, broke away from the Catholic Church so that he could divorce his wife, Catherine of Aragon, and marry Anne Boleyn. In retaliation, he and his daughter, Elizabeth, were excommunicated from the Catholic Church in 1570. Following her excommunication, Europe's Catholic countries refused to grant English merchants access to their markets. Elizabeth was struggling to survive. Politically and financially, she was in great danger.

"Philip, King of Spain and Lord of the Netherlands, and French King Henry II, signed a treaty of peace that joined them in opposition to Protestantism. With the Catholic countries boycotting her merchants, Elizabeth faced an economic crisis. She gave up trying for conciliation with the Catholic powers of Europe and sought alliances with the Ottoman Empire, Persia, and Morocco."

Aunt Frederica looked around the room and, sensing their interest, continued. "In desperation, Queen Elizabeth supported several young English merchants when they proposed a way to deal directly with the markets of the fabled East. Their way would allow the queen to bypass the European countries that controlled the routes to the East. The young English merchants wanted to cut out the middlemen and increase profits for themselves and for England. One of the first of the young merchants, Anthony Jenkinson, was a member of Lord George's family. He was only twenty-four years old when he set out to find new markets, but he had studied marketing in the Low Countries—The Netherlands and Belgium—and with the English factors, the merchants of the Levant Company. In 1554, he reached the city of

Aleppo, the end of the Silk Road. At that time, silk was pouring into Aleppo. He wrote that there were fifty-six flourishing markets in Aleppo! He settled there and began to ship goods from the East back to England. In fact, the family has been there ever since."

Aunt Frederica glanced around the circle of interested listeners. "Another young English merchant, James Harborne, was even more audacious. When he arrived in Constantinople, he asked the sultan, in the name of Queen Elizabeth, for commercial privileges for his country that were greater than those granted by the Ottoman Empire to any other Christian nation." She chuckled. "In 1579, Sultan Murad III wrote a letter to Queen Elizabeth—the first communication between an Ottoman sultan and an English ruler—assuring Queen Elizabeth that her merchants could trade and return home without interference."

Lady Florence looked pointedly at Georgette. "You see? Three hundred years ago, the Ottoman Empire helped our country to survive . . . and prosper."

"Well, what does it matter?" Georgette sniffed. "That was a long time ago."

"It was not that long ago that the Ottoman Empire assisted us." Louisa spoke softly but managed to capture everyone's attention. "Recently, five years ago, during the potato famine, the Ottoman Empire helped the Irish to survive. It was the only nation in the world to send help to the starving Irish people." She lifted her head and spoke directly to Lady Patience. "In May of 1847, Sultan Abdulmejid sent money and three ships—the Meta, the

Ann, and the Porcupine— loaded with wheat and corn. They landed in Drogheda, a small port north of Dublin." Her voice trembled. "Many Irish families escaped death by starvation because of the sultan's help."

* * *

After the ladies had withdrawn, Lord George did not wait for the port to complete the round of the table. "Those damn Russians and their dream of reclaiming Constantinople! They are going to force us into war. First, they tried to pull us into their plan to divide up the Ottoman Empire. Then they demanded that the sultan give them the right of protectorship over all Orthodox Christians in Ottoman lands." He bristled with rage. "Now the Russians have used their line-of-battle ships to destroy smaller Ottoman ships in an Ottoman harbor while the ships were at anchor! No wonder the newspapers are calling it the Massacre of Sinope!" He held out his glass for Foster to pour more port. "The newspapers are whipping up the public's demand for war. Damnation! War is not in our best interests."

Lord Charles twisted his glass on the gleaming table. "The Ottoman Empire has been making changes to try to appease the Christians and other minorities within the empire. They began with efforts to modernize the Ottoman Empire. It was hoped this would prevent internal nationalist movements, such as the Greek fight for independence. Of course, they also hoped it would prevent other governments—European governments—from interfering, supporting the complaints of minority groups within the Ottoman Empire. The goal was to emancipate non-Muslim subjects. It was designed to give them civil liberties and to grant them equality with Muslim subjects within the Ottoman Empire." He sighed. "The hope was that it would make them more content and less likely to try to break away from the Ottoman Empire."

Vicar Ashley had sat quietly while the other men drank their port. He debated with himself whether to join the conversation, and now he broke the silence that followed Lord Charles's words. "Among the educated Ottomans, the goal was far more ambitious. Sweeping, in fact. Their intent was reconciliation between the East and the West within the framework of Islam. They supported Ottomanism: a policy meant to unite all the different people living in the Ottoman Territories—Turks, Greeks, Armenians, Jews, Kurds, and Arabs. The policy began with the Edict of Gülhane of 1839, which declared equality before the law for both Muslim and non-Muslim Ottomans. The educated Ottomans were worried by the escalating interventions of the European powers in Ottoman affairs. They hoped that giving more rights to the minorities in the Ottoman Empire would reduce the danger of them accepting outside intervention on their behalf."

"I've heard about the movement," Lord Charles murmured. "There was a secret group, The Young Ottomans, who felt the Tanzimat reforms did not go far enough. They wanted a constitutional government."

"Yes." Vicar Ashley nodded. "However, many Ottomans did not agree with the changes. They saw them as foreign influences on the world of Islam. They did not support the changes."

"But there were changes." Ryker gave a cautious glance at his father. "There were some reforms. One major change led to a modern, conscripted army to replace the hated devshirme—the system of "lifting" or "collecting" practiced by the Ottoman Empire that sent military officers to take boys, ages eight to eighteen, from their families, often minority families, in order that they be raised to serve the state. The reforms also included changes in the banking system, improvement of the postal system, and abolition of slavery and slave trade. Perhaps most important, there was the establishment of the first modern universities and teacher schools in 1848. The reforms were led by Ottoman Europeans, educated bureaucrats, and they were supported by Sultan Mahmud II and later by his son, Sultan Abdulmejid." Ryker paused and then spoke more lightly, "For the first time in Ottoman history, officials were encouraged to wear western-style dress and the fez, instead of fur-trimmed robes and jewel-adorned turbans."

Vicar Ashley added softly, "Despite the reforms that improved their situations, the desire of the minority populations for independence has not diminished."

Lord George rose to lead them from the table. "While the Sublime Porte has tried to improve conditions for the minorities within the empire, we cannot ignore the fact that other countries—Poland, Austria, and Germany—are actively encouraging those minorities to seek independence."

Chapter 23

1854: A Time of Turmoil

During December and January, the newspapers continued to whip up public fervor for war. *The Times* wrote that the English people must not allow Russia to dictate conditions to Europe or convert the Black Sea into a Russian lake. Other papers pointed out that the tsar of Russia had begun the war without any pretext. Now, it was the duty of the Four Powers—Austria, Prussia, France, and England—to take all measures required to put an end to the war. The newspapers insisted that Russia had challenged the Maritime Powers, and they demanded that these aggressive acts be stopped. The reports of the Massacre of Sinope had captured the public's attention, and the newspaper articles fueled their outrage. The people were demanding war.

One morning, early in February, Munevver was sitting alone at the breakfast table, drinking her hot chocolate and watching fat raindrops that were almost snowflakes slide down the window when she noticed that Ryker seemed uncommonly alert when he entered the room. Usually, he drank two cups of coffee before uttering a word or even looking at anyone, but today was different. He said good morning to Quinn and then turned to her. "What do you have planned for today?" he asked.

"I imagine the day will be like every other day—work and more work," Munevver answered listlessly, and then, remembering that it was Aunt Frederica's at-home day, added, "I'm hoping Louisa will come for tea."

"You like Louisa, don't you?"

Such a strange question for Ryker to ask. "Yes, I do. She is kind as well as beautiful, and she never ridicules anyone or prevaricates." She thought for a moment and then added, "She is one of the most intelligent women I have ever known, and she is one of the few people I know you can depend on."

"I know," Ryker answered softly. "I'm afraid I won't be back in time for tea. Please pass on my greetings."

She studied Ryker. He was different this morning. His usual expression of annoyance was gone and he seemed changed—not happy but content. "Your business in the city will detain you that long?"

"Yes." He patted her shoulder clumsily and then was gone.

It was much later that Munevver learned that Ryker had secretly joined the navy and was among the many in the English naval armada that set off for the Baltic one cold day in February while excited crowds lined Portsmouth Harbor to wave them off.

Britain and France had already sent a combined force, a show of strength, that they hoped would deter the tsar from attacking Constantinople. Although that force had reached the Dardanelles a few days before the Russian attack on the Ottoman fleet at Sinope, it was too far away to come to the aid of the ships anchored in Sinope Harbor. Following the Massacre of Sinope, England's Vice Admiral Dundas had been ordered to sail up the Bosphorus and into the Black Sea. His instructions were to require every Russian ship he met to put back to their base at Sevastopol. The tsar saw this as an act of aggression, but he wanted to keep England and France out of his conflict with the Ottoman Empire, if possible, so he took no action.

Lord George never mentioned Ryker's absence. It was as though he had never been there. Instead, he threw himself into his work, and Munevver was required to spend even more hours in the study. Now, huddled over his desk, Lord George scanned the newspapers quickly. *The Times*, considered to be the finest paper in Europe, was against the Ottomans. It took the position that it was right for the tsar to be worried about the plight of Christians in a pagan empire that was breaking up. Prime Minister Lord Aberdeen believed in the good faith of the tsar and had little confidence in the Ottoman Empire.

On the other hand, *The Morning Press* supported the views of Foreign Secretary Lord Palmerston, who had no faith in Russia but a strong belief that the reforms instituted by the Ottoman Government, which would benefit the minority populations, would result in a renewed strength of the Ottoman Empire. *The Morning*

Press advocated for strong measures against Russia and applauded when, on February 27, 1854, England and France demanded that Russia withdraw all of her forces from Ottoman provinces on the Danube River—a demand that the tsar ignored.

Lord George threw the papers down and began to pace the room. "There is no turning back for the Ottomans. There will be war." He did not wait for a response from Munevver. "England and France have already sent their fleets to the mouth of the Dardanelles, ready to support the Ottoman Empire, if necessary." He stopped and stared out the window. "We'll be pulled into this damn war. We'll probably win, but it will cost us dearly."

"Is there news about the reaction of other countries?" Munevver asked quietly as her mind raced, considering the impact of the news on England's trade with the East, her lifeblood.

"Austria is insisting there be free navigation of the Danube River and the Black Sea. That's her center of commerce. She does not want Russia to have control of any of the provinces on the Danube." He turned back to the paper. "The sultan has demanded that the tsar withdraw his troops." He shrugged. "What else could he do?"

"How do we stand?" Munevver asked cautiously.

"There is talk about war, but there is always talk about war," he answered in a noncommittal tone.

"Even if we commit to war, it will take time." Munevver

estimated the problems of assembling the men, readying the ships, and sailing to the Mediterranean. "Three months . . . or longer." She forced herself to ask calmly, "Are we ready to go to war?"

"Ready to go to war? What an idiotic question!" He threw himself into his desk chair and began a bitter tirade. "We did not maintain the army after the Peninsular Campaign. Our navy is in poor shape and not at full strength, and our top military commanders are old." He hesitated, seemingly unwilling to admit the worst. Finally, he said, "I don't know how we'd finance a war. We have massive debts from the war with France. Napoleon's Peninsular Campaign nearly bankrupted us."

Munevver winced at the defeated sound of his voice. She had never seen him when he was not in full command of a situation. He always had the solutions to any problem that arose.

"And then there is that fool, Palmerton, predicting a French invasion of England. He's diverting attention and resources from our real problems. He has convinced the military to extend the breakwater on Alderney, and now he wants to build forts around Portsmouth to protect the shipyards from a French attack." Lord George's response crackled with biting cynicism.

"A decision about whether to support the Ottoman Empire or not will have to be made soon," Munevver offered tentatively. She remembered Florence Nightingale saying that Lord Stratford de Redcliffe was strongly pro-Ottoman. *Will he act on his own to prevent greater Russian intrusion into the Ottoman Empire?*

Munevver pointed at the unopened post in front of him. "Shall we start with today's correspondence? Perhaps Lady Nightingale has written to let us know if she has accepted Aunt Frederica's invitation to visit."

"We're on the brink of war, and you're chattering on about a social visit?"

"She's Aunt Frederica's closest friend. This is such a dreary time of the year. It would make Aunt Frederica so happy to see her again . . . and to learn all the news." When he did not respond, she added slowly, "If I remember correctly, Lady Florence's dearest friend, Lady Elizabeth, is the wife of Lord Sidney Herbert."

"Lord Sidney Herbert?" He gave her a sharp look. "He's just been made secretary at war." He handed her the letters. "Take care of it."

Chapter 24

Early March 1854: A Wedding

During the early days of March, Lord George had become increasingly short-tempered and everyone in the household tried to avoid him. Munevver had no choice. Day after day, she processed whatever he handed her to pursue. As she worked, she became aware of subtle changes in her father's business: longtime customers were stockpiling certain items, and he was having increasing difficulty meeting their demands.

It was the beginning of the second week of March, and Munevver paused by the window to check on the daffodils braving the chilly rain. She had just settled herself in her small office to begin a long day of responding to each order when Lord George appeared in the doorway. "I've decided it's time for you to be married." When she did not respond, he added brusquely, "There is no time to be lost. Each day, more men are being sent to the East." When she remained silent, he said flatly, "You and James must be married before he is shipped out." He paused, and then, unable to conceal a crafty, self-satisfied smile, he added, "There's no reason why you shouldn't continue to live here and do your regular work while your husband is away with the Light Brigade." He turned back toward his study and spoke without looking at her, "You'll be married here, in the chapel, in two days."

While Aunt Frederica worked frantically to arrange a small wedding, it was Fayne who held Munevver while she sobbed as bitter pain tore through her for the death of her most precious dream—the dream of a life with the man she loved with all her being and who adored her, a life with William. It was Fayne who planned how to help her beloved mistress. It was Fayne who whispered her plan into the ear of the beautiful, grown-up lady who had been a small child when she had been placed in Fayne's care so long ago.

Aunt Frederica mobilized the household and insisted that it work to bring about the event Lord George demanded. The windows of the frigid chapel were cleaned so that as much late winter light could fill it as possible. The day before the wedding, Aunt Frederica brought a slightly yellowed, white wedding dress to Munevver's room. "I think this will fit you with just a few alterations," she said as she motioned for Munevver to put it on.

"It is lovely." Munevver slid her fingers over the intricate lace trimming of the bodice. "I had thought I would wear my violet dinner dress."

"Although it is going to be a very small wedding, just the family and a few of our servants"—she hesitated— "it is likely that others will hear about it . . . talk about it." She lifted her chin. "Even though it's to be a very private ceremony, it must appear like a proper wedding for a lord's daughter. You must be appropriately attired. Otherwise, there will be a lot of gossip."

"There is going to be gossip anyway." Munevver slid into the dress her aunt was holding for her. "It's really a lovely dress," she said without enthusiasm. "Where did you get it on such short notice?"

For a moment, it seemed as though Aunt Frederica was not going to answer. "It is my dress. At one time, long ago, I thought I was going to wear it, but then things changed."

Munevver struggled to process the information. She tried to recall what she had been told. Aunt Frederica was her father's younger sister, and after their father had died, he had become her legal guardian. When his wife died very soon after Alexander's birth, Lord George had brought Frederica to his estate to manage the household and to raise his children.

The painful realization of what that meant for Aunt Frederica suddenly became clear to Munevver. When Munevver's mother died, Aunt Frederica would have been a young lady experiencing her first season. Since she had created a beautiful wedding dress, she must have been expecting to be married. Munevver could almost feel Aunt Frederica's pain when her brother told her that he expected her to look after his motherless children, but she knew Aunt Frederica would not appreciate it if Munevver said or did anything to destroy the armor of detached competence she wore constantly. "Thank you, Aunt Frederica. I am deeply appreciative that you are lending it to me."

The next day, late in the afternoon, Munevver, Aunt Frederica, and Lord George stood in the vestibule of the chapel. For Munevver, the sight of Fayne and two unfamiliar servants huddling at the back of the chapel was reassuring. The plan of action that she and Fayne had devised in such haste was already in motion. At each sound, Aunt Frederica would jump and then scan the area in front of the door.

When Munevver heard a collective murmur, she glanced up to see the bent figure of her grandfather's vicar slip into a side seat. *How did Grandfather, so far away in Yorkshire, know when to send him? Is he part of the plan? A part that Fayne has not told me about?*

Finally, two carriages pulled up in front of the chapel. The Duke of Leister and his two sons climbed out of the first carriage, and from the second, four already groggy young officers emerged.

As Vicar Ashley motioned Munevver and James to take their places in front of the altar, Louisa glided forward and handed Munevver a bouquet of dried heather tied with a white, satin ribbon. The sharp, woody scent of Yorkshire heather gave Munevver courage. Her father had sold her for his own benefit. She would soon be the wife of a man who did not know her, a man who had no desire for her or any woman. She could almost hear the whispers and snickers of those who knew James's predilections—whispers that would follow her for the rest of her life.

As soon as the vicar had completed the service and had pronounced them married, James had thrust a signet ring into her hand. That was the only contact they had. Within minutes, they were all in their carriages and on their way to Lord George's manor house where dinner awaited them.

Entering the main hall, Munevver could see evidence of the plan she and Fayne had made. Trays of drinks were being passed out by two sturdy footmen she had never seen before. Open doors to the dining room allowed enticing aromas to greet the guests. The large, formal table had been replaced by smaller tables scattered around the room. James and his friends, with drinks in their hands, were already drifting toward the tables.

After what seemed like hours, James and his comrades left to join others in the village tavern to celebrate his wedding. As they left, they called out boisterous, bawdy reassurances that they would return the bridegroom in perfect condition to carry out the duties of his wedding night.

Munevver had made her way back to her retreat over the front stairs. It was there that Louisa found her. She pulled two glasses from the pouch of Munevver's sewing table and added two fingers of raki to each one. Closing Munevver's cold fingers around her glass, Louisa began in a low voice, "Before he left, Ryker made me promise to tell you about James."

"Ryker made you promise?" Munevver could not conceal her astonishment. She knew Ryker was more relaxed in the company of Louisa than he was with others, but she did not know that he cared enough for her to confide in Louisa

Louisa blushed. "Perhaps I was the only one he felt he could trust."

"Or," Munevver spoke more confidently, "you are the only one he really cares about."

"What does it matter?" Louisa twisted her hands in her lap. "I am a vicar's daughter. Definitely not who your father would choose for his heir."

"Ryker is his father's son in many ways." Munevver leaned forward and patted Louisa's hands. "He gets what he wants." When Louisa did not respond, Munevver returned to what Louisa had said. "Ryker asked you to tell me about James? There's more to tell?" She smiled sadly at her friend as she settled into a chair in front of the window and took the first sip of her drink.

"Yes. You know that James is a sodomite?"

Munevver nodded as dread crept over her. *What is it that has worried Ryker and is bothering Louisa so much? My father has already sold me. What more dreadful consequences can this marriage hold?*

Louisa paced back and forth before coming to stand in front of her, and then she dropped to her knees and grasped Munevver's hands. "There are many names for one of the diseases that sodomites frequently acquire."

"Diseases?" Munnever whispered. Louisa had not

said illnesses.

"Yes. Horrible diseases that they get from . . . contact with another who has the disease."

"Go on." She could not suppress the horrible fear that was gripping her.

"I'm afraid that as a vicar's daughter, I've heard more than I should have, but I must share what Ryker told me and what I know in order to keep you safe. The worst disease is one known as the Grande Verole." When Munevver gave no indication of understanding, Louisa forced herself to go on. "The English call it the French Disease." She paused, wondering how she could best convey the information that Munevver needed to know. "Leave it to the French. They call it Morbus Gallicus."

"Syphilis?" Munevver whispered, unable to believe the full horror of what her father had done to her.

Louisa nodded. "For your own safety, you must accept the rumors as being true. You must assume that he is infected." At Munevver's involuntary gasp, she added, "His valet is vicious. He has told Foster that it is well known that James has the *French Disease*."

She paused at Munevver's shocked, "No!"

"You must not allow James to touch you." She struggled to continue. *Dear God! Has Aunt Frederica or anyone bothered to tell you what happens after the marriage? What takes place between a man and his wife?* "To protect yourself from getting the disease, you must not allow him to kiss you or touch you intimately."

Munevver's mind worked frantically, but she could make no sense of what Louisa was telling her. Finally, she said, "Like avoiding contact with a leper?"

"Yes, like leprosy, only worse. Syphilis is invisible for a while, but the effects of the disease work faster than those of leprosy, even more cruel, and far more deadly."

Munevver shuddered. "I must get away!" She looked out the window at the long drive leading from the manor. "How? Even if I can find a way to get away from this place, where can I go?"

"You must escape someway!" Louisa said firmly. "I will help you, but until you can get away, keep Fayne with you always. She will protect you."

"Does Fayne know about . . . ?" Munevver stared at Louisa.

"Yes, Fayne knows." Louisa started to leave and then turned back at Munevver's next question.

"Father? Did he know that James may have this horrible condition when he agreed to the marriage?"

* * *

Sitting beside Aunt Frederica at a small table, Munevver forced a smile as she accepted a delicacy from each tray offered to her by the silent Foster. It was the ever-protective Quinn who kept her glass filled with wine. Somehow, she managed to thank each person who stopped to wish her well. With each artificial expression of best wishes, Munevver's fury increased. It wasn't just the hapless James who was a threat to her. James's father, with his obsessive need for an heir, was far more dangerous. Fayne had told her what Lord Leinster had said. She would produce an heir for him, and he did not care how it was accomplished. Finally, she nodded at Fayne and rose to withdraw to the rooms that had been set aside for her and James. The difficult part of the plan lay ahead of them.

Silently, Munevver allowed Fayne to remove the wedding dress and slip a white, linen nightgown over her head. Her hair had been brushed and plaited into a thick, dark rope that hung down her back. With Fayne's help, she climbed into the massive bed and pulled up the covers. She did not know how long she would have to wait for James's rowdy friends to return him to the bridal chamber, but she and Fayne would have to be ready. The success of the plan depended on there being apparent evidence in the morning that James had performed as expected of a new bridegroom on his wedding night.

Hour after hour, Munevver and Fayne waited until finally, long after midnight, they heard the heavy tread of many feet and the soft voices of the hand-picked servants. James was deposited on the bed beside Munevver. She forced herself to remain silent as the ribald suggestions of his drinking companions faded with their retreating footsteps.

Once they were sure that James was in a drunken stupor, Fayne and one of the footmen removed James's clothing and applied the blood that they had procured to his body and to the sheets while Munevver curled deeper into a chair by the window to watch for the first lights of dawn. It would be a long time before his friends would return to retrieve James and take him to the ships that were ready to transport the men to the Ottoman Empire.

Munevver had to have the letter ready for James to sign. Her safety depended on his signing the letter she had written, saying it was his wish that his wife remain with her father until he returned. But who would witness his signature? Who would be important enough to oppose her father-in-law? Suddenly, she remembered her grandfather's vicar, now a bishop, who had been at the wedding. He would be the perfect witness! Grandfather must have sent him. Grandfather and Fayne had planned for there to be an important witness. Fayne would find a way for him to be there to witness James's signature. Suddenly, her feeling of abandonment lessened. She was not alone.

With a sigh, Munevver reached for her knitting. The click of the needles would speed the dark hours until morning.

Chapter 25

Spring 1854: War Looms

The reports of the Massacre of Sinope had so shocked the people of England that it was widely accepted that war was inevitable, and early in March, England and France took the first step toward war. They demanded that Russia remove her troops from Moldavia and Wallachia, the Ottoman principalities she had captured. Soon after, on March 11, 1854, the English fleet had set sail from England to travel to the Ottoman Empire to assist it if needed. All over England, the air was charged with the frenzied anticipation of war. The English people feared that their ships would be too late in arriving at the Dardanelles and that Russia would have seized Constantinople before the English were ready to defend it.

France made a final appeal to the tsar to avoid war. Russia responded by boasting that she would do to France in 1854 what she had done to Napoleon in 1812. English Prime Minister Lord Aberdeen was against war, but the people wanted a war, a glorious war. On March 28, 1854, one month after Queen Victoria had demanded that Russia evacuate her troops from the Ottoman principalities, England and France declared war on Russia.

At the onset of war, Britain had a one-hundred-thousand-man army, but much of the army was guarding and protecting the English Empire—an empire that included China, Ceylon, Burma, Afghanistan, Punjab, New Zealand, and the West Coast of Africa. The more territory that England seized, the greater became the strain on the English military to provide troops to defend those territories. The expansion of the empire was proving too great a drain on England's resources for relatively little return.

Lord Palmerston, who had become foreign secretary in 1846, had urged that the militia be increased. This measure was rejected in favor of fortifying the country's arsenals and dockyards against an invasion across the English Channel by the French.

Louis Napoleon Bonaparte, nephew and heir of the great man, Napoleon Bonaparte, had become president of France, and when his term was up in 1851, he staged a coup d'état and seized power. He was eventually proclaimed Emperor Napoleon III.

English politicians were wary of his intentions. They put in measures to add an additional four thousand men for the cavalry and infantry, one thousand for the artillery, and eight thousand to strengthen the national militia. However, with the introduction of steam-powered ships, the English Channel was less of a barrier to an invasion from France than it was when sailing ships were dependent on the wind. To make matters worse, England no longer had the systems in place that would enable her to campaign against a modern European Army. Not only were the systems perfected by Wellington and the equipment by which an army could be supplied, moved, and brought to action non-existent, there had been little or no effort to train the army. The one exception was the men of the Horse Guards, who had formed an exercise group in June 1853 at Cobham Camp. Ironically, within months of the Cobham exercises that Lord George had ridiculed, an English expedition force was sailing for the East.

In an attempt at modernization, the English infantry was changing its principal weapon. The old, smooth-bore muskets were being replaced by French-designed Minié rifles. The rapid-firing Minié would give the Allies a distinct advantage over the Russians, who were equipped with the older, smooth-bore muskets. The rest of the equipment in the English Army was scarce and old.

Military organization was unchanged. The army was led, from top to bottom, by members of the aristocracy, wealthy merchants, and landowners, most of whom had no training and no experience in battle. Each man's commission in the army had to be bought, usually purchased in the auction rooms on Charles Street. Lord Raglan, the officer who had served as military secretary to the Duke of Wellington and was his likely successor, was over seventy years old and had little battle experience. Not only were most of England's military leaders old and inexperienced in warfare, they dismissed logistic problems of supplies and transportation and ignored intelligence reports. They were content to rely on what they believed to be the invincible fighting spirit of the English Army.

The navy had a limited number of marines and few boats capable of transferring troops and horses from ship to shore. However, seamen were plentiful. Boys could enlist as seamen in the Royal Navy as young as fourteen by accepting the queen's shilling—an act equivalent to agreeing to serve as a sailor or soldier in the Queen's Armed Forces. They could choose between serving for twenty-one years or for life.

By early March, English troops began to converge on Plymouth and Portsmouth, ready to board the ships that would take them to the Ottoman Empire. They were known as the Army of the East, and when they set sail for the Ottoman Empire, they had two primary objectives: to protect Ottoman interests and to defend Constantinople in case it was attacked by the Russians.

It had been decided that men and horses would be transported by sailing ships instead of by the faster and more costly steamships. It was a decision that was later strongly criticized because by the time they arrived at their destination, the horses had suffered from being closely tethered below deck or suspended in slings on the pitching sailing ships. Many were injured and some died during disembarkment. Overall, one hundred seventy horses were lost in transport.

In early April, three weeks after England and France had declared war on Russia, Lord Raglan was sailing to the Ottoman Empire. Russia had laid siege to the Ottoman fortresses of Silestra and Shumla to prevent England and France from using the Ottoman's Black Sea Port of Varna as a port of disembarkment. The need for extended supply lines was proving problematic for Russia, and she was also worried that Austria and Prussia might join the war on the side of the Ottoman Empire.

English and French troops landed at the Port of Varna, a key port of the European part of the Ottoman Empire on the Black Sea not far from Constantinople. Although it had been designated in advance as the port of disembarkment, the English and French had made no plans for a drinkable water supply or for sanitation. Within weeks, cholera and dysentery were sweeping through the troops.

The French forces were well supplied, and their needs had been anticipated. The English soldiers were not as fortunate. The English commanders had not set up any hospitals, nor had they provided any ambulances to transport the wounded. The English Commissariat lacked horses, mules, and carts to transport tents and supplies from the ships in the harbor to the front-line camps. The English soldiers were forced to sleep on bare ground in their summer uniforms with no tents for protection from the rain.

At the same time, Russian troops began to move southward toward Sevastopol, the home of the tsar's Black Sea fleet that threatened Ottoman Black Sea ports, the straits—the Bosphorus and the Dardanelles—and Constantinople. Sevastopol was also Russia's storehouse in the Crimea. Now, as it had been throughout history, the Crimea was a strategic area. Whoever controlled the Crimea had access to the Ukraine to the north, the Caucasus to the east, Asia Minor to the south, and the Balkans to the west.

England and France were assembling their troops at Varna in preparation for coming to the aid of the Ottomans. Overall, the English Army was in poor shape due to a lack of supplies and to disease, especially cholera. The reality of their situation included hot, dirty camps with little water, poor food, and rapidly spreading cholera and dysentery. The people back home in England had not been told of the condition of the army—no supplies, little drinkable water, poor transportation, rampant disease, and no medical care.

By May 1854, Russia had moved enough troops into the Danubian principalities to force an offensive movement, widely believed by the English and French to be the first step of a march on the Ottoman Empire's capital city, Constantinople. On May 6, 1854, the English troops learned that they were to be deployed to help the Ottoman troops defend the fortress in Silistra that Russia had besieged.

Although Austria had not entered the war on the side of the Ottomans, it did not want a Russian presence on the Danube. On June 3, 1854, Austria told the tsar to lift the Siege of Silistra and to vacate the Ottoman principalities. If Russia did not do so, Austria said that Austria and Russia would be at war. On June 24, 1854, the Siege of Silistra was lifted. The Ottoman fortress was free! The Turkish troops, under the command of

English officers from the Indian Army, had driven off the Russians. The Russians withdrew their troops from Moldavia and Wallachia and moved back across the Danube River.

Not sure if the news that one hundred twenty thousand Russians were leaving the area of Silistra was true, Lord Raglan ordered Lord Cardigan to go north to Devna to find out if the Russians were still on the Ottoman side of the Danube River. In the heat of summer, Lord Cardigan pushed the men and horses hard. Many of the horses were damaged by the long hours, the heat, and the lack of food and water. In fact, after the march, seventy-five of the horses were unfit for work of any kind. In total, the Light Brigade lost one hundred of its finest horses on this maneuver. It became known as *Cardigan's Sore-back Reconnaissance* and was a permanent blemish on Lord Cardigan's reputation.

The goals of the English and French had been accomplished! They had come to the Ottoman Empire to help the Ottomans protect their provinces from the invading Russians and to prevent the Russians from capturing Constantinople. The Russians had been forced to abandon the Siege of Silistra and to withdraw from the Ottoman principalities of Moldavia and Wallachia. However, they had not been forced to withdraw by magnificent English victories, but rather by Austria's threat to go to war with Russia if she did not withdraw her troops from Ottoman territories on the Danube River.

Yes, the English and French had been successful in their mission, but the English people were clamoring for triumphantly successful battles achieved by their valiant troops. Now the question was whether England and France should bring their troops home—troops they had conveyed to the East at a huge expense—or invade the Crimea, destroy Russia's stronghold at Sevastopol, and put an end to Russia's naval power in the Mediterranean in order to prevent possible future aggression.

Chapter 26

A Preventive War: Taking the War from the Ottoman Empire to the Crimea

As the men joined the women in the drawing room after dinner, they continued their comments about the leading articles in the newspapers. Clamor for war against Russia—a preventive war—had increased. The papers were insisting England's policy should be to prevent further Russian provocations in the Black Sea area. The cry was for an attack on Russia's center of power—Sevastopol.

In response to the public demand for a preventive war, England prepared to move the war from the Ottoman Empire to the Crimea and France reluctantly agreed. The English and French leaders had little knowledge of the Crimea and no understanding of what a prolonged siege involved: transporting men, horses, equipment, and supplies over great distances; landing men and horses; long marches; and then the assaults on an entrenched and well-supplied enemy. Nor did they consider the lack of fodder for their horses in the Crimea, a barren tundra. They gave no consideration to the probability of a scarcity of drinkable water for men and horses in the dry steppes of the Crimea. Perhaps the most ominous planning omission during those hot days of July in London was the failure to anticipate the need to provide for men and horses during a Crimean winter.

"A preventive war! That's what they are calling for now!" Lord George exchanged challenging looks with the men standing in front of the fireplace. "This war in the East, this Crimean War, is already bleeding the English people." Lord George quivered with barely controlled rage. "There was never a promise to send our men to fight a preventive war!"

Speaking quietly but clearly from her seat on the sofa, Munevver surprised everyone by countering her father's statement. "It's not just the English that are being bled dry. The Crimean War has already forced the Ottoman Empire into debt contracts with nearly every foreign lender that exists." In an unusual moment, she met her father's gaze directly. "Their country is short of everything. If the war goes on, they will be in a desperate condition, even if they are not defeated."

Louisa, who had been sitting silently on the sofa beside Munevver, raised the question everyone was afraid to ask. "If we extend the war, go forward with a preventive war, is it likely that our men will have to endure another winter in the Crimea? Another winter without warm uniforms, tents, supplies, and medical care?" She glared at the men. "The vicar is the one who listens to the mothers' pleas after they receive a letter from their sons telling them how cold and hungry they are, or, even worse, how terribly ill they are with no one to care for them."

"Commissary General William Filder is the cause of much of the misery our men suffered through!" Vicar Ashley interjected heatedly. "He failed to issue lime juice for the men. It is there, nine tons of it stored in Balaklava Harbor. Unthinkable! English men suffering with scurvy! Because of Filder, men just seven miles from the harbor lacked fresh meat, vegetables, and fruit that would have kept them alive and healthy. Even more egregious, he failed to provide for the horses."

"It's not fair to put all the blame on him," Lord George offered with a grudging glance of respect directed at the vicar. "He was told to plan for a war in the Ottoman Empire, a short-term war helping the Ottomans remove Russian forces from Ottoman provinces." Lord George sighed. "Our men were supposed to be home for Christmas." He looked around the room. "The newspapers are creating a frenzy, and now the public wants a glorious victory, not just a lifting of the Russian Siege of Silistra and evacuation of their troops from the Ottoman provinces." He scowled as he continued. "Instead, the decision was made to push the Russians out of their stronghold at Sevastopol." He rubbed his eyes. "The English have decided to pursue a preventive war—to extend the war from the Ottoman Empire to the Russian stronghold in the Crimea in order to deter possible future Russian attempts to capture the Bosphorus . . . and Constantinople." He looked around the room in bewilderment. "Who ever heard of initiating a preventive war?"

"Well, in 431 BC, Sparta, believing Athens was becoming too powerful, a potential threat, launched a preventive war," Vicar Ashley offered with a wave of his hand.

"How did it end?" Lord Charles roused himself from the despondency Lord George's words had caused.

"Twenty-seven years later, Sparta was considered to be the winner." He shook his head slowly as he considered the disgruntled men facing him. "Preventive wars tend to be lengthy . . . and costly."

Chapter 27

October 1854: News Shared

The day had seemed endless, and now Munevver must hurry to change for Aunt Frederica's at-home tea. Although she felt drained from the long hours of work with the increasingly irritable Lord George, Aunt Frederica was the only loving force in her world and she did not want to disappoint her. Aunt Frederica would want to meet her guests with her niece, Munevver, properly dressed and smiling by her side. At one time, that would have been enough. But now, Munevver knew that the women would expect her to tell them what the newspapers were saying about the war, especially if the troops would be home for Christmas.

As Fayne slipped a pristine, white, linen blouse over her head and tugged it into place, Munevver's mathematical mind supplied the answer. If their loved ones were to be home for Christmas, they would have to leave the Crimea this week. She could only hope no one asked. Perhaps if she began by telling them what had been in the papers, no one would ask.

"Ah, there you are, my dear." The relief in Aunt Frederica's voice alerted Munevver. A quick glance around the room disclosed the reason for her concern. Georgette, in her dark-blue, silk dress with its snug-fitting, embroidered bodice and billowing skirt, was shown to perfection as she perched daintily on a ladies' side chair. Not only was she dressed more elaborately than the other guests, she was making no attempt to converse with any of them. Poor Aunt Frederica. She loved her goddaughter, but Georgette's unexpected visits tended to upset the quiet orderliness of the household that Lord George required.

"I am sorry to be late," Munevver said, hesitating before casting out a lure. "The newspapers, you know. So much news." Knowing that the women would not have had access to as many newspaper accounts as she had, Munevver prepared herself to share a lengthy description of the latest news stories with her eager audience who were desperate for any information about the war and their loved ones.

After a few minutes, Munevver sought to summarize the current status of the war. "England and France are preparing to remove their troops from the Ottoman Empire, where they had been assembled to support the sultan, and send them to the Crimea to force the Russians out of their stronghold, Sevastopol." There was a quick gasp of dismay. Munevver hurried on before they could ask any questions. "It appears that neither England nor France has much knowledge of the Crimea. In truth, they do not know much about their enemy. It has been broadly reported that the Russian forces are inferior and that there would be no serious resistance to the Allies' march to the Russian-held harbor of Sevastopol." She paused. "As you all remember, in July, it was widely accepted that there would be a quick victory. That's what the reporters wrote."

"They will be home for Christmas, won't they?" There was a desperate note in Georgette's voice as she asked the question that each woman in the room wanted answered. "They have to be!" she wailed as she hurried from the room.

What should she say? Every aspect of these women's lives and their children's lives was controlled by the men in their families. Fathers, husbands, uncles, brothers, or even male guardians regulated their lives. They weren't really asking if their men would be back for Christmas. They were asking if their men would ever return. And behind that desperate plea was the question no one dared ask: What will happen to me if he doesn't come back? But that was not her question. For her, the thought that haunted her was what will happen if he does come back? The note James had signed said that he wished her to remain with her father until he returned.

Trying to calm the anxious women, Munevver began to speak as dispassionately as she could. "We must keep in mind the great distance that lies between England and the Crimea." She hesitated and then stated what had to be made known to them. "It took about seventy days to sail from England to the Crimea." She saw from the dismay on their faces that they had understood what she had said. Their men would not be home for Christmas.

Later, after dinner, as Munevver sat half-hidden in the corner of the drawing room where the men had gathered, she absorbed the information that their unrestricted comments were revealing. The situation was worse than she had thought. The composition of the English high command in the Crimea was controversial. All the generals were old, and few had seen recent duty. There were numerous accusations of incompetence and mishandling of funds. One of the men insisted that, although there had been widespread criticism of the methods used to procure the supplies needed, the army continued to employ an antiquated and seemingly corrupt purchasing system.

When the conversation turned to specific military leaders, Munevver forced herself to pay close attention. One of the first lessons her grandfather had taught her was that behind every crucial decision there was usually one man, and a good businessman knew that man's preparation, experience, and, most importantly, aspirations. She concentrated now on what was being said. There was concern about leadership. Although it was known that Lord Raglan was in failing health, he had been appointed commander-in-chief of the Army of the East. He had served throughout the Peninsular War in Portugal and Spain and had lost his right arm at Waterloo. However, Lord Raglan had never commanded large bodies of troops. His knowledge was mainly confined to staff work as the Duke of Wellington's military secretary. The men also expressed concern about General Airey, who had served as military secretary to Lord Harding. Airey had been appointed quartermaster general by Raglan, and his main duty was running the general staff. It was said that despite Airey's lack of experience, Raglan relied on him for advice.

Lieutenant General George Bingham, 3rd Earl of Lucan, had been named the divisional commander for the cavalry, which consisted of two five-regiment brigades of light and heavy cavalry with twelve hundred fifty men in each brigade. An overbearing, suspicious, and disagreeable man, he was notorious for his repressive management of his estates in Ireland and large-scale evictions during the potato famine of the 1840s.

Although he had never been to war, General James Brudenell, 7th Earl of Cardigan, had been placed in charge of the Light Brigade. He was well known for his scandalous behavior with women—usually married women—and for his constant disagreements with his subordinates. He was a strict follower of military rules and traditions and served directly under Lord Lucan, his brother-in-law. He detested Lord Lucan, who returned his contempt with equal enthusiasm.

Captain Louis Nolan, a renowned horseman who did not wish to return to the dreariness of life with his regiment in India, was anxious to go to war. His writings had brought his name to the attention of the Duke of Newcastle, secretary of state for war and the colonies, who needed an officer with equestrian skills and knowledge of how to transport horses. Transporting horses by sailing ships was a difficult and dangerous operation that often resulted in the death of expensive animals and damaged the health of those that survived.

The voyage by sailing ships from England to the

Crimea would take at least seventy days. Lord Cardigan had already questioned the government transport policy, pointing out that the superior speed of steamships made them more suitable for the cavalry than the infantry. He warned that the delay and the risks of damaging the horses by using sailing vessels was great, but there were few steamships in England, and those that existed were not equipped to ship horses.

Brigadier General Richard Airey, aware of Nolan's books and reputation, petitioned Raglan to give Nolan a place on the staff. Two weeks before war was declared, Nolan was on his way to Constantinople. He needed to get there before the French agents could beat him to it. His mission was to find and buy remount horses that would be used to replace English horses injured or killed in battle. He was to buy Turkish horses that were hardy, smaller, and could withstand deprivation and fatigue.

Munevver filed the information away in her mind. The details of each man were as clear as those of any of the merchants her grandfather had insisted that she learn. She did not know how, but she had an ominous feeling that these men would play a role in determining her future.

In June of 1854, the secretary of war, the Duke of New Castle, said that, if the nation were to pursue a preventive war, it was best not to delay. He urged an immediate siege of Sevastopol, and July and August were spent making plans and preparations for attacking the Russian stronghold there. However, in August and early September, a cholera epidemic struck London. The epidemic that killed ten thousand people during those months delayed the nation's preparations for war.

Meanwhile, during July and August of 1854, the English and French troops, who were already in the Ottoman Empire, waited in camps in the hot and crowded Ottoman Port of Varna. They stood by in the relentless summer heat with inadequate shelter, poor food, and little water. Finally, on September 7, 1854, England decided to engage in a preventive war. They would take the war from the Ottoman Empire to the Crimea, specifically to the Russian stronghold at Sevastopol. But before they could attack Sevastopol, there were three Russian-fortified strongholds that must be defeated— Alma, Balaklava, and Inkerman.

The transport ships that were to take the English troops from Varna to Sevastopol were old and in poor condition. The troops were crammed in, but their tents and other provisions were left behind. Food, blankets, and tents were put on smaller ships that would come later. The fleet sailed eastward from Varna across the Black Sea to Sevastopol, a one-hundred-twenty-mile distance. During the crossing, a storm on the Black Sea caused seventy-five horses to perish. Later, when the horses were landed, some drowned and more were injured as they swam wildly in all directions until their handlers could get them to the beach.

The landing beach was in total confusion. The English landed twenty-six thousand men wearing summer uniforms. Horses and artillery were also landed, but no tents or provisions had been transported for the men or the horses. The men had only the food and water that they carried with them. They quickly discovered that there was only one spring to supply water for the entire army. Soon, the men were begging for water. In contrast, during the same time, the French landed twenty-eight thousand soldiers and the Ottomans, seven thousand. The French and the Ottomans had tents and provisions for their men.

It was not until four days later that the English Army's tents had landed. However, there were no wagons and no pack mules to carry the supplies the seven miles from the harbor to the front lines. Cholera and dysentery continued to spread, and fifteen hundred men were sent back to the sick transport ships.

To lift their spirits, the soldiers had been told that the Russians had dummy rifles and that they were driven into battle by guns pointed at their backs. In reality, the Russians were preparing to protect Sevastopol at all costs. They had built a bridge across the Sevastopol Harbor so that they could evacuate the civilian population. They had barricaded the streets, made plans for blowing up their forts, if necessary, and removed the guns from their ships so that the ships could be scuttled across the entrance to the harbor, thus denying English and French ships access to the harbor.

The Allied men and officers had disembarked from their ships in silence. The Russians knew they were there but did not fire on them. By sunset, it began to rain, and the men caught the rain water to drink. They waited where they had landed for their supplies. They were about thirty-five miles from Sevastopol, but there were four rivers between them and Sevastopol that had to be crossed: the Bulganek, the Alma, the Katcha, and the Belbek. Seven miles south of the first river, the Bulganek River, was the Alma River, and seven miles from the Alma River was the Katcha River. Four miles from that was the Belbek River, and five miles from that was the Tchernaya River, which forms the headwaters of Sevastopol.

On September 19, 1854, the advance of the English and French armies began. They moved forward, sixty thousand men marching in two great, double columns. Sevastopol was twenty-five miles away, but before Sevastopol, they would have to cross four rivers. They easily crossed the Bulganek River, with both soldiers and horses drinking the river water as they crossed. As they advanced, they found olive and pomegranate trees but very little water.

Lord Raglan had ordered Lord Cardigan to cross the small river, the Bulganek, and scout the other side in preparation for the main body crossing. Although the Russians fired on them, they did not pursue them. Lord Lucan and Lord Cardigan began to argue. Lord Cardigan wanted to attack the Russians, and Lord Lucan wanted to retire and wait for further orders. In the end, Lord Raglan, aware that they were on a hostile coastline without shelter, short of water and supplies, and dependent on being supplied by the sea, agreed with Lord Lucan and ordered them to retire.

The Russians were three miles away across another river, the Alma River. As the troops moved forward, the French were protected by the sea on one side and by the English troops on the other. The English had to advance without cover—sixty thousand men advancing on a hot day with no protection. The Russians, who had mounted twenty-five cannons on the heights, could fire at them with little fear of return fire.

The English experienced three hundred sixty killed and twenty-five hundred wounded. The English wounded were treated in the field by surgeons with unsterilized instruments and no anesthesia. The dead were buried alongside the Alma River in huge mounds, and the wounded were transported the three-mile distance back to the medical ships in jolting, wooden carts, arabas, pulled by donkeys or oxen. In sharp contrast, the French had covered hospital vans pulled by teams of donkeys that could swiftly transport ten to twelve wounded soldiers at a time back to their field hospitals.

Once they reached the harbor, the wounded were loaded onto small ships that would transport them to the larger hospital ships, which would take them back across the Black Sea to the hospital at Scutari across the Bosphorus from Constantinople. Little or no care was provided for the wounded as they waited. Once on board the hospital ships, they had to endure a four-to-five-day trip across the turbulent Black Sea to the Bosphorus, then down the Bosphorus to the old army barracks at Scutari that had been donated by the Ottoman Government to serve as a hospital for wounded English soldiers.

In the morning, the Allied Army moved forward over grassy ridges. The Russians, who were positioned on high, steep cliffs, thought that the cliffs would protect them, but there were paths, and the French Light Infantry managed to get up the cliffs undetected. Russia withdrew, leaving only two batteries of field artillery to hold back the advancing French Army. But the French troops failed to advance. At 3 p.m., a French messenger galloped up to Lord Raglan and said that the French position was desperate. The French were being massacred. The English must attack. At 3:05 p.m., Lord Raglan gave the order to advance across the Alma River.

The Russians fired on the straggling English lines, and many were killed or wounded. But suddenly, the Russians were dragging their guns away. Emperor Nicholas had declared that on no account should a single gun be lost to the enemy because he believed, erroneously, that the Duke of Wellington had not lost a single gun to the enemy. The English forces pressed on, but the Russians forced them back and then retreated to the protection of Sevastopol.

On September 20, 1854, after two days of fighting, English, French, and Ottoman troops defeated the Russians defending the Alma River. During the battle for the Alma River, the English sustained over two thousand casualties. It was not until the Battle of the Alma River that the men realized, for the first time, that they had underestimated the enemy. They would not take Sevastopol in three days, as had been widely believed. Now, they were forced to spend twenty-four hours a day in the trenches to protect the guns and to constantly repair their bulwarks. Then they would have twelve hours to rest. There was incessant Russian firing from 5 a.m. to sunset. Cessation of the big guns during the night allowed both sides to spend the night fortifying their defenses.

In the midst of the turmoil, Lord Cardigan wrote a

letter to Lord Raglan complaining about Lord Lucan. He felt that, after the successful Battle of the Alma River, the English and French should have continued to pursue the Russians to Sevastopol instead of stopping to bury their dead and carrying the wounded to the ships that would take them across the Black Sea to the hospital at Scutari.

On September 22nd, aware of the increasing precariousness of their position, the Russians scuttled seven of their line-of-battle ships across the entrance of the Sevastopol Harbor, making it impossible for the Allied fleet to help their ground troops. In response, thousands of English seamen were removed from their ships, provided with rifles with bayonets, and ordered to join the soldiers.

The march continued toward Sevastopol. On September 23, 1854, they crossed the Katcha River, and on September 24, 1854, they crossed the Belbek. The men were short of provisions, and there was no food or water for their horses. The English wounded were left lying on the battlefield. Medical care was extremely scarce. Amputations were done on the field without anesthesia. Although the Ottomans were using chloroform to anesthetize patients during their surgical treatment, English doctors from the principal medical office of the division, Dr. Gibson and Dr. Linto, had given orders that field surgeons should not use chloroform during operations. Dr. Hall, the principal medical officer of the army, had cautioned regimental surgeons not to use it. Despite these orders, there were a few doctors who used it anyway.

On October 2, 1854, the Russians evacuated the families and their possessions from Sevastopol under cover of night. Then, they turned their efforts to strengthening the defense of the badly damaged fortresses.

Back in England, when the ladies gathered for tea, the room was quiet as they waited for Munevver to update them on the news of the siege. When she had finished, there was silence for a long moment and then one of the ladies said, "I had a letter from my son." She pulled her shawl closer around her shoulders. "They are cold, so cold. They were landed at Sevastopol with no tents and no blankets. It is October, and they have only their summer uniforms." Turning her head away, she began to cry silently.

It was Aunt Frederica who broke the silence that followed her words. "The *Black Prince* and the other supply ships will be there soon. It seems so long ago that we were rushing during those hot days of August to get our boxes of warm clothes, socks, and blankets to the ships." She looked around the room at the shaken women. "The *Black Prince* will be delivering warm things for them any day now."

Munevver's mind computed the time and distance automatically. The *Black Prince* and the other ships would not get there before the middle of November. *It will be cold in England by mid-November. What will it be like in the Crimea?*

Chapter 28

October 1854: News from Crimea

It was not until October 5, 1854, that the English press printed the first reports of the Battle of the Alma River that had taken place on September 20th. Munevver was stunned as she read William Russell's graphic descriptions of the brave exploits by junior officers and even mere privates—young soldiers who had rushed forward to defend their comrades using their bayonets when all else failed.

The English officers had been surprised by their victory at the Alma River. The road to Sevastopol was open! But their officers did not order a pursuit of the Russian Army. Raglan and French Commander Saint-Arnaud knew that they could not transport siege equipment and supplies all the way from their base at Calamita Bay, thirty miles north of Sevastopol. Realizing that they needed a closer and more secure base, they decided to march around Sevastopol to the south to a narrow and more easily defendable inlet—Balaklava Harbor—just eight miles from Scvastopol.

When the English arrived at Balaklava Harbor, they discovered that it was too small to accommodate both English and French ships. The French moved westward to two adjacent harbors, Kazakh Bay and Kamiesch Bay. The advantage of Kamiesch Bay was that the Russians could not attack the French, as that would expose their rear to the English.

On October 7, 1854, the Russians withdrew to the banks of the Tchernaya River, the last stronghold before Sevastopol. Between the riverbanks and Balaklava, there is a valley that is crossed by low ridges. Ten days later, the Russians began to fire on the English and French— four hours of continuous bombardment. In addition, the Russians were able to fire on French and English ships when they approached to fire on the fortresses of Sevastopol. The French lost two hundred three men and the English, three hundred seventeen.

The English wanted to attack Sevastopol directly, but the French wanted to strike at their defenses first in order to weaken the Russian defense of Sevastopol. The English had to wait while the siege guns were unloaded and the sailors had pulled them into place, seventeen men for each gun.

The Russians fired on them constantly. Finally, on October 16, 1854, one hundred twenty-six siege guns had been dragged into the batteries, and on October, 17, 1854 at 6:30 a.m., the eleven-month-long siege of Sevastopol began. The Russians fired continuously on the Allied Forces as they carried ammunition to their forward positions. Many men were killed, and soon, headless, legless, burned bodies littered the ground.

During the day, English ships in Balaklava Harbor came under attack, and during the night, the Russians rebuilt their defenses. By October 23, 1854, Raglan's force had shrunk to little more than eighteen thousand men. More and more seamen were taken from their ships, given rifles with bayonets, and without any training, ordered to fight alongside the soldiers.

By the third week of October 1854, England had set up camp at Balaklava, and the Russians had moved twenty-five thousand men into the North Valley of Balaklava and had blocked the eastern end of it. Russian infantry, brass cannons, and divisions of cavalry waited silently. Then, on October 25, 1854, the Russians attacked the redoubts held by the Ottomans at 7:30 a.m. The English Infantry was two miles away. The English Cavalry did not come to the aid of the Ottomans, and four of their redoubts were overrun.

It was on October 25, 1854 that the most famous battle of the Crimean War took place—the Battle of Balaklava. It was the battle during which the pride of the English Cavalry, the famous Light Brigade, was decimated in a desperate battle to prevent a breakthrough by the Russians from the Tchernaya Valley. Out of a total of six hundred seventy-five men who took part in the English Cavalry charge on the Russian cannons, two hundred forty-seven were killed or severely wounded, and four hundred seventy-five of England's finest horses perished.

The Russian attack began at 7 a.m. on October 25, 1854. Because Lord Cardigan was still ill, Lord Paget was in command of the Light Brigade. As he and Lord Lucan rode to the Kamara Ridge toward Canrobert's Hill to check on the troops, they observed the flag signaling enemy advancing that had been run up by Ottoman soldiers, and shots rang out as the soldiers began to engage the advancing Russians. Realizing that a major attack was beginning, Lord Lucan deployed the Heavy Brigade in an attempt to cover the retreating Ottoman soldiers, but the Russians rode them down and killed them with their lances.

Lord Raglan watched the Russians on horses tackle the English guns with lassos, and he thought that they were going to drag them away. He sent a message to Lord Lucan "to advance rapidly to the front to try to prevent the enemy from carrying away the guns." He called after the messenger, Nolan of the 15th Hussars, to tell Lord Lucan to attack immediately.

Lord Raglan believed that the time had come to counterattack on the Causeway, and he ordered Lord Lucan to act. The cavalry was to advance and take advantage of any opportunity to recover the heights. They would be supported by the infantry, which had been ordered to advance on two fronts. This was Raglan's third order to the cavalry that day.

Lord Lucan ordered the cavalry to mount, and he redeployed the Heavy Brigade on the slope of the Causeway while placing the Light Brigade across the end of the north valley. Lord Lucan chose to interpret Lord Raglan's instruction as to wait for the promised infantry support before going on the offensive.

After thirty minutes of waiting, Lord Raglan and his staff became impatient. The Russians seemed to be contemplating withdrawal. It was the ideal time for a show of force, but Lord Lucan remained inactive. Using telescopes and field glasses, the officers could see Russian artillery teams approaching the redoubts with lasso equipment. The enemy appeared to be making an attempt to remove the cannons.

Lord Raglan dictated a fourth order to Lord Airey, and although Captain Calthorpe was next in line for duty, Lord Raglan wanted the message relayed as swiftly as possible. He insisted Captain Nolan carry the message: Lord Raglan wishes the cavalry to advance rapidly to the front and try to prevent the enemy from carrying away the guns. Troop of Horse Artillery may accompany. French Cavalry is on your left. Immediate. Signed R. Airey.

Both Airey and Raglan spoke with Nolan to clarify their intentions. Raglan shouted after Nolan, "Tell Lord Lucan the cavalry is to attack immediately."

Instead of picking his way carefully down the steep, seven-hundred-foot slope of the ridge, Nolan took a very direct course, riding almost straight down the escarpment.

The Russians had barely moved. The Odessa Regiment was drawn up in the region of No. 3 Redoubt. Twelve guns were positioned in a line so as to be able to shell-rake the valley.

Nolan cantered across the plain toward his destination. He asked where Lord Lucan was. After Lord Lucan and Nolan spoke, Lord Lucan rode over to Lord Cardigan and ordered him to advance, despite the fact that the hills were covered with Russian artillery and riflemen. Instead of returning to Lord Raglan, Captain Nolan asked Lord Cardigan for permission to join the brigade for the action. Lord Cardigan ordered the brigade to draw swords and then gave the order to advance at a walk, heading straight down the valley. The Russian Odessa Regiment on the Causeway observed their advance.

The brigade increased their pace to a trot and had covered about two hundred yards when Captain Nolan spurred his horse forward and toward the right in the direction of the Causeway. Lord Cardigan was incensed to see Captain Nolan galloping ahead. It was a breach of discipline to ride before a brigadier without good reason.

Rising in his saddle, Nolan waved his sword aloft and shouted as though trying to turn the advancing cavalry. At that moment, a Russian shell exploded between Captain Nolan and Lord Cardigan. Nolan was struck in the chest by a shell splinter, and although his arm remained raised, his sword fell from his grasp. Nolan's horse carried him back almost as far as the point where the brigade had started before the dead Nolan fell from his saddle.

Lord Cardigan rode onward, leading the brigade forward. The cavalry rode headlong into the middle of the Russian Army. Fired on from three sides, dozens of English soldiers fell, but the Light Brigade kept going. As the cavalry bore down upon them, the Russian gunners swabbed out their barrels and rammed charges down as fast as they could. The Light Brigade was now at a gallop, and at around fifty yards from the battery, swords and lances were leveled and The Light Brigade increased to a charge. They attacked the gunners as they met them. Lord Cardigan rode through the guns with his sword still held ready. Some yards farther on, he reined up at the sight of the Russian Cavalry deployed to his front. He had survived the charge unscathed. Some Cossacks were sent to capture him, but he wheeled about and rode back the way he had come. Lord Raglan was dismayed. How could his instructions have been so completely misunderstood or even deliberately disobeyed?

The number of men who took part in the Charge of the Light Brigade was between six hundred fifty-eight and six hundred ninety-nine. Only one hundred ninety-five English soldiers survived uninjured. Some reports indicated that one hundred ten were killed outright, one hundred thirty were wounded, and fifty-eight were missing or captured: a 40 percent loss of men. Nolan was the first man killed as he tried to turn the horses after he realized that they were charging down the wrong valley, riding directly into the Russian guns. Out of the six hundred seventy horses that made the charge, four hundred seventy-five horses were killed—three hundred eighty-one horses were killed outright during the charge, and others had to be put down shortly after.

Many men died of their wounds over the next few months and many were shipped out to the hospitals, but amputees were difficult to save, and those who did recover knew that they faced an uncertain future back home since there was little provision for the disabled in Victorian society.

Immediately after the Battle of Balaklava, a whispering

campaign began in the Army of the East about the disaster. Some felt that Captain Nolan was responsible for the disastrous charge. Others blamed Lord Raglan or Lord Lucan.

"What a disaster!" Lord George stared at the paper in his hand. "Such stupidity!" He pushed the paper toward Munevver. "Lord Lucan ordered Lord Cardigan, his sister's husband, to lead the Light Brigade in a cavalry attack against a battery of Russian cannons." He stared at the floor. "Such witlessness! Men in crimson uniforms on horseback with sabers drawn charging an entrenched battery of twelve guns."

One thought pounded through Munevver as she picked up the paper and began to read. *James was with Lord Cardigan. He was part of the Light Brigade.*

Lord George had handed a second newspaper to Munevver as he left the breakfast table. "Take care of this." The command was cold and closed off all questions as he strode out of the room. Munevver lingered in the empty breakfast room, and as she read the article her father had underlined, she struggled to assimilate the different account of the battle that the paper had proposed. Nolan was considered to be the one responsible for the fatal cavalry charge on the Russians at Balaklava! Munevver gasped. *How can that be? Nolan was an expert horseman, but he did not hold a command position.* Why had her father given the paper to her? What had he said? "Take care of this!"

"Never!" she vowed as she shoved the paper into her workbag. She would burn it at the first chance she got.

She would do no more of her father's dirty work! She would not tell Christianna what her father wanted her to say, that Nolan had proved to be a man without honor.

Still reeling from the horrible account of Nolan's supposedly treacherous behavior and death, Munevver had made her way to her office and now sat idly at her desk. What could she tell Christianna? How would she get a message to her? And what about her own situation? James would have been one of those valiant men on beautiful horses riding straight toward twelve entrenched Russian cannons.

Chapter 29

November 1854: Scutari Hospital

Ari moved quickly across the room to the bowed-out section of the salon overlooking the Bosphorus where his mother sat waiting for him. "How is your health, my mother?" He stifled a cough with a handkerchief as he bowed over the hands that she held out to him.

"All is well. Praise be to Allah." A quick glance had told her that Ari was not well. He was thinner, and his face had an ashen cast. Knowing he would not welcome any questions about his health, she motioned for him to sit beside her and signaled to the older woman, waiting by the door, to bring coffee. "What is the news?"

News? Shall I tell her about the Ottoman losses? Shall I warn her that food is in short supply in the city and that she should warn Omar to be more cautious than ever? No. It has to be something to distract her from her own problems and her eyes examining me.

"It is an interesting story that I have to tell you, but the introduction is long. So, you must be patient." His mother smiled as he had hoped she would and motioned for him to continue. "As you know, in September, the Russians were defeated at the Battle of the Alma River. The English and French won the battle, but the toll of dead and wounded was high. The French had nurses—Sisters of Charity—and they had surgeons. The English had made no provisions for their wounded. No field hospitals, no doctors, no nurses, no bandages, and not enough equipment for surgery. When the newspapers declared that the English War Office was trying to save money, there was a huge public outcry! Mothers were outraged that there was no care for their sons. They demanded that care be provided for the wounded men. Lord Sidney Herbert, secretary of war, wrote to his wife's friend, Florence Nightingale, who had studied nursing, and asked her to organize and supervise medical services for the English troops here in the Ottoman Empire." He paused, but his mother made an impatient motion for him to continue. "In addition to her studies in nursing, Florence Nightingale had other needed skills. Her father had taught her math, languages, science, research, and, most important of all, how to organize and run a large project."

"Did she come? Is she here?"

"Yes. On November 5, 1854, Lady Florence and thirty-eight nurses arrived at Scutari at the Selimiye Barracks. The Sublime Porte had agreed to let the English, who had not set up any field hospitals, use the Selimiye Barracks at Scutari as a hospital." He continued before she could speak. "English soldiers who had been taken there were dying of their injuries but also of typhus, typhoid, cholera, and dysentery. The mortality rate was over 40 percent." He paused for a moment, scowling, and then continued. "Scutari Hospital was filthy and overrun with rats, bedbugs, and lice. It was already overcrowded when the soldiers wounded at the Battle of the Alma River and still in their bloody uniforms began to arrive. There were not enough beds for them, and if there was an empty bed, there was no clean bedding. There was little food for them and no utensils. Using her own money, Lady Florence bought shirts, socks, cups, dishes, pillows, basins, tin baths, towels, soap, combs, lice powder, bedpans, and sheets. Because clean bedding was a huge problem, she arranged to pay women in Scutari to do the laundry."

Ari searched his mind for something he could add that would distract her from the questions he knew she was waiting to ask. "So, you see, the English are sending nurses to Constantinople to care for their wounded."

"The Selimiye Barracks are old and in poor repair," Janan Hanim offered tentatively.

"Yes, I know, but what can be done? The French have established good field hospitals for their wounded, but the English have done nothing." He shook his head. "To make matters worse, the fighting is in the Crimea, northeast of Scutari on the northern shore of the Black Sea." Ari added, in a low voice, "It is a long way from the battlefield to Scutari."

"How will the wounded get to the hospital?" Janan Hanim stared at her son in disbelief. For safety, she had secluded herself in the yali and relied on Omar for news, but he had not told her about the hundreds of wounded soldiers arriving at the harbor of Scutari. Scutari was just thirty minutes across the Bosphorus from her home and she had not known. "Why did they choose Scutari?"

"It has a good harbor"—Ari's voice was gruff—"and it was available. They will have to transport the wounded from the battlefield by arabas, carts, to their headquarters at Balaklava. Then they will have to take them to Balaklava Harbor where ships for the wounded will be waiting." He paused to consider the logistics. "It could be three miles or more of jolting travel in wooden carts to bring them from the battlefield to the tenders who will ferry them out to the hospital sailing ships. The hospital ships will take them across the Black Sea to the Bosphorus." Ari decided not to tell her that the hospital ships, built to accommodate two hundred fifty men, often carried fifteen hundred, and that there was no one to provide care for the men—wounded, vermin-infested, often naked or covered with one ragged blanket, and always thirsty—during the journey. "From the harbor at Scutari, they would be carried by stretcher up the hill to the hospital." He did not tell her that when they got to the hospital, there were already more than four miles of beds, less than one foot apart, occupied by wounded and dying men.

"The Black Sea is never serene, but it can be very rough at this time of the year." She shivered. "It would take several days to cross."

"Yes, at least four days, and unfortunately, there are many wounded English, French, and Ottoman soldiers." He stared at the floor. "The generals and politicians may have planned for the execution of this war, but they didn't plan for the casualties."

"I suppose it will be the generals and politicians running the hospital?" Janan Hanim sniffed.

Ari shifted uneasily. What would his mother's reaction be when he told her who the English had asked to organize the care to be given in Scutari? "The English have appointed a woman to be in charge of the hospital."

"A woman?" His mother's eyes sparkled with interest.

"Yes. They have appointed Florence Nightingale to be in charge of the care of the patients at Scutari. I met her when I was in England. I remember her describing her training at a hospital in Germany. I've heard she brought thirty-eight women, trained nurses, with her to care for the wounded." The incongruity of the life of women in England, where a woman was always accompanied by another woman, and it was considered to be scandalous for a woman to spend time alone with a man not her husband or a family member, and the thought of such a woman caring for wounded soldiers, stunned him, and suddenly, he felt a strong need to protect her reputation. "One of the women traveling with her is her aunt."

"You met this lady, Florence Nightingale, in England?" she questioned gently. "You talked with her?"

"Yes, she is an old friend of Lord George's sister, Lady Frederica. She was visiting the family when I was there. At that time, she was warning everyone who would listen that the English Government had not organized military medical care as the French had done after the Peninsular War." He shook his head. "Scutari is an old Asian city, picturesque and charming, but horribly inefficient." He shook his head as he remembered the elegant Lady Florence, whom he had met in Lord George's home. "I don't know how she'll manage!"

"Since you were introduced to her in England, we must return the courtesy. You must welcome her and her aunt. Please tell her that I hope they will come to visit me." Janan Hanim folded her hands in her lap and waited.

"Yes, Mother." He suppressed a groan. "I will go to Scutari and extend your invitation."

* * *

The route from the harbor to the massive, rectangular Selimiye Barracks, sitting on top of the hill with its four towers, anchoring each corner, was lined with slender, towering cypress trees that still released a faint, woodsy aroma into the early autumn morning. As Ari walked along the road beside the cemetery, filling the slope below the barracks and holding simple graves, some marked with a wooden cross and some with ornate sarcophagi, the stronger scent of illness and decay nearly overwhelmed him.

Upon asking for Florence Nightingale, he was conducted to a small office in the tower on the side of the barracks overlooking the Selimiye Mosque and the harbor. Fascinated by the activity in the harbor, Ari almost missed the whisper of skirts as Lady Florence entered the room.

"Ari Bey." Florence held out her hand for him to lift to his lips. "It is such a pleasure to see a friend in these terrible times."

"When I learned you had arrived in Scutari, I told my mother and she asked me to call on you. She requested that I extend an invitation for you and your aunt to visit her whenever you can cross the Bosphorus to Constantinople."

"How very kind of her. Please thank her." She gave him a direct look. "It is chaos here. There are no supplies. The barracks are filthy and not set up for caring for the wounded . . . and the dying." She lifted her chin. "But we're managing."

Uncertain how to proceed, Ari used the traditional Ottoman indirect approach. "These barracks were first built in 1806 by Sultan Selim III for his new army. He used stones for the ground floor but wood for the second and third floors. Unfortunately, the Janissaries, who had always been the elite military unit of the Ottoman Army, did not agree with his new army, and when they revolted, they burned down the barracks. It took a while, but in 1825, the sultan built these new barracks and he used stone." Not sure what else to say, he added, with a slight shrug, "At least you don't have to worry about fire."

"Fire may be the only thing I don't have to worry about." Florence paused, uncertain how much to tell a member of the sultan's court. "It was already overcrowded with soldiers desperately ill with cholera and dysentery when we arrived. Unfortunately, the untreated wounded from the Battle of Alma arrived at the same time we did." She shook her head. "We weren't prepared, but we had to find space for the sick and wounded soldiers who had survived a wretched journey across the Black Sea."

"I am with the Ottoman Government, but we met in England in Lord George's home, my friend's home. I would never betray my friend, and that extends to his family and friends." Ari shifted in his chair, ready to move if she did not wish to continue their conversation.

For a moment, Florence was silent, and then words seemed to erupt from her. "Barracks may have been planned to accommodate soldiers, but they are not set up to care for wounded soldiers who are also suffering with typhus, cholera, dysentery, malaria, and typhoid fever. The place is filthy! An open sewer flows under the floors of the building, and it is infested with vermin of all kinds. There are no warm blankets, no clean clothes, no basins for washing, and not even cups and bowls for soup. As far as treatment . . ." She shuddered. "The doctors use arsenic, mercury, opiates, and bleeding. I've tried to explain the *Sanitarian Method* of Edwin Chadwick. He showed in 1842 that life practices—lack of a sewer system and contaminated drinking water—were linked to the outbreak of illnesses." She shook her head. "I've described his scientific findings and his solutions, but the doctors refuse to listen."

"What will you do?" Ari knew what it was like to face superiors who would not even consider new information. "How will you manage?"

"The nurses and I have been cleaning the barracks and getting rid of the vermin. I've asked the medical director to do something about the sewer. The stench is overwhelming, and the patients are lying on straw mattresses or bare floors just inches above the raw sewage. I am determined to have beds for every soldier, but every battle is followed by ships bringing more wounded men."

"You have accomplished so much in such a short time." Ari could not disguise his amazement.

"I had some unexpected help. Catering for the troops was improved after the visit of the Sanitary Commission. A renowned London chef, Alexia Soyer, was appointed to be in charge of feeding the English troops, and that included those in hospitals," Florence explained.

Ari looked at her in disbelief. "Alexia Soyer? Wasn't he the French chef in London whom everyone raved about?"

"Yes. Then he went to Dublin in 1847 and set up soup kitchens to feed the Irish people who were starving as a result of the failure of their potato crops. Although he was an acclaimed, gourmet chef, he had learned early in life how to make delicious, nutritious meals out of low-cost items." She beamed at him. "Now he is using that knowledge to produce tasty, nutritious meals for the patients in Scutari Hospital using army rations."

"That is truly astounding! What about your supplies?" Ari inquired.

"We're short of everything, but I've been told that the

Black Prince and nineteen supply ships are on their way and should be here any day, by the middle of November at the latest. They are bringing tents, blankets, warm clothing, and boots for the soldiers. I've been assured that they are also bringing supplies for the hospital." She shook her head. "We are almost out of lice powder, and it is greatly needed."

Ari looked out the window at the darkening sky. "Winter is approaching very quickly. The Black Sea is always unpredictable, but even more so at this time of year. What will you do if the supply ships do not arrive in time?"

"I will go across to Constantinople and use my own money to buy what I need. I'm determined that every patient will have a cup and spoon. They are eating what little food is available with their hands." Florence shuddered. "Everything is dirty and lice-infected." She grimaced. "I had no choice but to set up a laundry." At his gasp, she added, "Fortunately, there are women in Scutari who are willing to wash the patients' clothes and sheets for a small amount of money."

"My mother and I admire your efforts. Not many would undertake such a challenge." Ari leaned forward and handed her a folded piece of paper. "Officially, there is nothing I can do, and I anticipate that I will not be in Constantinople much longer, but if you need help, contact my mother at this address and she will do what she can."

"Thank you." Florence hesitated before asking, "You say you may not be here much longer?"

"I've heard the possibility mentioned of being sent to Macedonia." He kept his voice carefully neutral. "There are problems there."

Lady Florence nodded in understanding as she remembered the heated discussion of uprisings in Macedonia. "It seems so long ago that we were all together at Lord George's home."

"I have not heard from Lord George in a long time." Ari was too polite to ask directly for information. "I visited them shortly before I left." He hesitated. According to Ottoman tradition, it would be unthinkable to ask directly about the women in the family. He paused, but the desire for news overcame his customary reticence. "I imagine the war in the Crimea has disrupted Lord George's business," Ari offered, hoping she would provide some information about Lady Munevver.

"From what Lady Frederica wrote, it seems that Ryker is with the navy somewhere in the Crimea." Lady Florence hurried on. "She wrote that Lady Christianna has been brought back from Yorkshire and, in the absence of a trainer, has taken over the care of Lord George's horses."

Ari strained to control his impatience and was rewarded when Lady Florence added,

"Lady Munevver continues to work long hours on Lord George's affairs."

Desperate for more information, Ari ventured. "Lady Munevver once mentioned that the changes in textile manufacturing following the demonstrations of more efficient methods at the Grand Exhibit had reduced the demand for English fabrics."

"No doubt," Lady Florence murmured cryptically and then added, in a neutral tone, "I imagine Lord George has a very wide scope of trading interests."

Unable to resist any longer, he asked, "Is she well?"

Florence hesitated. "Lady Frederica wrote that Munevver was married to Lord Leinster's oldest son, James, in March." At her words, Ari Bey felt a surge of anger, mixed with shock, that almost blocked out her next words. "She said that James left to join Lord Cardigan's unit immediately after the wedding." She hesitated and then supplied the information Ari seemed to be waiting for. "I heard that he shipped out with the Light Brigade the next day."

The black tassel on his crimson fez swayed erratically as Ari rose and bowed to Lady Florence. "I must not keep you." He motioned to the young man who had accompanied him. "Hasan is my mother's cousin. She has sent him to help you. She says he knows many languages. He can help the wounded and can bargain with the merchants for you." Reluctantly, he added, "Keep him close. In case of danger, he will protect you with his life."

"Please thank your mother. All help is welcome." Florence held out her hand. "It was good of you to come." A worried look returned to her face. "There is so much to do here and the wounded keep arriving." She shuddered. "We have to make it through one more week. The *Black*

Prince and the other supply ships will arrive then."

"May Allah grant you strength during these troubled times." Ari stopped at the door when he heard Lady Florence's soft voice, "We both know what James's father threatened. He is a contemptible man! If James is killed, Lady Munevver will be in danger. She must leave before James's father can claim her."

"I have no way of gaining such information, and even if I had the information, I have no way of contacting her." Ari Bey ground out the words.

"I have passed the word that I am to be informed immediately. I will get the news to Munevver," Lady Florence stated firmly. "Unfortunately, that is all I can do. She will have to find a way to escape."

Bowing his head, Ari Bey's words were barely audible. "When she asked for information about traveling to Allepo, I gave her directions to my mother's home. If she can get to Constantinople, my mother will help her."

Chapter 30

November 1854: Escape

Each day, Munevver woke, wondering what the news from the East would be. *Another horrible battle? Will this be the day?* Ryker had promised that somehow, she would be informed if James were killed. He had assured her that she would learn before James's father could come to claim his son's widow who, according to him, was carrying his heir. But how would she know? Who would bring her the news? Her father had an iron control over the household. No one would dare deceive him. Had she waited too long to escape?

Munevver had done all she could to prepare. The well-traveled but still-sturdy trunk she had found in the attic was packed with a few changes of warm clothing, the petticoats with the coins sewn into the seams, nightwear, stockings, slippers, and a warm cloak. She had crammed in the tin box of medicinal herbs and one treasured item from her childhood—the old button box from Yorkshire that her grandfather had given her. A worn, brown, leather book bag that had once been Ryker's held the travel book Ari had given her, her knitting bag, a book of poetry, some dried fruit, and packets of crackers.

Now, she paced her small office, delaying the moment when she had to start working on the documents Lord George had left for her. Just steps away, in Lord George's study, the three morning newspapers would be neatly stacked on the corner of his desk. Each morning, the papers bristled with news of ferocious battles, the number of men killed and wounded, and the disastrous conditions under which the English soldiers existed as they waited for desperately needed supplies. Usually, she could not wait for an opportunity to read the papers, but today she felt listless and strangely detached from her normal focus on meeting Lord George's expectations.

Munevver stared at the card on the silver tray Quinn was presenting to her, and then, with her pulse racing, she glanced at the old-fashioned, rosewood-encased clock on the mantel of the small, pine-paneled fireplace that ruled her day. Thank goodness Aunt Frederica, who was suffering with a cold, had not come down yet and her father's carriage had already left. He should be well on his way to London, but why was Lady Sylvia Featherstone calling so early in the morning, and why on her and not on Aunt Frederica? Lady Sylvia was Florence Nightingale's friend and had often visited when Florence was with them, but she had never called on Munevver before. A feeling of dread chilled her. She glanced around the small office and then nodded to Quinn. "Please show Lady Featherstone in."

"Shall I notify Lady Frederica?" Quinn asked quietly.

For a moment, Munevver wavered and then said, "No,

she is not feeling well. There is no need to disturb her."

"I will come right to the point." Lady Featherstone's tone was urgent, but she spoke softly, so softly that Munevver strained to hear her words. "I've had a message from Scutari, from Florence. She said it was crucial I tell you as soon as possible that James was badly wounded in the Battle of Balaklava on October 25th. He was transported to Scutari and died soon after he arrived."

"The twenty-fifth?" Munevver murmured as icy fear curled through her. A week ago, and then the journey to Scutari. Would James's father already know of the death of his son? Was he already on his way to collect her?

"Yes. She said I must inform you before his father was notified."

"It is very kind of you to come," Munevver replied stiffly, trying to conceal the terror she was feeling. James's father would insist his son's widow belonged with him while she awaited the birth of the baby—the non-existent baby James had assured him she was carrying.

Munevver shuddered as the memory of Lord Leinster's outrageous words flooded her mind. *"She'll be plowed deep and hard until I get my heirs. If James can't do it, I'll find someone who can."* Munevver trembled. He had bought her. He would have his heir, and he didn't care how it came about. She had to escape to a place where he could not find her.

Later that evening, her father's interrogation began as soon as the soup course had been served. "What was the purpose of Lady Featherstone's visit?"

For a moment, Munevver's courage wavered. She had spent the day carefully formulating the plan that had been just a hazy dream until now. "She said she was visiting friends in this area, and my godmother had asked her to visit me since she had not seen me in a very long time."

"What does she expect when she chooses to live in the South of France!" It had always infuriated him that the widowed Lady Sophiana had refused his offer of marriage after his wife had died. It would have consolidated two powerful family businesses.

Fearing that Lord George would discover the real reason for Lady Featherstone's visit, Munevver added carefully, "She suggested that I travel with her daughter, who is going to visit Lady Sophiana."

"Impossible," he said sharply after the fish course had been presented. "You have too much work to do here." He directed his next words to Lady Frederica. "I shall have to be in London for a few days but she," he said, motioning to Munevver with his knife, "can take care of the correspondence while I am gone."

Munevver's mind raced. The help she had prayed for had just been handed to her. She risked exchanging a glance with Fayne, who was helping serve dinner since two of the footmen had been conscripted into the army. Munevver accidentally sloshed her wine glass, and Fayne rushed to pat her sleeve dry with a napkin. She managed to tell Fayne to go to Lady Featherstone and ask if they could travel to London with her. If she could convince Lady Featherstone to allow her to accompany her to London, she would tell her that her godmother had repeatedly asked Munevver to join her in France for a few days. Munevver felt her pulse race. She had to get from London to Dover, cross the channel, and once in France, find transportation that would take her to Vienna and the Galatea steamship that would carry her to Constantinople.

* * *

Day after day, Munevver and Fayne huddled in coaches as they sped toward Vienna. With each stop to change horses, the terror of being discovered made it almost impossible for them to rest. Finally, they reached Vienna and boarded the Galatea, the steamship that would take them down the Danube River to Constantinople. They would have at least thirteen days of safety if they stayed in the tiny cabin with two bunks that Munevver had been able to secure.

Soon, they had developed a routine. Fayne would go to the crowded salon where meals were served and load a tray for both of them. Day after day, the food was the same—chicken soup, chicken and noodles, and bread pudding. When most of the passengers had crammed themselves into the salons to talk, read, or play cards, Munevver and Fayne would pace the decks, trying to get as much fresh air and exercise as they could before returning to the damp, smelly cabin where they spent the time knitting.

During one of their morning walks on the deck,

they overheard two men talking. They seemed to be discussing the news in the paper that one of the men gripped to prevent the wind from tearing it from his hands. Munevver strained to hear his words. It appeared that there had been a terrible battle on November 5th. He referred to it as the brutal Battle of Inkerman, the last stronghold before Sevastopol. There had been fierce fighting in a dense fog with unorganized, leaderless, man-to-man encounters with rifles and bayonets. Untrained seamen, two thousand or more, had been removed from their ships and given rifles equipped with bayonets. English and French troops, twenty-seven hundred soldiers, faced fifteen thousand Russians, fighting to defend their last stronghold, Sevastopol. Munevver felt faint as she heard the man repeat the words, "It was the bayonets that got the job done." Her mind whirled. He had said that seamen had fought in the battle. *Seamen. Ryker . . . and Gordy.* She shuddered as she remembered his other words, "There had been twenty-three hundred fifty-seven English casualties."

The voice resumed reading aloud. "At the end of the Battle of Inkerman, food, supplies, medications, and fuel/wood were in short supply. The trenches were muddy and cold. The soldiers suffered from frostbite, fevers, cholera, scurvy, and dysentery." He hesitated before continuing. "Many of England's young men who had survived the battle died from disease and semi-starvation."

Munevver strained to hear the words the man was reading in a low voice. "Three days after the Battle of Inkerman, Lord Raglan informed Commissary General William Filder that the army would winter in the Crimea."

He stopped reading and just stared at the paper, then he continued. "Lord Raglan has instructed Mr. Filder to make provisions accordingly."

Clutching Fayne's arm for support, Munevver whispered, "Our troops must winter in the Crimea! Dear God, the troops have already endured so much! How can they survive the winter without provisions! How can they live through a winter in the Crimea without warm clothing and supplies?"

Fayne guided Munevver back to their cabin. "Our ships are on the way with supplies for them." She wrapped a shawl around the trembling Munevver and then said in a soothing voice, "Remember, we had to get everything we wanted to send to our men to the *Black Prince* before the end of August." As she led Munevver to the cabin, she continued in a comforting voice, "The *Black Prince* and nineteen smaller supply ships are due to arrive in the Crimea by the middle of November." Fayne handed Munevver her knitting, hoping that the familiar activity would help her recover from the shocking news, but her own thoughts were of the families in Ireland. Women struggling to look after the animals and crops, trying to survive without their men. They had been assured that their husbands, sons, and brothers would be home for Christmas last year, and now it had been decided—their men would winter in the Crimea.

Unable to sit still and knit, Munevver had appealed to Fayne, "I simply must read the newspaper myself. I must know what is happening. I need to know it all." She pressed a small coin into Fayne's hand. "Please see if you can buy a newspaper from someone."

After what seemed like hours, Fayne returned with a newspaper concealed under her cloak. She handed it to Munevver, who sank down on the lower bunk and began to read.

In London, public outrage at the news of the horrible conditions the soldiers were enduring had led to the formation of a *Commission of Inquiry into the Supplies of the English Army in the Crimea.* In the public's eyes, the severe winter conditions in the Crimea, in combination with malnutrition, high rate of diseases, and lack of supplies that the soldiers faced were greater horrors than the disastrous Charge of the Light Brigade or the brutal Battle of Inkerman. The commission's findings provoked a storm of controversy with both Airey's and Filder's conduct called into question.

Chapter 31

November 14, 1854: Devastating News

Three weeks into their journey, as she was taking her usual later afternoon walk on the deck, Munevver overheard the words "Dear God!" burst from a well-dressed man standing near the rail of the ship, reading a paper. "They were already freezing and now . . ."

"What has happened?" Munevver cast all propriety aside and addressed the stranger directly. *Something dreadful must have occurred.*

"There was a storm with hurricane force winds, rain, hail, and heavy snow in the Crimea on November 14th. It lasted from daybreak until midafternoon. Unfortunately, there were many ships anchored in Balaklava Harbor, ships carrying supplies for our soldiers—warm greatcoats, blankets, and boots." He stared at the paper. "You remember the public outrage? The generals had made no provision for the troops. They have nothing to protect them from the frigid weather. The generals had insisted the fighting would be over well before winter set in." He paused. "It was a tough fight, but the public demanded that forty thousand greatcoats and warm boots for every man in our army be sent." He groaned. "Everything is gone. In just four hours, everything was lost—clothing, medicine, food, and forage for the horses—all lost in the frigid waters of Balaklava Harbor. Now our poor men will have to suffer through a long winter with no coats, no boots, no blankets, no medicines, and very limited food. Hundreds of tons of gunpowder and millions of cartridges were lost. Then there was the food for the horses. I don't know how they'll survive."

"The ships were in Balaklava Harbor?" Munevver wished she hadn't asked as Fayne turned pale.

"Yes. Thirty ships crowded into that small harbor. Thirty ships lost. Nineteen of our ships in addition to the *Black Prince*."

"Not the *Black Prince*!" Munevver cried. "She was carrying surgical instruments, bandages, stretchers, and flannel blankets for the wounded." She could not stop herself from adding, "So many socks, mufflers, and hats that had been gathered up through an appeal to the people to provide warm things for their loved ones . . . all lost." Munevver exchanged a desperate look with Fayne. In her mind, she could see Mrs. Coates, her fingers stiffened with arthritis, struggling to finish socks for Gordy. "The people are going to be devastated when they hear of the loss of the *Black Prince*!"

"So many ships lost. The *Wild Wave*, the *Mary Ann*, the *Progress*, the *Wanderer*, the *Resolute* . . ." His voice faltered. "Some of the ships ground against each other, and some lost their anchors and were dashed to pieces on the rocks." He rubbed his hand over his face. "I don't know how they'll get through a Crimean winter." He glanced at the paper again. "It's only the middle of November, and already it is snowing every day." He grimaced. "Winter has already come in the Crimea, and our soldiers have no winter uniforms." He shook his head. "They have no huts. They are still living in light-canvas tents." He snapped the paper down on the railing in disgust. "Even worse! It says that many of those tents were destroyed in the storm, and now the men are digging tunnels for shelter. English soldiers are freezing in muddy ditches! Not just the men. There is no shelter at all for the horses—just mud and frozen slush."

Another man had joined the speaker at the railing. "The greatest fear is the lack of forage for the horses. A month's supply was lost when the ships were destroyed." He shuffled his feet on the deck, avoiding their eyes. "They were so sure the war would be over quickly and the men and horses would be home before winter."

Ryker, Gordy, and so many more. They will have to survive without food, warm clothes, or shelter. "It would take more than two months to get supplies to them." Munevver spoke as though she were in the study with Lord George, analyzing a shipping problem. She forced herself to state the obvious. "Even if we could get the supplies, we don't have the ships."

The second man held out his paper. "It says that two hundred eighty-seven men lost their lives as a result of the hurricane."

Munevver nodded silently. If her calculations were

accurate, they predicted death for many more.

Fayne hurried the stricken Munevver back to the cabin. As soon as they reached the sanctuary of the crowded room, Munevver collapsed on the bunk. They both knew that, with the onset of the dreaded Crimean winter, the English Army, in its summer uniforms and canvas tents, would suffer appalling losses from the cold as well as from diseases.

It was Fayne, showing the strength of generations of Irish country women fighting to survive, who spoke first. "Dead soldiers can't fight. The commanders will find a way to get them warm clothes and supplies." She pulled out the knitting needles and yarn. "We begin again."

During the next day, the passengers talked of nothing but the hurricane and what followed—the constant snow heralding that winter had arrived in the middle of November. It was the beginning of what the newspapers called the *Dire Winter*. The reports described how soldiers did not remove their boots because they were afraid that they could not get them back on. Their feet swelled and they suffered from frostbite. They still wore the summer uniforms that they had on when they landed in September. Their diet consisted of hard biscuits, salt pork, and rum. They had no wood to cook the little meat that they could carry from the storehouse in Balaklava Harbor to their camps. Soon, many had developed scurvy and other diseases.

The newspaper articles were scathing as they pointed out that just seven miles away, in Balaklava Harbor, the warehouses were full of rice, flour, vegetables, and tea—even limes, which could have provided lime juice to prevent scurvy among the soldiers. The food was there, but there was no road between the harbor and the front line, and there were no horses or carts to transport the supplies through the seven miles of mud to where the soldiers were stationed. Although they had been ordered to build huts in preparation for winter, no wood had been provided and the barren tundra offered none.

Soon, men who had fought at Inkerman were filling the hospital beds in Scutari. Men suffering from wounds, frostbite, cholera, or typhus were carried to the port, where they lay crammed on lighters buffeted by the surf until they could be hoisted onto the hospital ships. Then there was a stormy four-or-five-day passage across the Black Sea to Scutari. Many who embarked on the ships never landed. Those who died on the ships taking them to the hospital were cast into the Black Sea. By the end of November, there were nearly eight thousand men in hospitals. The conditions were terrible, with shortages of surgeons, doctors, and supplies and appalling sanitary conditions.

The English War Office had two chiefs: the Duke of Newcastle was secretary for war and Mr. Sidney Herbert was secretary at war. The medical department was under the directorship of Sidney Herbert. As soon as he had become aware of the dreadful conditions in the hospitals, he had asked for the aid of ladies who already possessed experience in caring for the sick and wounded. He was searching for nurses to tend the soldiers, not the officers. One of the ladies he asked for help was his wife's friend, Florence Nightingale.

Within weeks of his request for help, Lady Florence had sailed from England. She arrived at Scutari on November 4th, accompanied by Protestant sisters and Catholic nuns, eighteen in all, and by twenty trained nurses. Florence Nightingale's first accomplishment was to improve the sanitary conditions, but she also brought in a chef to prepare appetizing, nourishing meals for the patients.

News that the hospitals were overflowing with ill and wounded soldiers, that they lacked care, and that nearly one hundred patients died every night caused a nationwide outcry of anger and grief. The people could not stand the thought of the young men of England suffering so greatly while there was wealth and plenty at home. The public reacted in two ways: finding a way to provide immediate relief, and identifying scapegoats and making them atone for the suffering they had caused. All of England became a workshop for the manufacture of warm clothing. Blankets, clothing, boots, and food were loaded onto steamships and sent to Constantinople.

However, long before this outpouring of public support arrived, Lord Raglan had dispatched a request to find things in Constantinople to make up for the loss of the *Black Prince.*

Beginning early in December, and continuing through the month of December, Sultan Abdulmejid sent warm clothing, boots, blankets, and tents to the supply station at Balaklava Harbor. By the end of December, the Ottoman Empire had supplied nineteen thousand new greatcoats, seventeen thousand blankets, and other needed items to the English troops. Lord Raglan was able to report that every man in the army had received a second blanket, a jersey frock, flannel drawers, socks, and some kind of winter coat in addition to a greatcoat.

The supplies helped, but during January and February, the number of sick men in hospitals increased to fourteen thousand. Although a speedy victory—a three-day defeat of Sevastopol—had been promised, it was soon evident that the Allied Forces would have to winter in the Crimea.

When the public learned that the men were on half-rations most of the time and that there was no way to get needed supplies to them—no horses or carts to transport the supplies, no forage for the horses, and no road for the men struggling to carry provisions seven miles back to camp—they were infuriated. Their desire to punish whomever was at fault for the poor treatment of their husbands and sons was rampant. The Duke of Newcastle began to censure Lord Raglan and also condemn the quartermaster, whose duty it was to provide for the army.

Lord Palmerston sent Sir John McNeill and Colonel Tullock to the Crimea to study the problem. They reported that the officers had shared the work and the hardships with the men. In fact, the officers had used their private means to provide for their men. Blame was cast on Commissary General William Filder for his failure to issue crucial supplies to the troops, supplies such as nine tons of lime juice. The very item that would have prevented the scurvy afflicting the troops—lime juice—was left in two hundred seventy-eight boxes in Balaklava Harbor. There were similar deficiencies in supplying fresh meat, vegetables, and fuel to cook it, as well as defective arrangements in locating local forage for the horses. All of these failures were charged to Commissary Filder and his connection with Sir Charles Trevelyan of the treasury.

In his defense, Commissary Filder said he had made adequate provision for supplies and fodder if the army had stayed in the Ottoman Empire, helping the Ottomans push the Russians out of their provinces as originally planned. Instead, the generals had embarked on a preventive war, moving to the Crimea, and to a siege of Sevastopol. When the war was expanded to the Crimea, Filder had requested two thousand tons of supplies from England but only received one-tenth of what he requested . . . and it took six months to get that small amount. Later, it was found that the treasury did not send a proper supply of forage for the horses from England.

Chapter 32

Summons from the Seraglio

The carriage Munevver had hired as soon as the steamship docked in Constantinople drew up at the entrance to the walled garden hidden by tall Judas trees that led to the harem section of the house. Munevver passed some coins to Fayne and motioned for her to pay the driver, who silently deposited her small trunk and book bag by the door and then hurried back to his carriage.

Munevver knocked hesitantly. What had made her decide to come to Ari's mother? Feeling like a coward, she acknowledged to herself that the crowds on the dock had made the decision for her. Although she had the name of a hotel that catered to foreigners, her courage had deserted her as she faced the noise and confusion that was Constantinople, and now she was here, on the doorstep of Ari's mother's home with only a card on which he had written a few words. What would she do if his mother refused to receive her?

The door opened, and an older woman, dressed in a

knee-length, dark-fitted jacket and loosely fitted grey, silk trousers gathered tightly at the ankles said, "Evet, Effendi Hanim?"

Munevver returned her greeting in the Turkish her grandfather had taught her so long ago and waited as the woman studied the card Munevver had passed to her.

After a moment, she motioned for Munevver and Fayne to enter. At a quick signal of her hand, two other women stepped forward to carry Munevver's small trunk into the entrance hall, and then the solid door was closed behind them. With a murmured "Lutfen," the woman indicated that they should be seated on the crimson-and-gold upholstered bench stretching along one wall of the small room tiled in shades of delicate aqua. The soothing gurgle of a small, pewter wall fountain was the only sound.

After a few minutes, the woman who had greeted them at the door returned and, after beckoning to Munevver to follow her, said in flawless French, "Janan Hanim Effendi requests that you enjoy the hammam after your long journey and then join her."

Reassured by the memory of her grandmother describing this custom, Munevver murmured a polite "Merci" and turned to the silent Fayne, hovering by the door, and asked her to wait for her.

"She will be served tea while she waits," the woman said with a note of impatience. "We must not keep Janan Hanim Effendi waiting."

Munevver hurried along the many corridors that seemed to be leading away from the garden side of the house and toward the Bosphorus. Her spirits lifted at the thought of a bath and shampoo after the long journey, but she also felt apprehension, as though there were a weight compromising her ability to breathe. What if Ari's mother rejected her? Where would she go? How would she find a caravan of pilgrims going to Mecca so that she could travel with them as far as Aleppo? If she found her way to Aleppo, would her uncle welcome her? Would she be safe? Even here, with Ari's mother, where she knew she was secure, the weariness of travel and the strain of constantly being on guard made her feel vulnerable. She had always prided herself on being able to analyze any challenge and determine the best way to handle it, but now she felt defeated as she hurried to keep up with the slight figure ahead of her.

As Munevver followed her guide through endless corridors, she tried to remember what she knew about Turkish baths. There would be a warm room with both hot and cold water, and she would be scrubbed with scented soaps and sponges to remove the dirt of her travels. She rolled her aching shoulders in anticipation of hot water flowing over them.

An hour later, she had been scrubbed three times and her hair had been washed twice. Her pubic hair had been removed with a depilatory, an evil-smelling cream the bath attendant had called "nura" that was applied with an ivory spatula and removed with the razor-sharp edge of a mussel shell. A sticky mixture of syrup and turpentine had been spread over her legs, allowed to dry, and then pulled off. Her feet had been smoothed with a rasp. She had never felt so clean or so mortified. How would she look Ari's mother in the eye when she met her?

At last, she was ushered into a large room with windows bowing out over the terrace that ran along the waterfront. Seated in the corner of a silvery-grey, velvet-upholstered divan with scattered pillows of crimson, green, and gold silk was a regal-appearing woman dressed in blue, silk pantaloons and a closely fitted, murrey-colored, collarless coat that revealed the neckline of a pleated, white, silk blouse. A triple strand of large pearls the color of fresh country cream was around her throat, and gold bracelets studded with rubies encircled both wrists. A small, plum-colored, fez-shaped hat with a golden tassel was worn on the side of her head.

For a moment, Munevver could not believe this could be Ari's mother, and then the slight lines around her eyes and the crinkling of the skin of her neck made her realize that this woman was about the same age as Aunt Frederica. Even so, she must have been very young when Ari was born. When Munevver was close to the divan, she made a very low curtsey and said, "Peace be on you" in Turkish.

"On you be peace and the graciousness of Allah." She motioned for Munevver to come closer. "Welcome to my home, my child. I trust your health is well."

"Evet, Hanim Effendi. I hope that your health is well . . . and that the health of your family is also well." Munevver swayed on her feet. The unaccustomed strain of traveling among strangers that she had held at bay for so long seemed to be released by the concern she read in the other's eyes.

"You are exhausted. We will talk later, but first, we must hurry," Janan Hanim said with a quick glance at the maid. "The Valide Sultan has asked us to come to her."

"The sultan's mother has invited us? Surely she meant the invitation for you alone. She would have no reason to invite me."

"We must not keep her waiting." She assessed Munevver from head to toe, trying not to wince as she registered the twisted left foot. "You must wear your best outfit."

"I have one other jacket in my valise." She thought of the beautiful, deep-mauve, silk twill material that Ari had brought back from the Grand Exhibit and given to Aunt Frederica. Her Aunt had noted that the color would suit Munevver better and had arranged for her modiste to make a close-fitting jacket out of the material for Munevver. The color of the silk made her eyes seem a darker violet than they were, and she loved it. She had never had the courage to wear it, to risk the interrogation of her father if he saw it. "It was necessary to travel very lightly."

Janan Hanim nodded to Fayne, who had been sitting silently on a bench at the back of the room. "Bring the other jacket." When Fayne held it up for her inspection, she could not cover her surprise. "It is not English."

"It was made in London," Munevver answered truthfully. "It was not suitable for traveling, but I was reluctant to leave it behind." She was not going to admit that the message from Florence Nightingale informing her James had died in the hospital in Scutari consigned her to a year of wearing black mourning, and then a year of half-mourning. Even here in the Ottoman Empire, there was an accepted period of mourning—four months and ten days—but the rules controlling what one could wear were less strict. She had decided not to wear mourning for James. In fact, she did not intend to let anyone know that her husband was dead. Traveling with just one maid, she knew it would be safer to be known as a married woman.

"It will do very well," Janan Hanim said briskly. Turning to one of her maids, she snapped out her orders. "Dress her to go outside. Use one of my carsafs." She looked back at Munevver. "We must show we honor the Valide Sultan." Her gaze swept over Munevver. "You need to wear your best jewels."

"I don't have any jewels," Munevver answered as a painful memory surfaced. Her grandmother had left her jewelry to Munevver, but when her father had insisted that she leave her grandfather's home in Yorkshire and come to live with him and help with the business, he had also demanded that she give her jewelry to him so that he could keep it safe for her. He had assured her he would give it back to her at the right time. *Was my jewelry included in the dowry my father paid to James's father?* She trembled with anger at the very thought.

"Not even some gold bracelets?" Janan Hanim asked

in disbelief. Every Turkish girl would have been given gold bracelets on her birthdays. She would wear them proudly for all to see, and they would be supplemented by other jewels—bracelets, necklaces, belts, broaches, and hair decorations—when she married.

Munevver shook her head as she hurried into the jacket, thankful that she was so slender that she did not have to wear stays.

As soon as they entered the enclosed carriage that was to take them to Topkapi Sarayi, Janan Hanim began her instructions. "It is customary to be silent as we go through the courtyards and corridors."

"Yes, Hanim Effendi. I remember my grandmother telling me that everyone must maintain silence as they pass through the gates and courtyards." For a moment, she could hear her grandmother's voice, repeating the words she loved to hear: *The Imperial Gate, The Gate of Salutation, The Gate of Felicity, and The Golden Way.* They were the magic words that preceded her grandmother's description of her friend, Lady Montague's, visits to the Imperial Harem. As a little girl, whenever she heard the words, she envisioned herself wearing a violet, silk dress embroidered with silver threads, walking through each gate. It was their names she recited whenever she could not fall asleep.

"Your grandmother told you about Topkapi Sarayi? Was she Ottoman?"

"No, she was of English descent. One of her friends was Lady Mary Montague. When Lady Montague was in Constantinople with her husband while he was ambassador to the Ottoman Empire, she wrote letters to my grandmother describing her visits to the palace harem." She paused, lost in memories. Her grandfather had drilled her in languages, marketing, and business relations so that she could take a place in his Eastern Trading Company, but it was her grandmother who had described the beauty of the palace harem.

"We must use all possible speed. We'll take a six-oar caïque down the Bosphorus and then a carriage to the Sarayi, the palace."

"A six-oar caïque?" The words slipped out before she could stop them. Only women of the royal palace were entitled to use a six-oar caïque.

"I see your grandmother taught you well," Janan Hanim responded with dry humor. "I was part of the palace, one of many young girls from Circassia given as gifts to the sultan from those seeking favors. After I had been there seven years, I was freed and given as a bride to Ari's father, who was being sent to Macedonia to serve as governor of the province." She lifted her head proudly. "That was long ago, but I still have some of the privileges of the Sarayi."

Munevver tried to remember everything her grandmother had told her as the enclosed carriage drawn by a small horse conveyed them along the tree-lined road toward the palace, which was situated on the highest terrace of Seraglio Point where the Bosphorus met the Marmara Sea. She could almost hear her grandmother's voice: *"The first gate is the Imperial Gate. It is a two-*

storied, white marble, arched pavilion that dominates the square before it. On each side of the arched portal, there are marble niches where the heads of the sultan's enemies are displayed after they are slain. The pavilion has two levels of windows, all closely shuttered. The iron door is opened by the gatekeeper at the first Morning Prayer and closed after the Night Prayer. The Imperial Gate leads to the First Court. It is also called the Court of the Janissaries, the elite soldiers of the Sultan's Army. Some call it the Parade Court. It is open to all."

Suddenly, Munevver thought of her grandmother's description of the bread. *"The courtyard has stone paths of shiny, black pebbles leading to the bakery, where the whitest of white bread was prepared for the sultan and served with butter from Moldavia and honey from Walachia. Bread of decreasing whiteness was prepared for the rest of the Seraglio occupants with the lowest-ranking slaves receiving black bread."*

Risking a glance from under her lowered eyes, Munevver noticed the features her grandmother had described: the infirmary and the waterworks that supplied the Seraglio, the whole palace, with water. In the middle of the courtyard, she could see a huge, widely branching plane tree that she knew was called the Janissary Tree. In the past, when the Janissaries disagreed with the sultan's treatment of them, they would gather under the tree and overturn their soup cauldrons to show that they would no longer accept the sultan's rice. They would not fight for him until their demands were met. On one side of the square was the Fountain of Ahmet III, and a corner wall abutted a corner of the Agha Sophia. The courtyard was unpaved, but stone pathways led to various gates. Only ambassadors, or very important people, could enter the First Court on horseback or by carriage. All others had to walk the length of the courtyard, approximately one-fourth of a mile, to get to the next gate and courtyard. Munevver winced at the thought of how walking so far on stones would make her ankle ache for the rest of the day.

Janan Hanim leaned closer and whispered, "Inside the First Court is the Palace School, which trains boys from a young age through their early manhood for government posts in the Ottoman Empire. There is also an infirmary for them if they become ill."

As Munevver listened to Janan Hanim's whispered words, she remembered how her grandmother would drop her voice as she shared the next bit of information. *"At the far end of the First Courtyard is the Gate of Salutation. It is also called the Ortakapi or Central Gate. It is the entranceway to the second courtyard. You will see it looming as you approach. It's a massive, grey stone structure with twin octagonal towers that are connected by a deeply crenellated parapet. The Gate of Salutation has two entrance arches—one big arch and then an inner, smaller arch. Everyone, except the sultan, his mother, and royal princes, must dismount from his horse or carriage and walk from this outer gate inward."*

Her grandmother would pause to make sure she had Munevver's full attention before she continued.

"The second courtyard, also known as the Courtyard

of the Divan, contains the Tower of Justice and the Imperial Council Chamber. Ambassadors and important visitors wait in small rooms for their audience with the sultan or his vizier. On one side of the courtyard is the Court of the Divan where the sultan or his vizier would listen to petitions. At the end of the courtyard is the Gate of Felicity. It's also called the King's Gate or the Royal Gate." Munevver hugged the memory of her grandmother's rising excitement as she said, *"No one could pass through the Gate of Felicity without the sultan's permission."* She would always wait before speaking to let Munevver's anticipation grow. *"As you come through the Gate of Felicity, you will see the Third Court. It is the private court of the sultan."*

Munevver smiled to herself. About this time, she would ask her grandmother how much longer before they got to the harem.

"At the far end of the Courtyard of the Black Eunuchs is the main gate to the harem, the Cümle Kapsis. It opens into a small, dark room, and opposite the main door of that room is the Golden Road, a paved walk with the most beautiful tiled walls." Janan Hanim paused and then said softly, "It came to be called the Golden Road because of the sultan's custom of scattering golden coins along the walk for his concubines on festival days."

Munevver nodded and let her grandmother's words fill her mind. *"The Golden Road leads to the harem, the four-hundred-room section of Topkapi where all the women of the sultan's household live—his mother, wives, daughters, sisters, and female slaves. His sons, those under the age of twelve, also live there with their mothers. The Golden Road connects the harem, the women's section of the Seraglio, with the men's section of the Seraglio, the Selamlik."*

Munevver was shaken out of her reverie by Janan Hanim's whispered question, "Did she tell you about the black eunuchs?"

"Yes," Munevver answered softly, trying not to shudder as she remembered the unbelievably cruel practice of castrating young African boys so that they could serve the sultan's harem. Munevver reviewed mentally what her grandmother had described. *"Inside the Cümle Kapsis, the main gate to the harem, a corridor leads to the black eunuchs' quarters. At the end of that corridor, the Golden Road leads to the paved courtyard of the Valide Sultan, the sultan's mother."* Munevver did not add that her grandmother had told her that the Valide Sultan's courtyard separated the women's quarters from the sultan's quarters, which were guarded by white eunuchs.

After asking Munevver to never reveal it, Janan Hanim had told her that the Valide Sultan's apartments were directly connected to the sultan's quarters by a corridor, the corridor of the Bath—hammam yolis— that leads from her hammam to his hammam. She had hurried on to describe the Valide Sultan's private sitting room as a corner room that extended over the lower level and had windows overlooking the Golden Horn. She had added that the Valide Sultan's salon, where she received guests, overlooked her private courtyard.

"We are almost at the Gate of Salutation, the Central

Gate," Janan Hanim murmured. "We will have to leave the carriage and walk." As she moved to open the carriage door, a black eunuch approached and told the driver that the carriage could proceed to the next gate.

The two women exchanged startled glances but did not speak, each wondering what had prompted the unusual courtesy. When the carriage stopped at the Gate of Felicity, they left the carriage and hurried through the gate and across the third courtyard passing the Palace School where the brightest boys in the empire— not Turkish boys but Greeks, Circassians, Georgians, Persians, and Armenians—were taught Arabic, Persian, music, falconry, and hunting. They were trained to carry out one of three duties: manage the finances of the Ottoman Empire, administer the provinces of the Ottoman Empire, or lead the army.

At the entrance to the harem, a black eunuch motioned them to follow him as he led them across the Valide Sultan's courtyard to her suite of rooms. As they crossed the courtyard, Munevver could not help gasping at the glimpses of intricately patterned Iznik tiles with their vibrant, red colors, ranging from delicate coral to crimson, against the purest white, decorating the wall of the Golden Road.

Starting at the entrance to the Valide Sultan's courtyard, the Golden Road then flowed across the Courtyard of the Kafes, the cages—a two-story apartment building adjoining the harem but separated by a black gate, the Djinn's Kapi or the Genies' Gate, which was closely guarded by black eunuchs. The Kafes that housed the brothers, sons, and sometimes nephews or uncles of the reigning sultan had no windows on the first floor, but the windows on the second floor overlooked the courtyard and the sea. The Golden Road terminated at the Courtyard of the Sultan.

Although her grandmother had described the Valide Sultan's rooms, Munevver was unprepared for the intricacy of the tiles covering the walls of her rooms. Panels of delicate designs created with blue-and-white Iznik tiles set within gold-embossed, red panels adorned the walls from floor to ceiling. The domed ceiling was engulfed in crimson tiles. At one end of the room was a raised dais with a massive, gold brocade throne. Its four posts supported a pleated, gold silk canopy. A large, pale-pink rug with an intricate overall pattern was centered in the room, and a divan upholstered in gold damask and made enticing by a profusion of small, velvet pillows with golden silk tassels continued around the room and under the windows. In addition to the bronze fireplace on one wall, which provided heat in the winter months, there was a large, brass mangal in front of the divan where she knew the women would gather to keep warm during Constantinople's frigid winter months. Although Munevver could not see any flowers, the room held the scent of fresh-cut roses.

Munevver remembered her grandmother telling her how young slave girls would walk through the rooms, swinging a silver-pierced pomander that would perfume the room with the scent of roses or jasmine. There were several women sitting on the divan with their embroidery, but the only sound to be heard was the tinkling music of an intricately designed silver fountain in a corner of the room.

Not knowing what to do, Munevver, with her gaze directed at the floor, curtsied low as Janan Hanim bowed to the Valide Sultan, sitting in the place of honor, the corner of the divan overlooking the Golden Horn. As she listened to their soft exchanges in Persian, Munevver's thoughts wandered. *According to what Grandmother told me, it is the Valide Sultan, the sultan's mother, who is responsible for the smooth running of the harem through her management of the primary harem staff: the Lady Stewardess (Kiaya), who serves as a manager or a head housekeeper and the Treasurer (Hazinedar Usta), who is responsible for all expenses for running the harem and for distributing pin money to those entitled to it and pensions for those banished to the Old Seraglio (Eski Serai). The Valide Sultan also supervises the Mistress of Robes, the Keeper of the Baths, the Keeper of the Jewels, the Reader of the Koran, the Keeper of the Storerooms, the Manager of the Table Service, and others.*

In addition to overseeing the management of the harem, it is the Valide Sultan who selects which of the many beautiful women in the harem will be led to the sultan's bed. The Valide Sultan also controls the access to power of the sultan's one hundred thirty women—the Kadins, the four concubines with the status of legal wife; the Ikbals, favorites of the sultan; and the Guzdeh (in the eye), those who have found favor in the eyes of the sultan. It is the Valide Sultan who has the power to promote the next sultan from among her many grandsons. Munevver suppressed a shudder, remembering her grandmother whispering that the Valide Sultan had absolute power over the life or death of every harem inmate.

There was a pause after they had inquired about each other's health, and then the Valide Sultan shifted her attention to Munevver and addressed her in Turkish. "You've journeyed a long way to visit my dear friend, Janan Hanim." The clear, grey eyes surveying Munevver seemed to deliver the message that the Valide Sultan knew exactly why she had traveled to Constantinople.

Munevver marshaled her most formal Turkish. "Aleppo is my destination. I am traveling to Aleppo to be with my uncle, who is not well." She paused, unwilling to deceive her hostess yet uncertain how safe it was to confide in her. "I have stopped in Constantinople before going to Scutari, where I hope to join a caravan of pilgrims en route to Mecca."

"Aleppo?" The Valide Sultan raised a hand toward the woman standing in the entrance to the room with a tray of tiny china cups from which the fragrance of coffee drifted toward them, and the woman hurried forward to place the tray in front of her. Without a word, she passed the first cup to Janan Hanim and then one to Munevver. Waiting until each of the ladies had taken their first sip, Munevver raised the cup to her lips and experienced Turkish coffee for the first time. She thought of the words of Talleyrand: "Black as the devil, hot as hell, pure as an angel, and sweet as love." The strong beverage seemed to give her courage to face whatever fate the woman sitting in the corner determined for her. It would take patience. She knew the Valide Sultan would not be direct in her questioning but the verdict would come.

"Forgive me for not asking earlier. Are your parents well?" Only the quick sip of coffee betrayed the Valide Sultan's desire for haste.

"Thank you for your kindness." Munevver did not linger on the usual pleasantries. "My father is living and well, but my mother died when I was a child."

"In childbirth?" The question was almost clinical as the Valide Sultan's gaze swept over Munevver from head to toe.

"No. It was a particularly hot summer in London, and there was an outbreak of cholera." Munevver examined her interrogator as her grandfather had taught her to do when facing an opponent. The realization that the lady was playing chess made her almost smile. *The Valide Sultan wants something!* No point in making it hard for her. "My aunt Frederica, my father's sister, managed our home after my mother's death." *Your move, my lady. It's time for you to take a risk or play safe.*

"You say you are on your way to Aleppo to help your uncle?"

"Yes. I lived with my grandparents from my early years until very recently. I assisted my grandfather in his work. He had been with the Levant Company, but when the company ended in 1826, he started his own trading company and taught me the business." She closed her lips firmly. She was not going to admit to these women that her parents had not wanted her, had cast her off, and that it had been her grandfather who had found her after she had been placed in a home for abandoned children in the country. It was her grandfather and grandmother who had raised her. "Now I help my father with his business in London. His younger brother, my uncle, handles the other end of the trading in Aleppo. He receives the products and starts them on the way to London." As Munevver gave this censored version of her situation, she sensed that the Valide Sultan already knew the full reality of it, but she persisted with her story. "When I learned that my uncle was not well, I thought I should go to Aleppo and help him."

"The tunic that you are wearing is a most unusual shade of mauve. It seems to be of Bursa silk. Did your uncle send it to you?"

We've come to the middle game. Munevver set her empty coffee cup on the tray. "No. Three years ago, there was a Great Exhibition in London. There were beautiful fabrics from all over the world. I believe the material came from there." She let her hands drop in her lap. "My Aunt Frederica had it made for me." There would be more to come.

"Yes, the English Great Exhibition," the Valide Sultan murmured. She turned toward Janan Hanim. "I believe your son, Ari Bey, was the representative from Constantinople?"

"Evet." Janan Hanim nodded in agreement, and detecting undercurrents of disapproval, decided to say no more.

Munevver's grandfather's words came back to her. *"Courage. Even if you are afraid, act with courage and honor.*" She glanced at the other women in the room. Something told her that it would be better not to speak in front of them. She raised an eyebrow, and the Valide Sultan waved her hand to clear the room.

"Ari Bey visited my father at our home outside of London when he first came to oversee the Ottoman Exhibit. He brought a young boy named Davud with him. He had planned to enter him in one of the English boarding schools. Since Davud was the same age as my younger brother, Alexander, my father suggested he stay with us for one semester and then they could enter boarding school together. He would study with Alexander under his tutor's guidance, increase his English, and learn the sports he would be expected to know," Munevver explained.

"Evet." The Valide Sultan accompanied the word yes with an impatient gesture of her hands that made the jewel-encrusted rings on her fingers flash in the light, filtering through the lattices.

"At the end of the exhibition, Ari Bey visited my father again. Because my aunt Frederica and I had not been able to go to the exhibition, he brought us samples of things from several countries." Munevver choked back the tears. *They cannot know how precious his gifts have been.*

At the sound of silver soles striking the tiled floor, Janan Hanim pulled Munevver to her feet and whispered, "The sultan is coming." Following the other women, who bowed, Munevver sank into a low curtsey and waited to see if the other women would resume their seats.

Chapter 33

November 1854: A Second Arranged Marriage

The sultan moved silently across the room and settled on the throne on the elevated dais at the end of the room. He began to speak without looking at them. "Soon, a message will be delivered from Her Majesty, Queen Victoria. It will inform me that she believes there is an English subject here, in Constantinople, the widow of one of her lords. That lord wants his son's widow"—he paused as though loathe to continue—"and the heir she carries returned to him. I have been told Her Majesty, Queen Victoria, is asking me to locate her subject and return her to England." He stared at Munevver.

There was complete silence in the room, and Munevver felt the blood drain from her face. For a moment, she was afraid she would faint. *James's father must have appealed to the queen to find me.* She drew a shuddering breath, remembering his words that she had overheard: "I bought her. I sold the honor of my family name to get her—the crippled daughter of a merchant! She is to give me an heir."

Munevver faced the divan and, lowering her eyes, began to speak in a low voice, "I plan to leave for Aleppo in the morning. My uncle is there. He will provide for me."

"Aleppo may be far away, but it is still part of my empire." He scowled at her. "The message said you carry his heir. Is this true? Have you been blessed with Allah's greetings?"

Munevver forced herself to take small breaths as a feeling of outrage swept over her.

Janan Hanim whispered in her ear. "He is asking if you are enceinte."

The sultan was asking her if she was pregnant! "I have not been so blessed," she managed to reply.

The sultan pointed a finger at Ari, who had been summoned to the Imperial Palace. "You are a widower. You have not remarried?"

Munevver could not stop the gasp that escaped her. *Ari? But a different Ari. A thinner Ari who appeared unwell. What is he doing here?*

"No, my Padishah. I have not remarried." Mutinous thoughts swept over him. *You gave me a woman from your harem who had not found favor in your eyes or, more likely, had angered the Valide Sultan. You must have known she had the Gusel Vereni, the beautiful decline, when you gave her to me.* It was dangerous to even think such thoughts but he could not stop. *Surely the sultan knows that four sultans, and many others in the harem, have died from consumption. He must suspect that the close living conditions of the four-hundred-room harem with little ventilation are conducive to the spread of tuberculosis.* It was very dangerous to say more, but he could not refrain from speaking. "I looked after her during her long illness and have not felt the desire to marry again."

The sultan gestured in Munevver's direction. "She is not a Muslim, but it doesn't matter. You will marry this woman, and she will no longer be an English widow in my empire." He waited with his hands folded across his stomach.

"Yes, my Padishah." Ari covered his mouth with a snowy handkerchief to silence a cough as he bowed.

The sultan pointed at Munevver. "Will you marry him, or do you wish to be returned to your husband's father?"

"I will marry him," she whispered, knowing that the sultan had full control over her fate. Any option was better than being returned to James's father.

After the sultan had nodded, Ari asked what he knew was expected of him. "Is it your wish that we leave Constantinople?"

"Yes." The sultan sighed and studied the man before him closely. "It is best. Ordinarily, no one would question an Ottoman man about his wife, but the English have no manners." After a moment he added, "You have served the empire faithfully, as did your father and grandfather before you."

"I am always your obedient servant," Ari answered, struggling to keep the fear rising in his throat from his voice. It was not likely that the sultan would leave the choice of relocation to him. What would he decide? There was unrest on the Russian border. He shuddered at the thought of enduring the frigid winters in Russia. Germany was pressing for access to the Bosphorus. Although he spoke the most elegant German fluently, he would be treated, very subtly, of course, as an undesirable in Germany. There were the usual problems with Syria and Egypt. And then there was the seething turmoil that was Macedonia. At the heart of the Macedonian question were the provinces north of the Aegean Sea—Salonika, Monastir, and Kosovo—populated by Greeks, Turks, Albanians, Bulgarians, Serbs, and Vlachs (Rumanians). They had long wanted independence from the Ottoman Empire.

All old problems with no good solutions. Would he be engulfed in the past forever? Would he ever be able to follow his own interests? Interests similar to those of The Young Ottomans: to build a new country, a country that offered a better life for everyone.

"You will leave for Ankara within the hour. The fewer people who know she has been here the better. We can deal with them."

"Yes, my Padishah." He forced his face to be expressionless. He was being commanded to leave his beloved Constantinople to move to Ankara. In his mind, the best that could be said about Ankara was that it was the center of activity of The Young Ottomans—young men in the Ottoman Empire, most of whom had served as translators or in foreign embassies. They rejected Christian and European interference in affairs of the Ottoman Empire and wanted a modern, constitutional government. They supported freedom and a motherland. He paused and then risked asking, "What will be my duties in Ankara?"

"Officially, you will be my representative. You will serve as minister of finance." The sultan extended his hand slightly toward Ari. "You will be my eyes and ears. I am aware that many of The Young Ottomans have taken refuge in Ankara, and I have heard that they have been very busy." He paused and then said deliberately, "It may be that difficult times are coming, but the danger is not just from the inside." He motioned to them that the audience was over.

Ari's thoughts were racing. *The Young Ottomans. They have no clear-cut, ideological program beyond rejection of Christian-European interferences in the affairs of the Ottoman Empire and a desire for some form of constitutional government. Their concepts are of freedom and a motherland, and their thoughts and words are spread through poems, plays, and journalism.* He forced himself to consider his position. *Their ideas are my ideas, but if I am posted there as a representative of the sultan, will I be accepted?* The sultan's unusual mention of difficult times and that the danger was not just from the inside had sent chills through him. *What will life be like in Ankara?*

"When?" Munevver whispered to Ari as she grasped

the cold reality of the situation—another marriage arranged by a powerful man who controlled her destiny. It had been futile to argue with her father, and now, to avoid being returned to her despicable father-in-law, she had agreed to marry a man who did not love her, a man who clearly did not want to be married to her. "If we must leave today, when will we be married?" Maybe there would be time for her to find someone to help her. Who could she ask? Ryker was with the cavalry somewhere in the Crimea. There was no way to get word to her uncle in Aleppo.

For a brief moment, she thought of William. William Del Feld had been fiercely proud of the Norman ancestors who had invaded England and fought their way north to Yorkshire, where they settled in West Riding. They had been too stubborn to anglicize their name to Field. Tall, lean William with the unruly, auburn hair and hazel eyes. William, who had taught her to ride and to shoot and had never considered her clubfoot to be an impediment. It had always been William, her first and only love. Caroline's older brother had been the protector of both of them when they were young, and she had fallen in love with him when she was sixteen. Munevver straightened her shoulders. There would be no help from William. She didn't even know where he was or if he had married. No, there would be no rescue by William.

"We're already married." At her startled gasp, Ari continued. "Under Islamic Law, marriage is a contract between two people."

"Surely we need a license?" Munevver sputtered. "Perhaps a special license?"

"No license is required." Ari raised an eyebrow. "A declaration of intent by both people in the presence of two witnesses is enough to constitute a marriage contract." He took pity on her and added in a softer voice, "We did both say before my mother, the Valide Sultan, and the sultan that we agreed to be married. Didn't we?"

Hearing his words, Janan Hanim slipped four gold-bangle bracelets from her arm and slid them onto Munevver's. Silently, the Valide Sultan removed a double strand of deep-purple amethysts the size of Castelvetrano olives and placed them around Munevver's neck. There were no expressions of best wishes for the couple, no happy felicitations. Marriage was not about the happiness of two people. It was about the continuation of the family and the passing on of the jewels symbolized acceptance into the family.

"It happened so fast," Munevver whispered as she touched the gleaming jewels. Faster than the brief marriage ceremony that had united her and James in her father's austere chapel. James had not wanted to marry her either, but at least her family had been there for her, and Louisa had made her a bouquet of dried heather.

She glanced down at her empty hands and realized she was still wearing the wedding ring James had thrust into her hand, apparently unwilling to put it on her finger. How strange. She had been a widow of a man she detested for nearly two months and she had not removed her wedding band. She lifted her chin and, ignoring Ari, who was gathering up the papers that had been left on the low table, slipped the ring from her hand and tucked it into her skirt pocket. She had to forget the past, and to have a future, the Munevver she had once been had to disappear. The onset of this new phase of life was far from ideal, but she was determined the future would be as good as she could make it.

Chapter 34

December 1854: Ankara

"Ankara? It's an ancient, windswept city set on the edge of the Anatolian Plateau with dry, hot summers and frigid, snowy winters." Ari shook his head in disgust as the covered carriage sped them from the Seraglio to the Bosphorus, where they would find a caïque to take them back to his mother's yali. "Because it's one hundred twenty-five miles south of the Black Sea, you might expect some moderation of the climate, but no, that's not the case. Ankara is part of the infinite steppes, an endless, arid land with blistering-hot summers, artic winters, and constant, savage winds. There is no water supply other than wells. It's home to Angora goats and dissidents like The Young Ottomans, poets, dreamers, and discontents." Ari stifled a cough with his handkerchief, then pulled his coat collar up to protect himself from the wind. "Diplomates who may have displeased the Sublime Porte often found it prudent to flee to Ankara. They talk about establishing a Vatan, a homeland, and a government that rules by consensus." His voice was laced with cynicism. "Believe me. No one chooses to move to Ankara."

"Yes, but it was once an important part of the Silk Road, a northern route used by camel caravans to bring silk, china, spices, and gems from China to the Ottoman Empire." Munevver spoke soothingly, as though to a fractious child. "Just think. It took over a year by camel caravan to bring merchandise from China to the Ottoman Empire, and then it had to be shipped to England."

Ari sighed. "It was once the meeting point of north to south travel and east to west travel." Irritation sharpened his words. "At one time, it was a very important place, but transporting goods by ships has changed all of that."

As they hurried into his mother's home, Ari spoke in a low, urgent voice to his mother. "You must warn the servants to say nothing about Munevver being here. We will leave immediately to spare the risk of anyone else knowing."

"Where?" Janan Hanim asked softly and then added, "how will you go?"

"We'll take a ferry up the Bosphorus to the Black Sea port, Rumeli Kauagi, and then a steamship eastward to Inebolu. From there, we will travel south by carriage to Ankara."

"How long will the journey take?" Munevver could not resist asking as she thought of the time she had already spent traveling.

"At this time of the year, probably three or more days on the boat and then six or seven days on the road." Ari shook his head. "It all depends on the weather and the condition of the roads. Winter comes very early in the steppes."

Janan Hanim's mind had been busy. "You will need warm robes for the carriage ride to Ankara and warm clothing. It will be bitterly cold on that high plateau."

Ari nodded. "From what I've heard, the conditions are primitive there. It is best that we travel as quickly as possible. We will take as much as we can with us, but please arrange for a second carriage to bring Munevver's maid and the household things we will need."

"Where will we stay?" Munevver asked cautiously.

"We will have two nights on the steamer, or maybe more, and after that, we'll be traveling by carriage. We'll stay in hans. There will be a han of some sort one day's traveling distance apart, twenty or twenty-five miles, all along the route."

"Are they hotels?" Munevver tried to remember what she had read about travel in the East.

"They are old caravanserais—stone shelters built for the caravans traveling the Silk Road. Most are very primitive, but there is one, the Ayranci-Ecevit Han, about halfway there, that will be clean and comfortable."

Janan Hanim patted Munevver's arm. "Come, I will help you. You must bring your own bedding, and it is best if you bring your own food, too. The accommodations can be very bad."

Munevver stole a glance at her husband's face. *Accommodations? Will we have separate rooms?* She wished she had someone she could ask about the wedding night. No one had talked with her about marriage when she was living with her grandfather, and certainly no one had said a word about it after she came to her father's home. They probably assumed she would never marry.

No one had told her anything when it was announced that she was to be married to James. Not entirely true, she remembered. Ryker had told her something. He had told her that James was well known for attending the theaters that served as the haunts of sodomites and for frequenting London's infamous Marden Lane. When she did not seem to grasp what he was trying to tell her, he had bluntly said that James was a pederast, a sodomite who preferred young boys to women. Now there was no one to ask.

Perhaps, like James, Ari would not want to consummate the marriage. Maybe no man would ever want to consummate a marriage with a woman with a deformed foot. Maybe all men saw her as defective, an undesirable cripple. Well, maybe not William, but that was long ago, buried in the past.

Within little more than an hour of arriving back at Janan Hanim's yali, they were on a ferry heading north to Rumeli Kauagi. Surrounded by the smells of Istanbul—the brisk, salty tang of the Bosphorus, the smell of fish, and the hint of coffee and crusty, warm simit—Ari frowned as he stared back at the yali that had been the center of his life for as long as he could remember. He had been sent to school in Paris and London, but he had always come back to Constantinople, to his mother's yali on the Bosphorus.

As they moved swiftly up the Bosphorus, Munevver, wearing the modest, full, Turkish trousers that women wore throughout the Ottoman Empire, an embroidered tunic that reached to her knees, and a warm jacket that buttoned to her chin, shivered as she felt the lash of the Poyraz, the wind that blows from the northeast and forecasts the arrival of a cold, driving rain. With her hair covered with a çarşaf and the lower part of her face concealed by a peçe, a short veil covering, she had lost her identity. She was an Ottoman wife now. She reached up to touch the çarşaf that Janan Hanim had hastily taught her how to arrange so that it covered all of her hair.

Not knowing what to say to her new husband, she stood by the railing of the ferry and shivered as they passed Leander's Tower, the Maiden's Tower. She remembered the tragic love story of Leandros, who would swim across the Bosphorus each night, guided by the light of a bonfire lit by Hero, the lady he loved, until one night, a storm quenched the fire and Leandros perished, trying to swim to Hero. Across the narrow Bosphorus, she could see the cheerful cluster of the lights of Scutari. With its excellent harbor, it was the gateway for trade going to and from the Black Sea and for commerce with the East.

In silence, she watched the Levantine shearwater gulls as they glided low over the glistening waters of the Bosphorus, teaming with fish. Flying closely together, their black bodies reminded her of the black clouds at home when they were laden with snow. Then the gulls would bank away, and their white undersides would be revealed. Their soft cries, which sounded like babies mewling, filled the air, sending shivers down Munevver's back as her arms came up to cradle her body. Would she ever hold a baby in her arms? She shook herself.

Should she tell Ari that her husband had not consummated their marriage? In fact, he had not even spent the wedding night with her. Should she tell him that she was still a virgin? Would he believe her? Her shoulders slumped. It was unlikely that the subject would come up. Ari had married her at the sultan's directive. He had always been kind to her, but he had never acted in any way that suggested he thought of her as anything other than a member of her father's family. No, she would say nothing.

Munevver straightened her back, determined not to be defeated by her husband's silent tribute to the home he loved. He might not be able to accept it now, but they had to go forward. They had no choice. The moment she had appeared at his mother's home, she had cost him his career, his home, and his beloved Constantinople. She had made him an exile. He would likely never forgive her, but they had to live together. They had to make it in a world foreign to both of them. If there was nothing else between them, she vowed that there would always be honesty. No things left unsaid. No insinuations. Her grandfather had taught her that, despite the pain, it was always easier to deal with the hard truth.

"I know we are traveling north to the Black Sea, but

the current appears to be very strong. It seems to be pushing us back." When he did not respond, she added, "Is it the wind affecting the current?"

Ari shook himself, as though to rid himself of a heavy burden. "The Bosphorus has two currents. One current, the surface current, runs from the north to the south. It is a colder, less saline current coming from the Black Sea. The second current runs south to north. It is a rich, warm, saline rope of a river forty meters below the surface. The wind, when it's strong, affects the surface current."

"I recall that it was once called the Hellespont. Xerxes, the son of Persian King Darius, built a bridge of boats across it for the second attack on Greece." She paused, remembering her grandfather describing horrific battles as they sat in his library before a fire at the end of the day in the peaceful tranquility of his Yorkshire home.

Ari turned his back on the view of his mother's yali disappearing from sight and stared at his new wife. "You know Persian history?" He did not try to disguise the surprise in his voice.

"Yes. I think I told you that I lived with my grandfather and grandmother as a child. My grandmother taught me to embroider, simple remedies for illnesses, and how to speak French. My grandfather taught me languages, history, and geography as they had affected the rise and fall of empires and the fortunes of traders," Munevver explained.

"He also taught you how to play chess," Ari said with

a slight smile. He took a step closer to his wife and, in a marked departure from customary Ottoman etiquette, asked a brutally direct question. "How did it happen that you lived with your grandparents and not your parents?"

Munevver forced herself to take a deep breath. Her grandparents knew the story, and her father, but she had never told it to anyone else. Not even to her best friend, Caroline, nor William. This was different. This man was her husband. He had agreed to marry her in a most difficult situation.

Her voice shook slightly as she felt compelled to answer his question. "When my mother was told she had given birth to a crippled baby, a daughter with a deformed foot, she refused to see me. She couldn't bear the shame. She insisted that I be sent away, to the country, to a home for abandoned babies. No one could know that she had produced a defective child. My father agreed, and I was given to a *Baby Farmer* who put me in a home for orphans, poor children, and bastards in Yorkshire." Munevver saw the question in his eyes. "It is in the northern part of England, far from London. Fortunately, my grandfather learned what his son, my father, had done before I was *rehomed*. He found me and brought me to live with him and Grandmother."

Ari frowned but made no comment on what she had said. Instead, he asked another direct question. "How did it happen that you came to live at your father's home in Surrey?"

Another painfully direct question. Munevver struggled to keep her voice steady. "My father found out that his longtime assistant had been diverting funds for his own use. He knew Grandfather had taught me his business practices." She tried to keep the anger from her voice. "You have to understand. My father uses people like chess pieces. When my mother died soon after Alexander's birth, he brought his younger sister, my aunt Frederica, to his home to look after his children and manage the household. So, when he needed inexpensive clerical help, he brought me back from Yorkshire to assist him." She looked at Ari directly and said in a flat tone, "He talks of the time when Ryker will join him as a partner, but I work for him. He has always made it clear that I will never be more than an office worker."

"Strange. When I met Ryker, he talked of joining the cavalry. He dreamed of being part of the Light Brigade. Has he become your father's partner?" Ari inquired.

"Ryker was much braver than me. He left home and joined the navy just before England declared war on Russia." She answered his unasked question. "You don't have to buy a commission to join the navy."

What finally prompted you to flee? The question had been burning in his mind since the first time he saw her in the Valide Sultan's salon, but he could not bring himself to ask her. Whatever the reason, it must have been drastic for her to leave her family and travel with just her maid to a foreign country. "We will be able to board the steamship as soon as we reach the Black Sea. There will be food of some sort provided. I'll ask to have it served in our cabin."

Munevver's heart began to pound. *Our cabin? One*

cabin?

"I suggest we sleep in our traveling clothes. The bunks are not very comfortable . . . or clean."

Munevver nodded. She would be safe for two days, but then she would have to tell him.

Chapter 35

Exiled in Ankara

Despite what Ari had told her about the harsh conditions of Ankara, Munevver was unprepared for the savage Asiatic winds that buffeted her as she rode in the open carriage to her new home. Three thousand feet above sea level, all she could see was rolling uplands, out of which rose jagged mountain ranges, cream-colored from the yellow gypsum deposits in them with the occasional blue flash of a chromium deposit. In the distance, she perceived the sharp edges of the Ilgaz Dag mountain range. When she had asked Ari if there was a pass through the mountains, he had said that they would have to go over the mountain to get to Ankara.

It seemed as though they had been riding in the small, springless, wooden carriage for days before they came to the Ayranci-Ecevit Han. From the outside, it appeared clean and well maintained. "I have reserved a room and asked for a hot bath to be brought to the room as soon as possible," Ari said in a low voice so that the driver could not hear him.

"Thank you." Munevver sighed, savoring the thought of sinking into a hot bath after days of traveling. She would wash her hair first and then scrub every inch of her body with the lavender soap she always carried with her. It did not have the lush scent of Turkish rose soap, but it reminded her of her grandfather's home.

Later, she slipped the white nightgown of finest lawn Aunt Frederica had given her over her head and climbed into the bed that she had covered with the bedding she'd brought with her from Constantinople. *Now I wait and wonder. Shall I tell him that I am still a virgin? Will he believe me? Will he care?* A sudden memory of Janan Hanim's last words stirred a feeling of uneasiness. "Happiness comes not from what we possess but from what we allow others to possess." *What did she mean?*

At the scrape of the door opening, Munevver shivered and pulled the covers up to her shoulders. Sitting rigidly on the side of the bed, Ari began to speak in English. "I have been thinking about our situation. If we wait until after you have your monthly bleeding, we will know that any child you bear is my child." When she did not respond, he continued. "It is the only way that I can know for sure."

She sat up and began to speak in crystal-sharp English. "It is one way. It is not the only way, but since it is your suggestion, we will abide by it." She blew out the candle on the rough table beside the bed and turned her back to him, burying her face in the soft sleeve of her nightgown. She would not let him see her cry. She had never let her father see her cry when she was hurt, and she wouldn't let this man see the pain his austere words had caused.

As soon as they were on their way again in the wooden wagon, Ari began to speak softly in English. "You said it is not the only way." He waited, and when it was evident that she did not intend to say anything, he asked directly, "How else could we know definitely?"

"You could have asked me if I was with child."

"Yes, but your husband died just a short time ago." Ari hesitated. "It's possible you could be pregnant and not know it yet."

"Is that so important to you?" Munevver snapped. *What is the matter with him? Yes, James had died just weeks ago, but he had been in the Crimea for months!* Suddenly, she became rigid with fury. Her husband of just a few days was implying that she had been promiscuous while James was away. She moved as close to the side of the wagon as she could.

"According to Circassian beliefs, every man is part of a clan. When he has a son, he creates a new extension of the clan, a new source of strength for his people. To father a son means to contribute to the continuation of his family, to carry out his rightful role in history. Yes, it's important."

Munevver had not responded, so Ari continued. "I am an Ottoman citizen, but I am not Turkish. I am Circassian, and I tend to follow their beliefs and practices. My people came from Circassia, north of the Black Sea. A long time ago, a great-grandfather, a brilliant student who knew five languages and had the manners of a diplomat, was given to the sultan. He was educated in the Palace School, sent to London and Paris for more advanced education, and then served the sultan, as has every firstborn son of my family since that time."

Ari paused. "They were all well-educated men who had traveled extensively. They knew the changes that other countries were making and they introduced new ideas. Some sultans listened and tried to carry out reforms. There would be progress, and then another sultan would not honor the reforms and the empire would slip backward. I have served the sultan faithfully, but I have also been aware of the hopes for a better future that are circulating through the empire, especially in Ankara." He hesitated and then added, "It will be my sons who bring about that better future."

Munevver made a decision. There was no advantage in considering Ari as her enemy. She would not let him see how his words had hurt her. They had to survive. Trying for a neutral voice, she asked, "You are not devastated at the change, of being sent to such a faraway place?"

Ari appeared to relax. "Change is coming to the Ottoman Empire. We may win this Crimean War, but it is not really our victory. Yes, we are sending our soldiers. They are poorly trained, ill-equipped, uneducated peasants, but they are loyal. They are the front line. They fight valiantly and they are being massacred. It is not just our soldiers who are giving their lives for the empire . . . our navy is being destroyed, too." He paused and then continued in a husky voice. "It is the French and the English who are carrying the brunt of the fighting. They are pushing the Russians out of Ottoman territory." Ari shrugged. "Not entirely because of their love for the Ottoman Empire. They know that an independent Ottoman Empire provides greater safety for their shipping and trading interests, at least for the immediate future."

He pulled the robe closer around them in an effort to stave off the bite of the wind. "After this war is over, we may still have a hold on our provinces, but we will have lost land, men, ships, and weapons. We will be even more deeply in debt than we were before the war." Ari shuddered. "I fear that we will lose the Ottoman Empire in my lifetime." He muttered, "It seems to be my destiny to see what I love lost."

Forgetting, for the moment, that among the people of the Middle East, touching was not customary, Munevver reached for Ari's hand under the carriage robe. Ari squeezed her hand briefly before he withdrew his hand and said with a rueful grin, "Or it may be my destiny to make a new life in Ankara." He gestured to the twin hills in the distance with the remnants of ancient fortresses still visible atop the hills and humble houses clinging to rocky outcroppings of shale extending down the slopes.

As they drove through the center of the town, Ari pointed out a bazaar with narrow streets, each devoted to one item—rugs, copperware, spices, food, and rough woolens. "Some things, such as milk, eggs, butter, and yogurt, will be brought to the house each day, but you will need to go to the shops for meat and vegetables." Munevver was soon to learn that shopping for food was a minor problem compared to having very little water, only what was supplied by a well that served several households, and almost no wood to cook their food or heat their home.

After pausing for a moment to stare at the house Ari had managed to rent with its lower half constructed of stone, the upper half of rough timbers, and the windows covered with wooden lattices, Munevver stepped inside when Ari held the door open for her. The room was long and low and appeared to serve as the reception area. Four doors opened off it, and at one side, a steep, wooden staircase led up to what she assumed was the sleeping area. A quick glance revealed traditional, built-in storage cabinets designed to hold the mattresses and bedding during the day, and a round, cast-iron stove. To Munevver's surprise, instead of the traditional, low divan around three sides of the room, the room was furnished with European-style furniture: a sofa, upholstered chairs, and a wooden dining table with matching chairs. At the back of the house was a cooking area and a small washing room with a stone floor, a spigot, and a cabinet de toilette.

The house was different from any she had ever lived in, but her mind acknowledged the logic of the arrangement. It was designed for survival in a harsh climate, but one item puzzled her. A small, highly polished but empty table stood at the end of the salon. It took a moment for her to recognize its function. According to what she had been told, when returning home each evening and entering the harem, the ladies' part of the home, an Ottoman gentleman would deposit a gift on a table that was always placed at the end of the salon. No honorable husband would come home empty-handed. The gift might be as small as a twist of sweetmeats or even a poem. To fail to do this was to imply that he was rejecting his wife.

To cover her momentary embarrassment, Munevver stooped to pat the sleek, white cat with oval-shaped, amber eyes ringed in green, waiting by the door. "What a strange-looking cat. Its fur is so silky. What's her name?"

"She doesn't have a name. She will be known by whatever name you choose."

"Opal. Her name is Opal." Munevver smiled. She had a friend in this new world.

Within days of arriving, they had settled into a routine. Ari was away from early in the morning until late in the afternoon, working as a finance minister with the local branch of the Ottoman Government. Although he tried to make friends with the "Young Turks" seeking ways to modernize their country without destroying it, they did not trust him and rejected his overtures of friendship.

For Munevver, the days were occupied by routine household chores, trudging to the shops, accompanied by Fayne, in search of whatever meat and vegetables she could find in the stalls along the center of the city and cooking their evening meal. As the weather turned bitterly cold, Munevver's focus was on finding fuel—wood, if she was lucky, but more likely, the foul-smelling, dried cow dung that was the only alternative fuel available.

As Munevver thought of the elegant, young wives who had left their aristocratic Constantinople families to join their husbands in Ankara, she was grateful that her grandmother had insisted she learn how to cook. The young wives clung to the tradition of meeting in the afternoon for tea in each other's homes. They spent most of the time complaining bitterly about the lack of heat, food, servants, and a hammam. Perhaps more than anything, they missed the luxurious, restorative features of a welcoming hammam.

Nothing had prepared them for the conditions they now faced in Ankara. They had spent their lives in luxury, their every wish taken care of by servants. Now they had to do their own shopping, cleaning, and cooking. She knew they would be visiting her tomorrow, and most of the conversation would be devoted to their unhappiness with life in Ankara.

While her hands were busy checking the supplies in the tiny alcove that served as a kitchen, the beginning of a plan to help them began to form in her mind, and Munevver pulled the largest pot she had from the corner. *Every day, each wife spends hours marketing for food and wood. They ruin their hands chopping onions and garlic, and then they each use precious fuel to cook the evening meal that has to be ready when their husbands return. What if we combine our efforts and make the evening meal in one home? Only one woman will have to chop onions. Only one woman will have to go to the market. We can rotate days, but how can we overcome the difficulty of finding meat to buy?*

As she began to think through her plan, she heard Lala, the village woman Ari had hired to come for a few hours a day to do the heavy work, slip through the door.

Each villager had a small bit of land, a few hens, a lamb, and a goat, and everyone in the family worked hard to ensure the survival of the family. _Lala may have access to meat._ Perhaps she could convince Lala to donate meat to the common meal in exchange for a bowl of prepared dinner for her family. When she tried to explain the plan in her precise Turkish, Lala ignored her. Munevver switched to Arabic and was pleased at the woman's slight nod. Munevver explained that tomorrow she wanted to make lamb and lentil stew. Could the woman bring a small piece of lamb?

When Lala shook her head, Munevver's spirits dropped.

"Sucuk," the woman offered softly.

"Sucuk? Sausage?" Munevver beamed. "Yes, yes!" _It will probably be goat sausage, but it will flavor the stew._ "Purslane?" she asked, hoping the woman dried the green herb that grew wild along the road. It would add a lemony tang to the stew.

Lala nodded and then glanced at the empty shelf in the kitchen and the empty drying ropes strung near the ceiling. She motioned to the shelf and, speaking in Arabic said, "Beans, bulgar, salt, nohut, olive oil, raisins, and spices."

Beans? Her grandmother had never taught her how to cook them, but she remembered seeing the women in the cottages soaking them overnight. She pointed to the ropes and listened carefully as the woman began to indicate the different spaces on the ropes. "Peppers, onions, garlic, tomatoes, and okra." She gestured toward the back of the house. "Carrots, potatoes, cabbage, turnips, parsnips, squash."

"A cold cellar? Is there a cold area to store vegetables?" Cooking here would be different. Munevver would have to learn to use the available material—bulgar when there was no rice, dried tomatoes and peppers, goat meat instead of lamb, and dried anchovies to replace the succulent lüfer from the Mediterranean. So many changes, but she would adapt. She had to survive, and someday, she would return to Yorkshire.

But not today. Today, she had a lot of preparations to make. She had invited three of the wives who had traveled from Constantinople to Ankara to be with their husbands to spend the afternoon. They had become good friends after Munevver had taught them how to soak beans in water with a pinch of soda overnight so that they would cook more quickly and become more tender. She had also suggested they add chopped rosemary or dried salsify, which grew wild along the road, to add flavor to the stews they were making. According to the ladies, their husbands had been surprised and pleased.

Munevver looked around the salon. During the day, the room was her haremlik, a clean, comfortable place to entertain the women who came to spend the afternoon. In the evening, it became the selamlik, where Ari would receive male callers . . . if they ever came.

As soon as the ladies had settled themselves rather awkwardly on the couch and had taken out their needlework, Munevver took out the sock she was knitting, as she had done for much of her life.

"You knit socks for your husband?" Pembe asked as she smoothed the delicate, three-inch-wide, gold-embroidered edging she was adding to a hand towel.

"No." Munevver answered slowly, "In my country, there are many soldiers and seamen who were wounded in the war. Some who returned have no families to help them. My aunt Frederica and I used whatever free time we had to knit warm socks for them." She glanced around the room. "The winters are not as cold as they are here, but they are constantly damp with snow and rain." When no one responded, she added, "Many of the soldiers have no homes." She cringed as she said, "They sleep on the streets."

"We will have wounded men returning soon." Hatice picked up a ball of yarn from Munevver's workbag. "After each Turko-Russian War, there have been men with amputations, trying to survive on the streets. They are entitled to an allowance, but it is always late or never paid."

Sari, an older woman, joined the conversation. "I have heard about a doctor, Dr. Abdullah Bey, in Constantinople. He talks about the need to help our soldiers when they are ill or wounded. He and some other doctors have been talking about a Society for Aiding Wounded and Ailing Ottoman Soldiers."

"You said he is a doctor in Constantinople?" Munevver thought of the strict hierarchy of medical professionals in the capitol city. There would be many well-trained foreign physicians for the upper class. There would be local physicians for those who could afford them, but there would be few doctors for returning soldiers, most of them peasant conscripts from Anatolia.

Sari hesitated. "His name was Dr. Karl Eduard Hammerschmidt when he was practicing medicine in Austria, but after the Austrian revolt in 1848, he came to Istanbul as a refugee. When the sultan refused the tsar's demand that all refugees who had escaped from Hungary and Poland be returned to Russia, Dr. Hammerschmidt accepted Ottoman citizenship and took the name of Dr. Abdullah Bey. Now, he is serving in the Ottoman Army, providing care for the sick and wounded on the battlefield."

"Amazing," Munevver murmured. She paused and then added, "The Turkish soldiers are fortunate to have a doctor who knows how to use anesthesia for battlefield amputations. The French and Russians both use chloroform, but the English do not." She gave an unladylike snort.

"Their reasoning was that the Iron Duke, Wellington, did not use anesthesia during the war with Napoleon, and there was no reason to alter that practice."

The normally shy Pembe spoke up, "I have a brother serving with the Ottoman Army. I haven't heard from him in a long time." She frowned as she studied the intricate, golden embroidery she was holding and then laid it aside. "We have enough embroidered linens to last through the next generation. We could all knit socks for our soldiers who will be returning."

"I have a brother serving in the English Navy." Munevver nodded approvingly at Pembe. "We were told they would be home for Christmas"—she hurried to clarify the time—"before the end of the year." She paused. "The last I heard, it had been agreed that they had to take Sevastopol before they could come home." She looked around the room. "Winter came very fast this year. All the soldiers will be so cold."

"It's agreed then," Sari said crisply, and then made a revolutionary statement. "From now on, we will spend our afternoons knitting warm things for our country's soldiers."

Hatice looked around the group, and then, with her eyes cast down said, "I would like to help knit for the soldiers, but I have to make a layette for my baby and I am very slow at sewing and knitting." She wrung her hands. "So much to get ready—long dresses, nightgowns, chemizes, blankets, and napkins. So many things that must be sewn, and then there are sacques and caps that must be knitted or crocheted."

"That is wonderful news. A new life!" Munevver glanced around the room. "We will help you." She paused as she remembered the sparse selection of material in the shops. "I will ask Ari Bey's mother to send us material—flannel, lawn, and pique. White, of course."

Sari hesitated. "We will need wool and silk yarn for the baby sacques and hats. Could you ask her to send some of that, too?"

"It is too much to ask," Hatice replied. "I am not part

of her family. She doesn't even know me."

"We are a family," Munevver stated firmly. "We will work together to make one layette, and then we will each use it for our babies." She thought of the soft silk and wool yarn that they would use for the tiny clothes and then looked down at her hands. Her fingers were rough from the cold and the hard work that she was not accustomed to. She had used all of the rose-scented hand cream she had slipped into her trunk and now had nothing. The yarn would catch on the roughness of her fingers. She was probably not the only one with rough fingers, but what could she do about it?

Her grandmother would have known. She had made her own hand cream. Munevver closed her eyes and was transported back to her grandmother's still room. She had watched her grandmother make many different hand creams. Some were scented with lavender and some with almond oil or orange shavings. Always, there would be some kind of oil, usually almond oil, and some kind of fine, white wax, such as bee's wax from honeycombs, and always Spermaceti—wax from the sperm whale. The fragrance would usually be provided by orange water.

What could she use that was available here and not costly? Munevver frowned ruefully as she thought of Ari's government allotments, which were always in arrears, and the steadily diminishing supply of gold coins Aunt Frederica had sewn into the seams of her petticoats. How long would they have to last? Should she save out enough to get back to Yorkshire? No. She had made her decision, and now she must live with the consequences, here in this unforgiving land. She couldn't waste money on hand creams.

The next day, Munevver completed the daily tasks and then moved resolutely to the kitchen and began to assemble her supplies. There was no silky almond oil and no spermaceti. It would have to be the heavy olive oil that the market offered and wax from the honeycomb. She would melt them together and use a little rice flour to thicken the mixture. It wouldn't be ideal, and she had nothing to scent it. Suddenly, she thought of the rosemary Aunt Frederica always tucked into trunks to prevent moth damage. Maybe there would be some in the crevasses of her trunk. She would look later.

As they began to pack up the ragout that they had made together, Sari put her hand on Munevver's arm. "A young family has moved into the house next to me. The man's name is Ahmet Kaan and the lady's name is Nasrin. There is a young son and an infant daughter. I asked her to join us, but she said her son is not well. He has a croaking cough. I wondered if you knew any way to help?"

"I'll go with you. Let me get some herbs that may help," Munevver suggested. She paused for a moment as she considered the local customs. She would be going there in the afternoon in the company of another woman. That was acceptable, but how would she come back? It would be dark in an hour, and no woman should be out on the street alone. "I must leave a note for my husband." And hope that he will come to escort her home.

The barking cough that met her ears as soon as they stepped into the tiny home alerted Munevver. She had heard the sound of croup among the workers' families on her grandfather's estate. The cold, damp winters of the North were known to cause croup among the very young.

She knelt down beside the mother, Nasrin, who was clutching her two-year-old son in her arms, rocking him while her gaze darted to the infant, fussing in a beautifully carved, old cradle. Even in the dim light, Munevver could see the tinge of blue around the toddler's mouth. He was not getting enough air. She touched his forehead with her hand. Fever, too.

Speaking calmly, she told the mother how to make willow bark tea from the bundle of herbs she had brought with her. *It will reduce his fever*, she thought as she held out her arms for the child. As soon as the woman had poured the boiling water over the herbs, Munevver showed her how to use a shawl to make a tent over the still-steaming kettle so that it covered the child's head and shoulders. The steam would make it easier for him to breathe.

As she held the cup of sweetened tea to the child's lips, she began to tell him a story about a little boy. When he began to cough, she slipped a small chip of horehound candy between his lips and told him to suck it very slowly.

After what seemed like hours, she heard the sound of Ari and another man talking in the doorway of the house and felt a sense of relief. Munevver had left Ari a message, telling him where she would be, and had desperately hoped that he would come. The other man must be the woman's husband, Ahmet Kaan. An old,

Kurdish name, if she remembered correctly. She knew from what Ari had told her that he was one of the leaders of the "Young Turks," and he had made it known that Ari was a representative of the Constantinople Palace and not to be trusted. As Munevver continued to tell the story, which was holding the little boy's interest, she heard Ari saying, in very formal Turkish, that he had come to escort his wife home when she was ready to leave.

At the sound of the two male voices at her door, Nasrin had drawn her scarf over her hair and held the edge over her face. Now her words tumbled out—Omar had been dying, unable to breathe. Then Munevver Hanim had come, and now Omar was breathing easier and there were fewer bouts of the horrible coughing. She would be eternally grateful to Munevver Hanim for saving her son's life. For a long moment, Ahmet and Ari remained silent, staring at each other, and then Ahmet motioned for Ari to enter.

Chapter 36

February 1855: The Reading Circle

Munevver had been told that the Turkish form of good morning was, *the sun has started its journey,* but the winter days in Ankara began in darkness. Each morning, Munevver got up early to prepare Ari's breakfast—at least two glasses of strong Russian tea, cheese, olives, a dried fig replacing the luscious, ripe figs of Constantinople, and any honey or jam she could find. She knew he missed the fragrant, warm rolls of home, but the only bread available was so dense that it was rock-hard the next day. She had given up trying to find any rolls, and now she toasted bread she had drizzled with olive oil and seasoned with herbs over the open flame for his breakfast.

By early morning, she had tidied the house, accepted delivery of yogurt and eggs from the man who came to the door, and dressed for her daily trip to the village to search for meat, vegetables, and the rare bit of fruit. Munevver sighed, anticipating that the only choice would be between dates and figs. Memories of the crisp apples of Yorkshire, and even better, the taste of ripe strawberries smothered in cream, teased her as she pulled her scarf closer to protect her face from the biting, dry wind. Once those chores were done, she prepared for the afternoon visit of the women, the unhappy expatriates from Constantinople whom she had come to think of as friends. It was a rare day that two or three did not come.

As the cold, dark days of winter dragged on, the women had gathered earlier and earlier each afternoon in one or another's home to knit and talk, but lately, they had been silent and listless. "We used to play backgammon on days like this in my mother's harem," Pembe murmured wistfully.

"Oh, home." Sari stared at her idle hands. "We would start the day in the hammam. Then we would dress and have lunch—tender, juicy lamb, crisp börek with its melted, white-cheese filling, velvety eggplant baked in olive oil, an assortment of olives, and always fruit at the end. So delicious!" She looked at the stove where the communal pan of beans, onions, garlic, carrots, shredded cabbage, and dried herbs was simmering. "After lunch, a miradjus, a storyteller, would come." Sari added, "She would recite the most enchanting stories for us while we did needlework."

"My younger sister, Christianna, was always restless when she had to sit embroidering during a long afternoon." Munevver hesitated. She had never shared any information about her family or life in England, and she did not know how they would respond.

"Christianna. That is a lovely name." Hatice's eyes brightened with interest. "What does she look like?"

"She does not resemble me at all. She has beautiful, golden hair and dark-blue eyes." Somehow that did not capture Christianna. Did she dare tell these elegant ladies from Constantinople that her little sister preferred horses to people? She cleared her throat and continued hesitantly. "We did not have storytellers come to us, but quite often I would read stories, novels, to my aunt Frederica and Christianna while they did some kind of needlework."

"Modern novels?" Pembe glanced up from her knitting.

"Yes, modern ones. The last one I read was *Bleak House* by Charles Dickens."

"It sounds sad." Pembe frowned.

"It's about a family inheritance that is devoured by legal costs," Munevver explained, omitting the part about the suffering and humiliation. "There are other novels that you might like better." Munevver ran a list through her mind: *The Scarlet Letter*, too sinful. *Madam Bovary*, infidelity would not be a good topic for discussion. *Ruth*, fallen woman with illegitimate child. *No. None of those will do.* "I know two you might enjoy. *Jane Eyre* was written by a woman, Charlotte Brontë, in 1847. Later, she wrote *Villette*, the story of a woman who flees England and a tragic past to become an instructor in a French boarding school. Another novel that everyone is talking about is Alexandre Dumas's, *The Queen's Necklace*. It's a mystery that was published in 1850 about an incident in the 1780 court of King Louis XVI."

"They all sound interesting," Sari said with a smile, "but they are probably written in English or maybe French."

"I could translate them into Turkish if you are really interested. Then we could take turns reading aloud."

"How soon?" Pembe asked softly.

"I have a copy of *Jane Eyre* with me." She paused, remembering that the English public had been highly critical of the hero, Mr. Rochester's, numerous liaisons. *What will the pampered and sequestered Ottoman ladies think of a story about a young woman who has to find a way to earn her living? One who falls in love with a man who has an insane wife locked away in the attic?*

They were looking at her expectantly. She hesitated. She would have to open her trunk again to get the book. Could she resist the temptation to take out the dance card with its tiny pencil that she had hidden in the lining of the trunk? Could she hold it in her hand? Search for the pages on which William had written his name? It was too late to back out. "I can have a translation of the first chapter of *Jane Eyre* ready for next week, if you like." *Isn't Ari always saying that the world is changing? If he is right, it is changing for these women, too.*

Chapter 37

December 1854: Ankara

When Ari returned late that afternoon, he seemed lost in thought as he nibbled the salted sunflower seeds Munevver had arranged on the low table by his chair. He looked up and smiled. "No matter how limited our supplies, you always manage to have a few tasty bits." He lifted his evening glass of raki in a silent salute.

"Has it been an unusual day?" she asked quietly. It was both Christmas Eve and her birthday, but Ari had made no mention of either. During the long day, Munevver had not been able to prevent her thoughts from turning to Christmas at home. The house would have been scrubbed, waxed, and polished from top to bottom. Mrs. Coates would have been making puddings for weeks. Lord George would have delegated the selection of the perfect tree to his steward. Aunt Frederica would have conferred with Mrs. Coates about the menus. Foster would have visited the wine cellar and brought up delicious wines.

For a moment, a sense of depression threatened to overwhelm her. Later, when Ari was asleep, she would very carefully select one memory to relive. Although she wanted to deny it, she knew it would be the memory of her seventeenth birthday. She would let herself relive those magic moments when William had signed her dance card for two dances and then taken her into dinner on his arm. The evening when he had said he would speak to her father the morning after her eighteenth birthday. He had given her a whole year to wait and dream.

Ari hesitated, choosing his words carefully. "Ahmet Bey invited me to a meeting today."

"Oh?" As far as she knew, Ari had never been included in the meetings of the men who seemed to be the most politically active.

"He said that his son was doing well and thanked us."

Munevver felt a blush cover her cheeks. Ari had just given her the most beautiful gift. He had acknowledged her as an asset, not just a burden thrust on him by the sultan to solve a problem. She waited, but when he did not continue, she decided that from now on, she would operate not as the submissive piece of property her father deemed her to be but as a full partner. "What was the meeting about?"

"It seems some men from England will be coming to Ankara in a few months."

"What is the purpose of their visit?" Without realizing it, Munevver had slipped into her father's direct mode of analyzing new information.

"When there is blood in the water, sharks travel great distances." Ari clipped out the old adage and then continued more gently, "On the surface, it appears to be the same reason as always. In the thirties, it was just the Russians who called the Ottoman Empire the Sick Man of Europe and offered suggestions for how the sick man should be divided up. Since then, there have been more who are eager to seize parts of the Ottoman Empire, but it is hard to know what lies behind their zeal." Ari shook his head. "At least with the Russians, we know what they want—ports on the Black Sea, the straits, and Constantinople." He moved restlessly in his chair. "We don't know what these unknown visitors want."

"What has changed?" Munevver had listened to the wives repeat their husbands' views of the political situation in the Ottoman Empire, but she had never asked Ari what he thought.

"They are aware that this latest Turko–Russian War—the war the Europeans call the *War in the East* and the soldiers call the *Crimean War*—is hurting us badly. We have lost an enormous number of men." Ari hesitated. "As you know, the greatest part of our army is made up of peasants from Anatolia." His voice, raspy from constant coughing, now held a note of despair. "There will be many, many widows when this war is over. Who will help them? Who will tend the farms? Who will produce the crops we depend on for revenue? How will we replenish the army? Where will the men come from? Ships? How will we ever rebuild our navy? The Russians have ironclad steamships. We have old, wooden ships and must depend on the power of the wind. They have ammunition that explodes on impact and causes great fires. We have heavy cannonballs with a very short range that cause little damage. We must adapt or perish, but where will we get the money?" He groaned. "We have no choice. We will have to continue to placate the European powers. Even before the war, they controlled our finances, and now they will determine our future."

"These men who are coming . . . do you know who they are?" When Ari did not respond, she asked again, "Are they government representatives or individual businessmen? Whoever they are, what is it that they want to accomplish?" Munevver's mind was racing. *Not an increase in the current commerce. England already has a favorable trade agreement in place—the 1838 Anglo–Ottoman Commercial Treaty. The Ottomans export raw silk, madder roots, raisins, wool, and wheat, and they import English cotton cloth, woolens, hardware, cutlery, refined sugar, iron, and steel.* She remembered her grandfather telling her that from the 1830s on, the sultan had been forced to balance the European powers' efforts to interfere in the Ottoman Empire against their trade—trade that he depended on to survive.

Munevver lowered her eyes, unwilling to have Ari read what she was thinking. *They may be coming to ferment internal strife. They may be engaged in destroying the Ottoman Empire from within by encouraging uprisings against the policy of the Sublime Porte as they had during the long Greek insurgence. Always there will be some advantage in it for them, some financial gain. What does this barren part of the Ottoman Empire have that will produce a profit?*

"The official reason for their visit is to strengthen ties with the people of the Ottoman Empire." Ari's voice was carefully neutral.

"Interesting that they are coming to Ankara and not Constantinople or Edirne or Izmir," Munevver commented carefully.

"They have probably heard that there are men in Ankara who want changes in the internal affairs of the Ottoman Empire, men who claim they want to modernize it." Ari hesitated before adding, "There are a few younger ones who have been outspoken about wanting changes in the military, too. The present system of recruitment by levy of male populations between the ages of twenty and twenty-five is corrupt and hated by the people. A well-to-do draftee can send a substitute; pay someone to take his place. Considering that otherwise he would have to serve six years in active duty and then serve seven years in the reserves, many will do anything to avoid the conscription."

"Yes. Even here, in Ankara, I have heard the women grumble about their sons being seized and forced into the army. It is a harsh sentence for widows. Without sons, how can they tend the animals, plant wheat, and harvest the crops?"

Ari nodded. "Then there is another factor to consider. I fear the Europeans have been misled by the sultan's tours of the empire." He waited until he could catch his breath after a paroxysm of coughing that resulted in specks of blood on the handkerchief he used to cover his mouth. "They are calling them *Tours of Love*," he scoffed as he began to pace the small room. His words came out angry and clipped. "They view the sultan as weak, unable, or unwilling to fight fiercely to defend the empire. It's not just this sultan. It started with Mahmud II when he toured some of the cities. Officially, the tours were to celebrate the sultan's birthday, but the real reason was to increase the visibility of the empire's ruler. The Sublime Porte wanted to gain approval of the population and the usual method—building mosques, schools, hospitals, and fountains—did not impress the people in the provinces.

"Sultan Abdulmejid's tour, the 1846 tour, was called the Tour of Love, love for his subjects. He gave money to churches, synagogues, and holy places. He emphasized equality between the three main religious groups in the Ottoman Empire: Christians, Muslims, and Jews. He used the father/child metaphor—my love and justice are strong for all and all are my sons. He emphasized education and public health and built schools and large hospitals for the poor. Wherever he went, he had doctors inoculate children against smallpox, and he gave them small gifts of money after they were inoculated. To some extent, it was successful. Gradually, the metaphor of father and child belonging to the place where they first saw the sun had changed to belonging to the same state, a common fatherland. It was the beginning of the concept of one country instead of the present Millet system of self-governing religious communities organized under their own laws and led by their religious leaders—in essence, individual provinces within the Ottoman Empire." He threw up his hands. "*Tours of Love*. They did irreparable damage. They made us appear weak to the world!"

When Munevver did not speak, Ari dropped to the divan where she was sitting and asked, "What do you think is really prompting them to come to Ankara . . . now?"

Startled by this direct question, so different from Ari's usual behavior, Munevver felt cold all over. There must be tremendous anxiety among the young men if he had brought himself to ask her opinion.

Ari continued. "You are unique. You have gained a vast understanding of the world—the entire world, not just the Ottoman Empire—and you do not pass judgment." He lifted her hand to his lips and said humbly, "We would ask that you share your knowledge and thoughts."

She began slowly, aware that her words would bring pain. "My grandfather always said that all of England's policies and military interventions were determined by concern for her trade—safeguarding trading routes, controlling sources of supplies, and maintaining high profits for the investors. England is ruthless when it comes to protecting her financial interests."

"Why do you say ruthless?" Ari asked with a guarded look.

"Take the example of teak. England has always been a country that depends on its navy, on its ships. For a time, majestic English oak trees supplied the tall masts that the sailing ships needed. In time, it was necessary to find other sources of suitable timber. The Balkans—Denmark, Sweden, and Norway—supplied England's shipyards until the Napoleonic Wars put a stop to that.

England tried other sources, timber from Canada and the United States. However, it was subject to dry rot and had half the life span of timber from the Baltics. Then England discovered another source: the teakwood trees of India, especially those of the Province of Pogu, renamed Lower Burma by the English after they annexed it. England fought two wars with India, and in the end, she had ravaged the teak forests and owned India."

When Ari remained silent, Munevver continued in a hushed voice. "The English merchants have believed from the beginning that, with French and English support, the Ottomans will win this war." Her expression was grim. "It was also generally accepted that the Ottoman Empire would be severely weakened." She looked at Ari directly. "The Ottoman Empire controls vast lands and waterways. It is in England's best interests that the Ottoman Empire remain intact for the immediate future."

"The longer future?" he whispered.

Reluctantly, Munevver forced herself to speak. "It seems likely that many of the provinces within the Ottoman Empire will follow the example of Greece and seek independence."

"It has always been a danger," Ari acknowledged.

"Yes, but now the empire is in great debt, dependent financially on many European countries. The army will be in shreds after the end of this war, and the people will be in desperate straits," Munevver explained.

"The men from England . . . they are coming to incite

turmoil?"

"No. There is no need for them to do that. I think they are coming to make connections with the different factions within the Ottoman Empire—connections that will benefit them. It is likely they will befriend them, and then they will be in position to claim protectorship of certain territories when the empire collapses."

"Certain territories?" Ari ground out. "What are they looking for?"

Very slowly, Munevver began to speak. "All trade depends on transportation. Once, it was camels and sailing ships, but now most of it is by steamships . . . or trains." She paused. "My grandfather has vast coal mines on his land. Miners dig it out, and then the coal is loaded onto trains that take it to his ships. The ships then transport it to buyers." She looked at Ari to see if he was following what she was trying to convey. "As a form of fuel, coal is less bulky than wood, but it is very heavy."

Ari nodded. "We are dependent upon it."

"I remember my grandfather telling me that long ago in China, fields would burn. By 600 BC, the Chinese were able to refine oil that bubbled up from the ground for their use."

Ari moved impatiently. "They tell the same stories about places in the southeastern part of the Ottoman Empire. The local people have found a way to use it as fuel."

Munevver nodded. "I heard that at the Great Exhibition, they were talking about an American, Samuel Kerr. He had refined a substance he found in his backyard and had been able to use it to fuel his lamps." She shrugged. "He called it carbon oil."

After a long pause, Ari said in a low voice, "We don't even know who they are, the men who are coming."

Munevver let her mind work as her grandfather had trained her. There were only so many men in England with an interest in the Ottoman Empire or who knew its natural resources. "New ventures tend to attract younger men eager to make their fortunes and establish themselves socially," she murmured. "And"—the words came out slowly—"young businessmen's wives, desperate to make their children successful, often work behind the scenes to promote their husbands." Suddenly, she began to speak more rapidly. "Englishmen are frequently accompanied by their wives when they travel to a foreign country." Munevver waited, and when Ari did not respond, she added, "It is customary for the wives of officials in foreign countries to receive the ladies and to plan some entertainment for them."

He looked up and shrugged in defeat. "We don't know the names of the men. Even if we could devise some form of entertainment, how would we know which wives might be coming with them?"

An unexpected, mischievous smile lightened Munevver's customarily composed face. "If a lady plans to travel, she first visits her dressmaker, and then she visits all of her friends to share the news with them."

Munevver smiled at Ari's confusion. "She plans far ahead and she shares the information."

"A brilliant idea, but unfortunately, we have no contact with English society."

"Perhaps not. If I ever had any contact as Lord George's daughter, it was extremely slight, and I am sure that I lost the little I had a long time ago." She continued teasingly. "Of course, Florence Nightingale maintains a voluminous correspondence with English officials, politicians, and businessmen who might be possible donors to her causes . . . and their wives."

"Do you think she would know?" Ari asked in disbelief.

"I will write her tomorrow. She had asked me to tell her about life in Ankara." Suddenly, the joy went out of her voice. "My letter will take weeks to get from Ankara to Scutari."

Ari jumped to his feet, his eyes blazing with enthusiasm. "I'll include your letter with the official correspondence going to Constantinople tomorrow." He seemed happier than she had ever seen him. "Let me pour us both some raki."

Much earlier than usual, before the first glimmer of the grey morning light, Munevver woke and forced herself to go back over the evening—the discussion about the men coming to Ankara, her promise to write to Florence, and then the two glasses of raki. There was a memory of being held in Ari's arms. For the first time, Ari had pulled her close and caressed her. It seemed as though he wanted to make love, but it had not happened.

What had she done wrong? No one had told her the steps of lovemaking, what each partner did. In dancing, the actions of the couple were clearly understood. The man extended his hand, and the woman put her hand in his. But there was no information given to young women about the process of consummating a marriage. It was what young women worried about and feared, but they received no guidance.

Munevver must have missed an important step that had caused him to stop, but it was all hazy in her mind. The unusual pleasure of being held in Ari's arms, feeling safe and protected. Kisses, usually so rare, had covered her face and neck. Hands, wonderful, slim, strong hands, had stroked her and she had reveled in it. The weight of his body, and then nothing. What had gone wrong? What had she failed to do? She forced herself to leave the warmth of the bed and go to the bathing room to wash and dress. No one talked about facing the person after, but surely, if she were dressed and her hair arranged, she would be better prepared to face Ari.

For a moment, neither spoke, and then Ari broke the silence. "I am sorry." He was silent for an instant and then forced himself to continue. "I should never have tried." He started over. "I should have known. It's this damn coughing, always coughing. I feel drained of strength all the time."

It wasn't her fault. He had not found her repellent. It had something to do with his illness. Her violet eyes were sparkling with tears. "I should have told you that I know nothing about what married people do."

Ari looked at her in disbelief. "You were married. You are a widow."

"Yes, but James didn't desire me. He left the chapel as soon as the wedding was over. He and his friends left right after to celebrate." Munevver stopped, unwilling to go into more detail. "In the morning, he said he was leaving with his regiment for the East. He asked me not to tell anyone. He was afraid that they might tell his father that he had failed to sire an heir."

"How can that be? You are still a bakire? A vierge?" he stammered in French. "You are so beautiful. Your hair is the shining blue black of the Bosphorus in the moonlight. Your skin is the pure white of the Iznik tiles in the Seraglio. Your eyes, your beautiful, violet eyes, would entrance the soul of any man. They have owned me since the first time we met."

Munevver felt the hard pain of failing that seemed to be crushing her soften at his words. "My brother tried to warn my father that James was a mandrake, a sodomite. He was well known for preferring the companionship of boys . . . young boys."

"Your father didn't listen to him?"

"James's father was determined to have an heir, and my father was blind to everything except that I would be a duchess when James became the Duke of Leinster. He saw the marriage as creating opportunities to help the family—a titled husband for Christianna and titled wives with generous dowries for Ryker and Alexander. Business opportunities that had been closed to him would be open. Nothing else mattered." Munevver paused, wondering if she should tell him more. "I overhead James's father as he left the church after our wedding. He was with some of his relatives. He said, 'I've sold the family name to a filthy chit, a merchant, and I'll damn well have my grandsons.'"

Munevver curled deeper into her chair. "His father terrified me, so I made a bargain with James. I would not tell anyone that he had not consummated the marriage, and he would sign a note saying that, as my husband, he wished me to stay under my father's protection until he returned from the war." She shuddered. "As soon as I learned he had died in Scutari Hospital, I knew I had to leave. I had to flee before his father could claim me."

"I hope you won't mind my saying that I am thanking Allah for his wonderful gift." Ari's eyes gleamed, and for the first time since she had seen him, he seemed happy. "It is my greatest hope that I will be able to enjoy it fully when I have recovered from this terrible bout of bronchitis."

"How can you thank him? I am the cause of your being forced to leave Constantinople. I know how much you love your glorious city. You are a true Ottoman, and Constantinople is the center of the world for you. I'm sorry I made you lose it."

Chapter 38

1855: Winter's End

Munevver hurried to hand Ari a cup of hot tea as a series of coughs racked his thin frame. He no longer tried to hide the blood-stained handkerchiefs from her. As his supply dwindled, she suspected that he was burning them. Handkerchiefs were not the only thing in short supply. It was almost the last of their tea, and there had not been any boxes of provisions from Constantinople for weeks. "The roads will be open soon, won't they?"

"Not soon," Ari rasped. "The passes are still clogged with snow." He struggled to speak, "When you are shopping, would you buy some handkerchiefs for me? I seem to keep losing them."

"Yes, of course." Munevver smiled at him. There was no way she could get to the stores, and even if she could, they were practically empty. She made a mental note to remove the bottom flounce from her best linen petticoat. It would make at least two dozen handkerchiefs once she hemmed them. His handkerchiefs from home were finished with a double row of exquisite hemstitching.

The most she would have time for was a single row, but she would put the handkerchiefs under his other ones and perhaps he would not notice.

Munevver picked up the newspaper he had brought home. Although it was old, she read it eagerly. "It says the Russians are surviving the winter siege of Sevastopol and are in good shape." She turned the page. "On the other hand, it says that the Allied Forces lived through one of the coldest winters in flimsy tents." She put the paper down. "I remember how they assured the English people that the troops would be home for Christmas." She pulled her shawl closer. "Now the English troops are stranded outside of Sevastopol, living in trenches without a dry place to shelter, scant food, and no supplies for their horses that are dying every day. Worst of all, huge numbers of the soldiers are sick or wounded and are not getting the care they need."

"The Allies are planning a Spring Offensive," Ari managed to say. "I've heard that despite the frigid conditions, from December 1854 through February 1855, English and French engineers have been destroying the docks, forts, and barracks on the south side of Sevastopol Harbor. They also demolished the aqueduct that supplied water to the docks." He rubbed his hands together to warm them. "They are determined to drive the Russians out of Sevastopol."

Slowly, the months passed, and on May 3, 1855, the English, who wanted to break Russia's supply lines maintained by their control of the Sea of Azoff, sent their three-decker war ship, *The Royal Albert*, accompanied by five other ships-of-the-line, from their anchorage off Sevastopol to the Black Sea. In order to deceive the Russians, they set their course in a northwest direction, toward Odessa, the one warm-water port on the Black Sea. Odessa, formerly an Ottoman province, had been lost to the Russians in the Treaty of Jassy that ended the Russian–Ottoman war of 1787–1792. At the same time, the French had set sail to cut off Russia's access to the Sea of Azoff, southeast of Sevastopol. The goal was to discontinue the provisions—men, munitions, and food—that were arriving steadily from Russia by way of the Sea of Azoff to supply the besieged Sevastopol.

Although all seemed to be going as planned, it soon became obvious that the French ships were changing course. They were now headed southwest, back toward Sevastopol. They were abandoning the joint plan to close off Russia's flowing supply chain that had kept Sevastopol safe during the cruel winter. Emperor Napoleon had sent orders by telegram to the French commander, requiring him to bring up the French Reserve Corps from the Bosphorus.

"How could the French do such a thing?" Munevver sputtered. "Don't they realize that if they don't shut off Russia's supply line, our troops face another hot summer and brutal winter? Will they have to maintain the siege of Sevastopol through another winter?" Munevver shook her head. "The leaders had promised that the troops would be home by Christmas 1854! Now they are facing another Christmas and another winter in the Crimea!"

Chapter 39

March 1, 1855: Burial in Ankara

"I can hardly believe it!" Ari's voice, roughened by the constant coughing he had been suffering with for weeks, was filled with horror as he studied the newspaper. "Lord Stratford de Redcliffe arranged a dinner on January 31st at the English ambassador's embassy, and he has asked Sultan Abdulmejid to attend! Sultans do not go to embassies! They do not attend events where unveiled women mix with men and even dance with them." He shuddered. "It's not enough for de Redcliffe to pride himself on his ability to pull the strings in Topkapi. Now he has to make it clear to the world how much control he has over the sultan. He commands the Ottoman Empire! We may survive this war with Russia, but we will not be free. England owns our treasury, and Lord Stratford de Redcliffe dictates our policies." He ground his teeth. "He has convinced the sultan that if he modernizes the Ottoman Empire—if all subjects, irrespective of race or religion, have equal rights under the law—he will gain influence and stature among European countries that will benefit the Ottoman Empire."

"As I recall, Lord Stratford de Redcliffe's father was disinherited because of an unfortunate marriage," Munevver said softly. "It's as though he has spent his life trying to compensate for his father's diminished status in society. His father was ambassador to Constantinople in 1824, and he has been ambassador since 1842." Munevver stared off into space. "He has made the ambassadorship his own kingdom. My father never said it definitely, but he implied that de Redcliffe had influence over which merchants made the most advantageous trade contracts with the Sublime Porte."

"No doubt." Ari rested a moment and then continued. "It may be hard to believe, but de Redcliffe did have his rebellious moments. He was a close friend of Byron. He even wrote poetry." Ari smiled weakly as he reached for another handkerchief to cover his coughing. "Haven't earlier sultans tried to institute the same reforms that de Redcliffe is recommending?" Munevver handed her husband a piece of horehound in a desperate attempt to stop his coughing.

"Yes, and there has been opposition. When the people heard that Christians refused to serve in the Ottoman Army, that they pay a fee to be exempted, they were outraged. Ottoman families are losing their sons and husbands in this war to prevent Russia from seizing Constantinople and the straits. Muslim widows and orphans all over the Ottoman Empire weep, but the Christian subjects and others do not. They have not lost their sons and husbands. They prospered!"

Ari struggled to catch his breath. "If we win this war, we will have avoided Russian control. We will have kept them out of our empire, or at least that is what the proposed treaty is supposed to do. The Ottoman Empire is to be admitted to the concert of European nations, and in exchange for that, we will have to agree to the Black Sea being neutral. No one can build any fortifications there, and it would be closed to all warships. In return, the European powers pledged to maintain the integrity of the Ottoman Empire. In effect, they will prohibit other nations from interfering with the sultan's administration of the Ottoman Empire. That protection means we are now controlled by the Europeans—the English and the French. What will happen when they no longer need to travel through our country to carry out their commerce? Steamships and railroads will put an end to overland trade routes." He groaned and turned away from her. "We are going to lose our empire."

Munevver watched over her young husband as he dragged himself to work each morning and returned in the late afternoon, feverish and with an ever-worsening cough. She tried every herb she had, but they gave him only momentary relief. She begged him to see the doctor in the Turkish military hospital, but he refused. Finally, in desperation, she sent a message to the English representative in Ankara, asking him to send a doctor. By the time one arrived, Ari was in bed with a fever that left him drained of all will to do anything.

"Munevver," Ari whispered. "When it is time for you to go home, my mother will help you." He shook his head as she started to protest. "Go to her. She knows my wishes. She will make the arrangements to return you to your home." He lifted an emaciated hand. "I have left instructions. She will get you back to your grandfather." Ari struggled to speak again. "Take her with you. She will be all alone."

Three days later, Munevver faced a decision that had to be made immediately. Where could she bury her young husband? He was Circassian, not born a Muslim, although he had followed the Muslim customs all his life. She considered the options Ankara offered: a Greek Orthodox cemetery, a tiny Armenian cemetery, an even smaller Jewish cemetery, and a Muslim cemetery adjacent to a lovely, old mosque with its turban-capped tombstones for men and tulip-topped tombstones for women. The choice was clear. She would go to the mosque and beg them to allow her gallant, young husband to be buried in the graveyard by the mosque. He had never attended their mosque. They would not know him.

Slowly, Munevver pulled the worn Muslim prayer beads her grandfather had used to teach her that there were many religions in the world from her pocket. She rubbed them briskly on her skirt so that she could smell the pine scent one more time. Then she looped them around her husband's wrist. With Lala and Hatice accompanying her, she walked the rough road to the mosque and pleaded for permission to bury her husband there.

Numb to everything, Munevver divided the few items in her home among her friends and made arrangements to travel to Constantinople, where she would urge Ari's mother to return to England with her as Ari had wished. It was the last thing he had asked of her. He feared that his beloved mother would be alone in the world, and he could not bear that.

As she traveled ever closer to Constantinople, her plans began to solidify in her mind. *My destination is Yorkshire, but I have to see them again. The pain of not seeing them, not communicating with them— Aunt Frederica, Alexander, Christianna, and Ryker— has been dull but constant. They are my family. I will return to my father's home in London for a very brief visit and then make my way to my grandfather's estate in Yorkshire. I can almost see the sunshine and smell the heather.* An ever-present fear clenched her. *Are there enough gold coins left to pay my way? Why haven't I kept better track of them? What can I sell? The signet ring James thrust into my hand? The gold bracelets Janan Hanim has given me? The necklace the Valide Sultan put around my neck after I was married?*

Munevver was returning home a failure. She had been married twice and widowed twice in less than three years, and now she was a penniless widow. Neither man had loved her, not even wanted her. Each had been trapped into marrying her by a despotic man. She winced at the painful thought of never having someone to love, never knowing the love of a man. Even more excruciating was the knowledge that she would never have children. Munevver blinked back the tears. If she could not find happiness for herself, perhaps she could help Christianna. If her sister was in Surrey, she would ask her to return to Yorkshire with her. They would make their home there, far away from their father.

News of the death of her beloved son had robbed Janan Hanim of all sense of purpose. She listened patiently as

Munevver relayed Ari's wish that she accompany her to England so that she would not be alone. "How could I leave Constantinople? I have lived here all my life. I know the rhythm of its seasons, the scent of each hour of the day, and the life-giving force of the Bosphorus. I would be nothing without them."

As Munevver heard Janan Hanim's words, she knew she would be leaving the Ottoman Empire as she had entered—alone, except for the faithful Fayne. The next morning, as soon as they had finished in the hammam and eaten breakfast, she returned to the subject that had to be settled. "I plan to return to England as soon as possible. If you feel that you can't come now, will you consider it for the future?"

Before Janan Hanim could answer, a maid approached her with a note on a silver tray. After a quick glance at it, she held it out to Munevver. "The Valide Sultan wants you to come to her immediately."

"I can't think of any reason why she would request me to attend her," Munevver said hesitantly, remembering the hostility of the Valide Sultan the first time they met. "I don't have much time before my ship leaves. Perhaps there is some misunderstanding?"

"No. The message is clear. You are to come as soon as possible." Janan Hanim frowned and then said, reluctantly, "It is most unusual. I fear she wants something from you."

"What could she possibly want from me? I have nothing to give anyone." *All I have are the few remaining coins Aunt Frederica hid so long ago. They will be barely enough for food during the long journey home.*

"You must not keep her waiting." In a low voice, Janan Hanim asked one of the servants to arrange for a carriage.

As the carriage approached the Gate of Salutation, Munevver shuddered at the thought of walking across the vast cobblestone second courtyard before she could enter the Gate of Felicity that led to the harem section of Topkapi Palace. As she prepared to step down from the carriage, she noticed two black men with a richly decorated sedan chair approaching her. They opened the door of the chair and motioned for her to enter. It seemed she was not going to have to limp across the uneven courtyard.

When Munevver entered the four-hundred-room harem section of the Seraglio for the second time, she was instantly aware that the air was heavy with the lingering odor of many women and eunuchs crowded into a small, unventilated space. Without sunshine, the tiles that had gleamed so beautifully on her first visit now appeared dull. As she followed the eunuch down the Golden Road that would take her to the Valide Sultan's courtyard, the tiles lining the walls with their red designs, which had once looked so vividly alive, now resembled patterns of dried blood.

Munevver was bowed into the Valide Sultan's salon. The regal-appearing woman seated in the corner of the divan overlooking the Marmara Sea did not seem to have aged since the last time they had met. Without speaking, she motioned Munevver forward.

Forcing herself to assume the outward calm that she used when her father was his most irascible self, Munevver sank into a low curtsey and then rose to stand silently with her hands clasped in front of her. Janan Hanim had been right. The lady wanted something from her, but what? She would wait for her hostess to reveal the purpose of this requested visit—one of the first lessons she had learned from her father.

The Valide Sultan motioned Munevver to the upholstered side chair by the divan that was customarily provided for European ladies in full skirts. "May Allah grant you endurance in this difficult time."

Endurance? Was that what she was to strive for? Not retribution for sending her husband, who was known to have little tolerance for the cold, to his death. Unable to trust herself to make the proper response, she nodded in acknowledgment as she settled into the chair.

"I understand you are going home. To London?"

"I will go to my father's home outside London first, but then I will be going to Yorkshire. To my grandfather's home." When there was no response, she added, "I believe he needs me." *It is really I who need him. I need someone who wants me, who loves me.* Munevver sat rigidly erect, waiting for the Valide Sultan's next move.

Once coffee had been served, the Valide Sultan waved her hand to clear the room. "I have a service that I would ask of you." She paused and then beckoned to a small boy waiting in the doorway to enter the room. Munevver studied him closely—a slim child with curly, dark-brown hair, a well-balanced face with a broad forehead, a nose that would be regal in time, eyes that appeared to be silver in the dimly lit room, and a well-shaped mouth. He was dressed in blue, silk pantaloons and a richly embroidered crimson vest over a closely fitted, ivory-colored, silk shirt. On his feet were yellow, silk, backless slippers. He seemed to be about four years old and already had the air of command.

"This is Selim. He, too, has experienced a great loss. His mother was called by Allah three days ago." She gave Munevver a sharp look. "Unfortunately, there are no ladies in the harem who are able to serve as his foster mother."

The information stunned Munevver, and she felt a ripple of fear travel up her back. She forced herself to nod, acknowledging that she understood what had been said. *But why is the Valide Sultan talking to me about such a sensitive matter?* Her thoughts raced as she began to put bits of information together. *This charming child must be the Valide Sultan's grandson, and since his mother has died, his life is in danger without a foster mother to look after him—to protect him every hour of the day and night from the other mothers in the harem who are ever eager to decrease any competition to their sons' future claim to the throne.*

The Valide Sultan continued in a carefully controlled, low voice, "I have kept him with me in my rooms since her death, but I cannot do that much longer."

Munevver's heart beat faster. His grandmother had two options: return him to the care of the slaves in the harem where his life would be in constant danger, or send him to the Golden Kafes where he would be locked up for the rest of his life, or until he was selected to be the next sultan—a very slim chance without a powerful mother to advocate for him. Against her will, she heard herself ask, "What is it that you would ask of me?"

"Take him with you. Raise him as your son in London. Adopting children is an old Ottoman custom. We call them *children of the soul*." The Valide Sultan's voice trembled for the first time. "It is the only way to keep him safe."

How can the Valide Sultan ask such a thing? She doesn't know me, doesn't seem to like me, and yet, she is willing to entrust her grandson to me. "I am not returning to London. I am going back to my grandfather's home. It is not a cosmopolitan city like Constantinople or London. It is isolated country living. The air is clean and crisp. The land is covered with sweet-smelling heather. The sky above the meadows is filled with flights of red grouse, and the fields are home for lambs and cattle. My grandfather's stables are the center of a business that trains horses for the military." Munevver shook her head. "As you can see, it is not the place for a young"—she hesitated—"gentleman to grow up."

"He would be safe," the Valide Sultan said flatly. When Munevver did not respond, she began to speak rapidly. "You arc an intelligent, young woman. You speak several languages, and I've been told you help your father with his trading business." She nodded her head briskly. "I have decided you will do very well." When Munevver did not say anything, she added, "You have no children, and with two deceased husbands, it is unlikely you'll marry again."

Ignoring the pain caused by her words, Munevver found herself studying the little boy. So far, he had not said a word. *Does he understand what his grandmother has said?* "What is your name?" She tried to keep the anger she felt toward the Valide Sultan out of her voice as she put the question to him in Turkish.

"My mother called me her Little Lion," he answered in a low voice.

"Do you understand what the Valide Sultan has asked of me?" *He is so young, so frail. Is it wise to ask him such a question?*

He nodded slowly and whispered yes in Turkish.

Dear God, the boy knows. He probably also knows the danger he is in. She turned back to the Valide Sultan and spoke in French. "My ship is leaving this afternoon." *I will have a son after all. My son's name will be Liam, another form of William. Surely God will not begrudge me that small gift.* "I will take Liam with me as my son if he can be ready to leave immediately."

"He is ready now." The Valide Sultan's voice was curt.

Munevver turned back to the boy. "Is there anything you wish to take with you?"

"My sister," he whispered. "I promised my mother I'd look after her."

His sister! Older? Younger? It appears that her new son is a man of honor who wishes to keep his word to his mother. "What is your sister's name?"

"My mother called her Star Light."

"Ah, a lovely name." Munevver turned to the Valide Sultan and drew on the knowledge that she had almost been a duchess. "My son wishes his orphaned sister to accompany him."

"Impossible! You don't know what you ask!"

"It's not what I ask. It's what my son asks. He is obviously a gentleman, a man of honor who meets his obligations."

The Valide Sultan seemed to soften slightly. "You don't understand. His sister will be looked after most carefully. Young girls in the palace are brought up by all the women. They are taught languages, music, dance, poetry, and painting. When they are a little older, they are trained in management of a large household, an important household. They learn about finances, purchasing, and so on. Sons of elite families, ambassadors, and royalty considered them to be a very fine gift from the sultan. Not only do they bring valuable skills to the marriage, but they retain their ties to the Seraglio." She leaned forward slightly to emphasize her point. "They have the sultan's ear for life."

In the face of the woman's opposition, Munevver realized she had no weapons to use to rescue Liam's sister. "I'm sorry," she murmured to him. "We must accept Allah's will." She held out her hand. "Come, Liam." She glanced down at the yellow, silk slippers. "We have a long walk to reach our carriage, but I will help you."

"A sedan chair will carry you both back to your carriage," the Valide Sultan announced with a dismissive toss of her head. "I don't want anyone to see you leave." She hesitated and then asked firmly, "You are going directly to your ship?"

"Yes. I have said goodbye to Janan Hanim." Munevver's voice faltered. "I asked her to come with me as her son wished, but she said she could not leave Constantinople."

"Of course she can't! This is her home." Her voice softened. "She is of the palace. We are her family for life."

Her words caught Munevver off guard. She had known that Ari's mother had been a gift from the sultan to his father. She tried to remember what Ari had said about his father. He had been the governor of the province of Macedonia and had been killed in an uprising. She nodded. Of course Janan Hanim had come back to Constantinople, to the home she had known as a small girl when her widowed mother had brought her here from Georgia to become part of the sultan's household.

The Valide Sultan raised one hand to capture Munevver's attention. "Everything has been arranged. Transportation and guards will be provided all the way to your grandfather's home." Her gaze swept mercilessly over Munevver, registering every detail of her shabby appearance. "I have made arrangements for some things to be brought to the ship for you and for the boy. It is safer that you do not leave the ship." She drew a sharp breath. "Even in Paris, you must not leave the hotel. I have arranged for Charles Worth to attend you there." For a moment, her expression softened. "He creates magnificent dresses in the richest satin made in Lyons. He is not very well known, but I think he will be very successful in the future." She nodded at Munevver's astonished expression and added smugly, "I've heard that he already designs for Elizabeth of Austria and for Empress Eugenie." When Munevver began to protest, the Valide Sultan waved a hand to silence her. "Janan Hanim does not want you to return to your family looking as though she neglected you."

Chapter 40

April 1855: Returning Home

Munevver had arranged for two small cabins for her and for Fayne, but now, looking at the tiny space of her cabin with its two twenty-four-inch-wide berths stacked one above the other, a closet on the opposite wall, and a narrow strip of space between them that could accommodate a small, wooden chair, she wondered how she and Liam would fit?

She shoved her battered trunk under the bottom bunk. At least Liam had no luggage. Now dressed in a white, cotton shirt, short, woolen pants, and a matching jacket but still wearing toe slippers, Liam was investigating the cabin with delight. He had probably never been outside of Topkapi Palace.

What am I going to do about shoes for him? Munevver eyed the inquisitive little boy, who had not uttered a word since they left the Seraglio. The Valide Sultan had said she would have suitable clothing delivered to the ship, but there had been no shoes in the bundle waiting in her cabin. What could she do about shoes? April was warm in Constantinople, but it would be cooler as they traveled northwest on the Danube. She could only hope that Fayne might be able to find him some shoes if they stopped at a port along the way.

Munevver glanced down at her frayed traveling outfit in dismay. She had worn it when she left London in a frantic flight to escape James's father, worn it day after day in Ankara, and now was wearing it to return. She had nothing suitable to wear when they arrived! How could she face her family in rags? She would rather die than appear in front of her father like this.

Suddenly, she remembered the Valide Sultan's words. She had arranged for new clothes to be waiting for Munevver and Liam in Paris. She would not be returning like a failure, a destitute burden on the family.

Taking a deep breath, Munevver spoke briskly in Turkish. "The top bunk is your area. You may sleep and play there. The bottom one is mine." She waved a hand in the direction of the opposite wall of closets and said, "For our things." She pointed toward the small basin in a built-in chest. "The hammam." Then, gesturing to the narrow strip of bare floor between the bunks and the closet, she said, "Our salon."

This would be their world. Munevver had taken note of the masses of people crowding into the line for steerage passengers. She shuddered as she remembered her journey to Constaninople—the steamship's common room, used during the day for meals or for sitting and talking, and the crowded, smelly salon. It was cramped here in their cabin, but they would be safe. She made a mental note to remind Fayne to avoid the common room. When Liam remained silent, Munevver continued. "You will have English lessons each day." At his surprised look, she explained, "I know you speak several languages, but where we are going, you need to be able to speak English."

How were they going to get through the days? Munevver had her knitting and two books, but he had nothing. Lessons? Yes, but how was she going to fill the rest of the hours? From the little she had observed of children, they seemed to jump around a lot, play with toys, and had stories read to them.

After a moment of silence, Munevver began a monologue in Turkish, telling Liam what she was going to do. She opened the worn trunk that had traveled so far with her and tried to remember where she had put the tin box of Yorkshire buttons, the collection of handmade, wooden, bone-and-ivory buttons she had been given by her grandfather so long ago. As a child, she had spent hours using the buttons to form the shapes of bridges, houses, and castles. She smiled, remembering how her grandfather had used them to teach her to count, and later, she had used them to help Alexander with multiplication.

When Munevver found the battered tin box, she placed it carefully on her bunk and continued her search for the heavy yarn she knew was there. She would use it to crochet a hopscotch court. She rummaged some more. There had to be something heavy that could be used as the puck. Finally, in the corner, her fingers found the frayed bag of beans that she had always carried as a child in the hope of finding someone to play toss and catch. Yes! It would work perfectly in the confined space of the cabin. She would make the grid this evening while Liam slept, but for now, she would show him how to count with the buttons. Maybe she could find twelve black buttons and twelve white buttons that she could use to teach him how to play draughts.

There would be many long hours to fill, but they were going home! At last, she was on her way home.

Chapter 41

Surrey, England

They had been traveling nearly four hours after leaving London, and now, from the window of the luxurious carriage, Munevver studied the sweeping, green lawns cleanly scythed on either side of the drive that curved through the quiet country toward its ultimate destination—her father's home. Never her home . . . always her father's home. Despite the war, somehow he had found enough staff to maintain the lawns in pristine condition. She breathed in the scent of freshly cut grass. Could she ever rid herself of the odor of burning dung? She straightened her back. She would only be here for one night, and then she would be on her way to Yorkshire. On her way to her real home.

There had been times during the last two years when she thought she would never see her grandfather's home again. She had almost lost faith in her dreams. She felt a twinge of guilt as she remembered Janan Hanim insisting that it was her honor to arrange transportation for Munevver to her father's home outside of London and then all the way to her grandfather's Yorkshire home. Munevver smiled now as she remembered Janan Hanim telling her about the Circassian custom. It was the host's obligation to see his guests safely to their next destination. All Janan Hanim would say was that a friend in the Seraglio had told her a carriage would be waiting for her when she arrived in England, and similar carriages would convey her to her final destination.

Munevver had been stunned when she saw the magnificent, black coach with its brilliant crest—four squares within a blue circle with a red, crown-like top— on the door. It was not a crest she recognized. The coach had taken them from the dock to an elegant London townhouse, and it was not until she heard the coachman speak to the butler that she learned the owner of the coach was Lord Stratford de Redcliffe, the ambassador to Constantinople. It seemed so long ago, in 1852, that she had read that he had been elevated to the peerage as Viscount Stratford de Redcliffe of Somerset County.

The housekeeper had rooms ready for them, and a dressmaker was waiting to make adjustments to the dresses and evening gowns that Munevver was assured had been selected for her according to Janan Hanim's precise instructions.

Now, standing in front of the heavy, oak door of her father's home, tears blurred her vision as she watched Quinn slowly open the hefty door. "Good afternoon, Quinn," she said in a voice she kept steady by sheer willpower. "It's good to see you again."

"Welcome back, Lady Munevver." Quinn raised an eyebrow the slightest bit as he studied the child standing silently beside her, holding her hand while the faithful Fayne waited behind them.

"This is my son, Lord Liam." Munevver swept through the door and directed a glance at the footman in the hall. "Perhaps someone could carry my trunk and portmanteau to my rooms?"

"And the young lord?" the footman asked.

She looked down her nose at him. "Make arrangements for him in my suite." She turned back to Quinn. "Please put Fayne in a room near mine." As Quinn motioned them forward, she added hesitantly, "Is it Aunt Frederica's at-home day?"

"Yes, Lady Munevver." He took pity on her and added helpfully, "It is Lady Louisa's and Lady Frederica's at-home day.

Lady Louisa and Lady Frederica are both at home. What is Quinn trying to tell me?

She looked at him directly without speaking and waited.

"Perhaps the news did not reach you." Quinn spoke quickly, "Lord Ryker and Lady Louisa were married shortly after his return." He turned promptly and motioned for her to follow him.

Ryker and Louisa married! Munevver felt a delicious feeling of happiness spread through her. They were perfect for each other. Ryker would have the steady, supportive love that he needed, and Louisa would have a husband who adored her.

"Thank you, Quinn. It will be so good to see them again." She turned to Fayne and said, "I am glad that I wore an afternoon dress instead of a traveling outfit. I will not need to change for tea, but I do want to wash my face and hands before I join Lady Frederica and Lady Louisa." She hesitated and then made her decision. "I would ask that you bring Liam to meet Lady Frederica and Lady Louisa at the end of tea."

Pausing outside the door to the drawing room, Munevver felt gratitude again for her mother-in-law's help. Janan Hanim had tried to anticipate every unpleasantness Munevver might encounter on her return and make it as easy for her as she could.

Munevver smoothed a hand down the side of the garnet, silk twill afternoon dress she had chosen in Paris. The mirror had reassured her that the design, although very strange to her eye, was flattering. The tightly fitted bodice accentuated her high, firm breasts, while the pointed bottom of the bodice emphasized both her narrow waist and the flair of her hips. The fullness of the skirt was swept to the back in a bustle that made her legs appear impossibly long. She would be eternally grateful for the corrective shoes that a shoemaker under Janan Hanim's instructions had made for her. The shoes were lighter and built up in appropriate places so that she could walk with less of a limp. Sweeping into the room, she ignored Aunt Patience and, stopping in front of Aunt Frederica, made a low curtsey.

"Oh, Munevver! My lovely Munevver. You're home at last." Aunt Frederica turned to face the roomful of curious women. "My darling niece has been living abroad and has just returned."

What a lovely, sugar-coated description of what I have endured. Munevver smiled at her aunt. "It is wonderful to see you again." At her aunt's nudge, she turned and greeted Aunt Patience and the other women. Only after that was finished did she feel that she could join Christianna, Louisa, and Georgette in the window alcove.

It was Louisa who greeted her first. "I am so glad to see you again," she said softly as her eyes made a swift assessment of Munevver.

"I believe that I can call you my sister," Munevver murmured. "Quinn told me the wonderful news. I am so happy for you and Ryker." She linked her arm through Louisa's. "We'll talk more later."

Christianna nodded at Munevver but remained silent as she huddled in the far corner of the window seat. Munevver smiled at her and, recognizing her sister's withdrawal, made no attempt to hug or kiss her. As Munevver turned to Georgette, Louisa spoke quickly, "You may not have received the notice. Georgette and my brother, Edmund, were married shortly after you left." She paused. "They have been blessed with a lovely little girl."

"Oh, may I extend my belated best wishes for both events," Munevver managed to say smoothly.

Remembering Georgette's dismay when she heard that the troops would not be home before the end of the year as had been promised, she had an uneasy feeling that she knew what had happened but she would ask Louisa later.

Georgette nodded in acknowledgment but did not add anything to the conversation. She seemed tense, as though waiting for something to happen.

Munevver turned to survey the room. The whole atmosphere was different from what she remembered. There were fewer smiles, no exchanging of family news, and there were several women she did not recognize. What were so many strangers doing here? There was a certain feeling of awkwardness about the gathering. They did not seem to understand the function of an at-home day. The ladies of the family were at home to receive guests—usually friends, neighbors, or relatives. The guests greeted everyone, made polite small talk, and stayed no more than thirty minutes. They did not grill other guests or ask personal questions.

At her aunt's slight hand gesture, Munevver moved reluctantly to join her. She murmured politely as Aunt Frederica introduced Lady Masham and Lady Cowdray. As they began to ask pointed questions about her relationship to Lord George, Munevver's mind was turning over information. She knew those names. They were not old friends of Aunt Frederica's, nor were they neighbors. They were two of the names on the list that Ari had shown her in Ankara. These women were the wives of merchants seeking to exploit the weakened Ottoman Empire.

Munevver froze. Her father was using her aunt to promote these people. Why was she shocked? Hadn't he exploited her? She felt a wave of hot anger surge through her and then forced herself to be calm. Tomorrow she would be gone, on her way home, to Yorkshire. All she had to do was get through this day. She could do that. She owed it to Aunt Frederica.

"You were there, in the Crimea, I believe." Aunt Patience sniffed delicately. "Although, I've never understood exactly why we chose to send our men there. But tell us, are the Russians truly defeated, or will we have to send our sons to fight them again?"

"History informs us that the Russians are never completely defeated." Munevver answered as diplomatically as she could before turning to acknowledge Uncle Charles, who had ventured to join the ladies for tea as he so often did. "Dear Uncle Charles," she whispered, taking in the empty sleeve of his coat. He bowed and kissed her hand.

"Welcome back, Munevver." He lowered his voice. "Was the escape worth all that followed?"

It was the first time she had faced the question. For a moment, burning memories of the hardship of the flight, the difficult months in Ankara, and the slow death of Ari prevented her from speaking, but then her answer came clearly. "Yes, Uncle Charles. Oh yes!" She choked on the next words. "My travails were nothing compared to what you endured. I am so sorry!"

"I am one of the lucky ones," Lord Charles said softly.

"So many did not get to come home."

"Gordy?" Munevver whispered.

"Young Gordy learned about the reality of hand-to-hand combat, but he is in Yorkshire now working in your grandfather's stables."

"Thank God!" Munevver murmured. "I don't know what Mrs. Coates would have done if he had not come back."

When the last of the visitors had left, Fayne slipped into the room with Liam. Taking Liam by the hand, Munevver announced to the suddenly quiet room, "This is my son, Liam."

It was Uncle Charles who recovered first. "What a fine boy," he said as Liam made him a perfect bow.

"Your son?" Aunt Patience sputtered. "How can that be? He's too old to be your son!"

"Liam is my son, my adopted son." Her glance challenged anyone to ask any further questions. "And now, I believe I will rest before dinner." She swept out of the room with Liam's hand firmly clasped in hers. At least she could have a hot, fragrant bath before dinner and the inquisition she knew she would have to endure.

With his usual efficiency, Quinn had instructed the maids, and a supper for Liam had materialized almost instantly. Munevver relaxed as she noted that the tray contained a variety of easy-to-eat things and a local pear beautifully sliced . . . food designed to tempt a small boy. While she waited for the footmen to bring the hot water for her bath, she ran the options she had for dressing for dinner.

She had not had any new gowns since she left England, and now the skirts and tops that she had packed so hastily and worn for two years were in no shape to wear for dinner. On the other hand, the silver-striped, silk dress that had been waiting for her in London with its low neckline, close-fitting bodice, elbow-length sheer sleeves, and the volume of the skirt pulled into a bustle at the back in the latest fashion was the most elegant evening dress she had ever seen. The question was, did she have the courage to wear it?

She pushed open the door of the wardrobe hesitantly. Perhaps it would be wiser to wear one of her old dinner dresses, if they were still there. She grimaced. The only other dresses she owned were those she brought with her from her grandfather's home. Four-year-old dresses. So much had happened in four years. She had married twice, been widowed twice, and survived the time in Ankara. What difference did it make what she wore to dinner? She had never been able to please her father, and tonight would be no different. She motioned toward the silver dress. "I will wear that one."

Later, after she was dressed and Fayne had arranged her hair, she reached into her leather book bag and removed the necklace the Valide Sultan had put around her neck on her wedding day. The double strand of almond-shaped, plum-colored amethysts gleamed in her hands. Slowly, she lifted her hands and slipped the strands over her head. As she felt the heavy jewels against the front of her gown, she thought of them as a shield. She would need all the protective armor she could find to get through this evening.

There was a gentle knock on the door, and then she was swept into Aunt Frederica's arms. "Oh, my darling Munevver. I am so glad that you have come back."

For a moment, Munevver savored the comfort of Aunt Frederica's embrace, and then said what had to be said, "I will be leaving in the morning, but we will enjoy this evening together." She reached out to Christianna, who was standing silently by the door. "I've come back for you. Just as I promised." When Christianna barely nodded, Munevver turned to her aunt in bewilderment.

"Christianna . . . is easily overwhelmed." Aunt Frederica hurried to fill the silence.

Aunt Frederica turned toward the little boy, eating his supper by the fire. "Welcome home. We are so glad to have you with us."

Munevver laid her hand on Liam's shoulder and spoke in soft Turkish, "Liam. You remember my aunt Frederica and my sister Christianna. You met them in the drawing room." She smiled at him as he regarded them intently. "We are going downstairs for dinner, and Fayne will stay with you until I return."

As she followed Aunt Frederica into the drawing room to await the announcement of dinner, it seemed to be bursting with people. After a moment, she realized that the wide skirts of the women's gowns supported by wire frames were creating the illusion of more people than there really were.

Her father, who was positioned in front of the fireplace surrounded by gentlemen, ignored her. It was Ryker who, using a sturdy cane, limped across the room to greet her. For a moment, she thought she would disgrace herself by crying. She knew he had been injured at the ferocious *Soldiers' Battle of Inkerman*, but it had not been real until she saw him now—thin, his face lined, as he struggled to move across the room. Ryker, her invincible older brother. She welcomed the kiss he gave her on the cheek with a shy smile. "It is wonderful to see you," she said in a husky voice. "I was so pleased to hear that you and Louisa had married." She paused and then added, "She has loved you all her life."

"I am the most fortunate of men." Ryker's usual cynicism was missing. "You and Louisa have always been a steady source of support I could count on."

"How are you doing?" *How can Ryker stand to work, day after day, with our father? He is as trapped as I have been.* She gasped suddenly. Alexander? No one had mentioned him and she had not seen him. She grasped Ryker's arm. "Alexander? What has happened to him?"

"He is well and content." There was a note of satisfaction in Ryker's voice.

"Tell me," Munevver insisted.

"He is at a fine boarding school, one that has produced

many medical men." Ryker smiled at her quick gasp.

"How did you convince Father to let him go?" Munevver whispered.

"It was Uncle Charles who helped me. He convinced Father that it would be healthier for Alexander to be in a school that encouraged outdoor sports."

"And he agreed to do something because it was in the interest of Alexander's health?"

"Well, Uncle Charles might have mentioned that it would be less costly than hiring and providing room and board for tutors and instructors in riding, fencing, rowing, and so on."

There was a lull in the conversation as the guests who did not know Munevver tried to assess her degree of importance in the family. Fully aware of the judgment in the gaze of the women and the appraisal of the men, she lifted her head and moved toward the fireplace. She must greet her father.

Willing herself to limp as little as possible, she moved forward with her back straight and her head high. The men surrounding Lord George were suddenly quiet, evaluating her as though she was a horse on the market at Tattersalls. She smiled to herself as she realized that none of these guests of her father were likely to be among the exclusive four hundred members of Tattersalls. "Good evening, Lord Arundal," she said in a calm voice. As she curtsied, she felt the other men's judgmental eyes sweep over her.

"I see you've returned," he said coldly. "How long will you be honoring us with your presence?"

Munevver felt as though she had been struck across the face, but she would not let him know how he had humiliated her. She looked around the group of men surrounding him before answering. There were no familiar faces. These were not the men her father usually did business with. He must be struggling to bring in new money. She forced herself to smile. "Regrettably, I will only be here a very short time. I'll be leaving for Yorkshire tomorrow morning."

"Yorkshire! Impossible!" Lord George snapped. "I can't spare my carriage for that long a trip." As he registered the surprised look on his companions' faces, he hurried to add, "Not at this time. Er . . . perhaps later."

"My travel plans are nothing for you to be concerned about," Munevver responded in an icy voice. "My mother-in-law insisted on arranging my transportation—from her home to my final destination." She smiled in the general direction of the group. "All the details of my journey were organized by my very gracious mother-in-law . . . and her friends in Constantinople," she added over her shoulder as she moved to join her aunt.

When the ladies had retired to the drawing room to await the arrival of the gentlemen, Aunt Patience's voice had easily overridden all the others. "Munevver, it appears you have returned in time for the season." She gave a malicious smile as she glanced at the other women.

"Since you have been married twice in just two years, I'm sure you will be able to show the younger ladies how to bring a man up to scratch in a short time."

"Ah, Aunt Patience. You must have forgotten that both of my marriages were arranged by men—powerful men." She turned toward the piano. Perhaps if she began to play, she could escape more of Aunt Patience's disparaging comments.

"I know your father arranged your first marriage." Aunt Patience smiled contemptuously. "He was determined to make you a duchess." She paused. "Unfortunately, he didn't count on the vicissitudes of war." She looked around the room to make sure she had the attention of the other ladies. "Pray tell, who arranged your second marriage?" She hesitated and drew her words out for a more dramatic effect. "I believe it was less than two months after your husband's valorous death at the Battle of Balaklava."

Munevver turned from the piano to face the room. She had known this moment would come, and there was no way to avoid it. "My second marriage was arranged by Sultan Abdulmejid," she said with quiet dignity.

"I have no idea who that is," Aunt Patience said dismissively. "It's certainly not an English name. A local tribal chief perhaps?"

"Sultan Abdulmejid is the Sultan of the Ottoman Empire." Munevver moved closer to Aunt Frederica, who was standing at her shoulder. She glanced around the room, searching in vain for support in parrying

Aunt Patience's viciousness. There was none. "When he learned I intended to go to Aleppo to be with my uncle, he decided I would be safer traveling in his empire if I were the wife of an Ottoman citizen." She considered her next words carefully. "His mother, the Valide Sultan, is a close friend of my mother-in-law, Janan Hanim." Munevver forced herself to smile as she lifted her arm with its array of golden bracelets and let her hand slide down the twin ropes of amethysts. "They both attended our wedding." When no one spoke, she caught Aunt Frederica's eye. "With your permission, I would like to retire. I am suddenly overcome with the fatigue of traveling."

The next morning, Lord George scanned the breakfast room as he entered. Aunt Frederica was at the end of the table, as usual. Ryker was sitting on her right and Louisa on her left. He cleared his throat before saying briskly, "Ryker, you are behind on the paperwork again, but Munevver can help you with it. She must delay her departure until a more convenient time." He frowned. Munevver was always the first down to breakfast, but this morning, there was no sign that she had been there.

He had just finished eating when he heard the crunch of carriage wheels approaching. At the sound of voices in the entrance hall, he motioned to Ryker to accompany him to the front hall. They were just in time to see Munevver assisted into a large, glossy, black carriage with a coat of arms on the side. He watched it pull away in silence. Turning to Quinn, he asked in an ominously quiet voice, "Did you recognize the coat of arms?"

"No, my lord," Quinn answered. "I am not familiar with it."

"I believe it belongs to Lord Stratford de Redcliffe," Ryker answered in a neutral voice. "It's a new crest." He nodded reassuringly in Quinn's direction. "He was elevated to the peerage quite recently."

"Lord de Redcliffe!" Lord George exclaimed. "Our ambassador at Constantinople?"

"Yes," Ryker answered, and when his father did not say anything, he added, "they say little takes place in the Ottoman Empire without his approval."

For a moment, Lord George was speechless. Munevver had connections to the highest levels in the Ottoman Empire. She was being escorted home by the man who determined Ottoman trade with all the European countries and he had let her go. It was not until late that afternoon that he was able to speak to anyone about what he saw as her betrayal. In an unaccustomed move, he joined Aunt Frederica for tea. "Did she say when she would be returning?" He tried to put the question casually.

"No, she didn't mention it." Aunt Frederica offered him a plate of tiny cucumber sandwiches. "She was looking forward to seeing her grandfather again and being in Yorkshire."

"Well, I suppose she'll be back for Christianna's birthday celebration." He frowned. "It's later in the summer, I believe."

"Christianna's birthday is in February, but she went with Munevver. She said she wanted to see her grandfather's horses."

"Horses, damn!" He began to pace in front of Aunt Frederica. "Why didn't she ask my permission?"

"Ask you?" Aunt Frederica looked astonished. "You have never taken any interest in Christianna's activities, her visits to friends." She shrugged. "She wanted to go with Munevver. You know it would not have been proper for Munevver to travel alone . . . well, with only little Liam and her maid." Her expression softened. "Such a dear little boy but so quiet." She lifted her head and gave her brother a direct look. "Christianna needed a change." Surely he was aware of how apathetic Christianna had become. "She is so withdrawn. She creeps about the house avoiding everyone, and when there are callers, I can't get her to leave her room. You must have noticed how reclusive she has become. She hardly speaks." She folded her arms and said firmly, "She will be safe with Munevver."

Chapter 42

Return to Yorkshire

"You've brought us a laddie!" Her grandfather's voice was husky as he reached out his arms to Munevver and Liam. "A fine laddie!" He hugged them tightly before releasing them and greeting them more formally. "Munevver, welcome home." He brushed the tears from his eyes with the back of his hand. "You have been sorely missed." He turned to Liam. "I know you are my grandson, but what is your name?"

"Liam. I am Liam," he whispered as he studied the tall man looming over him.

"A fine name," Lord Clarence pronounced firmly. "I've waited so long to have a grandson in my home. I believe I'll call you Laddie." He held out his hand. "Come. You'll be wanting to see the horses. There's a new colt, a baby, just born last night."

Liam gave a dubious look at the tall man and then moved closer to Munevver.

"Ah, you're thinking your mother would like to see the

colt, too." Lord Clarence extended his arm to Munevver. "It's been a long time," he said with a gravelly voice, "but I think you'll find not much has changed."

Slipping her arm through his, she leaned her cheek against his shoulder. "It's been a very long time," she choked out. "There were times when I didn't think I'd ever be able to come back, to come home."

"And are you here to stay?"

"Yes, I am here to stay. I am twenty-one now. No man can make me leave you."

"And the laddie?"

"He is my adopted son." She looked around to make sure that they were alone before she began to speak in a low voice. "A friend of my late husband's mother asked me to save him, to take him away. His mother had just died. He was alone, and there was no way to protect him from almost certain death." She turned her head so that she could look him directly in the eye. "We must never speak of it again." She sagged against his arm. "I know people will talk about me, that I have been married twice and widowed twice." She paused. "There is nothing I can do about the past, but I want people to accept Liam as my son."

"Ah, people." He groaned. "Where single women are concerned, they tend to believe what they want to believe."

"Surely anyone can see that he is too old to be the son

of my first husband." She shuddered. "James was injured in the Battle of Balaklava in October of 1854 and died in Scutari Hospital soon afterward." With a stricken expression, she whispered, "It is James's father I am terrified of. He's a despicable man. He was willing to do anything to get an heir." She shuddered. "I will never let James's father get his hands on my son."

"When did your second husband die?" her grandfather asked gently.

"In January of this year." Her voice faltered. "He was sick, so sick. We were in Ankara, and the winters there are harsh, bitterly cold all the time. The doctors could do nothing to help him."

"People can be very cruel," Lord Clarence said gently. "Even here in Yorkshire, where our family has lived and provided for the people for over seven hundred years, they can say hurtful things."

"We've traveled so far to find sanctuary. What can I do to safeguard him?"

"Marry. Marry a good man as soon as you can."

What man, good or otherwise, will want to marry a twice-widowed woman with a clubfoot, no dowry, and an adopted son?

* * *

"Porridge. It's porridge, Laddie." Muncvvcr's grandfather nodded enthusiastically at the bowls filled with creamy oatmeal that had been placed in front of him and Liam. "It's the best way to start your day." He rubbed his hands together before pouring a generous amount of heavy cream over both of their bowls and then drizzled thick, golden honey over the top.

Munevver held her breath as she waited for Liam to pick up his spoon. His breakfast in the harem would have consisted of cheese, freshly baked bread, a few olives, and a juicy fig or apricot. For a moment, he sat motionless, staring at her grandfather, and then he picked up his spoon and copied the huge man's movements.

Nodding approvingly, her grandfather addressed Liam, speaking seriously but in simple terms. "Yesterday, you saw the horses."

Liam nodded, his gaze wary.

Turning to include Munevver in what he was about to say, Lord Clarence motioned toward the land that lay outside of the breakfast room windows. "You are my grandson." He waited for Liam to nod. "Someday, all that you can see, and beyond, will be yours." When Liam did not respond, he repeated it in Turkish.

Liam shot a puzzled look at Munevver.

She looked at her grandfather. What was he up to? In England, according to the law of primogeniture, the entire estate passed, on the death of the present owner, to the firstborn male descendant, and if he was dead, to the next closest male descendant. He spoke slowly. "A long time ago, when Munevver first came to me, I found a way for her to inherit everything I own when I die. I'm sure she will want you to be her heir." He looked at both of them and, seemingly satisfied, changed the subject.

"Yesterday, you saw some of our horses. Starting today, you will learn about the estate: the people who live on it, the crops, the cattle, the sheep, and the coal in the mines." He rubbed his hands together briskly and motioned for Liam to finish his porridge. "Later, you will learn about the ships, but we will begin just as your mother did when she was your age."

"My little desk?" Munevver whispered as she remembered the day that she had found a gleaming, cherry desk, a perfect copy of her grandfather's huge one, positioned next to his in the massive library.

Chapter 43

William

"Little has changed," her grandfather murmured as he looked around the library. "It's the same as it was when you were a little girl." At the sound of footsteps, he beamed. "Well, maybe not entirely. I think my steward has changed since you lived here." He hurried to meet the tall man with broad shoulders, long legs, and slim, finely honed body entering the library. "I want you to meet him."

Munevver had risen and turned to face the door at her grandfather's words and now stood, wishing she had something to hold on to for support. William! He seemed as tightly coiled as ever. He was thinner, and there were lines around his eyes and mouth that had not been there the last time she saw him. His hair was still a deep, glossy pecan color and his eyes the sparkling amber hazel she remembered so well.

William! Once she had dreamed every day of seeing him again, of feeling his touch, of hearing him claim her for his own. Now, fury spread through her so intensely that her eyes burned. Munevver had waited all that terrible day for her father to say something. She had waited in vain for a note from William . . . anything.

Then there had been the humiliating experience of the arranged marriage with James with everyone knowing his proclivities. Munevver heard again the snide whispers each time she entered a room. Worst of all, there was no one in the family with whom she could share the pain, the degradation, and the betrayal of her father. He had sacrificed her, knowing the indignity she would suffer.

Munevver forced herself to take small breaths as Fayne had taught her. There had been no one in the family she could confide in. They all feared her father's retribution. It was Fayne who had stayed with her constantly during the horrible days after her marriage when she could not stand to face people. In the end, it was Fayne who had aided her escape and had sacrificed everything to travel with her to Constantinople. It had been Fayne who had helped her make the time in Ankara bearable.

The blinding rage she had felt when she first saw William had changed to searing pain, a level of anguish she had never felt before. "You didn't come!" The words sounded as though they had been torn from her, and as she started toward the open door, she was unable to halt the outpouring of agony. "You said you would come!"

She hissed at him as she ran from the room and stumbled up the ornate stairway, not hearing his agonized, "I came."

Lord Clarence put his arm around Liam, who was shaking as he tried to hide behind the desk. "Don't worry, Laddie. Your mother has had a shock, but she will be all right soon." Munevver's grandfather looked at William and, seemingly satisfied with his measure of William's intent, said, "If I were you, I'd follow her up the stairs as fast as I could move. Her room is the second on the right, and the key is over the door." He glared at William as he took the stairs, two at a time, and shouted, "Grovel, man! This requires lots of groveling."

William turned the knob, hoping that the door was unlocked, and when the door opened to his slight push, he felt a sense of relief. Munevver had not barred him. She was standing in the middle of the room. Her face was colorless and her eyes wide with shock. William closed the door but did not venture farther into her room. "I came, Munevver!" He could not control the tremble in his voice. "I came the morning after your birthday. I came too early for a proper visit, and Quinn asked me to wait in the hall outside of your father's study." He pulled out his handkerchief and wiped his face. "I told your father I loved you and wanted to marry you. As soon as possible." William shuddered. "He . . . he said he had plans for an excellent marriage for you, an advantageous marriage. He would make you a duchess. He walked me to the door and asked me not to contact you, or him, again."

Munevver stared at him, and as her face crumbled, she covered it with her hands. William had come. She had not been a failure.

William moved quickly, pulling her tightly against him. "I had no way to tell you. I had given my word that I would not contact you again."

Munevver let herself be molded to the long, hard length of his body. She had waited so long to be in his arms, and now, delicious, warm, unfamiliar feelings engulfed her. She pressed closer and let her hands slide around his waist. As she felt him tremble under her touch, she moved her hands upward and opened them wide to hold as much of him as possible. At his quick gasp of pleasure, an exquisite flash of happiness flooded her. She realized that she knew the steps of love. She cupped his face in her hands and let her thumbs caress the corners of his mouth. "You really love me?"

"I've loved you from the first day I saw you. The day your grandfather brought you home. You were not quite three years old, and I thought you were so beautiful."

Munevver turned her face into his shoulder, afraid to lose the magic of the moment but driven to face the reality of time. "I am no longer a young girl. I am a twice-married and twice-widowed woman. I am an impaired woman who may carry the family curse." She forced herself to continue. "You? What of your life?" *Tell me quickly. Tell me that you are married and have children. I must get the pain over with as quickly as possible.*

His life? William groaned even as he pulled her closer. His life, his hopes, and dreams had ended the day Munevver's father had dismissed him as unworthy. He forced himself to speak. "I don't know if you are aware that my older brother died a little over two years ago."

"No, I did not know." *William is now the heir and will be sought after by every father with unmarried daughters.* "I am sorry," she said simply.

"There was an accident. He broke his leg, and at first it seemed to be healing, but then septicemia set in and he died, slowly. I had been about to leave to join the cavalry, but my father insisted that, as his only living son, I remain." He shook his head and muttered bitterly, "While others have been off fighting for their country, I have been here, managing the family estate."

"Grandfather said you have been helping him, too," Munevver whispered as her hand fluttered up to touch his cheek.

"A little. Just enough to keep him company from time to time." He remembered her grandfather's words. Grovel. He would do anything to make Munevver his own. He decided to forgo groveling and try begging. "Marry me now. Today!"

"There would be a terrible scandal. People will say vicious things. You would hate it."

"I would hate going home alone, knowing my love is so near. I've waited a long time, years. Marry me now and let them gossip." He shook her gently. "Are you concerned about people criticizing you for not observing the proper mourning period after your husband's death?" He looked at her in disbelief. "Would you make me wait another two years?" His voice was rough with emotion. "Nothing—no words, no social slights—can hurt us as much as being apart."

Her love made her want to erase all the pain he had suffered. Munevver put her arms around as much of him as she could. "I was married to an Ottoman. Their mourning period is four months and ten days." She smiled sadly. "I don't think I can say that I loved him, but believe me when I say that I mourn the loss of his young life."

"Is that mourning period over?" William asked as he watched her intently.

"It's a few days short of being over, but my husband was Circassian, and their mourning period is forty days. So, yes, my period of mourning is over." Munevver smiled at him. "He wanted me to go home as soon as possible, to go back to my life in Yorkshire." Her voice dropped. "He asked his mother to arrange for my return." There was a soft tap on the door, and then there was Tobias, her grandfather's ancient butler, announcing that the vicar had arrived and Lord Clarence requested that they join them in the library.

Grandfather, dear Grandfather! Somehow, he would make everything right. They would be married. There would be no more fruitless waiting. No long, empty days and sleepless nights.

* * *

"Find the rhythm," Munevver muttered to herself.

Remember how the midwives in Ankara had helped the women during their labor. They had rubbed their backs with warm olive oil. They had given them sips of special teas, but mostly, they had murmured to them that birth was normal, the universal process by which all mankind had entered the world. Crying out in protest of Allah's will was not acceptable or helpful.

There were no Muslim midwives with warm olive oil in Yorkshire. The deep snow drifts blocked the way of any midwives who might have come to her. She looked at William, who smiled reassuringly. "I've helped with the birth of many colts. The process is the same." He wiped her face and offered her the tea left in the cup. "Mrs. Coates's sister is on her way up from the village to help us. She delivered most of the babies in the village. Try not to worry. Until she gets here, we'll manage together."

The hours passed and the contractions increased in force until Munevver thought that they had taken over her entire body and soul. It was as though nature decided that she was secondary to the deliverance of a new life. Finally, she heard the wail of the baby as it took its first breath.

Trembling, she waited to ask the question that she had lived with for months and that was overwhelming her now. Then she heard William say, "Don't swaddle the baby yet. Munevver needs to see her beautiful daughter." As she looked at him pleadingly, he said, "She is perfect all over, but let me show you her feet first." His voice was unsteady as he held the partly wrapped baby so that Munevver could see her feet—tiny, perfectly shaped pink feet. There was no hint of the clubfoot that she had feared. "Annice. Her name is Annice." She snuggled the baby closer. "It was my grandmother's name." Then, as she looked around the room, she asked, "Where's Liam? He has just become an older brother, an Abi. He will be her teacher, her guide, and her protector for all of her life."

Chapter 44

Who Is My Father?

Holding Munevver in his arms, William tried to absorb some of her distress. "What if he doesn't find his sister? He will feel he has failed his mother again." Munevver could not help the tears that slid down her cheeks. "The memory of Liam pleading to take his sister with him haunts me still. I tried, but I could not convince the Valide Sultan to let his sister come with us." She sobbed. "I failed him, and he has had to live with that sense of not honoring his mother's last request—to protect his sister."

William rocked Munevver gently in his arms and then was unable to hide his own anguish. "He's not going away to search for his sister. He's going to find out who fathered him." He looked away, unable to bear the compassion he saw in her eyes. "I've loved him as though he were my firstborn son, but for him, it is different. Every man has a burning need to know his real father, the man who gave him life, his clan." He paused. "The need becomes intense as he approaches the time to start his own family."

"Liam? He's too young to start a family!" Shock and fear colored Munevver's words.

"Oh, my love. Our Liam is twenty-two." He pulled her more snuggly into the circle of his arms. "Life has matured him more quickly than some." He could not keep the worry out of his voice. "I only hope his journey will not cause him pain that cannot be eased."

Sheltered by his arms, Munevver began to speak slowly. "I've never spoken to him about his father. What could I say? I didn't know who his father was." She hesitated, not knowing how much William knew of life in the harem. "Every time a chosen woman lies with the sultan, it is recorded the next morning in a black book, the *Book of Couchings*. The chief Black eunuch records the sultan's sexual activities, the date, and the name of the woman. The records are kept in order to establish the child's parentage." She paused. "The book is kept by the sultan's mother.

"Liam is traveling as an Englishman. He will not have access to the Seraglio, and certainly not to the harem part of the Seraglio." William tightened his arms around Munevver. "He has a fortress within a fortress to storm."

"I gave him a letter to Janan Hanim, Ari's mother." Munevver raised her head and met her husband's questioning gaze. "She was very kind to me during that difficult time in Ankara. I'm not sure I would have survived without her help. Ari asked me to bring his mother home with me." She groaned as she relived the feeling of failing Ari. "She refused, even though she had no family, no one other than the women of the Seraglio.

I think Liam realizes how much it bothers me that I was not able to look after Janan Hanim."

William pressed a reassuring kiss to her forehead. "Do you think she will be able to help Liam?"

"She is the only one who might be able to." Munevver's voice quavered. "Or at least keep him alive." When William remained silent, she added, as though the information explained everything, "She's of the Seraglio."

"I don't understand." William frowned. "I thought she lived in an old home on the Bosphorus."

Munevver drew a deep breath. "Often, when high-ranking military officers died in defense of the Ottoman Empire, their young daughters were sent to the care of the sultan's mother. They lived in the Seraglio and were taught many things—languages, music, embroidery, dancing, and how to make Turkish coffee." She smiled as though lost in pleasant memories. "Ari's mother, Janan Hanim, was sent there when her father was killed. She became a favorite of the sultan's mother, and they remained friends after she was given in marriage to Ari's father, a high-ranking envoy who spoke several languages." She moved away from the comforting circle of William's arms. "Those Seraglio ties last a lifetime, sometimes for generations." She shivered. "If anyone can help our son, it is Janan Hanim."

* * *

"It's been over a year. What if he doesn't return?" Munevver's voice was hoarse as she expressed her greatest fear.

"A man will always return to his mother. His mother is his first love and his most faithful supporter." William gave her a wry grin. "A father, on the other hand, is a teacher, a taskmaster, a disciplinarian, and . . . a competitor." He carried her hand to his lips. "A man returns to his mother because of his love for her. If he returns to his father, it's usually because of the need to survive or perhaps a sense of duty or obligation." William passed his hand over his face. "Rarely, very rarely, is it because of love."

William pulled her into the circle of his arms. "I know you have spent hours creating a salon for Janan Hanim. I've seen the divans you've had made to go around the room, the tiled fountain in the corner, and the gardens with fragrant flowers and herbs that you have planted outside her windows. Surely your work and faith will be rewarded."

The days passed slowly, and then one day, Munevver heard the children shouting in the courtyard, "Abi, Abi!" The moment she had been waiting for so long had come, and now she could barely stand. She leaned on her godchild, Emine, the daughter of Georgette and Edmund, who had come to live with them a year ago when both parents died of typhoid fever. In the year that Liam had been gone, Emine had metamorphosed from a shy child into a beautiful, young woman.

Now, after so many hard days of waiting and worrying, Munevver laughed as she saw the children swarming over her beloved son who had returned. And then he was beside her and had picked her up in his arms and swung her around and around. "I'm home, my mother." Suddenly aware of William standing beside them, he went down on one knee, kissed William's hand, and said, "My father."

It was later, after dinner, when Munevver asked the question that had been on her mind for so long. "Were you able to locate your sister?"

Liam nodded. "Janan Hanim helped me. She found out that my sister had been given in marriage when she was sixteen to a young man of a good family who had been appointed governor of Monastir." He spread his hands in a familiar gesture. "Of course, I had to go to Monastir to see her. I had to know that she was well."

"And was she well?" Munevver whispered.

"Yes. She is loved and honored by her husband and they have a son." He beamed at Munevver. "Just think of the goodness of Allah. My little sister has a home, a loving husband, and a son."

Munevver felt as though a huge burden of guilt had been lifted from her. Liam's sister had survived—not just survived but flourished. The goodness of Allah, yes, but in her heart, she thought that the will of Allah had most likely been carried out by the Valide Sultan. She had kept her promise that Liam's sister would be well cared for.

"Did you learn what you needed to know?" William forced himself to ask.

"Yes. I am Liam Del Feld of Yorkshire." He looked at his father for acknowledgment. William's arms came around him instantly. "You are Lord Liam Del Feld."

Standing beside his father, Liam let his gaze return to the beautiful, young woman at his mother's side. William took pity on his son. "Her name is Emily, but we call her Emine."

"Emine," Liam murmured. "In Turkish, it means one who is fearless and courageous."

"She is the daughter of Lady Frederica's godchild, Georgette, and Edmund, the vicar. A year ago, when her parents died of typhoid, she came to live with us." William's speech halted abruptly, and then, as though compelled, he pulled Liam aside and spoke in a low voice so that no one else could hear his words. "She was raised by the vicar as his daughter, but she does not know her father, the man who gave her life."

"Nor do I," Liam said quietly.

Leaning against William, Munevver began to speak softly. "I have learned from life that while a man may give the seed of life, it is the man who gives you protection, guidance, and love who is your true father."

"She is younger than I am," Liam muttered, "and so beautiful." He forced himself to meet his father's eyes. "Is she betrothed?"

"No," William answered slowly and then looked to Munevver for guidance. At her slight nod, he added, "You know my holdings well. Choose an estate that you would like to be your own."

Liam drew slightly apart from them. "I am your son, but I am also a son of the land where I was born, the Ottoman Empire. When I was in Constantinople, I realized that I wanted to devote my life to helping my country, the country where I was born."

"You will go back?" Munevver gasped.

"Perhaps from time to time." He drew himself up and announced with pride, "I have been appointed to the position of envoy, a representative of the Sublime Porte. I will be working in London." He waited uneasily for his father's response.

Munevver's mind raced. *How can that be? He has no family in Constantinople to petition for such an important position for him. He is unknown, most likely seen as a gavior, an unbeliever. Someone has helped him. It could not have been accomplished without the approval of the Valide Sultan, but who has carried out her wishes?*

"A friend of Janan Hanim's has offered me a place to live." Liam seemed hesitant.

"A friend?" Munevver murmured.

"Lord Stratford de Redcliffe," Liam mumbled and then his pride flared. "I am Liam Del Feld. I do not want to be beholden to anyone!"

"There is no need!" William declared firmly. "You must have the Del Feld London home. It is not as luxurious as de Redcliffe's, but it will serve you well." William grinned mischievously. "Quinn has been there for months, waiting for someone to come to stay there."

"Quinn?" Liam's eyes watered as he remembered the kind man who had brought him cheese and a beautiful pear for his first meal in Lord George's home.

"Yes, Lord George dismissed him in a fit of rage and he had nowhere to go." Munevver's voice was indignant. "How could he do that after so many years of devoted service?"

"I would be honored to have Quinn's assistance," Liam said in a husky voice. "There is so much work to be done, and I fear the Ottoman Empire is in a perilous position."

"As it has frequently been throughout the centuries." Munevver smiled at her son and patted his shoulder. "And yet it survives. There have always been those who rise to the challenge of ensuring her survival, and now it is your turn."